The Raggedy Edge

Michael S. Turnlund

ISBN 9781453717554

Printed in the United States of America

To Robbie

Prologue

Some said that people had become unpatriotic and had forgotten how to love their country. Others said that all empires must die and the ardent sectionalism sweeping the country was an expected and normal outcome. A vocal few called it God's judgment on the nation. But for the average citizen, the I-don't-vote-because-it-doesn't-seem-to-make-a-difference majority, the political turmoil in their world was simply a product of exhaustion. Apathy, yes, but mostly exhaustion. Two decades of economic malaise, a steeply declining standard of living, and Washington's inability to make any effective change – except makes things worse, in spite of an endless litany of promises – created an indifference brought on by an emotional and spiritual tiredness that sapped both the intellect and the heart. No one really cared anymore.

This became most apparent when some enemies of the state, as posited on a seemingly endless list, devised a means to bring down the federal government. It came to be called *swarming,* an unfortunate term but one that caught the publics' imagination. A person could just visualize a mob of suicidal martyrs attacking their target like a swarm of determined, unrelenting hornets with fatal stings. Though this imagery never quite matched the reality, swarming was still terribly efficient. Unnervingly so.

In hindsight it is obvious that swarming, as a means to an end, came about as the inevitable consequence of an "arms race." When backscatter x-ray technology made the classic strap-on-a-vest suicide bomber suddenly obsolete, it was only a matter of time before someone devised the means to get the bomb *inside* of the martyr and out of the view of the increasingly ubiquitous scanners. But making the explosives ingestible was genius. The martyr simply had to swallow scores of tiny plastic-coated bomblets, along with a few radio-activated triggers, and he or she would be transformed into death incarnate. In effect each martyr could become a human daisy-cutter who was able to stealthily mow down any person within a 10-yard radius with a flesh and bone scythe. All it took was the push of a button on a transmitter.

What wasn't anticipated and which made this new technology so grievously effective was the fact that when the warrior-martyr was armed for his mission he was no longer condemned to a one-way trip to paradise. Instead, if the target could not be acquired, the warrior-martyr could simply disappear into the crowd, return home and wait for nature to pass the bomblets through his body, where they could be recovered and reused. Martyrdom now became optional and not *de rigueur*. Whereas in the past a few dozen brave souls might have been recruited to serve as human bombs, today thousands could be found that were eager to demonstrate piety by participating in the cause *without* the absolute necessity of dying. With this ample supply of would-be assassins scores of bombers could now be released to simultaneously attack a target. Hence, the idea of the swarm.

The success of this tactic went beyond the grandest hopes of its earliest proponents. Surely it was god's hand. Whereas in the past a strong security curtain would offer high-profile targets a certain degree of protection, this was no longer true. Anyone was a potential assassin. Public appearances by potential targets were no longer practical. But what became especially unnerving was the recruitment of "cleanskins" – light skinned, blue-eyed, anybodies that didn't fit the stereotypical profile of suicide bombers. They could be anywhere and anyone: office staff, a child's nanny, the janitor. . . anyone.

And it got worse. When efforts to directly attack the targets failed, indirect targets were substituted. The spouses or children of the primary targets were sought out and murdered. Or their nieces and nephews, their parents, anyone somehow related to the target. This became so problematic that many schools and nurseries would no longer accept the kin, sometimes the remote kin, of high-profile targets. It only took a few well-publicized bombings of a childcare facility or a college classroom before panic set in.

And it still got worse. Initially swarming was a phenomenon of the Middle East and then later Europe. By the time it had reached the United States organizers of this weapon had perfected their strategies and tactics. Soon, each and every person in the presidential order of succession was directly or indirectly targeted, from the President herself down to the Secretary of Homeland Security. They were hounded by the zealots, and if the not themselves, then their families. In effect, accepting a position in the United States government that put a person even remotely into the line of succession for the executive office would put at risk the very lives of each and every family member. For most it was too much to ask.

The hoped for effect was achieved. After the assassination of the President and her domestic partner, quickly followed by the murder at summer camp of the vice-president's granddaughter, everyone was put on notice. Then as if by clockwork swarming attacks were levied against the rest of the executive officers of the United States government. Soon members of Congress were also targeted. Within a years time it became difficult to find competent people willing to accept a position in the government. The government of the United States became effectively catatonic.

Therefore General Jonathan Abrahmson, the most senior American military officer, hero of the Third Gulf War and head of the Joint Chiefs of Staff, announced that he would assume the position of executive *pro tempore*. He assured the American public that elections would be held as soon as practical, during which time the federal government would reestablish security. His first official pronouncement was to declare a state of emergency and the suspension of certain rights, such as *habeas corpus* and freedom of assembly. The Republic now stood, he said, on the precipice of its greatest challenge since the Civil War and at all cost order must be restored. It wasn't long before the rebellion was set into motion..

+++

Chapter 1

The morning started well, but then what morning hadn't? Otty's retirement was recent enough that he still delighted in getting up each morning to see what challenges he *didn't* have to face. And he had already established a routine. First coffee, then mail, then the news. He was going into the second step of this delightful regiment as he entered his home office with coffee in hand.

He spun the soft, black leather desk chair around to face him and sat down. As he settled in he verbally directed the computer to open up his mail file and to display it on the screen. A soft buzz began emanating from the desk and in a moment a rectangle of white light was projected onto the wall across from him. He took another sip from his steaming mug as he waited for the picture to come into focus. He knew it wasn't the image that was out of kilter; it was as sharp as could be. It was his aging eyes which sometimes took a moment to find their way, especially this early in the day.

Then a strange thing happened. No sooner had the screen come up he began to hear his brother's voice. The computer had opened up directly into a vidmail file and there was his brother's larger than life face, smiling and talking to him as if he himself was sitting across from the desk. Smiling! That was odd. Karl was the perpetually serious type, even as a child. To see his image grinning and casually chatting made Otty feel strangely ill at ease. To add further to the mystery captions were superimposed over the bottom of the screen, reflecting the words that his brother was speaking. This is peculiar, Otty thought to himself. Not only had his brother sent him an incongruent message, he must have thought he had gone deaf.

"Computer, stop!" he said softly, though with more than a hint of alarm. But the image didn't freeze; it kept staring kindly at Otty and rambling on in that familiar voice. Otty ordered the computer a second time to end the projection, but again it resisted his command. He moved to override it manually.

Out of habit he quickly brushed the ebony desktop in front of him with his fingertips. Dust tended to interfere with the holographic keyboard and he didn't want any more issues with his computer. He then verbally directed the computer to activate the key board and in a flash of red light a shimmering grid of letters, numbers, and other assorted buttons was projected out onto the surface of the desk. His fingers rapidly tapped the wooden surface as he worked to turn off the vidmail projection and determine why it wasn't following his commands.

His efforts were successful and his brother's image and voice disappeared into the morning stillness. He examined the vidmail file before reopening it. Strange, he noted, there was no date that indicated when it was sent. He paused as he considered this for a moment and then reopened the vidmail with a tap on the desk. He settled back to again watch his brother's image reappear. His older sibling was dressed in casual clothing and was sitting in front of the bookshelf in his study.

> Hi Otty. Thanks for the letter. Say, Tessa and I
> are escaping to the cabin for Solstice with the kids
> and grandkids in tow. We thought that you and

Ellie and the gang would like to join us. Let's
make it that family reunion we've talked about
having. Bring camping gear and maybe a few
extra treats. You know I like your cooking. Lots!
Everything in scratch. Let me know, sooner than
later. Oh, and by the way, I found that lost copy of
that old science fiction novel we both love. Do
you remember? Bye.

Karl's kind face indicated the end of his message
with a wink of an eye, a nod of the head, and big toothy
smile before disappearing. Otty snorted in response. He
hadn't realize his brother was capable of doing any of these
gestures so naturally and surely not at the same time.

He grabbed a pencil from the desk and replayed
the vidmail, pausing it frequently, until he had written
down all of the tall words that were appearing on the wall.
He wondered why his brother sent this message with
captions. That in itself must be significant. He considered
the words on the paper in front of him and and began to
circle elements of the message that seemed important. As
he did so a strange sense of foreboding crept into his mind.
The whole idea of a message within a message sent by his
brother, a rationalist to the extreme, made a tightness in his
gut. A sudden thought struck Otty that he wasn't the only
person reading this message. This can't be good, he
mused.

On a lark he forwarded a copy of his brother's message to his friend Howard, reciting a brief audio-attachment that explained his puzzlement with this vidmail and expressing a hope that he might have an opportunity to examine it before their previously scheduled get-together. "You know what to do," he chuckled as he signed off on the letter and forwarded it with a command to the computer.

He pondered his thoughts as he gently swung himself back and again in the chair. After a few moments Otty set the pencil down and reached for his phone bud. He paused to clearly enunciate his wife's name and then placed the phone in his ear. A ringing sound was followed by a woman's voice. "Hello Otty," she said kindly.

"Hi, Ellie," he answered her. "Where are you?"

"Halfway home," she answered. "What's the matter?"

She knows me so well, he thought to himself. Immediately she had sensed the unease in his voice. Amazing. He had learned a long time ago to not even attempt to keep a secret from her. He swore she could read his mind.

"I got an vidmail from Karl," he said.

"Oh," she said with a breath. "Anything the matter? What did he say?"

Otty paused. "More than I am sure of," he said matter-of-factly.

"What is that supposed to mean?" she asked with amusement.

"Two heads are better than one. Just checking when you were going to be home. See you when you get here."

"Alright, Otty. Be there in a few. By the way, have you put the puppy out recently?"

"Oh no, I forgot!" Otty exclaimed in sincere dread, "Gotta go!" He tugged the phone from his ear and tossed it onto the desk. He called out the dog's name. No response. A bad sign, he thought.

He searched the house. This was a simple as it was only a small cabin. He found the puppy sitting in the kitchen looking guilty. Otty's nose hold him why. The odor led him to the mudroom.

"Puppy," he said sternly, "I should change your name to poopy." He grabbed some paper towels and disinfectant and cleaned up the evidence. The culprit, a rather large black Labrador pup, sat in penance, ears down, with his tail dusting the floor. Otty sighed.

"It isn't your fault, pup. I know you're trying. I should have remembered." He reached over and scratched the dog behind the ear. Sensing that the worst was over, the dog pranced about and then settled before the door, staring expectantly at Otty.

"You're smarter than me, that's for sure." Otty let the dog out to run.

"Stay away from the skunks," he shouted.

The dog knew his neighborhood, if you could call it that. He lived with his masters on a ten-acre plot along Blue River Road. The Blue River, a large creek really, was a tributary of the Purcell River. Blue River Road was a half paved, half gravel, track that had originally served as an access for logging operations in the surrounding mountains. A small community of sorts had developed along a one mile stretch of the road. Loggers, retirees, and an odd collection of counter-culture types shared what little private land was available along the paved access in this area dominated by national forests. A railroad track shared in the meager bounty of level ground, running parallel to the river.

Otty and Ellie had retired to the area from Purcell about five years earlier. Their intention wasn't to escape the world; Purcell was already far enough off the beaten path. Instead, Otty got a job offer he couldn't refuse: he served the eclectic population of Blue River as pastor of the Blue River Community Church. Though he had retired from a professorship in history at the state university, the sum total of his theological training was zero. But he loved the people, and they loved him, and the rest just fell into place.

+++

Myla hadn't intended to spend the night in Purcell, let alone her life. At least the part of her life that mattered. She blamed it on her car. She smiled to herself as she contemplated the thought.

She stared fixedly at the red traffic light, waiting for it to turn green. "The only stoplight in town," she mused, "and it is always red for me." She remembered that it was red fifteen years earlier when her old hybrid finally gave up its ghost. The light turned green but she couldn't move forward. She had blocked traffic in the one busy intersection in Purcell until that handsome cop came over to help push the car out of everyone's way. Strange way to meet a husband. She smiled again, looked both ways and advanced under that now green traffic light that was she knew existed only to develop her patience.

She passed down the main road to the turn-off that headed to her home. How quickly the years had passed from that first arrival in Purcell. She was fresh out of nursing school in Boston and on her way to that big adventure of life. Her destination was Seattle where a first job interview awaited. She intended to drive to Washington state and not fly in order to see the countryside, using the energy of sheer optimism to keep her car intact for the journey. But it wasn't to be.

Myla piloted her car toward the eastern limit of town. Purcell was a compact community, its dimensions formed by nature. The little city was boxed in by the low mountains to the west and north. The Purcell River formed the southern boundary. There was an open expanse to the east, which two-generations earlier was farm land. Anymore, it was simply a quilt of rural neighborhoods that erupted in disconnected plots, dominated by the ersatz country estates of wealthy retirees. Myla lived in an older neighborhood within the city limits. "It's real," she once explained to a friend back East, though it was hard for her to define what that meant. Ultimately, it was simply her home and she looked upon it with the sentimentality a comfortable, but under-achieving, middle-class lifestyle brings.

Myla was currently content. Today she felt that ease of mind that life didn't bring frequently enough. It was sunny, the kids left for school in happy moods, and it was a day off. She enjoyed her work, but days off were better still. The only thing that could improve her spirit was for Jarad to be awake so they could visit. She glanced at the digital clock on the dashboard screen of the car as she pulled quietly into the driveway. It was a little past ten o'clock. Jarad would be soundly asleep. He would be back to day shift next week. Tonight was his last graveyard shift for this cycle. She could wait. Waiting came naturally to the wives of cops.

She brought in the groceries, trying to be as quiet as possible as to not disturb her husband. The house was cold. She left her coat on while she set about reestablishing some comfort to her nest. It was times like this that she missed the instantly gratifying indulgence of central heating. But the cost was out of the question. Heating by gas or oil, even electricity, was the prerogative of those who had money to burn, literally. Plus, most thought of burning with wood as being a strike against global warming since it was carbon neutral and renewable.

The thought of facing another winter with wood heat suddenly caused her to resent the advent of autumn. She stoked the wood stove, carefully positioning the wood to get a good burn. In a moment of indulgence she decided to leave the door to the wood stove open so the now exposed flames could directly heat the front room. She repositioned the fire mat with her toes to protect the carpet. As if in response to her effort a tiny glowing missile of ember bounded out of the stove and onto the mat. The fire within the stove popped and crackled in threat. Myla stood for a moment before the naked heat, and then returned to the kitchen to put away the groceries. Passing by the telescreen she paused to turned it on, but quickly changed her mind. "No," she thought, "I don't want to hear any news. Why spoil the mood." But just the thought caused her to sigh. "The world is so dark," she thought, glancing at the sunny day outside through her living room window.

+++

Ellie honked the horn when she pulled into the driveway. This was the family code for groceries, come and help. Otty met her under the carport and helped her carry in the few bags. He made a pot of coffee as she put things away. Then they sat facing each other at the table, both leaning on their elbows, sipping their coffee while considering the paper that Otty had laid on the table. He had spun it around so his wife could read it. She did so in silence.

"Yes," said Ellie, "I understand why this raised those little hairs on the back of your neck." She reached over and patted his hand. "It is really strange. I wonder what it means."

"Well, here's what I think," Otty replied, picking up the paper. "First, he uses weird phrasing. You know how precise Karl is in his language. That is a red flag. Assuming that I am correct, it is a simple matter of reading between the lines."

"A simple matter, with Karl?" she shrugged. "But that is odd, if only because it is coming from him."

Otty nodded and continued with his thesis. "First off, he used a vidmail with a text message superimposed over it. He could have used a regular email, but then I wouldn't have seen him. It was seeing him that tipped me off. I don't think text alone would have worked."

"The message in the message was meant for us. Karl must . . ." he paused. "Karl must have assumed other people would also be reading his mail."

Ellie stared at him unseeing for a moment. "I hope that you are wrong," she replied. "Thinking that other people might be reading Karl's mail means that he has been marked," she said. Otty nodded.

"Yes, and Solstice with the family at the cabin," Otty said softly, looking at Ellie's eyes. "And he invited us!"

"I noticed that right away," Ellie said. "That cabin is teeny-tiny. There isn't going to be room for all of them, let alone us. He even included Breanne and the kids."

"Yes. That is also alarming. That tells me that this is a real emergency."

"Emergency?" Ellie repeated, her voice expressing doubt. "What kind of an emergency?"

"I don't know, but if anyone does it is my brother." Karl was what Ellie called the family spook. Officially, he was an analyst and he worked for the government in Maryland, just outside of Washington, D. C. But no one in the family really knew what he did. And they sort of learned over time not to ask.

Ellie pushed the paper back to her husband and pointed at a line. "What is this about a family reunion you and Karl had planned? I never heard anything about this." She looked up at Otty.

"We've never discussed a family reunion. But he is reminding me about a conversation that we had about a year ago. I think he's telling me to head for the hills, so to speak."

"What do you mean?" Ellie said, alarmed.

"Well, you know Karl. He would never say anything directly. But he told me that we were living in 'strange times' – his words – and he was thinking about moving up to the cabin. For a vacation."

"So, what does that have to do with a reunion."

"He said that when his family went to the cabin for vacation, it would be advisable for our family to go on vacation as well." Otty looked at Ellie. Her soft brown eyes were framed by her the arch of her brows, a sure sign that she was getting worried. Otty took her hand.

"He's telling me to get somewhere safe. And if being safe meant all of us being crammed into that little A-frame cabin he has in the mountains, then things must be pretty serious."

She pointed at the paper, again. "So, here where he states "escaping" he doesn't mean that metaphorically?"

"No, I think he means it literally. That is part of the message within the message."

"And look here," he continued, "Bring camping gear, to the cabin? I think he's telling me that things are going to be rough. And my cooking? Karl doesn't like my cooking. You know very well I don't cook. Strictly bachelor stuff. Microwave." Ellie nodded, looked down at her coffee and smiled a worried smile.

"Let me re-read this passage, how I understand it. 'Bring some extra treats, lots, everything in scratch.' Notice he said 'in scratch' and not 'by scratch.' It doesn't make any sense, unless he's telling us to stock up on food. Basics. And lots of it."

Ellie leaned back in her chair and rubbed her neck with her hand, the other gripping the table. "Maybe you should call him," she said. "Write him. He even asks you to contact him."

"No," Otty said, nodding his head. "It's too late. Either he is gone, which I hope, or," he paused. "something else. Ah, we shouldn't worry. I don't think that the sort of people who read these things would even be suspicious."

"I hope not," Ellie said, softly. "By the way, what's with this science fiction book he has found?"

Otty picked up the paper again and re-read the line. "That is odd, isn't it. I can only think of one book that he and I ever shared any interest."

"Which is?" she said impatiently, drawing out her words.

"*Alas, Babylon.*"

"*Alas, Babylon*," she repeated. "Is that supposed to be significant?"

"I suppose not, but it sure impressed Karl and me forty-odd years ago. It was a really old book then, too," he replied.

"So, what does it mean?" she asked, again drawing out her words, seemingly trying to lead him along.

"Well," he replied, using her tone of voice. "I was the one who had the book. It was an old paperback. Karl didn't have it. I think I sold it along with a lot of my other books when I was in college. That's the point. He is alluding to a book he doesn't even have. But the meaning is clear to me."

Ellie looked at him expectantly, silent and waiting.

"Without going into details about the whole story, it is a tale about one brother, who I think worked for the air force, warning his other brother about the a coming nuclear war between the United States and the Soviet Union."

"The Soviet Union?" she asked. "Yes, that is an old book." She paused, thinking. "So Karl is warning us that there is going to be a nuclear war?" she asked in an incredulous voice.

"No, I don't think so," he replied softly, squeezing her hand. "But, he is warning us about something big, I suppose. Effectively, I think that Karl is warning us about some sort of big event."

"What?" she asked, her voice becoming more shrill. "Lord knows we don't need any more 'big events!'"

He looked at Ellie. Her mien was that of bewilderment. He now wished that he hadn't brought this letter to her attention, realizing it will only cause her to be worried. He suddenly felt selfish. "Yes, he does," he said quietly. "I think I might wander over and see Howard. He'd be interested too." He reached for the coffee pot. "Hey, next week, you want to go shopping? Serious shopping?"

+++

The gibbous moon blanketed a pale cover over Jarad's police car as it sat on the north end of Purcell in one of his favorite perches. Here was on an expansion of the blacktop where the state highway ran through town and just before the point where the speed limit increased. Jarad liked this spot because it was hidden from the view of northbound traffic and provided a safe launch to pursue speeders. Many tourists passing through Purcell seemed to be in such a hurry to leave town that they would anticipate the higher speed limit posted a half-mile up the road. "Okay, lets be honest," he chuckled to himself, "It's a speed trap, but it is an honest speed trap."

Jarad toggled the remote laser built into the front fender by swiveling a little joystick that sat between the two front seats. He pointed the laser to favor the northbound lane by aiming it with a small video monitor positioned in the center of the dashboard. The beam would now capture the speed of any vehicle trespassing through it. He knew that the laser was redundant, because the squad car was also equipped with a receiver that monitored the signal emitted from each passing vehicle's transponder which broadcast their speed. But many people had learned how to block those transmissions. The laser was his old-fashioned, low-tech backup.

Jarad was oblivious to the squeaks and squeals of his leather belt against the vinyl seat as he resettled himself into the cushions. He was getting seat sore from sitting so long in the car. The ache reminded him that he was well into his shift. He watched the steam from the coffee he held in his left hand cloud the driver's door window. Out of habit he reached across with his right hand and drew a smiley face in the patch of moisture. It was barely perceptible in the dark thin gauze of mist.

He turned and looked out the windshield with the eyes of a man who had the time to sit and think. That was one good aspect of working the graveyard shift, he mused. Like the rest of the small Purcell police force, Jarad rotated shifts. Tonight was the last of graveyard and then back to days. He really didn't mind working the middle of the night. Generally things were quiet and he had a lot of time to contemplate what ever needed chewing on.

Jared knew that Purcell was actually always pretty quiet. On occasion he had to respond to a fight down at one of the bars in town or maybe a domestic abuse incident. Every cop in town had learned that it was only a matter of time and beer before one of the too many unemployed mill workers would slap around his wife. Or perhaps partner was a better term, Jarad thought. People didn't marry much anymore.

That thought led him to think about his own relationship with Myla. Fourteen years. We've been married for fourteen years. Jarad smiled to himself. He still felt like a newlywed. Myla would roll her eyes if he told her that, but he knew she felt the same.

After an hour and no luck, Jarad refastened his seatbelt. It was time to refill the coffee thermos. He pushed the ignition button and the motor came alive. Jarad revved it a couple times, feeling the vibration of the big diesel rocking on its engine mounts. Though his police car was getting a little long in the tooth, he was glad that the city hadn't replaced it. He well understood that this was partly because of economics. The city was not in a position to afford new police cars any time soon. For Jarad, the city council could wait as long as they pleased because he wasn't ready to give up this raw power for one those electric hybrids. Across the country, hybrids and all-electrics had become the norm, from little three-wheeled economy cars up to the big long-haul trucks that ruled the interstates. Only a few police cars and hot rods still eschewed the demands of economy. A sort of competition, Jarad supposed. But even this was changing. Soon, only those who owned antique hot rods would experience the thrill of a powerful engine. Nothing stayed the same.

As he flicked on the headlights a big southbound semi-truck hit the brakes hard. The driver wasn't speeding, but well honed reflexes work faster than the conscious mind. The truck slunk from the darkness of the highway into the golden bathed boulevard of Main Street. Jarad wheeled the police car behind the truck and followed him the short distance into town. Like most professional truckers the driver watched the cop car with covert paranoid glances to both mirrors, left to right, and then back again. The trucker breathed a sharp sigh of relief when the car turned into the parking lot of the Conoco station. The City of Purcell Police flashed from its right flank as it pivoted under the canopy lights.

Jarad parked the car near the front door of the only 24-hour market in town. Out of habit he always parked in shadows away from the lights to the left of the building. This routine wasn't due to stealth, but to avoid the mobs of bugs attracted by the bright lights of the canopy that lit up the darkness like some gaudy casino in the Nevada desert. Jarad hadn't remembered that it was already fall and all the bugs were gone. Their lives had ended en masse with first hard frost weeks earlier.

Jarad entered the temple gates of 24/7 coffee, cannabis, and beer, blinking his eyes as they adjusted to the brightness. A lazy "hey Jarad" came from an exceedingly rotund figure struggling to swing a mop in front of a half-empty dairy case.

"Anything new?" he asked, panting.

"Same old, same old," Jared replied, putting his empty thermos next to the coffee dispenser.

"Be back in a sec," he said as he walked to the restroom. "Out with the old to make room for the new." James, the heavy man, chuckled with his whole body the way only the overweight can.

"Take your time," he said, "I'll fill it up for you. I know, four sugars. Right?" Jarad gave him a quick salute without breaking stride. He glanced at his watch as he leaned against the door, pushing it with his shoulder. "Four hours till sunrise," he thought. "Then I can go home. I also got to remember to order some more firewood."

+++

Chapter 2

Jarad was looking for his best pair of jeans. "Where are they?" he asked quizzically.

"Look on my side," Myla shouted in a muffled return from somewhere downstairs. "I might have hung them up on the wrong side."

Jarad started leafing quickly through Myla's clothes. He smiled, thinking "my side," the whole closet was her side. He was left with just a corner of the walk-in closet for his clothes. He found his best pair of Levis hanging among several of Myla's blue nursing scrubs. He wiggled into the jeans as quickly as he could. He never understood how his pants were chronically too tight in the waist. Time to go shopping for a new pair.

He stepped out of the closet, tucking in his shirt. He grabbed a belt off of the dresser as he exited the bedroom, slipping it through the belt loops as he hustled noisily down the stairs. He was met at the bottom step by his son and daughter, both of whom were slipping on their coats. Though they were twins, as twelve-year olds they couldn't be more different. Annie was the dominant one of the two and acted more as an older sister to her same aged brother. Cameron was the passive one and never seemed to be ruffled by his sister's more assertive nature.

"Come on dad, we're going to be late again," his daughter said firmly. Annie never stated more than the facts. She is so much like her mother, Jarad thought, just tells things the way they are.

He held the door for his daughter and son and followed them out to the car. The morning was that perfect sort of morning, the kind that made him glad he lived in Purcell. The autumn air was crisp but dry, and the sun was just over the horizon, its rays too bright to look at, but too warm to want to turn away from. Even better, he and Myla both had the day off. Really, it would be a great day even if it were raining torrents.

He sat himself in the front seat on the passenger side. Myla preferred to drive. This suited Jarad just fine for sometimes he felt that he spent his life behind a steering wheel. Myla backed out deftly into the road and then accelerated quickly in the opposite direction, shooting gravel in every which way as the front tires worked to gain traction.

She looked at her husband. "You're not going to give me a ticket, are you?" Jarad laughed, and gave her that winning smile she so adored in him.

"Well, miss, I would but I just happen to have forgotten my ticket log. I'm afraid I'll have to let you go, but I must warn you to please drive safe," he said in mock seriousness. She smiled back at him, batting her eyes with exaggerated effort before returning to the business of driving the car.

"Thank you, officer," she said. "And I'll remind my husband to put on the snow tires before winter comes."

Jarad laughed again. "Oh, no," he chuckled, "honey-do, honey-do." He yawned, shaking the sleepiness from his body. "I'll be sure to put that on my list," he said with his mouth agape. He leaned over the dash in order to scan the hills and ridge lines. He noted the perfect demarcation between the white on the top of the ridge and the green below. "By golly, I think I see a snow line." He looked at Myla and arched is eyebrows in mock wonder. "Must be that time of the year. It seems early."

They headed west toward the other side of town. Their church was situated completely opposite their home in relationship to Purcell. As they approached the center of town they passed by several of the larger, mainstream churches. Jarad noticed that the nicest and newest cars always found their home in these parking lots every Sunday. He also knew the owners of almost every single one of them. Such was the tiny community of Purcell. Everyone knew everyone else's business.

They continued west. Myla used Schaffer Cut-Off as a short cut to Mountain View Road. The road, like most in Purcell, was pock-marked with ruts and potholes. Infrastructure maintenance was chronically under funded by the town and county government. Just like the state, Jarad reminded himself. And the country.

"Slow down, honey," Jarad howled when the suspension bottomed out in a rut. Myla snorted. "Alright, alright," she said, as the car bobbed about on its springs.

She followed Mountain View about mile and a half and then pulled into the parking lot of Mountain View Church. But instead of finding a parking space, Myla pulled over onto the gravel shoulder.

"I don't want to go to church today," she said flatly. She stared ahead toward the alfalfa field next to the church before looking at Jarad. He looked back at her for a moment before saying anything.

"You're reading my mind," he said softly.

"I don't wanna either," a girl's voice volunteered from the back seat. "We're already late," it reminded them.

"Thank you, Annie," her father replied. "Your opinion is always welcome." He shook his head. "You know why we are late, don't you?" he said to his wife rhetorically. "It's because we don't want to be here."

"It's terrible, but that is the way I feel," Myla said. "And this is our church."

"Yah," Jarad drawled, "It's our church. This is where I've attended since I was a boy, and this is the church we got married in. And we still have friends here, well at least a couple. But in some ways it isn't our church anymore, Myla. It's changed. It's changed too much." He paused and rubbed his fingers over his chin as was his habit when contemplating something. "It hasn't been the same since Dr. Bronson arrived."

Myla hissed. "*Doctor* Bronson," she said with heavy sarcasm placed on his title. "Not pastor, not Bob, but doctor. Always doctor." She turned in her seat to face her husband. "He is just weird, Jarad. You know," she continued, "I'd honestly rather not attend any church than have to attend this church. I'm sorry if that offends you, but that is just the way I feel." She crossed her arms and lifted her chin. "I'm communicating, Jarad."

Jarad looked at his wife and then stared out the windshield. "I tell you what, Myla. Let's just take a break. We don't have any obligations right now. No Sunday school. No nursery. Let's just do something else the next few Sundays, and think about it. If Doctor Bronson or one of the elders calls to check on us, I'll talk to them." He reached over and cupped the back of his wife's neck with his hand. "It's okay," he smiled. "I tell you what, this is a special day. Let's go out for breakfast."

The two spectators in the rear seat cheered spontaneously. Then, as if on cue, they began to argue over which restaurant in town should be graced by the presence of the Traverson family's business.

"I love you, Jarad," Myla said with a straight mouth. She batted her eyes again, shifted into drive and sped out of the parking lot and heading back into town, racing the electric motor. "I feel a burden off my shoulders." she paused. "And my heart."

He smiled thinly at her, his gaze then drifting unseeing at the countryside. He felt better too, which only made him feel oddly guilty. But he began to relish the idea of breakfast.

+++

Purcell had avoided much of the social unrest that had befallen many areas of the country. This was probably due mainly to its poverty rather than its isolation. There wasn't any truly isolated places any more since the advent of the televisor. The televisor was a combination television, movie screen, and telephone and had become ubiquitous. It was versatile as it could both send and receive live images. Many families used it to visit with each other over long distances, and of course businesses found it to be a great means of communicating internationally. For many students it removed the need to physically attend school.

At one time Purcell was a mill town. The past decade or so had seen the mill operating only sporadically, falling in and out of receivership as different owners tried their luck at the crap shoot of commodities marketing. Every time the mill closed and then reopened, salaries fell. Still, the mill had paid some of the highest wages in the county, so many former employees held on and tried to stay in the community by living off of meager savings or selling assets a piece at a time, or working combinations of part-time jobs. But between chronic recession in the national economy which stifled the demand for lumber and the inevitable lawsuit filed by some environmental group whenever a timber sale was approved, the largest mill had now sat shuttered for over two years. Conventional wisdom in the county was that now there were no longer enough loggers in business to fall trees and haul them to the mill even if it did re-open.

Some would surmise that tourism would be a logical alternative to an economy based on exploiting natural resources. After all, Purcell was – in the words of publicists – "nestled among towering peaks and virgin forests, a veritable playground for the nature lover to discover." This was true, except that the towering peaks were really only high ridge lines and the forests were third growth.

Tourism did have its place, but it did little to alleviate poverty. The only real money to be made in the tourism business was by the business owners: motels, shops, resorts, and such. Otherwise, wages paid were meager. After all, what high skills are needed to flip burgers, drive tour buses, and change bedding? And as many tourism entrepreneurs were to unfortunately discover, tourism is driven by the larger economic picture. The poor national economy had long since buried the few viable enterprises in the county years ago.

No, Purcell survived mostly because of the rich retirees who found the area profitable to exploit. It was their superfluous monies that greased the local economy. But it wasn't really enough. Purcell was dying. This home of some two thousand souls would one day be a monument of shuttered homes and businesses, another ghost town to haunt the west. But in the end her fate mattered little to those who currently called her home. Life was to be lived in the present. The future would take care of itself.

+++

Otty had spent the rest of the week in abject frustration. His nature normally was one of comfortable optimism and self-assuredness constructed from a lifetime of success heaped upon success – though the measure of each might be modest. He was also a man of devout faith, but currently prayers had not soothed him nor offered any answers. As he told his wife half-humorously he was "just a little discombobulated."

Ellie was disconcerted by her husband's change in mood and seeming mental waywardness. She had only seen him once before in such a befuddled state of mind and that was quite recently. That was when little Amanda from church was found dead in her crib and her family called in the middle of the night for Otty to come and provide them succor. Crib death. Such a lovely little baby, she remembered. Two months old. Tragic. The entire event left Otty somewhat emotionally and spiritually disheveled. Planning for the funeral he had paced the same hallway where he now cast his shadow, quietly asking himself "what should I say." The picture today was the same, but instead he whispered "what should I do."

But for Otty this was different. This was bigger. He could always prepare himself and his family for any impending crisis. He and Ellie had already discussed strategies and made tentative plans to prepare for the "event." The bigger question to Otty was if he should tell, no, warn others. Would they believe him? Or would he just generate panic? Or, worse yet, disillusionment?

The historian in him was reminded of the Adventist movements of some two hundred years previous. Christians of various stripes had been caught up in the hysteria of a purported return of Christ. A date had even been pinpointed on the calendar. True believers had sold all their worldly assets and freely distributed the money. What value is gold in heaven when there it is only used to pave the streets? But when the day came and went, and believers had found themselves greeting only the dawn and not their Lord, disillusionment and shame had shattered faith. No, Otty did not want to re-enact that vignette from history. Not that he was expecting the immediate return of Christ. Still he didn't want to be guilty of crying wolf. Neither was Otty ready to be cast as a prophet, because in the upside-down world in which they existed anyhow, the Apocalypse would be associated by many with any crisis.

Otty quit his pacing and sat down at the table. But no sooner had his weight settled on the chair than he bounded again to his feet. He put himself to the task of making a pot of coffee. We had better add coffee to the shopping list, he said aloud to the walls.

+++

"Lieutenant, the chief wants you. He's got a death threat."

Jarad looked up from his desk to put a face to the voice. It was Judy, the single employee of the police department that wasn't a cop. She was harried and exasperated as usual. He gave her a startled look.

"Someone has threatened the chief?" he asked, perplexed.

"No." She gave one of her patent sighs. "He's got a death threat for you to check out. He's in his office." She huffed and spun her plump figure and faux-blond head around and disappeared down the way she came. Jarad laid down the pen he had been holding suspended in the air and pushed himself away from desk. He weaved through the narrow and somewhat cluttered hallways to Captain Dreever's office. He paused at the open doorway when he noticed that the chief was speaking on the phone. The balding man bobbed his liver-spotted head back and forth with impatience. He grimaced as he listened to the other party. He would wear such a face when he had made his own mind up about something or other and had to endure the counsel of others who held a contrary opinion After a moment the chief acknowledged Jarad with a wave of his hand, beckoning him to enter. He then motioned for Jarad to sit in one of the two chairs situated before his desk.

"Yes, Bob, I got him here right now." The chief paused for a moment as he listened and then continued, "That's a good idea. I'll have the lieutenant give you a heads-up on whatever he finds out.

Yes, this afternoon. No, its not a problem. Team work. That's right. Bye." The chief disconnected the call by tugging the phone bud from his ear.

"That was our friendly sheriff and he wants in on this too. I am sure that Judy has informed you with all of the specifics," he said with a smirk. "Let me fill in any details that she might have missed."

"She said that you got a death threat," Jarad said.

"She could only hope," the chief spat. Judy was one of those type of people who was essential but unpleasant. No one cared for her, but everyone needed her. She was the sticky glue which kept everything together, but which was unpleasant to touch.

"Anyhow, I want you to run down to this address and talk to this man," the chief handing Jarad a piece of scratch paper. Jarad looked at the name but it meant nothing to him.

"This is really peculiar," the chief continued. "He said something about a death threat, but that he had it under control, that this is all a formality. I don't know what the hell he's talking about, so I told him I'd send someone out right away. That's you." The chief made a facetious grin. "Any questions?"

Jarad nodded is head in the negative. "I've never had to handle a death threat before, so this will be interesting." He stood to leave.

"Yup, interesting," the chief agreed. "But let me caution you. Do you know anything about GILM?"

Jarad's face registered ignorance. "G-I-L-M," the chief continued. "It's an acronym. The God is Love Movement, or something like that. That ring any bells?"

"Yes," Jarad acknowledged, now recognizing the name from a passing news program on the televisor. "That's now here, in Purcell?"

"That's what you got in your hand. When you're all settled with him, come back and we'll both ride out to see Bob."

Jarad could have walked the short distance to the Episcopal church, but he thought that a police car would serve as a good calling card. When he arrived the parking lot was empty except for a single car and a pair of brand new full-size vans.

When he entered the foyer of the church he was greeted by a tall young man in a dark suit whom he didn't recognize.

"My I help you," he asked politely.

"Yes, I am here to see a Mr. Swess."

"Sure, Reverend Swess was expecting someone from the police department." The young man's placid countenance seemed appropriate for the building but not for his tremendous size. Jarad noticed that he was even larger and broader than when he first appeared. His suit was tailored perfectly. The young man looked at Jarad's badge.

"Follow me, Officer Traverson," he said. As they passed down a hall another young man, similar in size, dress, and demeanor, moved from a seating area and out to the foyer. Evidently he was the backup to Jarad's guide. The fellow nodded and smiled at Jarad as their arms almost touched in the hallway. Jarad looked up a head length to return the nod but not the smile. He was on business.

Jarad knew the church fairly well. He had attended summer Bible school here as a kid and, later, various church functions when he was a teen. As was true in most of the Purcell area churches, if there was pizza or ice cream to be shared the kids would come, regardless if they attended church somewhere else or not at all. Such were the vagaries of teen faith and the opportunities for a free meal.

He was led to the banquet room that had been converted into an office. The tables were grouped together to create a larger central island that was banked with computer monitors, printers, and organized stacks of paper. A man sat at the only desk in the room. He immediately rose from this chair when Jarad entered the room with his guide. Jarad shook the proffered hand.

"Welcome, officer. ." he glanced at Jarad's name tag, "Traverson. Thank you for coming so promptly. This is very kind of you and very professional. I didn't expect such immediate service. My name is Jonathan Swess." He waved away the young man. "Thank you, Harley. I'll be fine alone."

The man was similar in age to Jarad, slight of build, blond hair neatly trimmed. Oddly, he wore lightly tinted sunglasses, behind which Jarad could just see the man's eye carefully examining him. He wore a suit that appeared to be the same as those of Harley and the other young man. Dark, well tailored. "What can I do for you," Jarad asked him.

"Let's sit down and discuss that very thing." He pointed to a collection of chairs that were positioned around a small table. The table held a clutch of religious magazines and tracts.

"None of this is unexpected," he said once they were seated. "In fact, the very opposite. It was very much expected. I just didn't think that it would happen so soon. I've only been here a couple days." His demeanor was masked in a practiced passivity, but didn't seem to overtly hide any suspicion or fear. He seemed to be speaking candidly. He sat with both feet on the ground and his hands together in his lap. His cuffs were fastened with cuff links. For whatever reason, Jarad felt he was in the audience of a one-man play.

Jarad removed a note pad from his pocket. He confirmed the man's name and current business address. He noted that he had arrived from Spokane where he had been working with a church for about a year. He was originally from Sacramento. He didn't know anyone in Purcell, having only met the Episcopal minister the day he arrived. He had come with that man's invitation. He wouldn't disclose his current place of residence, but did state that he believed he was perfectly safe.

"Officer, there really is nothing you can do. It is simply important that I report the threat. In fact, I will give you the document." He returned to his desk, grabbed a large envelope and handed it to Jarad.

"It was folded in half, addressed to me, and taped to the outside door of this church," he noted. There was a single sheet of paper within the envelope. Jarad removed it and examined the paper. It was a plain sheet with words scrawled in black marker. The message was simple and blatant: Leave town or you are a dead man. GILM is not wanted here. We know who you are and you will be constantly watched. If you do not heed this warning, your death is your own doing. Cheers!

"My I keep this?" Jarad asked.

"Of course," he said, making a casual wave with his right hand. "I've already made a copy for my records."

The man crossed his legs and cupped his hands over the knee. He settled in to speak. "Let's talk openly, Officer. I know that the Purcell police department can not insure my safety. Nor would I expect them to. Death threats have become the norm for GILM workers. Some have died. They have been martyred. Accordingly, the church has organized its own means to insure the security of its workers. You have met Harley, for example. He is one of six young, highly trained, professionals who have been asked by the church to provide protection for myself and other GILM workers here in the field. They are our bodyguards, so to speak. We consider them to be missionaries." He paused to allow Jarad to respond, watching him jotting notes on his pad.

"Do you have any idea as to who might be threatening you?" Jarad asked.

"Yes, of course. He, or she, or they, whomever it is are among those whose narrow definition of God and faith precludes them from seeing the light, honestly. God is love. He, or she, however a person conceives of God, is love. That is our message. God is too big to be caricatured by the narrow definitions of the traditional faiths. Look at all the grief the world has endured because of the intolerance of people who have not been able to step out of the box of their limited concepts of God." Swess' voice became emphatic as he spoke. His hands left their perch on his knee and were given life by his words. Jarad felt like he was hearing a sermon.

"Simply put, Officer Traverson," he continued, "these are people of intolerance and disrespect. They want the world to conform to their narrow description of God and, if not, then they or at least some of them. . . I don't condemn them all," he said, spreading his hands magnanimously. "But, it only takes one to cause harm."

"We are here to spread the good news to the world, to the people of Purcell. And, that quite simply, is upsetting to some people. But the gospel is offensive. Anyhow, I will not be bullied by this threat. I, we, are here till our work is done."

"And how long might that be?" Jarad asked.

"Weeks, months, a year," he said, throwing his hands up in the air. "How long it might take. We work on a different schedule than most people, Lieutenant. A different time frame."

"Cosmically, or what?" Jarad asked, speaking his own thoughts.

Reverend Swess smiled. "You could say that," he replied. "We will never leave Purcell. I might some day, but GILM never will. Because the love of God changes hearts and minds. Once that is done, where those people live, so lives God, so lives – in a fashion – GILM. We are simply servants waiting for the sign." He raised his palm to cut off Jarad's question. "And that sign is. . . something we don't know. But we will know when it comes. It will be clear." His face reflected the conviction he felt with in.

"And then?" Jarad asked.

"And then peace, love, kindness. A restoration really. A restoration of that kingdom that the Lord had originally intended for us. Maybe in my lifetime, maybe not. That is my purpose. That is why I am in Purcell."

They exchanged a few more words before Jarad stood to leave. Jarad thanked him and shook his hand. He reminded Reverend Swess to let him know if any addition threats or problems became apparent. He handed the man one of his business cards.

"Thank you, thank you," he said, "You've been very kind. Let me show you the way back to the foyer."

Jarad assured him that this was not necessary. He explained that he was familiar with the church building. Reverend Swess smiled upon hearing that information and invited Jarad and his family to church. Jarad thanked him and left. Suddenly and silently he found himself paired with a giant who seemingly appeared out of the proverbial thin air, walking in step with him to the end of the hallway and into the foyer. His stealthy escort faded from sight as quickly as he had appeared. Harley stood waiting near the door, nodding as Jarad passed.

He returned the nod as he existed the building. As he was heading toward his police car a woman's voice called out.

"Jarad! Hi Jarad." He looked up to see a pleasant woman in a dress walking toward him carrying a cardboard box. It was

Susan Holmes. Jarad had known Susan most of his life and she now worked as a secretary for the church. Secretly, Jarad had always admired Susan's voluptuous form, especially now as the burden she was carrying pulled the flowery fabric taut over her chest. Reuben would have painted her.

"Hi Susie," Jared called out innocently. "How are you?"

"Great," she said enthusiastically. "I am having the time of my life." Jarad moved to take the box from her and to carry it inside the church. She shook her head and said that it wasn't really that heavy.

"Good news for you and Mountain View Church," she said cheerily. "Doctor Bronson has just indicated to us this very morning that he is very interesting in learning more about the Movement. Isn't that exciting?" She smiled broadly and genuinely at Jarad. He noted that she had the visage of a true believer. His heart winced.

"I suppose so," he replied neutrally. "Good to see you, Susie, but I gotta go. Business, you know." He gave her a big smile in return and headed for his car. Things are going to be interesting around town for a while, he mused.

+++

"I wish we had a time line, it would sure make this process a lot less chaotic. I keep thinking that I am forgetting something." Ellie looked at the pile of papers around her. She had lists for food stocks, for medicines and supplements, clothing. . . it was endless.

"How do you prepare for a disaster when you don't even know what it is," she hollered to the walls. "This is absolutely ridiculous. We are running around in a panic."

"Otty," she yelled out the back door. She could hear his voice faintly as he responded to her call. She wasn't sure what he said, but she knew he could hear her. "Otty, come on in. I need you."

A few minutes later Otty appeared in the kitchen. He had been unloading firewood from his pickup truck. He mumbled something about enough cords of wood for now, but Ellie wasn't really listening.

"Otty, we need to stop. We're not getting anywhere. All we have done is work ourselves into a lather. We need to stop."

Otty removed his outer shirt. He had been in a good comfortable rhythm that kept him warm despite the coolness outside. He leaned against the kitchen counter.

"You're right," he responded. "You're right and I'm exhausted." They looked at each other silently for a while. Neither wanted to speak. Otty turned to check the carafe for coffee. He never seemed to tire of the stuff. He swirled the near empty pot in his hand. With his back to his wife he resumed their conversation.

"Honey, I think that you're right on another point, as well." He knocked the old coffee and filter from the basket into the food disposal. He rinsed the basket out with water and returned it to the coffee maker.

"I'm going to send an email to Karl," he said as he measured out coffee into the filter. "Perhaps a response wouldn't be unexpected. And you're probably right. Maybe things aren't as urgent as we might think. As I might think." He filled the carafe with water, bringing the level up to the six-cup mark. "How does that sound?" He carefully emptied the water into the reservoir.

"I think, yes. The sooner the better. Besides, you still haven't prepared for Sunday."

Suddenly Otty stood upright and froze, as if shocked. "Good golly," he said. Then he guffawed until he had to sit down from a lack of breath, such was the release of nervous energy.

"At least I have a topic for Sunday's sermon," he gasped between spasms of laughter. He raised a finger, "Being prepared for the unexpected." he said solemnly. He again howled in delight.

When his coffee had finished brewing he refilled his cup and took it outside with him as he returned to his wood pile. He paused with the splitting maul in his hands, balancing in one palm and feeling its heft. With the other hand he ran his fingers over the blade to measure its sharpness. It didn't need to be honed and he resumed his previous pattern of swinging the maul over the rounds of wood, burying the edge into the grain of the wood, and then removing it with a long-practiced twist to the side. Freeing the maul he repeated the process, repositioning the raw wood as need so as to best reduce it into fragments into the right size, like sections of an orange.

As he worked he directed his thoughts to consider his wife's words. He knew he needed to bring other people into this, if only as a sounding board. He also began writing in his mind a response to Karl's message. "Dear Karl," he would begin and then stop, not knowing how to proceed. His mind raced back and forth between these two thoughts: preparing and responding to Karl. The more he considered these two problems, the less his maul would swing. Soon he found himself staring the fresh round of wood in front of him with both hands tugging at maul which was buried deeply in the flesh of the wood and which stubbornly refused to release the steel. He just let go of the handle, which remained positioned above the section of wood like an errant arrow. He walked to the door, cracked it opened and spoke into the gap. "I'll be right back. I'm going to drop in on Howard and say hi." Hearing his wife's acknowledgment he spun on his heels and moved out onto the road.

He had to ramble down a worn gravel drive for about a half-mile to reach his destination. Downhill. Getting to Howard's house was always easier than returning from it. But the effort was always worth it as Howard was probably his best friend; at least his favorite. He and Howard were the founding and sole members of the local John Polkinghorne Society.

Otty rarely moved much faster than a leisurely pace. This was partly because it of his nature, and partly because of his knees, which hadn't aged as well as the rest of his body. But he was eager to talk with Howard and he didn't even realize that he was almost into a jog.

As he reached Howard's house he rapped his knuckles against the door in a coded pattern and then grabbed the doorknob to let himself in. It was locked. Reflexively he tried to open it again, like a drunk who couldn't believe that the tavern was closed. Odd, he thought. Then he heard a small dog bark.

"Hold on, Otty," a muffled male voice called from the other side. The knob rattled a bit and then the door swung opened, revealing the gray bearded countenance of an old man attached to a plump body swathed in flannel and suspenders. An equally elderly Chihuahua peeked from around one stout leg. Otty stepped in and closed the door.

"Vandals. I had vandals last night," he complained. "Some tom-fools were lurking around my place. They drove Bitsy nuts." His little dog whined when he said her name, as if concurring with his words.

"Vandals, here?" Otty asked, surprised. "How strange. I haven't seen or heard anything unusual. Who were they, did you see?"

"No. I heard some noises outside last night after I had gone to bed. I figured I had another bear rummaging around. But then I heard the back door open and I knew it wasn't a bear. Dammit. It scares the bejeebers out of an old man to have an intruder. The dog must have scared them off."

"How did you know it was more than one?" Otty asked.

"Because I went outside this morning and there were footprints everywhere, different ones. I would say that there were two of them.

Out of habit Otty kicked off his shoes and settled himself on the single sofa, an ancient affair covered with an old, ugly quilt. It was positioned under the only window in the undersized wood-paneled front room, along side a small wood burning stove that sat on the fireplace hearth. Otty could hear the fire crackling within it. From the kitchen area which shared the same basic room, Howard poured steaming tea water into a couple of mugs, bringing one to Otty.

"Hell's fire, Otty, I moved here so I didn't have to live in fear." He sat down and leaned back in his ratty recliner, his short legs propped up, his feet pointing at the wood stove, one hand carefully balancing the tea. "I feel like I'm back at the 'U'. Lord, I hated that town. Couldn't wait to get away." Howard and Otty had both worked at the same university but in different departments and even then were only acquaintances. They both retired to Blue River, unaware what the other was doing. It was here where they became friends.

Howard sipped his tea and then set it daintily on the table next to his recliner. *"Pues, qué tal?"* he asked in Spanish.

"Bien," Otty replied, *"pero esto."* He handed Howard the same paper he had shared with his wife a few days earlier. "I got this from my brother. Did you get the vidmail I forwarded?"

Howard took the sheet of paper and read it silently, his bearded chin resting on his rounded chest. "Well, it means nothing to me. But I must say that your brother is quite sophisticated when it comes to computer technology. He pulled some tricks I've never seen and which took me a couple of hours to figure out. But I did." He looked up at Otty, his eyes beaming with the self-satisfaction of a job well done.

Otty shrugged his shoulders. "What did he do? What did you find out?"

Howard talked in terms Otty didn't wholly understand. Howard was impressed by something that was "embedded" and it was "untraceable" and "clocked." Otty just listened and nodded, trying to look like he understood.

"Good thing that you are predictable, Otty," Howard said with a smirk.

"How's that? What do you mean?" Otty responded, surprised and curious.

"You used your old computer and not the televisor to read your mail. None of this secret message stuff would have worked on the televisor. Only on a computer."

Otty grunted a chuckle. "I guess I am guilty as charged. To change the subject, Ever heard of *Alas Babylon*."

Howard didn't respond but bounced in his recliner until the stubborn mechanism retracted and allowed him to rise. "Want some more tea," he asked, turning stiffly. Otty nodded a negative. "Be right back," he said, shuffling off toward the back bedroom which he used as a storage unit. The old widower had crammed it full with the legacy of a lifetime of collecting this and that. After a few moments he returned holding an old paperback, which he gently handed to Otty. "Careful with it," he warned, "it's old, like me. You know, it wasn't really that great of a story. I don't know why I've kept it."

Otty looked at it briefly and handed it back to him. "Yep, that's it. I used to have a copy but sold it a long time ago. Perhaps I can borrow it some day and reread it."

Howard reclined again in his chair and reread the paper that Otty had given him. "Well, Otty, your brother is a bright one. I suppose then, that this entire message is somehow a code?" Otty nodded. He knew that this old computer science professor would be able to see inside the box.

"So tell me what it all means."

Otty explained to him everything as he understood it. Afterwards he asked, "so what do you think?"

Howard arched his eyebrows and puckered his lips, as animated personalities are apt to do. "Sounds like the you-know-what is about to hit the fan." He laughed. "This is gonna be interesting, to say the least."

They talked for a few more minutes while Otty finished his tea. As he left Howard's place he wandered behind the house to take a look at the tracks. Sure enough there were bootprints in the mud, some of which had been now been covered in little paw prints. The bootprints were of two different types, one of which had a distinctive chevron pattern. The prints were concentrated around the outside shed and under the windows. Mud prints were on the back step.

He had better keep his doors locked, Otty thought to himself. He headed back home, slowly, uphill.

+++

As she watched herself in the mirror Myla reached up behind her head and braided her hair. Deftly her hands weaved the frosted locks into two tight braids, one on each rear quarter of her blond-from-a-bottle coiffure. As she secured each end with an elastic band she slowly spun to make sure that nothing was amiss with her uniform She would never forget her embarrassment a couple years ago when a patient asked her if she had a brown-colored dog. Myla responded yes and asked her how she knew. The lady pointed to Myla's scrub bottoms which were covered in dog hair. She still blanched at the thought.

Myla liked being a nurse even though it was stressful at times. St. Boniface General Hospital was the only hospital in the county and while it was small it received every sort of patient, whether life-threatening injuries from a logging accident or the supposed spider bite on the child of an overly-concerned mother. She had worked there some fourteen years, but she was already one of the old-timers. Boniface General had a hard time attracting and retaining nurses. The big cities offered better wages and more opportunity. And while Purcell was located in a lovely area, a person still had to make a living. Beautiful scenery didn't pay the bills and times were difficult.

She had already made sure that the kids were next door with Jennifer, who would watch them till Jarad got home around five. As she gather up her keys and purse she called for the dog. Champ, the family's moppy brown water spaniel trotted out good naturedly from one of the kid's bedrooms and stood by the rear sliding glass door that opened up to the fenced backyard. He knew the routine. The sight of the dog caused her to absent-mindedly brush her bottom as she slid the door shut behind the dog.

She pulled on a sweater and stepped outside the front door. As the door shut she doubled-checked the knob to be sure it had locked securely. Anymore it was imperative that all doors and windows be locked, whether the house was occupied or not. The same was true with the car. Since the bombing of Washington, D.C. a couple years earlier and the subsequent deepening of an endless

economic recession, crime had edged upward. Even in St. Boniface
County. Anything not battened down was subject to new ownership.

She started her car and glanced at the charge level of the
batteries and the fuel level of the fuel tank. Both were fine for now.
She wouldn't have to stop for fuel nor plug in the car at work, which
was okay as far as she was concerned. She disliked pumping diesel
oil even more than handling the heavy electric cord of her car. It
never retracted onto its reel as it was supposed to and she inevitably
brushed it against her clothing, getting them dirty. This was
especially true during winter. She sighed with the thought. She
would deal with both another day.

As the car silently pulled away Myla contemplated the
routine of her existence. She was the type of personality that always
found comfort in routine, but that only seemed to guarantee that she
would regularly fall into a rut. And she felt that how she currently
felt – in a rut. Always the same shift at work, always the same faces,
the same uniform, the same everything. Only the patients changed,
but then they were in the same beds in the same rooms with the same
doctors, and suffering from the same illnesses. Myla sighed again as
she pulled up to the main road. She has been taking this same route
to work for forever and a day. She wanted a change, she needed a
change, but change was always fraught with risk. And a risk taker
she was not. Plus she knew she was fortunate having a good, steady
job.

Before she consciously realized it, she found herself already
at the parking lot of the hospital. As she headed away from her car
toward the building the locks on her car reset automatically. She

headed for the employee entrance located near the emergency room. She could have found her way to her unit blindfolded.

+++

The three cops sat as a triumvirate within the office of the sheriff. Jarad had been sharing with both the chief and the sheriff what little had transpired on his visit with Reverend Swess. Jarad was frustrated that there was so little tangible information to share. It was the intangible that he found so nagging.

"So, what do you mean that you don't trust him? What evidence have you got? We got to have something more than a gut feeling," the sheriff huffed.

"I know, Bob," Jarad replied, "but everything seemed so contrived. Is this note authentic? How can we know? Sure, we'll zip it off to the FBI for prints and whatever else they think might be helpful, but I don't think it matters. I suspect that this threat was simply a ruse for an excuse to bring the muscle."

"Those boys are missionaries, right?" the chief asked. "That is reason enough, don't you think? Maybe they just happen to be plus-size missionaries!"

"True, on the surface," Jarad agreed. "but these are big boys. Granted, I only saw two of them, but Swess said there were six. First, this is an unusual collection of over-sized men. They're linebackers. And six of them? Did the president have that many body guards? But that's only part of it. Swess is not being upfront. He has another reason for being here. I just know it. "

"Is this paranoia or a professional hunch?" the sheriff asked. "There sometimes isn't much of a difference. I know that there has been many changes in our county. Hell, in the past ten years this county has gotten more than its fair share of counter-culture types. We've gotten that colony of The Resurrected Saints, I mean the Primitive Resurrected Latter-Day. . . what the hell are they called?"

"The Resurrected Primitive Church of the Latter-Day Saints," Jarad coached him.

"Yes, them, the polygamists." the sheriff snorted. "They got their colony out east now – good people, I'm not criticizing nobody. And then we got the first legal brothel in Purcell in who knows how many years. Remember how that got so many folks worked up. Protests in front of the courthouse and all that. But the Kitten Palace pays its taxes and minds its own business, etc. Things settled down and returned to normal. And then, of course, Liberty Ranch was set up. Again, that riled people up. I think folks just think the worst of others that are different than themselves. Just because the Ranch doesn't allow men to enter the compound doesn't mean that they are up to no good. It is a school, for goodness sake."

The Sheriff continued to blather on inarticulately. "And a lot of people retired here. People from outside of the area and who happened to live lifestyles that were. . .", the Sheriff paused, his hands in the air, looking down at the table as he searched his mind for a word. ". . not typical of what you find here in Purcell and the surrounding environs. And as I told folks, like it or not, these people are not breaking any laws. And now we got GILM. So what? People will get upset and say negative things because they don't understand. No one likes things that are different. But they will get over it. As I was saying. What has happened in those past ten years from all these changes? Nothing. And nothing is going to happen with GILM."

"Bob, you might be right," the Captain agreed, eager to be done with the Sheriff's pontificating. He yawned and leaned back in his seat and laced his fingers behind the back of his head, his arms as wings. He had heard all of this before. The Sheriff was on one of his moral high-ground trips. "This whole thing might just blow over. But I am concerned about this alleged death threat. With everything you mentioned, we never had people threatening violence." He resettled his arms on the table before him, his fingers fiddling with a pen. "And as Jarad said, perhaps this is a concocted reason to bring in muscle. That causes me concern."

The sheriff shrugged. "Maybe, maybe not. How can we know?" he asked emphatically, his voice stretching thin. He leaned an elbow on the table and turned to face Jarad, accusingly. "I just don't want any of us here to make a mountain out of a molehill." He turned and crossed his arms against his burley chest satisfied that his point was made.

"Perhaps you are right. All I can say is that we'll try to keep on eye on him. This GILM thing is big," the chief said. "And now it is here in Purcell. Beyond that there isn't a whole hell of a lot we can do." He looked at the sheriff and then at Jarad. "Any other thoughts?" Both were silent.

+++

Chapter 3

Fall was a faithfully prompt visitor to the latitudes where Purcell lay. By the middle of September the first hard frost had fallen, laying to rest the labors of the area gardeners as the tomatoes and beans, corn and squash, and myriad of other well-tended delicacies died the death of blackened leaves, murdered by the sudden cold. But Fall was just and fair, sharing her martial skills with those of the artist, adding color change to the surrounding forests as the deciduous trees traded their green for the earthy tones of brown, yellow, and deep, ruddy red. The cool crisp sunny days alternated with cold, ice-tinged evenings. It was the very sort of weather that sweaters were invented for.

But Fall didn't loiter as winter did. She kept an itinerary by which people could know her schedule. Soon and definitively winter would creep down the mountains and ridge lines, tracing his advent with white demarcations as he slunk closer and closer to the valley floor, where most the residents kept their abodes. And then, suddenly, one morning all would wake to find the first snowfall on the ground, signaling the change in season as Fall finally fled to points south and Winter settled in for his customary stay. Fall is only a visitor, whereas Winter is a resident.

Fall was an active time for many residents, especially those who truly worked for wages and spent more time thinking about how to make a life rather than its ultimate meaning. For such folks this time of the year was one to gather firewood for the winter, shoot a deer for the larder, and draw in the last of the summer harvest for the cellar. Fishing was more than a sport and huckleberries were preserved not as homey gifts for Solstice, but for the morning bread. Life was a contact sport.

After the assassination of the President and the horrific devastation of Washington D.C, the people of the United States seemed to lose the collective wind in their sails. Perhaps if this had been a solitary event, it might have rallied the spirit of the collective can-do Americanism. But not now. Everyone was simply too tired from the continuous onslaught of one crisis after another. The bombing of Washington had followed on the heels of the dirty bomb detonated in the mouth of the Niagara River and then a similar one in Mobile, Alabama. Then the bombing of Giant Stadium during the Super Bowl, the ruin of the Statue of Liberty by a bomb-laden airplane, and the dramatic though botched attempt to blow up Los Angeles International Airport. And not to overlook all the seemingly endless and disparate problems Europe, Asia, and the rest of the world had been facing. Ethnic and religious strife, countless groups opposing each other and any and every government. To most Americans, chaos was the only word to describe the world around them.

Nonetheless, it was the third Iraq war that seemed to symbolize this sense of the endless conflict and entanglement that the United States could not, or would not, end. A generation of war in the Middle East and elsewhere exhausted much of the spirit and hope among the citizenry in the Republic. And with the world economy in a continuous slow unwinding, ambitions became smothered as working life took on an almost feudal existence, one foot in front of the other as each was glad to earn his or her daily bread and grog. Bread and grog. Even the children were tired.

+++

A soft rap at the door brought Otty back to attention. His thoughts had wandered as he contemplated the reasons why this Reverend Swess was interested in meeting with him. He had received the Reverend's vidmail requesting an appointment. Otty replied with a confirmation of the date and time and but felt trepidation ever since, albeit mixed with a strong dose of curiosity. Otty was familiar with GILM, but was surprised that it had already reached such a rural area as Purcell and it modest hinterlands. He would soon find out more.

"Come on in, the door's open," Otty said loudly but invitingly. He stood and maneuvered around his desk to greet his visitor. Make that visitors, he noted, as a second figure followed the first into his office.

Otty extended is hand to the first man. Otty recognized Reverend Swess' image from both the net articles and the man's vidmail. To Otty it was a nondescript face except for the remarkable gray eyes. The men exchanged sounds of greeting, ending with Swess indicating with a sweep of his hand the third figure in the room.

"This is my assistant, Jonathan. He is a missionary with our organization." The giant man nodded at Otty, but remained silent, his hands remaining knotted before him. Otty was impressed by the young man's stature. It was the sort of size that stood out in a crowd, like a seven foot man. The young man's kind face seemed in contrast to his massive frame. He remained standing by the door while Swess took the proffered seat.

"Yes, it is a pleasure to meet you pastor," Swess said as he sat down.

"No, please," Otty interrupted. "Call me Otty."

"Otty," Swess replied quizzically. "That is an unusual name."

"My initials, o and t. But always Otty, since I was a child."

"I see," the man replied. "Very clever."

"So, what can I do for you, Reverend Swess?" Otty asked as he settled himself in his chair behind the desk. Swess furrowed his brows as a person does to intimate the earnestness of one's words.

"I represent an organization . ." he paused, "that is out to change the world." He looked at Otty squarely. Did he see a challenge in the visitor's eyes. Perhaps there was some underlying resentment that Otty was unwittingly harboring, but he sensed an element of showmanship mixed with serious intent.

"Do you want to part of that change?" his guest asked him. "Like St. Paul, to turn the world upside down?"

A sales pitch, Otty thought to himself. He's either recruiting support or converts. The bemused but interested countenance on Otty's face did not betray his feelings. He had sat on innumerable thesis committees and knew when someone was trying to present a hypothesis that went against most trends of thought. His mind chuckled.

"Change?" he asked, feigning interest.

"Yes, change. I have been visiting the area churches and inviting pastors and congregations to join with GILM and to change the world."

"I see," Otty replied, nodding his head. "And I suppose you have met with some success?"

"Oh, yes, almost universal support. The local churches I have met with have been practically unanimous in their assent." He smiled broadly at Otty, exuding the confidence of a man who never doubted the eventual success of his efforts.

"And now I come to you," he said, pausing to examine the room. He scanned the books on the shelf to his right. He noted the cross hanging on the wall and some sort of framed diploma or credential. The specifics didn't interest him.

"But forgive me," he said in a contrite falsetto. "I am getting ahead of myself. I assume you are familiar with the movement?"

"GILM?" Otty asked. "Yes, I am. I have been following your organization with some interest over the years." Otty's interest in GILM was both academic and theological. He understood it as both a religious and social phenomenon. What started out as a grassroots ecumenical movement to counter the growing polarization of the Christian Church in America had evolved into a worldwide religious movement that sought to unite all religions in the name of peace. It had become particularly successful in Europe.

"Excellent," his guest said with obvious delight, his gray eyes sparkling enchantingly. "Then I can expect your support? I . .

we. . would appreciate your presence at the community rally Sunday afternoon. It would mean a lot to us."

Otty tacitly acknowledged his words with a brief wave of his hand. He plunged into thought, his hand scratching his cheek absent-mindedly. That same hand then pulled at his nose and chin.

"With all respect," Otty cautioned, "I am familiar with GILM, but that doesn't mean I support it." Otty watched as his words caused Swess to almost imperceptibly sway in recoil. His smile never wavered.

"Yes," he said with assurance. "I understand your hesitancy. But, perhaps, this is a question that needs to be shared with your board, even your congregation. It might be that you owe them the opportunity to assist you in this decision." He paused and resettled himself in his chair. "But I must confess, I cannot fathom why anyone would be opposed to joining the movement. It is only about love. It is about uniting people. It is about peace." A small slather of foam formed at the corner of his mouth.

"It is not how we perceive God that is important," he continued. "Some view him, or her, as a person, another as an emanation, still another as an ethical necessity. It doesn't matter. We may disagree on such minor details, but surely we can agree on what matters most of all. And that is love. Undoubtedly, you can't be opposed to love?"

He looked at Otty almost accusingly. "The whole world is coming together. Why would you want to be left behind? Even more, why would you set yourself and your church apart, even in opposition, to all that is good and right?"

Otty smiled and gestured a shrug with his hands. "Who said anything about opposing love? It is jut that we are a little body and sort of out of the mainstream of things. Changes just come a little slower here, I guess."

Swess inhaled deeply, betraying the indignation he felt welling up inside of himself. He isn't accustomed to being told no, Otty surmised. A kind, though flaccid, demeanor masked Otty's own inward turmoil. He felt threatened, a revelation which surprised and concerned him. But he didn't have time right then to analyze his emotions.

"Perhaps you are a student of history, pastor," he suggested in a formal tone. This question gave Otty a start. Had his guest done his own background research? The man's gray eyes pierced the space between them. An eyebrow arched.

"When was the last time Muslims, Jews, and Christians agreed to agree? That, my friend, is what GILM is all about. Just recently, you remember how France had practically erupted in ethnic warfare? You saw those images on the telescreen of the Champs Elysees in flames? The smoldering remains of the Louvre? GILM ended that! And who brought peace to Jerusalem after so many others had tried and failed? It was GILM! And our work still continues, today, now. We will never rest until we have brought peace to the world." He sighed again, and then lifted himself up to standing.

"Remember the words of Jesus," he said firmly. "Those who are not for us are against us." The meeting ended as Swess rose from his chair.

Otty stood with him and shook his extended hand. It was cold. He moved himself to offer his hand to the young man, but this silent giant was already exiting the room. Otty followed the pair of them out of his office and into the foyer of the church. His guests left the building directly without exchanging another word with him. A Lincoln sedan had anticipated their leaving and sat parked immediately in front of the doors. Shaded windows precluded Otty's from seeing the driver or anybody else in the vehicle. Both men slipped quickly into the car and it sped away as soon as the doors had closed. Otty watched the vehicle depart as its powerful electric motors whined softly and gravel was shunted noisily out from under the tires and sent bounding into the cold grass.

Otty slipped back into the warmth of the church and sat on one of the old wooden benches under the bulletin board. He realized that he had been warned, but was unsure of how to respond. Should he take the man seriously or simply shrug him off? Otty searched his feelings, trying to make sense of them. He was surprised that he felt so rattled by the visit and the man's words. Then suddenly, his mind found the emotional response it was subconsciously searching for. Otty now realized that Swess was attempting to bully him, which only made him feel even more vulnerable. With nowhere else to turn, indeed with no desire to go anywhere else, Otty picked himself up and headed for the sanctuary, his favorite place for prayer. He heard Swess's words haunting his hearing. "Remember the words of Jesus. . ."

"What?" Otty asked himself, "Is Jesus now wearing a GILM flag on his lapel?"

+++

Jarad cruised through the dark streets of the west side of town in this squad car . Here is where most of the wealthier families lived, and consequently saw most of the property crimes that were committed in the area. Jarad knew that there was practically little he could do to stop these thefts, but a display of the colors never hurt. Anyhow, he was glad to be doing something.

It was Friday evening and the sun had set, so he knew that some girls would be 'posing.' Posing was a national craze among the high school set that had recently settled in Purcell. Teenage girls would wait until it was dark and then stand before the front windows of their homes, the lights on bright, and display themselves to the men and boys who would watch from their parked cars at the curbside. Some girls would dance, others modeling suggestive motions and poses, always scantily clad in lingerie or even less. It was considered risqué but innocent fun by most adults, who would fondly recall from their youth their own adventures and exploration of the erotic. The unwritten rule was that the audience would never leave their vehicles and one parent would always remain home, secluded away in a bedroom or den in feigned ignorance of what was going on. The girls' safety needed to be assured.

Jarad slow down to a crawl as he maneuvered around the collection of parked cars in front the Bronsky house. He glimpsed Lily, their precocious 14-year old daughter, clumsily performing some sort of sensual movements that only the young male spectators, shivering in the breath-misted cars, could find attractive. Some of them waved meekly at Jarad as he slowly drove by. Jarad wasn't concerned about the boys; his intention was simply to pass through and to make his presence felt. But it never hurt to keep an eye out for trouble.

+++

It was probably the largest gathering in Purcell in living memory. The GILM rally in the high school auditorium brought in people from all around the county, though most came more out of curiosity than faith. But whatever the motives an assembly of this size generated its own dynamics. Enough of the GILM true believers were present to add fire to the fuel of anticipation. The room was dark except for stage lights which focused their beams forward toward the raised platform. Small digital cameras were perched in strategic vantage points to record the evenings proceedings for posterity, as well as other GILM purposes.

Reverend Swess sat on a metal folding chair with like seated representative ministers from the community, many in the colors or costumes of their particular sect. The rest were garbed in simple dark suits and ties. All carried broad smiles. It didn't matter the denomination, every preacher loves a crowd and this was an enthusiastic one.

At the appointed time the Presbyterian minister came to the speaker. His presence there drew a mixed response from the crowd, some cheered and others clapped. Most of the members of the audience simply sat quietly. It seemed a bit too rowdy for a church service, if that was what this was. What else could it be with so many clergy present?

"Welcome, everyone," he said. "This is a wonderful day. This is a new day, the first day of a wonderful future." The crowd received his words with a volley of applause. GILM workers in distinctive rainbow-colored vests jumped up from their seats, clapping with the abandonment of the zealot.

He waited for the applause to settle before he resumed his greeting. He talked with the practiced cadence of a professional speaker, pitching his voice upward as he pitched his sale outward. The assembly of people responded as if on cue. During the prolonged applause, the minister waved forward the next clergyman, an elder from the Mormon stake house. He led a group prayer, emphasizing both the universalism of God's love and the universalism of God's identity.

He, in turn, was followed by other church leaders. One led a congregational song whose lyrics were projected on the wall behind the podium. The next gave a brief overview of the history of religion. She noted that it was a history "replete with misconceptions, misunderstandings, and miscommunication, which meant in the end we simply missed God." The crowd rewarded her clever play on words with vigorous applause.

On that triumphant note, she then waved forward the speaker who was the focus of everyone's interest. Reverend Swess came forward seemingly oblivious to the cascade of clapping, hoots, and whistles that greeted him. He gave the Methodist minister a warm if not demure hug, touching her cheek with his, as she backed away from the front. He faced the crowd, gripping the front of the lectern and resting both arms upon it, leaning forward. He remained silent, nodding his head in each direction, smiling warmly.

He then pumped his hands, palm upward, encouraging the audience to increase the intensity of their applause. Those sitting in the pull-out bleachers began to stomp their feet, as when the home team scores a crucial goal in the closing seconds of a basketball game. Once the noise level had reached a thunderous intensity, he stared toward the ceiling and raised his hands as if in prayer, a pious effort to direct the crowd's cheers in the appropriate direction.

Then, suddenly, he shouted into the microphone, "people of Purcell, stand and praise your God." With that, he again lifted his hands, stared toward the ceiling, clapping his hands vigorously. The other ministers on the podium stood and mimed his movements. Smiles gave way to prayer, and some even began to weep.

But even before Swess had given his address, dim shadows animated the walls as people left the auditorium singly or in pairs. Many had already seen and heard enough. Before the evening's program was through, only a core group of true believers remained to fill the front seats of the bleachers. Though he did not visible acknowledge this exodus of people, it did not escape his notice. These sinners would pay, some day, for their insolence.

+++

Chapter 4

By most people's reckoning, the middle of October was too early in the season for the first snow. Not unusual, just too early. Even the most ardent winter enthusiast realized that an October snow meant almost a half year of shoveling. Only the naive were giddy.

Typically, the snowfall at the beginning of any one season in Purcell was heavy. Not heavy in volume, but in weight. The high moisture content being a quality of both the the last snowfalls of the season and the very first, before old man winter settled in making that dry powder the skiers preferred. This first cast of whiteness was only a harbinger of what yet lay ahead in the future.

The power company was ready. John Masker had been watching the weather forecasts everyday for weeks. It was his job as the branch manager for Northern Power and Electric in Purcell to have crews ready for the inevitable blackout caused by the first, heavy snows of the season. He watched both the quarter-sized flakes flutter indifferently in the harsh apron of light cast by the xenon lamps in the parking lot and the grid display on the wall that told him where electricity was and wasn't flowing.

Strangely, the snow had only just begun to fall before the first blackout of the season caused Purcell to become as dark as the surrounding forests. When John Masker turned to his screen to isolate the break in the grid, he was met with an unexpected and ominous precedent. Not only was the whole of Purcell black, so was the county. In fact, as far as he could ascertain, so were all of the surrounding counties. His screen was black in every direction.

+++

Jarad knew the kids would be delighted. He had awakened at six to stoke the wood stove and noticed that the clock face was black. No power, no school. He moseyed over to the window in the front room and peaked through a sliver in the curtain. Snow. Well, he thought, that's what they had predicted. From the kids' perspective, it's getting better and better.

He carefully opened the twin metal doors of the stove and stood for a moment before the open flames. The heat felt good against the bare, nakedness of his legs. He rotated in front of the fire like a vertical rotisserie, before grabbing a couple pieces of wood and carefully nestling them over the coals.

"Shoot!" he exclaimed under his breath. "No power, no breakfast." He thought for a moment and then went into the kitchen. There he scooped a couple heaping tablespoons of coffee into the tea kettle and topped it off with water. He set it on the wood stove and spun open the draft a bit to increase the level of heat. Camp coffee was better than no coffee, he thought to himself. It was times like this he was glad that they heated their home by wood.

He returned to the bedroom and quietly dressed in the darkness. Mentally, he planned his meal. Eggs and bacon, and maybe some pancakes, all cooked over the wood stove. The lack of power didn't mean he couldn't enjoy a hot meal.

Jarad was going to let the kids know that there wouldn't be any school today, but then decided that it didn't make any sense to wake them. He went over to the printer to get the morning newspaper, but remembered that there wasn't any power. No power, no telescreen, no newspaper. Alas, fair Warwick, he moaned. At least I can eat, he thought, heading back to the kitchen.

The sound and smell of sizzling bacon in the front room brought Myla out of bed. She stood in the dark hallway trying to blink her mind clear.

"Powers out," Jarad said in greeting.

"I see that, honey," she yawned. "Smells good," she said, inspecting her husband's enterprise. She shuffled into the kitchen and returned carrying an empty coffee mug. "I smell coffee." She gave her husband a kiss on the cheek as he poured her a cup.

She crossed the room and drew open the curtains. She observed the whiteness that covered everything. "Snow already, and it isn't even November," she stated matter-of-fact. She retired to the couch and curled up, drawing her feet up under her housecoat. "Have you called the school?" she asked quietly.

"No, I didn't think too," he said honestly. He looked up from his task of frying eggs. The bacon fat popped and gurgled as it was squeezed between the eggs and the heat. "I just assumed that the power was out everywhere." He pointed with the spatula at Myla's wrist. "What time is it?"

Myla looked down at her watch. "Seven-thirty. The kids still have to make it on time. Let me call."

She reached across to the table opposite the couch and picked up the phone. She placed it in her ear and switched it on. "Dial school," she said evenly into air about her. The phone responded with a beep, indicating no service.

"That's odd," she said quizzically. "The phone is down."

Jarad handed her a plate of bacon and eggs and then refilled her coffee cup. "The power outage probably affected the cell towers." He sat on the opposite end of the couch to eat his breakfast. "I'll go for a quick ride after I'm done eating and check things out," he smacked. "It would be a good idea to run by the station, just to make sure that they haven't been trying to contact me."

It took Jarad twenty minutes to clear the driveway. The two inches of snow that had fallen had already begun to melt, which made it that much harder to shovel. He thought that it was peculiar that an outage would be caused by this little amount of snow. He assumed another cause. Perhaps a car slid off the road and made a mess of things. The power company linemen probably had to string a good measure of line and re-set a power pole. He'd seen it happen before. The county still hadn't upgraded into underground power lines.

The neighborhood was still dark. The sun was just now making its appearance, indicated by the opaque luminance of the clouds to the east. As he drove by the kid's school he noticed that only a couple cars were in the parking lot. The windows were all dark. He moved to call his wife, but stopped when he remembered that the phones were not operating.

The plows had already cleared the main thoroughfares. He turned onto Cleveland Street and headed toward the station. Melted snow would sprinkle his windshield whenever he passed under any overhanging branches of the large trees that bordered the drive. The lights were on at the hospital, which seemed spectacular in the dark, gray morning light. Besides the police station and the sheriff's office, only the hospital had auxiliary power.

Things seemed normal as he pulled into the station. He smiled at Judy as he entered, stomping his boots on the concrete landing to knock off snow before crossing the threshold.

"Morning, Judy," he said with his sweetest voice.

She glanced up from her desk and then down again. "Morning, Lieutenant," she replied flatly in her I'm-busy-so-don't-bother-me voice.

He went around the corner to a large room that served a variety of purposes, including housing his desk. He fumbled quickly through the papers in the in-box situated on the corner of the desk, but noticed nothing urgent. Everything could wait till he went on shift at noon. He opened a drawer and removed his service phone. He switched it on and put it to his ear. No dial tone. He returned it in the drawer and pushed it closed.

He headed back into the hallway and toward its terminus. He peeked into the chief's office. The chief was sitting with his chair spun around, facing the only window in the room.

"Good morning, Chief," he said. The older man turned his chair around to face his desk and Jarad.

"Morning," he said gruffly. "Something strange is going on and I think you should know." He leaned on his desk with his elbows and clasped his hands together.

"I radioed Pully and had him cruise on over to the NP & E office and get a status on the power situation, and maybe any scuttlebutt about the phones," he said. "John Masker, the manager, you know him?" he asked. "He said that he had no idea of what was going on. He doesn't know about anything local that could have caused this outage. It's bigger than the county."

"So what does that mean," Jarad asked, leaning against the door jamb.

"It means that I need you to start early. See you in an hour."

Jarad left and headed home. Myla was not going to be pleased.

+++

"Otty, darling, the power is out."

Otty opened his eyes as his wife nudged him on the shoulder. He groaned. He didn't like to getting up early. And anytime not of his own accord was too early. He yawned deeply and tried to focus on his wife. He reached underhand for his glasses, which he always left on the nightstand next to the bed. Fumbling, he accidentally knocked them to the floor. Ellie picked them up and handed them to him.

"Sorry, Otty," she said softly, "I thought that you'd want to know."

"How long?" he asked.

She paused. "About two hours."

He sat up and pulled the covers away, pivoted and placed his feet on the floor. He sat there on the edge of the bed, trying to force his mind clear.

"Did it snow?" he asked, remembering the forecast from that prior evening.

"Just a couple inches," she replied. Otty could sense the tension in her voice.

"It was probably a just a broken limb taking down a power line," he mumbled, trying to sound encouraging. He stood up and headed for the dark bathroom. "I'll just be a moment dear," he said as he left the room.

After a few minutes he appeared in the kitchen. He noticed movement in the mudroom and peeked his head out the door. Ellie was perking coffee over the stove. Thank goodness for propane he though to himself. She gave him a smile when he stepped into the little entryway, which served as a combination entry way, closet, and shoe room. Shoes were not worn in their home. She handed him a cup of coffee, knowing that she didn't need to ask. The dog came up and touched its nose against Otty's hand. He gave the dog a brief petting and then moved across to the window, peering outside.

"If power doesn't come on in the next couple days, I will suspect that this is what we've been expecting," he said in a soft monotone. "I'm going to walk over and see Breanne and the kids. Why don't you come along."

"Absolutely, I wouldn't have it any other way," she replied. "But first, let's have some breakfast." Otty smiled. He knew everything was going to be alright.

+++

At first, the loss of electrical power raised few concerns. Power outages were the norm during the winter months in this part of the country. In fact, the utility crews counted on the extra hours in the field during November and December as a means to earn additional money for the Solstice holiday. After that, overtime was an annoyance. It tended to interfere with skiing, ice-fishing, and sleep.

The first day there were few problems in Purcell. For the children, it meant a three-day weekend. Then a four-day weekend. But by the fifth day it was no longer pleasant. Many folks heated by gas or electricity and these were unavailable during the blackout, forcing them to stay with friends or family members who utilized wood for heating. Welcomes began to wear thin. People vented their frustration at the employees of the local NP&E office, who were at a loss for answers. Even the police and the sheriff's office were harangued with requests to do something, but no one had any answers or solutions.

The biggest source of anxiety of all was simply not knowing. What was going on? What was being done about it? Where should one go for answers? Communication had become centralized with the telescreen. It served as television, internet, and telephone for those who hadn't kept their cell phones. It even delivered the morning newspaper to a subscriber's printer. But without power, the telescreen couldn't function. And without active communication, the world that had become so small suddenly become so big.

+++

Otty and Ellie walked hand in hand, helping each other manage the slick surface as they trekked to their daughter's house, 100 yards away in the adjacent lot. She lived in an old, dumpy, double-wide mobile home that sat next to the road. It was not a

particularly nice place, but it was the best that Otty and Ellie could afford to provide with their limited means.

Arriving at the house, Otty was intentionally noisy has he loudly knocked the snow off of his boots by stomping them on his daughter's front porch. He listened for the sound of any activity within the house before giving the door a few raps and calling out an inquiring hello. Ellie stood next to him, silent, holding her coat tight against herself. She was cold. After a moment, they heard soft footfalls. Their daughter opened the door without so much as a smile, positing a brief 'hi dad, hi mom' in the doorway before disappearing back inside the room from which she had come. The two entered into the mudroom and removed their coats. The house was warm, Otty noted, which was a good sign. To their endless frustration, Breann often tended to be indifferent to the needs of those around her, including her children. She was by any definition a negligent parent.

Otty loved his daughter and adored his two grandkids – his only ones – but whereas he had mellowed over the years she seemed to have developed an emphatic need to be contrary to everyone's opinion or position. He didn't understand it. Ellie believed that their daughter was simply trying to find her way in the world. Otty was patient, but by his reckoning the only things she had found were a couple children fathered by two different men and an inability to support herself. They did their best to help take care of their daughter, their only child. Maybe that was part of the problem.

Otty slipped through the messy setting of dirty clothing, food wrappers, and unswept floors, and cleared himself a spot on the couch in the front room near the wood stove. Breann took a perverse pride in her lack of housekeeping, somehow rationalizing it as a demonstration of her independence as both a person and as a rebel against the norms of society. Otty thought that she was just lazy, but he had learned to never vocalize those thoughts -- at least not around his daughter.

It wasn't that Breann had total disregard for the assistance of her parents. She did appreciate them; as best as she could. As with many people in Purcell, she struggled to find steady employment. And since the government could no longer afford to maintain a comprehensive welfare system, she had to rely on the help of others. In her world, those others were her parents. She was thankful. Still, Breann had trouble acknowledging this fact to their faces.

She reappeared with her mother in tow. "I need to go to Purcell today," she said to her, "would you mind watching the kids?"

"Of course not, dear," Ellie cooed, "I would be delighted to."

"They should be up before too long. I let them sleep."

She slipped on a heavy coat and then grabbed car keys, phone bud, and wallet off of the kitchen counter. She stuffed the wallet into a rear pocket. Breann didn't use a purse. Purses, cosmetics, and jewelry were symbols of oppression. By Jove, Breann was not counted among the oppressed.

"How's your fuel?" Otty asked, wanting to offer his assistance so she didn't have to ask. It was difficult for Breann to ask for help.

"I'm okay," she responded neutrally. "I got a half tank and a full charge. I'll be fine, don't worry."

She turned to her mother, who was peeking through a bedroom door, checking on her grandkids. Breann whispered, "I should be back before supper, but would you mind feeding them?"

"Of course not, Breann. Anything else?"

She paused, her hand on the doorknob. "Yeah, could you check Sammy. He might have a fever. He said he didn't feel good when I put him to bed last night; that he was hot. But you know how I hate touching sick kids." She shook her head with a grimace and bolted out the door. It seemed like she couldn't wait to get away from the house.

+++

Chapter 5

Communities, like individuals, often do not realize how woefully unprepared they are for calamity until it strikes. Although there might be some nominal attempts at readiness, such as stockpiling supplies, training emergency personnel, or developing contingency plans, too often this preparation can not match the reality of the need. Because once preparations are undertaken the question is always asked as to how much preparation is enough? And then it ends, for it soon becomes too costly in both time and money to justify the expense of constant readiness. Only the superficial is budgeted, as it is deemed adequate and cost-effective by the powers that be.

This was the predicament Purcell found itself in. There were few resources in place to meet the needs of the under-prepared citizenry. Over the course of the pass couple decades, electricity had taken over the task of other forms of energy. Almost everything ran off of the grid: transportation, communication, heating and lights. Therefore with the grid down, the hospital and its diesel powered backup generators had became the community shelter by default. Few people had any other choice. RVs and campers became squatters outside the facility, running umbilical cords to draw power from the generators. But this solution created another problem. Where was the diesel going to come from that was needed to keep both sets of generators functioning? This was a question the city government pondered.

People also began to steal from each other, a harbinger of
the desperateness that was yet to come. First it was firewood that
began to disappear, forcing those who had stacks of cord wood to
bring their precious supplies into their homes. Unused bedrooms
and guest rooms were stocked with split rounds of fir, pine, and
larch. This caused the more daring thieves to raid the houses to get
what they needed. Once this inhibition was breached, it was easier
to repeat. And the elderly were easy prey. Soon, Purcell experienced
an unprecedented level of burglary and larceny. This led to the first
murder in the city's history, though the fact went unrecorded for
many weeks.

The police and the sheriff's deputies could not manage this
spectacular increase in crime. The mayor considered declaring
martial law, but relented when he was advised by the sheriff and the
chief of police that it couldn't be enforced. Instead, a neighborhood
watch program was developed that used volunteers to patrol the
streets after dark. They were equipped with radios to communicate
with the police station. Many armed themselves out of fear for their
own safety. But the program was scuttled when it was realized that
many of the volunteers were using their position to actually
coordinate the break-ins. It seemed no one could be trusted.

Most of the churches had united under the GILM banner
and marshaled their meager resources to meet the need in the
community. Church volunteers went door to door, soliciting in-kind
donations and then distributing them to those in need. When
donations dried up, the county food bank was drawn down. Soon,
the only thing edible remaining at the food bank were large bags of

TVP – textured vegetable protein – that looked and smelled like cheap dog food. Hunger in the community had not yet reached the deep, dark valley where even TVP is a godsend. It soon would.

In addition, it was difficult to get around. The snow resumed in quiet regularity, accumulating in the unplowed streets. Only a few important arterials were maintained, but even this effort was questioned. Unless fuel was brought in some time soon, the diesel used in the plow trucks and what remained in the two local fuel stations would have to be diverted to the tanks supplying the hospital generators. It was only the inevitable question of when.

+++

Jarad parked his patrol car near the emergency entrance of the hospital. This was partly due to the fact that it was plowed and partly because this was the wing of the hospital where Myla worked. The rest of the building, including the office spaces, the waiting areas, and even many of the hallways, were full of refugees from the cold.

As he entered the swinging door Jarad heard his wife's voice echo down the dimly lit hallway. Most of the lights were off in order to save fuel for the generators. He followed the sound of the echoes up to and then past the nurse's station. He saw Myla standing near two large doors which he hadn't ever noticed before. She was talking with a plump, well dressed, middle-aged woman. Neither of them seemed happy.

"I am sorry that there is no more toilet paper. What more can I say?" Myla said very firmly, in a voice washed with tiredness.

The older woman turned to face Jarad as he approached from behind Myla.

"There was no reason to call the police," she said vindictively to Myla. "We need toilet paper and I just wanted to know where the hospital storage was."

"Again," Myla stated, "there is no more toilet paper. Perhaps you and some of your friends could return to your homes and bring back some from there. We have no means of getting more, ourselves." She gave the woman a glare. "So please back away, if you don't mind, so I can close, and lock you damn people out!" The force of Myla's words seemed to push the woman backward. Jarad helped Myla to secure the doors. The lock was balky from lack of use. This was the first time that these fire doors had ever been locked.

She turned and leaned against the doors as if testing their strength. Dark rings hung under her eyes. She looked at Jarad with an exhausted face through which he could still see that determined gutsiness which never seemed to diminish. Lord, I love this girl, he thought to himself. He put his arm around her and drew her close to himself, enveloping her with his arms. She nestled her nose into his neck. For a moment neither said a word.

"Let me finish my rounds, then I'll be ready to go," she said softly. She moved her arms from around Jarad's waist and up toward his chest, giving him a strong hug. She moaned deeply. "Connie is late. I hope she comes. These crazy twelve hour shifts are killer." She sighed again and unbound herself from Jarad's embrace.

"Why don't you follow me," she said with a pouty smile. "I miss you and I need your company." She grabbed his hand and tugged him along. Jarad followed in the semi-darkness. She entered a brightly lit room. He waited at the door and watched his wife do whatever it is that nurses do.

In all, there were only six patients, all sharing two rooms. None of them were seriously ill, though most were not yet ready to go home – especially under the current circumstances. All but one of them was asleep. The doctor had ordered sedation for a couple of them because of their anxiety.

"Hello, officer," a gravelly voice said from the far gurney. Jarad craned his head and then entered the room. He eyed the anonymous face of a man of indeterminate age. He was of medium size and build, but even laying down he projected an air of authority. He seemed at ease with his current situation. Jarad nodded to him without speaking.

"So, how are things in our fair community?" he asked. "Any news on what has caused all of our grief?"

Jarad nodded a negative. "It sure has turned our world a kilter," he told him. As was his habit, Jarad scrutinized the man. "Do I know you?" he asked.

The man chuckled softly. "Actually, you do," he said, extending his hand into the air. "Peter Rafferty. Our paths crossed a few years back, if I remember correctly." Jarad took his hand and gave it a brief though firm shake, as men do when meeting for the first time. But Jarad still couldn't recall where he knew him from.

"I'm sorry," he told the man sincerely. "You look familiar, but I can't place the name or the face."

"Well, I understand," he said kindly. "Think back two years ago, May or June, I think. Border security. You know, that Alberta thing."

Jarad nodded his head as recognition came to his mind's eye. "Yes," he said, "you and another fellow. I remember."

The province of Alberta chose to secede from Canada right after the long anticipated departure of Quebec. This move caused a political upheaval north of the frontier, and was posed by some in Washington as a possible threat to border security. Not only did new protocols have to be established between the United States and the now sovereign nations of Quebec and Alberta, but also between the two wayward provinces and Canada. Rafferty and his partner were sent by Homeland Security to assist Purcell and the County in monitoring the situation. It was feared that any one of the many purported terrorists cells in Canada might take advantage of the tumult to sneak across the border into the United States.

Jarad smile and patted the hospital bed inquiringly. "So, what are you doing here?"

"Well I decided that I liked this area when I passed through that time. And since I was retiring, I figured Purcell was as good a place as any. I am single and it is easy to locate almost anywhere." The man smiled. Jarad noted the loneliness in his dark eyes.

"And. . ." Jarad asked, encouraging him to continue.

"I was shoveling my walkway and, like an old man, I fell and broke my butt bone." He paused, "I don't know what you call it, but here I am."

"Sacrum," Myla murmured from across the room. She was obviously listening in on the conversation.

"That's right, my sacrum. The doctor said I am fortunate that it wasn't my hip. But I'm okay. I'll be out of here tomorrow. Right nurse?" he called over at Myla. She looked up from a portable computer pad she was writing on. "Cross our fingers," she said.

"Do you have a place to stay?" Jarad asked.

"Yup, I'm set up pretty good," he replied. "But, I might need a ride."

"No problem," Jarad said. "Just have the nurse on duty radio over to the station. We should have someone available to come by and give you a lift."

They shook hands again, exchanging a few more words. Myla came up behind him just as he was about to turn and leave.

"Ready?" she said to Jarad. She smiled at the man. "You be good to Connie," she told him in mock threat. She grabbed her husband's hand, tugging him along. "Let's get out of here before I get another admit."

They were both exhausted. Each had been working long hours that were fraught with tension as the world around them turned in on itself, and seemingly everyone in that world turned to them for support. Myla shared with her husband the problems going on at the hospital. Not only was it never designed to be an emergency shelter, but it had become overcrowded and barely manageable. It was also being stripped of any and every supply. But the worst was the fact that it was down to Connie and herself to carry the load in what was left of the medical care. "Hey, I got a family too," she said, emphatically "but you don't see me bugging out." She yawned a long draft of the outside air.

They drove home in the police car. The haze of smoke from the many wood-fired stoves drifted among the trees, casting a depressing gray pall to the snow that covered every surface. Small white dunes lined the streets as unused vehicles became buried in the frequent flurries. Jarad drove slowly among them, following the tracks made by other unknown travelers.

When they pulled into the driveway, Myla turned to face her husband. "Jared, this can't go on. I'm going to go insane. We've got to leave."

She threw herself back into the scat and sighed heavily. Suddenly she burst into tears, drawing her hands over her face. She cried deeply and hard, turning herself away from her husband. Jarad unbuckled himself and reached across to his wife, trying to encircle her in his arms. She let herself slump into his grasp.

"Jarad, we've got to leave. But where are we going to go? Where are we going to go?" She breathed deeply and forced herself to stop sobbing. He used her husband's sleeve to wipe her eyes. "This is so unfair," she said softly.

Jarad held her as best as he could. He didn't know how to respond. He had been so engaged in his own responsibilities as a cop that he now realized that he had not been the husband that Myla needed. Nor the father his children needed. Suddenly, Jarad was angry with himself. How could he have been so blind? How could have been so out of touch with the current reality? Was it selfishness? Did the world really depend on him?

Jarad smelled his wife's hair. You are so beautiful to me, he thought to himself. He touched his lips to the back of her neck, snuggling. "You're right, Myla," he whispered, "Let's get the hell out of here."

+++

People began to leave. The first to go were the chicken-littles, those who saw any trial as a portent of their own doom. Within a dozen days of the loss of power and with a growing sense of uneasiness, such folk had already fled to safe harbors, wherever they might lie. But most people remained, confident that power would be restored in due time and normality would return. As it always had.

But when the days without power began to be counted in weeks, the trickle of people leaving Purcell turned into a modest stream. Even those who were initially ambivalent to their situation changed their minds by casting their vote with the herd instinct. Vehicles were loaded with clothing, food, mementos, and tired children. Fuel was begged, pooled, or stolen and little caravans were organized. Within a month's time over half of the town's population had left. Some to families and friends elsewhere, others with less specific plans. Simply away. As with refuges across the world and across time, simply banding with the like-minded and the like-suffering was reason enough. Commiseration en masse and always toward the cities.

Yet, a few promptly returned to Purcell, now a shelter that was only days earlier scorned. They retraced their steps, filled with tales of violence. The city of Spokane, the only real city of any size in the area and a natural destination for refugees, had established roadblocks manned by city police and county deputies to keep people out. There was 'no more room.' Passage was allowed on Interstate 90 but only for those vehicles that had sufficient fuel or battery charge to make it through the city and out to the other side. Past that point, the police were not concerned. Their job was to maintain the integrity of the perimeter established around the city.

For want had turned many former neighbors into brigands and highwaymen. As desperate times created desperate people, theft and murder became simple things. The civility of Dr. Jekyll was no match for the crazed, animal instincts of Mr. Hyde. The wolves had descended upon the sheep and the sheep knew not what to do.

+++

Jarad returned to his office after dropping Myla off at home. He felt differently inside, relieved actually, that he and Myla had decided to leave. His first impulse, just minutes earlier, had been one of shame. He felt a strong sense of obligation to his coworkers, the chief, and to all that his badge represented to him. But only minutes of contemplation had steeled his resolve to leave, to be away, to be safe. The impulse of a husband and father trumped those of a cop.

He sat slumped in his office chair. He was trying to remain focused as he attempted to compose yet another burglary report. He amused himself for a moment with the idea of duplicating a similar report he had filed just yesterday, altering only the names and addresses. But this game only reminded him of his impotence in protecting people. He knew that there was little the police force could do to fulfill its duty or people's expectations. He wondered if this is what law enforcement was like in wartime conditions. A tinge of fear echoed in his mind as he pondered the erosion in the civility of the people he was sworn to protect.

He was startled out of his haggard state of mind by the shrill voice erupting from the intercom. It was Judy and Jarad had never imagined her capable of such an expression of emotion. He left his desk without waiting to hear the end of her message and moved swiftly down the hall toward the entryway. His hand had subconsciously grasped his holster.

He was greeted in silence by two teary-eyed women, Judy and another whom he didn't recognize. She was a younger gal, bundled in a dirty pink winter coat and over-sized boots. She was in obvious distress as her bloodshot eyes corkscrewed around the room. She and Judy burst simultaneously into fresh tears when he parked himself in front of the two of them. The young woman began to wail.

Suddenly, as if on cue, she collapsed. Jarad was just able to capture her in his arms, keeping her from falling onto the sodden carpet. Judy rushed around the counter to help him carry the woman into the multi-purpose room. They laid her on a small love seat that served as a couch in the sitting area. Moisture streamed unattended from her eyes and nose. Her moaning had softened to a whimper as she lay akimbo on the cushions.

"Oh!" Judy cooed between hiccuped sobs. She tried to dry her tears with the heels of her hands. The smeared mascara had created a raccoon's mask around her red, damp eyes. For the first time Jarad realized that they were blue in color. She gracelessly plopped herself on the chair next to the young woman. There, she gently gathered up and held the woman's hand in the grasp of one of her own while the other brushed the tousled hair from the woman's filthy, pallid, tear-smudged face. Jarad stood stiffly next to the little sofa, mesmerized by the anguish incised into the young woman's countenance.

"Her husband and baby are dead," Judy said flatly. She looked up at Jarad. "They were shot."

"What!" Jarad exclaimed, his voice rising in inflection. Suddenly he felt a little light-headed as the room around him took on a surreal cast. He knew murder was his business, but he hadn't ever experienced it professionally. A tremor coursed through his upper arms as he fought back the gnawing feelings of fear that he found harder and harder to keep at bay. He was alarmed and afraid, but like a good cop he didn't want to show it.

"She told me what happened. That is when I called you." She looked down at the silent form next to her. The woman had ceased making any sounds. Was it not for the slight rise and fall of her chest, she seemed to be dead. "Poor thing," Judy said softly, tears again wetting her cheeks.

Jarad knelt down and spoke to her softly, trying to get a response. He then hesitantly moved his hand to her shoulder and gave it a few gentle tugs. The young woman seemed oblivious.

"Leave her be," Judy said softly. "Let her sleep. When she gets up I'm taking her home. She needs someone to look after her."

"That is fine, but I need to get some information from her. I need to know what happened. Who did this and . . ."

"I can tell you what she told me. She won't be of any use to you as a witness. Not in her current state, any how."

Judy recounted how the young woman stumbled into the foyer as if she was inebriated. She startled rambling on that her husband and son were dead. They had been stopped by armed men at a roadblock. She was driving. Her husband got out of the car to face the men. The baby had been fussing, so he was holding it. The men were agitated and demanded money, fuel, food, anything of value. When he reached for his wallet inside of his coat, one of the men hollered that her husband had a gun. A series of shots rang out, killing her husband and the baby he was holding.

"That is all I know," Judy said. She sighed deeply. "I don't know what happened after that and how she escaped, but here she is." Jarad looked down at the tragic figure. Considering her future, he wondered if she had escaped at all.

"I'm go check out her car," he said, turning away. He knew that it would probably be a meaningless task, but he was relieved to be leaving the room.

He shielded his eyes as he was greeted by a bright noonday sun reflecting off of the snow. He had left his sunglasses on his desk. An ancient, dirty Mercury sedan in otherwise excellent condition sat idling in the parking lot with its driver's door wide open. The old car must have been a collectible, called into use as an escape vehicle. A scan of the exterior revealed a couple of jagged punctures in the front windshield and hood. Bullets holes, Jarad surmised. The missing rear window confirmed the fact. Nothing remained except a gaping maw with jagged crystalline teeth and a chrome gum line.

Jarad opened the rear passenger door. The rear compartment was empty except for a baby seat tethered to the immaculate vinyl cushion. A baby's bag and a stack of photo albums were tumbled on the floor. Shards of glass mixed with snow had collected in the seam of the rear bench where the cushions came together.

He slammed the door shut with too much force. He turned and leaned into the still open driver's door, resting his weight on the steering window. He scanned for the engine stop button before remembering that these old cars was turned off by the keys. He located the key on the dash and gave it a counter-clockwise twist. The engine died in response.

In his entire law enforcement career Jarad never had to contend with savage violence and murder. That was something for big city cops. He felt a sudden and almost overwhelming urge to get his wife and children and run away, to be done with this insanity. But he fought down the impulse. He had to remain strong at least for little while longer. Then he'd run. He was glad that he had asked Myla to start gathering together supplies and to stuff them into their car. He wanted to be ready. He wished he was with her now.

He pulled the radio from the harness attached to his belt. He gave the call button a push, waited a moment, and then shouted into the microphone.

"Chief.'

There was a long pause before an old, raspy voice responded. In his excitement Jarad cut him off. "Chief," he said again, "we got problems. I think things are coming to a head." "Jarad," a tire voice responded, "Send Judy home, lock up the station, and get over to the Sheriff's office as soon as you can. I just got some news. Really bad news. And things are far worse than you could ever imagine."

+++

For a moment Otty was racing a varying hare that he had inadvertently flushed from a stand of young cedars. But the hare didn't seem inclined to finish the race and with a sudden twist disappeared into a thicket of willows. Otty's mind turned briefly to hunting and wondered how many hares it would take to feed his family.

It seemed that no sooner had he begun his journey than it was over. Howard's little A-frame cabin appearing quickly. Otty shifted his weight on his skis and brought the tips together, plowing on the inside edges to decrease his speed. He circled around to the side of the cabin and stopped short of the door. He deftly removed the skis and leaned them against the cord of wood that was stacked on the porch. He swiveled his body to remove the rucksack with the attached snowshoes. Just the sight of them reminded Otty of the slow return trip he would be undertaking in a couple hours. He stacked these against his skis. Lastly he rapped his familiar greeting on the door before helping himself inside, kicking the tips of his boots against the threshold to knock away any snow.

The house was warm and filled with the smell of cinnamon. As was his custom, Howard was making tea for the two of them. He hailed Otty from the kitchen A skinned hare hung over the kitchen sink. As usual, Otty mused to himself, Howard was a step ahead of him.

They settled down in their usual places. Otty noted that the room seemed to exude that delightful musty smell of ease and old memories, things he hadn't really noticed before. Was he getting sentimental? He and Howard talked a bit about everything and anything, each savoring the tea and each other's company. In time the conversation settled into a more somber and serious tone. By looking at Howard's eyes Otty knew instinctively that something meaningful was cooking in the old boy's mind.

Howard began to speak. "There is something important I want to discuss, but first I think that we need to rally as a community. Maybe organize is a better word," he said. He elaborated on how he thought that Blue River needed to make an organized effort to canvas the area for people in need. In addition, he proposed that abandoned or empty homes be stripped of any useful items like food, clothing, and fuel, and that these things be distributed to those in need. He felt that Otty's position as pastor of the only church in the area qualified him as a neutral authority to organize such an enterprise. "Anyhow," he said, "I just wanted to run that by you."

He cleared his throat again before continuing. Otty had recognized a long time ago that Harold's habit of throat clearing was a means to shift his thoughts from one topic to another. Here we go, he thought to himself.

"Now, picking up on our previous conversation. ."

"Which one?" Otty interjected.

"When you were here last," he said. "You know, the collapse of the power distribution grid."

Otty chuckled. "Just making sure," he said with a smile.

"So," Howard said with a wink, "picking up on our previous conversation. I've done some research. . ." Otty cut him off. "Research?" he asked incredulously, "how can you do 'research'? Is your telescreen up?"

"Let me rephrase that," Howard said with a devilish tone of voice. "Let's just say I've been perusing old issues of my magazine collection." Otty laughed a deep, needed laugh. His visits with Howard were his respites. Subconsciously he always tried to make the best of them.

"Howard, you are a pack rat. You save everything" he said, teasingly.

"And aren't you glad! Besides, they burn well," he said, pointing at the wood stove. "As I was saying, it is as I remembered. The grid is centrally controlled and very small sections can be manipulated independently."

"Why is that, I wonder."

"Think about it Otty. With the advent of all those alternative power schemes, especially when Congress made that push for energy independence and all those energy production sites began springing up. Soon we had wind farms, wave farms, solar farms, and then, of course, all those nuke plants began to come on-line. Well, instead of a few dams and power plants to keep track of, we now had thousands of little energy production sites scattered all over the country, some producing at night, others during the day. The grid had to be upgraded and more finely controlled. Ergo, the current system."

Otty paused for a moment and considered Howard's words. "So what you're telling me is that the grid is a flexible system. Makes sense."

"Yes it is. It is very flexible, but also centrally controlled. Otherwise there would be no way to effectively monitor and control the flow of power as the various farms and plants were put in and out of operation."

"Okay, so what does that mean Are you telling me that the entire system collapsed because somehow the central control failed? Sabotage, for instance?"

"Possibly, but I don't think so. If central control was lost, then the grid would simply operate in a patchwork fashion, like a series of islands in a sea of power lines. And we would just be one of the unfortunate ones without power in our small section of the grid. But I don't think so."

"So. . . what do you think?" Otty asked, slowly.

"I think that that our section, and maybe other sections, perhaps all sections have been turned-off."

"Intentionally?" Otty asked.

92

"Intentionally," Howard agreed with a nod of the head..

"Why?" Otty asked, more so thinking aloud than an intended question.

"That, my dear friend, is *the* question."

+++

Jarad drove slowly to the Sheriff's office. Anticipation was making him practically sick. The sounds of the chief's voice replayed in his mind again and again as he drove. Not the words he said, but the sounds. Jarad realized he was experiencing a powerful feeling of anxiety. "This is worse than my wedding day," he said to himself.

Purcell was like a ghost town. Nobody was on the streets. In fact there were few footprints in the snow. He passed the Safeway store, its sliding doors torn from its tracks and set carelessly against the exterior wall. The store had been ransacked weeks ago, which the police didn't even try to prevent. They had only showed up to keep order. Jarad could still remember the surreal environment inside the store when he had first arrived after being notified that the store had been broken into. While some people were pushing carts down the aisles, reading cans and boxes, carefully and thoughtfully making their selections as if shopping on a stringent budget, others were careening around, shoving any and everything haphazardly into their carts, constantly looking over their shoulders. Considering the circumstances, Jarad though that the wild-eyed were the sane ones.

When he pulled into the parking lot of the Sheriff's Department, only two other vehicles were there that were not covered in snow, the chief's and the Sheriff's. The station looked eerie even in the daylight because of its lighting, which now seemed oddly garish in contrast to the obscure and dark windows that had become the norm for the rest of the town.

He found the two men in the Sheriff's office. It was warm there, which suddenly cheered Jarad. He didn't realize he had been so cold, being so consumed with his own thoughts and emotions. Neither man greeted him, except with tired wan glances. Jarad simply sat down, unwilling to break the silence.

"Well," the chief began, as if continuing a conversation,"that we are all in one fine fix." He paused, seemingly more from exhaustion than for effect. His face was haggard and unshaven, giving him the appearance of an old, wayward bum. "You know how hard it has been trying to find out what the hell is going on. Well, Bob got a hint."

Jarad looked at the Sheriff. His head was straight back against the cushion, an arm laying across his eyes to shield them from the overhead lights. He wasn't responding to the chief's words.

"And?" Jarad asked, quietly but expectantly.

"And . . . . it looks like things are over. Everything. We're gonna have to give up the ship."

"What do you mean?" Jarad asked perplexedly.

"It means that Bob here was finely able to talk with someone who had some inkling as to what in the world is going on. As you know, Bob made it to Spokane and while there he talked with an assistant to the chief of police. This guy, I don't can't remember his name, said that he had heard from some Air Force officer at the base near Spokane that there has been some sort of coup in Washington, DC, and that this entire electricity fiasco is being orchestrated as a result."

"So, Bob has heard from some guy who had heard from some guy that there has been a coup in Washington, D.C." Jarad sounded dubious. "It makes sense, I suppose, but I wish we had something more concrete."

The Sheriff dropped his arm and sat up squarely in his seat. "Just shut the hell up, you dumb, stupid, fool!" the Sheriff growled at Jarad. "I am sick and tired of your ignorant skepticism. What the hell do you know about anything?" Jarad's temper began to stir and was set to respond to the Sheriff's challenge, when he suddenly realized how strangely different the man looked. Old, suddenly very old. And thin, even emaciated. The lower lids of the man's eyes were watery and sagging grotesquely downward. Jarad's riposte died on his lips. He sat there mutely, looking at the Sheriff.

"Bob, stop!" the chief interjected. "Just leave him alone. I agree with him, by the way." The Sheriff turned toward the chief, began to speak, and then decided against it.

The chief snorted and responded to Jarad. "Either way, in a couple days we should have a better idea as to what is going on. The mayor is trying to concoct some hookup to Olympia and hopes to get some sort of confirmation from that end. We should know in a couple days."

Jarad remained mute. His mind was processing the information and he was unsure what his next step should be. He had nothing to say.

"I grabbed some of the last TVP from the food bank. It's in the trunk of the car. I want you to take a bag, just in case. Otherwise, let's get back to work."

The chief and Jarad rose from their chairs and left the Sheriff alone in his office. The two walked out to the chief's car. The chief pointed his key fob at the car and the trunk door popped open. Jarad noticed that there were probably a half dozen 50 pound bags in the trunk. He took the one proffered by the chief.

"By the way, I've heard that every single dog has been adopted out of the animal shelter," he said wryly to Jarad, trying to lighten the mood. "I bet every single one of them got invited home for dinner."

Jarad smirked, but took the bait. "Too bad the paper isn't still in circulation. I could see the headline now, "Man bites dog."

The chief rolled his eyes, attempted a smile, but only managing a grimace. He slammed the trunk lid shut. "What happens now, that we've run out of dogs?" he asked, abstractly. He let out tired sigh, his breath frosting in the cold. "Get back to work, lieutenant, " he said kindly.

The two men parted, Jarad carrying the bag of food to the trunk of his own car. The chief called out after him. "At least for a couple days." The chief and Jarad silently stared at each other for a long moment, and then both turned to their respective vehicles without so much as a goodbye.

+++

Chapter 6

If there had been lights on, as was common before the power outage, someone might have noticed the two shadows slinking around the yard, hugging the fence line. But there were no lights and no witnesses. Just the darkness.

The two dark forms shimmied up against the back of the house. A bare hand reached out and gave the door knob a twist, but then quickly withdrew. Both figures then moved simultaneously in opposite directions, reaching for windows and trying to find a way in. Soon one was found as a window moved upward. As if on signal the second form followed the first into the house, hoisting his figure headlong into the blackness.

All was silent, but moments later an old man's voice cried out in alarm, followed by an eerie, animal-like shriek of a younger man. Silence again, but that too quickly ended with the sharp report of a small caliber gun. A couple minutes later the back door was swung open savagely and two figures raced into the dark, howling like hyenas. The door and the window remained open. The silence resumed and continued uninterrupted through the rest of the night.

+++

Jared hiked the distance from his car to the house. He could only drive to within a block of his destination before he was stopped by the snow that had heaped itself upon the unplowed street. As he left his patrol car the doors locked and the alarm was automatically set.

He crossed the neighborhood to the alley behind the house. He wanted to check for any tracks and where they might lead. Unfortunately, all tracks were lost within the myriad of prints that formed the path which rent the snow covered gravel driveway. At the scene of the crime, which was his primary interest, he could make out three distinct sets of footprints, coming and going from the house. He reasoned that two belonged to the suspects and the third to the neighbor lady that had ventured into the open door only to discover the frozen remains of her dead friend. She was so startled and so angry that she had walked the whole distance to the police station. Jarad had appreciated her spunk, but rued that there was little he could do to justify her efforts.

He entered the house. It was as cold inside as it was outside. He found the man's body in the short hallway that connected the kitchen with the front room. The victim was heaped in a frozen pile of dirty clothes and a thin almost childlike body, which had been tossed like an old rag doll onto the floor. Jarad noted that the man's collar was twisted up behind his neck. The assailant had apparently grabbed the man from behind and spun him around before dispatching him with a shot to the back of the head. An opaque mirror of black frozen blood pooled around the victim's shoulders. Surprise mixed with fear was permanently cast into the dead man's icy countenance which stared expectantly at the wall. A toothless gape was framed in white grizzle, giving the man a morose but comical look. Jarad found the whole scene terribly pathetic.

He carefully stepped over the corpse and examined the two back bedrooms. Nothing. One window was open, but no evidence of pillage. Returning, he again maneuvered around the corpse, leaving a single boot print in the frozen black sheen as he entered the bathroom. The vanity was open and its effects were strewn across the floor. Nothing remained on its shelves but the white, pasty residue from where a toothbrush had lain.

Jarad backed out and ventured into the front room. There he encountered a familiar sight. The man had made his bed on the sofa and the carpet around it was littered with the debris of junk food. Empty cans of tuna fish and cat food were carefully stacked against one wall. Jarad was not surprised. Pet food of any sort was prized as a meal in most every household. He was grateful that he hadn't yet found it necessary to feed himself or his family such things, but he would if required. Pet food was too precious to waste on pets. Indeed, pets themselves had been disappearing for weeks. In hungry times meat was meat. He took another glance around the cold house and another at the frozen figure on the floor. With a grunt and a shake of the head, he exited through the open door. He knew the body would wait. It wasn't going anywhere.

+++

"Here she is," Howard said. Otty looked at the receiver with inquisitive ignorance. He knew it was a radio, but it had too many switches, knobs, and gauges for it be fathomable.

"Okay, great," he agreed, "now what?"

"Well, as I said I need power. And I have an idea," Howard responded, with a quick tap of his temple with a finger. "I think I know just the place to fine what I need, but I can't get it. I'm getting too old for moving about much. I need you to get it."

"Get what?"

"Power, a solar cell," he said emphatically. "I think I know where there is a solar cell large enough and portable enough to power the radio. But I need you to get it."

"You said that. So, where is it?" Otty was tired and he felt himself getting exasperated. Why am I so ill tempered? he wondered. He knew it wasn't Howard's fault, it was simply that he felt he should be putting his time to better use. His self imposed to-do list was already plenty long.

"Take it easy, Otty. I know you're feeling a wee bit overwhelmed." He gave his friend a squeeze on the shoulder. "Why you would be, I don't know." He smiled a sympathetic smile. He then pointed his arm toward the far end of the room, giving directions. "If you head out the tracks about 3 miles east, along that stretch with the swale that separates it from the road grade, you'll see it. I am not sure what the function of the solar panel is, but I think that it has to do with powering a receiver that registers and transmit the positions of the trains as they pass. And since we haven't had a train in months, I figure that Burlington Northern wouldn't mind if we borrowed it."

"Alright," Otty agreed, "I know where you are talking. But I don't remember seeing a solar cell along the tracks. But why there? What about that Dome home up the road? It will have one for sure."

"Yes, it probably will. But then you are talking a seven mile trip one way, up hill, in the snow. Plus, what if they are occupied?" He asked.

Otty nodded his head in agreement. "Well, I don't think that they are occupied, but I agree that the one along the tracks is a lot closer and it is on level ground. Assuming it is there."

"Yep, assuming. . . .just remember to take along a hacksaw and some wire cutters," Howard reminded him. "And a sled if you got one, to pull it along in."

"I thought you said that it was portable."

"Oh, I am sure it is," Howard said in mock earnestness. "But portable is a relative term. I just meant that you should be able to handle it by yourself."

"Should be able to?"

"Should," he agreed. "But you might want to bring along a helper. You know, someone about forty years younger than yourself." He beamed a smile at Otty. "And don't you worry, I won't be going anywhere."

+++

It was snowing lightly as the two men trotted in snowshoes over the crusty snow that lie between two parallel mounds of snow-covered railroad tracks. Otty had asked Jeremy, one of the young men who was a member of his congregation, to help him collect the solar panel. Otty carried a hacksaw, a spare blade, and a few other tools in his knapsack. Jeremy carried a rifle. He had hopes of possibly shooting some game. Anymore, everyone hunted on a continual basis.

It was slow going, mostly because the men wanted to save energy since they were not in any hurry. Time was one thing that they had a surplus of. As they moved forward in the late morning light all they left behind were parallel tracks of shuffled snow, the cold air and the dense, frosted woods muffling all sounds. Their frozen breath streamed behind them like the exhaust of two miniature steam engines.

"Let's break for a moment," Otty huffed, putting a hand out in front of his companion. He stopped, twisting around as if looking for a place to sit down and rest. Seeing nothing, he remained standing, his labored breaths smoking from his open mouth. They had traveled quite a distance and it wasn't as level as he remembered. And he was not looking forward to the return trip, but he hoped that the prize would make it all worth while. He would do just about anything to know what was going on in the world. Otty considered that for a moment. What was it worth to know, he pondered silently.

"How much farther do you think," Jeremy asked in a distinctly less labored voice. Otty pointed. "Just ahead of the bend, if I remember correctly."

Suddenly realizing that they were closer than he initially thought, Otty took off in a trot, slogging through the powder with a bit more vigor. He was surprised at how animated the excitement of reaching their destination had made him. Perhaps he was more anxious than he realized to discover the truth of their situation, and this solar panel might be the key to obtaining that knowledge. Jeremy let out with a hoot as the excitement of the moment captured him. He trotted quickly to keep pace with the older man.

They had forced themselves forward about a hundred yards when Otty stopped, sounding a tired "here." "It should be right about here," he said, sweeping his arms around himself. He scanned the bank, locating the large metal box that contained the receiver.

"Where is the solar panel? Shouldn't it be somewhat close to this contraption?" Jeremy asked, brushing the snow away from the metal top.

"I would think so," Otty agreed. "Maybe we are in the wrong spot." He craned his head to look further down the tracks. Mentally, he tried to position himself on the road that ran parallel the tracks, about fifty feet to his immediate south, imagining where the solar panel should sit. Trying to remember what it was like to drive on that country lane made it seem like it was years, not weeks ago.

"No, we're in the right spot," Jeremy said. He swept the snow away from a section of metal pole , the top of which had been roughly cut at a slight angle. A couple wires stood like lame sprouts above the end. "It just seems that someone got here before us."

+++

Chapter 7

For the first time in a long while, Myla was feeling optimistic. She had brought both of the kids with her to work and they were playing outside with the refugee children, most of whom they knew. Watching the kids play gave her a sense of normality. And the decision to leave Purcell gave her hope, even if they weren't sure where they were going to go. She began to see the light at the end of the tunnel and it was far brighter than those in this dreary hospital.

Jessica, their longtime babysitter, had gone to live at Liberty Ranch. She had always had a connection there with some friends and decided that now was the time to move – at least until things turned around. The Ranch was a sophisticated island of self-sufficiency. It had its own energy resources through wind turbines and solar panels. It provided for almost all of its own food through gardens, hydroponic systems and fish ponds. It even had its own police force. It was surrounded by a large security fence designed to keep out intruders. Jessica said that she would finally feel safe.

So many people had left Purcell, that fewer and fewer came to the hospital for care or shelter. This was also a practical result of the fact that the hospital had effectively ceased to function and had now been absorbed by the growing body of refugees. As a consequence, Myla had only a single patient and he was dying. He was a diabetic, and since the hospital and the local pharmacies already distributed all of the area's drug supplies, his body was now rejecting his pancreatic cell transplants. Consequently, he had slipped into a diabetic coma. As insulin injections were virtually a thing of the past, there was little Myla could do except keep him comfortable.

Using quilts and blankets she had brought from home, Myla had built a nest for the kids in the pyxis, the medicine secure room that required a code to enter. Myla did not chose the pyxis for its security, but because it was close to her station and hadn't been yet commandeered for some other use. It was virgin land, waiting to be settled. And it was clean.

Myla sat alone in the nurses station, thumbing through one of the magazines that she had already read a dozen times before. For the first time in a very long time, she actually felt bored. In its own way, it was really a nice feeling. The kids were having fun with some of their friends and her patient was asleep. This sudden change of pace from endless 12-hours shifts to virtually nothing to do generated a strange sense of ennui. What should she be doing? Why was she here? What good was she doing? And, what did it really matter?

Her brief venture into inner contemplation was interrupted by the movement of shadows against the wall beside her. She looked up and found herself facing three men, none of whom she recognized. The eyes of their ragged, dirty faces were fixated on her person. She felt like a cat trapped in a corner by three hungry, feral dogs. Instantly, she wanted to run, but knew she couldn't escape. Her breath became hurried.

"Can I help you," she asked as calmly as possible, setting down the magazine.

The thin, gaunt man closest to her gurgled a deep-throated giggle that sounded like an animal. He licked his deeply chapped lips and then curled them into a smile. "Yes, princess, why don't you open up that door and let us do some shopping," he said, pointing at the door to the pyxis with a thin, filthy finger. Myla didn't move.

"There are no more drugs, not even aspirin. You'll have to go away."

The man laughed, shrilly. "No," he said in an oddly taunting voice, "I think you're lying."

Myla subconsciously began to move slowly away from the men. "Why would I lie?" she asked in as reasonable voice as she could muster.

"I don't know," he said, indifferently. "But I don't care. Maybe you got other things we might want here." The man slipped off his coat and let it slump to the floor. He continued to stare at her, mouth agape, his tongue rushing from one side of the mouth to the other as if hurrying in excitement. To Myla's horror he began to pull his tattered shirt out from his stained, blue jeans and then tugged aggressively at the end of his belt, working to unclasp it. He began to giggle louder and louder. By this time Myla was against the wall, trapped between a high counter top and cabinets. She began to shake but was strangely mute. She wanted to scream but for some reason she had lost control of her voice. She could only manage a quiet, hoarse rasp.

As if on cue the two other men rushed to Myla, tugging her away from her erstwhile shelter, each man clutching an arm too tightly. Myla began to kick as they forced her to the floor, but the thin man was too quick for her and grabbed both of her legs around the knees. She began to thrash her body about, but her movements only helped the thin man in tugging down her scrub bottoms which soon began to rip. Finally she let go a scream but it was quickly muffled by a dirty hand that partly obstructed her sight. She tried to bite the hand, but only managed to taste it with her tongue, a sensation that made her nauseous. She could feel but not see a hand pulling at her panties and she found herself helpless to resist. She was captured.

Suddenly, a boy's voice shrieked, "no!" The thin man, who had been attempting to mount Myla, roared like a frustrated lion as the boy tugged at his leg, digging nails in the hairy flesh, trying to pull the man off of his victim. The thin man swore as the other men laughed coarsely at the sight of this puny knight trying to rescue his lady. The thin man turned on his knees and swung at the boy, hitting him square in the jaw and sending him flying against the far wall. The hero crumpled in a heap on the dirty carpet, remaining silent.

"You bastard, that's my child," Myla screamed as loudly as she could. She kicked him sharply in the jaw with her leg that had become temporarily freed.

Angered by the blow, the thin man attacked Myla, hitting her in the jaw, cutting her lip. She again screamed, as blood colored her teeth. She spat the blood and saliva at the man.

"Stop!" a deep voice shouted. The two men holding Myla both looked up at the voice and simultaneously released their grip.

They then quickly stood up, raising their arms in the air. The thin man remained on all fours, his head down, greasy hair hanging, hiding his face. He didn't move. Sensing an opportunity, Myla drew her legs up and rolled over to a corner, tears initially blinding her to what was taking place.

"Get up," the voice commanded, harshly. Slowly the thin man stood to his feet, naked except for his open shirt, his pants down around his ankles. He stumbled a bit in the tangle of jeans and looked slyly at the intruder. All he could focus on was the barrel of a pistol pointed at his face. He followed the gun up toward the stern countenance of a cop. "No harm, officer, no harm done," he panted. "Just having a little fun."

"Pull up your pants, pervert," the voice said. The thin man reached down to his jeans and slowly began to pull them up. Suddenly, he turned quickly toward the cop with a knife. It was met by an explosion that erupted in the hallway, followed by a second, and then a third, each splattering the cupboard behind it with crimson. The thin man stood frozen, as if impervious to the bullets before toppling forward onto his face, with his thin bare rump in the air.

Jarad stood wide-eyed in front of the dead body, still pointing at it with his gun. He briefly looked around the scene, noting his wife in the corner crying softly and his son groaning on the floor, his frame slowly rolling back and forth. Jarad faced the other two men with his gun, which was still stiffly projected outward from his body, held rigid by his two hands.

He glared fiercely at the two men. "Get the hell out of here, before I kill you both!" he roared. The two scarecrows were immediately animated and quickly disappeared down the dark corridor toward the exit.

The small voice of Cameron drew Jarad's attention away from the fleeing figures. "Mom," he said softly, again and again. In response, as metal drawn to a magnet, Myla crawled quickly over to her son, clothed only in her scrub top, pink panties, and blue booties. "Oh, my baby, my big hero," she sobbed softly, carefully turning him over, inspecting him for damages. "Oh, my baby," she said again, and drew him into her arms as she sat against the wall. Instinctively she tried to hold him as the little boy he was in her mind, though in reality he was nearly as large as she was. She rocked him back and forth, as best as she could from her awkward position on the floor.

Jarad squatted next to the two of them, caressing each in turn, his hand gliding over their heads and down to their cheeks, whispering softly. "Oh, honey, I am so sorry. I should have been more careful with your safety. I am so sorry."

Myla had quit crying now as the call of motherhood had transferred her thoughts from her own survival to those of her child. "Oh Jarad, who could know?" She looked up at him, her moist brown eyes full of both fear and solace. She grabbed his hand and hugged it by trapping it against her face and then kissed it. "I love you," she said firmly. "Let's take care of this boy."

They carried him to an empty gurney. She inspected the wound on his swelling jaw where he had been struck and the lump on his head where he had hit the wall. Besides the bruises he appeared to be fine. While she continued to dote on their son, Jared went to take care of the dead man.

The body had drained more blood than Jarad had imagined was possible. He found it difficult to avoid walking in the sticky mess which seemed to be everywhere. The dirty corpse seemed to float in it. In addition, the bullets had left dark splotches of their passage in the cupboards behind Myla's desk. As the adrenaline subsided from his system, he began to become increasingly queasy. He had never before fired his gun in the line of duty, let alone having killed a man. And simply imagining what might have happened to both his wife and child was enough to cause him to become filled with guilt, though mixed with an increasing level of rage. He was dazed with the conflicting pulls of fear, anger, and repulsion as well as a sense of duty to the community versus duty to his family. He wished all of this would end.

"I'll be back," he called out to his wife as he grabbed the dead man's collar and began to pull.

"Where are you going?" Myla responded anxiously, alarm in her voice.

"I'm not going anywhere," he said as reassuringly as he could. "I'm gonna toss this garbage into the trash." With that, he dragged the body outside, leaving a streaked trail as he went. It was only then that he noticed the growing crowd of spectators that had responded to the noise and commotion. Pausing for only a moment, he ordered one of the men to help him toss the corpse into a well picked through dumpster. Looking at the body nestled in among the garbage, Jarad thought it was entirely appropriate.

+++

Purcell had become a dark, somber, even pitiful, place. Not that Purcell had lost the grandeur of its natural setting. Rather, it had lost its homeyness, its sentimental comfort, its familiarity – all of which are the hallmarks of anyone's hometown. In every way Purcell had become a memory. But for those who remained, busy with the need to survive, such thoughts would come later.

In hindsight it is surprising that there hadn't been any fires. With the loss of electricity and the subsequent use of alternative forms of heating and lighting, an accidental fire would be a given. But graciously this occurred later, rather than earlier, since there was no way to combat an uncontrolled burn. The Purcell Volunteer Fire Department no longer had the capacity nor the volunteers to respond to any outbreaks.

It was probably a candle that started the conflagration, though it could have been any number of other things, including arson. Nonetheless, with the winds blowing strongly that early morning, it quickly spread in all directions. The westerlies that prevailed most of the year would often circle in a cyclone effect over Purcell as they encountered the dished wall of low mountains to the north. This phenomenon ensured the equitable distribution of the spread and effects of the flames.

+++

"Jarad, get up, quickly," Myla shouted at him, vigorously shaking his shoulder. They had decided to return to their home and spend the night there, rather than stay in the hospital. This was a good decision, as far as their dog was concerned, who had been left behind to guard the premises.

"What?" Jarad asked, as he sat up in bed with a start. "What's wrong?"

"Fire, Jarad. There is a fire somewhere. You can hear it!" she said excitedly. "Hurry!"

Jarad pulled on his trousers and rushed outside in his bare feet. It was a gorgeous late fall day, clear and sunny – the sort that caused a person to be thankful to live in this area. Jarad noticed neither the sun nor the cold, as he ran out barefoot into the snow-covered street to determine where the fire was, and more importantly, where it was heading.

The smoke seemed to be everywhere in the early morning sky, but the sound of crackling, like a giant bonfire, came from the neighborhood one street beyond his own. He cast glances both up and down the road and noticed that others were fleeing to the north, away from the sounds. Soot and hot embers were beginning to fall like snow.

His wife was standing in the doorway, watching him. He shouted, "Myla, this is it. Let's go!" They had prepared for departure days ago, having already packed up the car with most of everything that they thought was important. All that was left to do was to strip the beds of their covers.

He rushed back into the house, leaving the door open. It didn't matter. He slipped on the same socks he had worn the day before and put on his boots. On the kitchen table his radio started to squawk. Someone was trying to contact him. He considered ignoring it, thus finally severing his commitment to his work and his responsibilities and then simply flee to his parent's old vacation cabin along the Blue River. But he couldn't. He grabbed it and switched it on.

"Traverson here," he said, breathing hard.

"Jarad, come to the office. Right now!"

"Chief, I need to get out of here. There is a fire rapidly approaching my house. I need to scramble."

"Just come by here one last time. Repeat, come by here one last time."

"Okay, Chief. I'm on my way."

One last time, Jarad thought. One last time? Is this the end? Was he done? What did the chief have in mind? He didn't have time to ponder. He grabbed his belt and holster, if only out of habit.

"Myla, follow me in the car. We're stopping by the office."

Myla was loading the kids and the dog into the car. The dog was excited and wagged his tail vigorously, oblivious to the danger. He was just happy to be going for a ride.

Jarad made for the police car, but turned and faced the house one last time. Deep down he didn't want to leave. This was house his home, and leaving it was like severing a connection to all what meant to be who he was. But he knew he had to go. Life would go on. And right now, everything he held dear was in that dark green Chevrolet wagon.

He strapped himself into his squad car and backed out onto the street, turning on the police lights. In his final public appearance as a police officer, at least he could offer the semblance of doing something official. His wife followed closely behind. He drove slowly, partly because of the condition of the road and party to monitor the progress of the fire.

It was difficult to know what was going on because he was unable to get a perspective on the extent of the conflagration, its course, and from where it had traveled. But he was glad to be traveling in a direction he thought to be away from it, with his family in tow. He slowly wound through the streets of Purcell toward the police station. The roads were in the best shape they had been in weeks, simply because the snow had stopped a couple days earlier and the subsequent sunny days did their part to melt or compress the rest. The further he progressed, though, the greater the foot traffic increased. The few people that remained were streaming out of town to escape the flames.

They arrived without incident at the station. Myla waited outside in the car with the kids. Even though it was cold outside, she had turned off the engine in order to save fuel. And in spite of the fact that they would only be at the station for a few moments, Jarad quickly plugged the car into one of the outlets normally reserved for police vehicles. He wanted to top off the batteries -- just in case. After this was done he ran into the building.

"Chief," he called out immediately upon entering, his voice echoing in the dark room. Jarad a heard a distant response from the back of the building. He headed for the armory. There he found the chief busy taking apart a rifle.

"Jarad, glad you're here. We need to be quick so we can both get the hell out of town." He handed Jarad an assault rife. He then pointed at a small multi-purpose bag hanging on a hook on the wall. "Grab that yellow bag. That's for you. It's ammunition. I split it 50-50." Jarad reached for the bag and lifted it up off the hook. From its heft he knew that it contained quite a few boxes of ammunition. These were the weapons from Homeland Security surplus which were held in reserve for extreme situations. "I don't understand," he said, turning to the chief.

"Yes, well listen. The Sheriff's dead. All of this stress killed him. He never did hear back from Spokane. We're the last two peace officers in the county, for all I know, and we are now both out of a job. I've just resigned and now I've just fired you, both effective as soon as you leave this building. As you know, everyone else is gone anyhow. I'm leaving, and I figure you best better too. But, there is no way on God's green earth I'm gonna let these arms fall into the hands of those brigands."

He threw the gun he was disassembling into a pile on the floor. There were four or five others there as well. "I've pulled their bolts and I'm gonna take them with me. I'll toss them somewhere where no one can find them. We've got all the ammo."

He grabbed his gun and another multipurpose bag and joined Jarad in front of the counter. "Look Jarad, I know that wherever you go, you'll do the right thing. I just wanted you to be as prepared as I could make you. Do you have any plans?" Jarad

explained his intention to hole up in his parents' cabin on the Blue
River, assuming it hadn't been occupied by some other family.

"Good, I am sure you'll make it fine. Just be cautious about
roadblocks north of town on the highway. Please get there before
dark."

"And you, Chief? What are your plans?"

"I'm heading east, out past Dumont road. My in-laws'
place. Barb is already there. We should be alright." Jarad knew the
place. He didn't view it as ideal, but it was better than where he was
living now.

They shook hands, each looking the other squarely in the
eyes, neither speaking. Jarad then spun on his heels and headed for
the way he came back in. Exiting the office he looked out toward
the city center. In the brief time that he was in the station the smoke
and flames had advanced even further to this end of town. The
strong breeze on his face told him why.

"Jarad, we got to go," Myla called from the car. He yanked
the cord loose from the outlet and tossed the cord into the snow. He
jumped into the front passenger seat. He dropped the bag onto the
front floor and nestled the gun barrel, downward, along side the seat.
Myla looked at the rifle and then back at her husband. "Jarad, you
drive. I don't want to drive. I might hit someone."

"No, honey you drive." She was about to protest when he
silenced her with a finger to his lips. "I got my reasons," he said
softly but firmly. He buckled his seatbelt, and looked over his
shoulder at the kids. Each was silent, watching him. He gave them

a smile. Turning around he said to Myla, "Let's head north on the highway."

Myla drove quickly toward their destination. Oddly, they were the only vehicle in sight. People walked in small groups carrying bundles or pulling sleds. Some motioned for Jarad and Myla to pull over and to help them, to give them a lift, but Myla kept driving. She and Jarad had their own worries, and besides, their wagon was stuffed full as it was. Today was not their day to play the good Samaritan.

As they neared the edge of town, Jarad opened up the yellow bag and drew out a box of ammunition. "What'cha doing dad?" Annie asked, watching her father.

"I'm loading the rifle, honey," he said with as much ease as he could project into his voice. "We're gonna be heading up to Grandma and Grandpa's cabin and maybe we'll see a deer along the way. How does venison steak sound to you?"

"Good," she said, neutrally, unconvinced. "Do you think that our house is going to burn down?" she asked, getting to the heart of her concern. "Will we ever be able to go home again?"

Jarad was for a moment nonplussed. He wasn't sure what to say. To be honest or to be comforting? Could he do both without lying? "I hope so honey," he said with honest conviction. "I hope so, but it is not in our hands. What is important is that we are together."

"It's in God's hands, right dad?" she asked. He nodded his head. "Then those are good hands to be in. I'm glad to be with you and mom."

"And what about me, Annie," Cameron asked, mildly indignant.

"You too," she said with a dramatic sigh. She gave the dog a hug.

They were finally leaving the town behind them, having no desire to view the fire. They were anxious to be away. The road was surprisingly passable, considering that it hadn't been plowed for weeks. The advent of the nice weather was working in their favor.

The crowds had just about disappeared as they began to drive up the long grade north of town. Their route took them next to Liberty Ranch, whose brick and steel security fence was visible from the highway. Strangely, there appeared to be a work crew using a county backhoe making some repairs to the barrier. How could these county people not be aware of the fire, Jarad thought as their path moved them closer. Then he realized that these men were not county workers, nor were they building up the barrier. They were attempting to tear it down. Silently, he watched as some of the workers raised rifles to their shoulders and fired into the breach they had created in the brick fencing. Liberty Ranch was under assault. Jarad returned to his task of filling the gun's magazine as well as an additional clip. Things were getting crazy.

"Jarad, I don't like this," Myla said loudly and with concern. He looked up to see an improvised roadblock about an eighth of a mile ahead, constructed from saw bucks and planks. A few cars and trucks were parked haphazardly to either side. There was a single man alongside the roadblock, awaiting their approach.

"What do you want me to do," she asked, nervously.

"I'll tell you in a second," he said quickly. He turned around. "Kids, I need you to lay down and don't look up and till I say it is okay. Do you understand?" he asked, firmly. The kids both nodded and quickly laid down on the seat between them, Annie pushing the dog down to the floor. "Stay," she told him.

"Myla, approach the barricade as if you're going to stop. But when I say, step on the throttle and just bash right through it. Okay?"

"Bash right through it? That might break something."

"Honey, this a trap to rob us. There are probably other men hiding behind out of sight. Do you understand?"

"Yes," she said nervously. "I wish you were driving."

"No, I need to work this," he said, feeding a bullet into the chamber of the gun by drawing back its bolt. He unfastened his seatbelt and moved his seat back to give him some room to maneuver – just in case.

As they approached the barricade the man began to motion for them to stop. He appeared unarmed, but Jarad spotted the butt of a rifle stock leaning against one of the vehicles to the right of the man. He was most definitely armed.

They approached to within twenty-five yards when Jarad shouted, "Go!" The car momentarily spun its front tires in the snow before gaining some traction, and then lurched forward. The man became more emphatic in his motions before he realized what was happening. He then turned to get out of the way of the approaching car. He made a motion to grab his rifle but lost his footing in the slick conditions and fell hard on his back.

The car rapidly approached the barricade. Just as Jarad had hoped it was not very substantial. The wooden barrier snapped loudly as the car pushed savagely through it, none of which hindered the forward motion of the vehicle.

"Keep going, Myla, don't stop!" Jarad shouted.

Suddenly, a series of dull thumps sounded from the rear of the car and then the rear window disintegrated. Instinctively Jarad ducked, but then turned around in his seat with the rifle at his shoulder. "Kids, cover your ears!"

The small space in the car echoed harshly with the explosive noise of gunfire, causing both kids to scream. The dog jumped up in mad panic, clawing to get away from the loud noise. Jarad knocked the poor animal back down to the floor with the rifle barrel before firing off another burst of bullets at the men behind them. For just as Jarad had suspected, after the car had burst through the barricade five or six more men appeared, a couple of whom began firing at the car. Jarad's return shots hit one of them, who slumped gracelessly to the ground and which caused the others to scatter to safety. He kept the gun pointed in their direction until the road turned and they were out of sight.

Myla was shaking as she drove, the car careening down the road. "Slow down, Myla, were through. We're okay now." The car slowed. Jarad looked back at the kids and gave them a thumbs up as nonchalantly as he could. They both sat up and looked around. Cold air was tumbling in through the windowless rear hatch. Jarad turned up the heater switch.

He looked at Myla and gave her a wan smile. He was relieved to be through that obstacle, though he knew they weren't yet entirely safe and that there were probably more troubles ahead. One at a time, he thought.

"Something's wrong," she said. "Something with the car. I think we have a flat tire." Sure enough, the left rear corner of the car was riding low. A flat tire would have to be changed if they were going to reach the cabin.

"Stop at the top of the grade, honey," he told her. "I'll change it there."

"Is it safe to stop? I don't want to stop."

"We need to stop, or we'll become stranded."

They drove on slowly for another couple miles, the left rear tire beginning to slap rhythmically against the wheel well. When they finally crested the hill Myla stopped the car in the middle of the road.

"Everyone stay in the car," Jarad said, stepping out with the rifle. He scanned all around the immediate area before going to the rear of the car. He spotted two bullet holes low in the rear hatch and a third where the left rear taillight used to be. He looked at the flat, which was now only a wheel banded by the frayed remnants of a snow tire.

"Okay everyone, you can get out," he said softly. He walked to the front and exhaled a grunt of disgust. Both headlights had been busted. They would have to get going quickly or they would be driving blind in the dark. He wondered what phase the moon was in.

He returned to the rear of the car and opened the hatch in order to access the spare. He leaned the rifle against the fender. He began transferring items from the back of the car to the road surface, shaking glass shards from each item. Myla called to him, interrupting his task..

"Jarad, look." He glanced at his wife, who was staring to the south. He moved to catch a glimpse of what had gained his wife's interest. What he saw took his breath away.

The entire town of Purcell seemed to be ablaze. Thin black smoke billowed upward and toward the east, being pushed by the winds. He could see the hospital burning and he wondered where all those people would go. Triangulating the hospital with the radio tower, he located the general placement of his house. From all appearances, he couldn't imagine that it had survived. Myla was thinking the same thoughts and she began to cry. Jarad drew her close, but continued to watch the holocaust below. He felt like he was watching the destruction of a world. He felt empty inside.

+++

Otty was enjoying life. He couldn't remember the last time he had so much fun with such a simple pleasure. It had been worth the effort. Boiling up ten gallons of water so he could have a hot bath was the work of genius. He only wished that it stayed hotter, longer, but it was still better than a sponge bath. Ellie said tomorrow night was her turn.

Otty felt trapped. The bathroom was cold but the water was warm. He didn't want to step out of the tub and into the cool air, but then he couldn't stay in the tub forever. Anyhow, the water was losing its heat. Oh well, here goes, he thought, and he stepped out on to the cold floor, shivering. He was toweling himself dry as quickly as he could when Ellie stepped into through the door.

"Otty, you got to hurry. You got to see this!"

"What? What's wrong?"

"Nothing here, it's Purcell. It's burning!"

Otty hurried and dried himself and stepped into clean clothes. Normally, he would have savored this moment as well, for laundry was increasingly difficult to keep up, but his mind was now elsewhere. Purcell burning? How tragic!

He finally got all bundled up and ready to go outside. Ellie had been pacing as she waited for him. She took his hand and they hurried out the door. She led him up the road to the "perch" -- an outcropping that provided a vista of the valley and Purcell. There was a small crowd of on-lookers, all silent. The ones who had been there for a while stepped aside to make room for Ellie and Otty. He gasped when he saw the sight.

Though the sun had almost set, Purcell was clearly visible in the distance. A deep, orange-red glow like the embers of a campfire shimmered on the horizon, clearly indicating what fate had befallen the community. It would have been beautiful in any other context. Otty's thoughts ran the same gamut as everyone around him: Who made it safe? Who perished? What happened?

All he could do was watch and wonder.

+++

Though it was only twenty miles from Purcell to the cabin, it had already been hours since they left Purcell. The roads which had started out surprisingly good had progressively gotten worse the closer they got to their destination. The combination of altitude and lay of the land had conspired against them. They were soon reduced to a crawl.

"Honey, I don't know if we have enough charge or fuel to make it" Myla said matter-of-fact as she slowly maneuvered the car under the trees, following the snow crusted road as it meandered along the ridge line that followed the river. It was still daylight, but the sun was falling too quickly in the western sky. The shadows of the trees were growing increasingly longer, darkening their path.

Jarad leaned over from the passenger seat and peered at the dash. The fuel level was less than a quarter full, while the battery charge was more than half. "That doesn't make sense, we should have a lot more fuel than that. That tells me one thing. Stop when you can, I want to take a peek."

Myla stopped in a open patch of road where most of the snow had melted. Jarad stepped out and then disappeared out of Myla's sight as he looked under the side of the car. He quickly reappeared.

"Damn it, I should have looked for this sooner. I was afraid one of those shots might have possibly hit the battery pack. I didn't think about the fuel tank. We've been losing diesel."

He sat for a moment, lost in thought. "Let's sit here for a bit and charge the batteries," he said. We've got more battery charge than fuel, which we are losing as we drive. Let's just charge up our batteries and then make a run for it. It will be close, but I think that we'll make it."

"Okay, if you think so." Myla pushed in the command on the touchscreen of the dash. "I guess we wait, then."

"Yep, but to conserve charge we're going to have to turn off the heater fan."

"What? The kids are going to freeze," Myla said, criticism tempering her voice.

"Sorry honey, but they'll just have to bundle up. They'll be fine. Won't you kids," he called over his shoulder. There was no response. He craned his head to look at them, and found them both asleep, each snuggled into their coats and bedding. They had already found their own way to cope.

"Obviously, they are doing okay," Jarad whispered, smiling at his wife. She looked at her children and then to her husband. "Good, let them sleep. Let's get this done before its dark. Remember, we don't have headlights."

Within twenty minutes the batteries were fully charged. Myla drove on until the diesel engine finally quit, after which the electric motor had seamlessly come on-line. They were getting closer to the cabin..

It was now quite cold in the car and their breath was frosting. To keep from icing the front windshield they kept their conversation to a minimum. Jarad watched the scenery pass by. He noted how strange the railroad tracks looked, covered in crusted snow. Obviously there hadn't been any rail traffic through here recently.

They rounded a bend and came upon a herd of elk standing in their path. The large animals huffed in surprise and all made to disappear up the hillside, away from this large silent intruder. Jarad was tempted to pull out his rifle and to shoot one of the animals, but decided against it. He didn't want to wake the children, and he knew that there would be plenty of time later for hunting. On top of that, there was no way he could handle the carcass by himself in the pending darkness. Not at this point in time.

It had gotten dark. The sun set quickly at these latitudes and they were still a distance from the cabin, though frankly Jarad was unsure how far. They were rapidly consuming what battery charge they had. The only saving grace was the fact that they had a near-full moon, whose light was amplified by the snow, giving them some semblance of visibility to navigate by.

"I think we just got a mile or so to go," Jarad said. "There should be a red house coming up on the left side. Remember? The cabin is the next one after that." No sooner had he spoken when a mailbox appeared along side the road. "There we are, just a bit more."

"None too soon, we are out of charge," Myla said, her head nodding toward the flashing yellow light on the dashboard. "We'll just go as far as we can and then, I guess, we'll just have to hike the rest of the way." She sighed, frosted breath escaping from the loose-knit scarf she had wrapped around her neck and chin.

"Honey, just think of all that has gone on today. We're doing great." He rested his hand on her shoulder. "This is the last hill, give her all she's got."

Though the gauge indicated empty the car continued to crawl up the hill, the soft whirl of the electric motors and the sound of the snow crunching under the tires were the only noises.

Jarad raised his hand to point. "Right. . . . there," he said, indicating with his hand in the form of a pistol. Myla turned in what should have been the driveway and stopped the car. The little cabin was dark.

"Great, looks like nobody's here. That is what I was hoping" Jarad said, opening the car door and heading for the house. In a moment he had the door unlocked. He waved back at Myla, "We're home."

+++

Chapter 8

Jarad slowly awoke, surprised at his sense of ease and peace of mind. He pondered how this could be knowing he had escaped Purcell and was now condemned – in a fashion – to gross uncertainty in a little cabin in the woods. He realized he was finally free from the crushing stress of the past few months. At least now he had hope. He had peace, for the moment. Lying on the floor in a musty sleeping bag in a cold cabin was a heady luxury. He breathed in the chilly air, surprised that it wasn't arctic cold. Life was good.

He quietly extricated himself from his polyester cocoon, careful not to disturb Myla and the kids. He noted that each had pulled their heads into their sleeping bags as a measure against the chill. He set about building a fire in the stove, hoping the protest of the squeaky door hinges and the rattle of the vents wouldn't draw them out of their well-earned slumber.

After the fire was established, he briefly scouted out available resources in the cabin. The wood supply was well-seasoned but meager. Maybe a month's supply if they were careful. The kitchen was empty of any foodstuffs, except for a few stray envelopes of pasta meals and gelatin desserts. He was glad that they had the foresight to bring along the supplies that they did. He was also relieved to discover that the toilet worked – running water was a boon. This would make Myla happy. He opened the kitchen tap until the water ran clear and then filled the coffee pot. He set it on the wood stove to heat. The coffee was still out in the car.

He had slept in his clothes so he only had to throw on his boots to step outside. It had resumed snowing. He was glad that it had waited up till now. He tried to imagine how much more of a struggle their journey yesterday would have they had with the added challenge of fresh snow. He shook his head and resumed his task. He was able to empty everything out of the car and bring it inside before Myla stirred. He bent over her enveloped form and planted a kiss on her head. She groggily sat up, pulling the bag up around her shoulders. He returned to the stove and carefully spooned coffee into the percolator's screened retainer.

"Morning," she said with a yawn. She scratched her scalp and then rubbed her eyes with her hands. Jarad smiled at her with kind but watchful eyes. He was sure that she would feel a similar sense of elation.

"Toilet works," he said quietly.

"Wonderful," she said neutrally. She lowered the sleeping bag from her shoulders and let it heap around her waist. She stretched and yawned again.

"It's nice and warm. Thank you for the fire." She stood and paused for a moment until she gained her bearings and then softly padded off to the bathroom. Jarad watched her leave and then turned to examine the coffee pot. He lost himself in thought as his mind became mesmerized by the pulsing of the hot coffee into the clear top of the percolator. For a moment, nothing was important. He knew that many anxious and demanding moments awaited him, perhaps even today. But right now, at that moment, nothing mattered. Jarad didn't have to think, so he didn't. The smell of the coffee disrupted his reverie, but it wasn't unkind. Coffee was just the item he wanted.

He handed Myla a mug of coffee on her return. "Kids still asleep," she said softly as she whispered her thoughts. Her eyes surveyed the room. She saw the bags of groceries and supplies in the kitchen, realizing that Jarad had already emptied the car.

"We're going to need toilet paper," she said matter-of-factly. She looked at Jarad with bright eyes. "I must say, I am glad to be here."

Jarad moved over to her and drew her close to him. He gave her a gentle but firm squeeze. He then stood and walked over to the hutch, quietly opening and closing drawers as he searched their contents. Finding what he wanted, he drew out a foot long piece of wood and set it on the table. He sat next to the board and began to shuffle a deck of cards.

"Baby," he said to his wife, "let's play some cribbage."

Myla looked at him, her face pierced with a smile. "You know, it seems like forever since we've played. I'd love to beat you at a couple hands."

Jarad stopped shuffling the cards and straightened his smile. "Well, you better get over here, because I still got to make breakfast." He set the cards down and folded his hands in front of himself, resting them on the table.

"Let's see: coffee and pancakes, maybe some juice. Then I am going to bundle up Cameron and he and I are going to go exploring. I want to find an abandoned house. We will then proceed to break into said house and search it diligently for supplies, expressly toilet paper. Then, we will bring the toilet paper home to you." He winked at her and gave her his it's-going-to-be-alright look. "See, it's all figured out. Now come over here and put your money where your mouth is." He patted the empty chair next to him.

She smiled, swaying her head from side to side. "Jarad, you're a lunatic." She took the seat next to him and reached over to embrace him. "You're my strength," she whispered softly, sighing deeply.

He gave her leg a tender squeeze. "We'll see," he said in mock warning. "Remember, to the victor goes the spoils."

"And what spoils do you have in mind, mister?"

"You," he said softly, kissing her gently on the lips. When was the last time that they had made love, he pondered in his mind.

She laughed again and pulled the pegs from the board, positioning them to the starting holes. They both looked up at the unexpected hello emanating from the entryway window. The dog barked in warning.

+++

Otty tromped away from the Johnson's trailer. He was out "making his rounds" and Tyler Johnson told him that he heard a vehicle that night. "I heard it down the road, and I thought I heard some voices and doors shutting, that sort of thing. But I didn't check them out" So after his brief visit, Otty refastened his snowshoes and shuffled off in that direction.

He paused to remove his glasses and blow the snow away from the lenses. The snow had returned. It was a beautiful sight, which was not lost on him.

The still air allowed the large flakes to fall in uniform vertical paths. The crispness of the air caused Otty's nose hairs to freeze and frosted the developing mustache across his upper lip. He had slogged through about a quarter mile of travel before he paused to rest. A frozen mist marked his breathing as he sat upon a windblown tree, which provided a convenient perch.

Suddenly his nose began to search the air like a hound as it caught a scent of wood smoke. He noticed a hazy gray column of smoke rising lazily to his right. He resumed his trek and made for this next destination.

It was the Traverson's cabin he noted as the old rustic home came into view. Someone had occupied it over night, Otty thought to himself, judging by the still unfilled ruts in the snow that ended at the Chevrolet wagon parked haphazardly in front.

Otty paused about twenty feet from the house and bellowed a hello, trying to sound as nonthreatening as possible. He then shuffled a few steps closer to the building before hollering again. He slowly proceeded even closer, removing a mitten in order to give the door a rap, when it opened unexpectedly. A man's face with a guarded expression greeted him. Otty recognized the man, but he couldn't recall the name or why he was familiar.

"Hello," Otty said, as warmly and jauntily as he could muster. He pulled the scarf away from his face and the cap from his head to reveal as much of himself as possible. He hoped his stubble didn't make him appear too sinister.

"Otty Oleson," the man said with mild surprise. "Come on in." The door opened wider to offer him entrance. Otty huffed a thank you as he gathered his wind. He bent over to unleash the snowshoes, and leaned them up against the house. He stomped his feet before he stepped inside the little cabin.

"Nice and toasty," he exclaimed as he nodded at the woman sitting beside the table. "Did I interrupt your game," he asked, nodding at the cribbage board.

"That's okay," Myla said kindly. "You just spared my husband certain defeat."

Both men chuckled at the challenge. They then took turns reacquainting themselves. All three knew one another, but from quite a few years past. Otty had served years ago as an elder at the church they attended, or at least formally attended.

"So, I heard Doctor Bronson joined up with GILM," he said to Myla as Jarad handed him a cup of coffee at the table.

"Yes, and we were about the only ones who left," she said. "Of course, in all honesty, we contemplated leaving even before then. . ." she paused. "I guess that was as good of an excuse as any."

The conversation moved on to current events. Jarad filled Otty in on questions he had about Purcell and how the power outage had impacted the town. Myla elaborated on points that Jarad overlooked or had forgotten. For both of them, it seemed as if they had lived years through the tumult, and not the weeks it really was.

Otty commented on the sight of Purcell burning. This left them all in thoughtful silence for a moment.

In short order the two children were roused by the talk and joined their parents at the table. They sat quietly on each side of their mother, eying their visitor carefully. Jarad had told Otty his plan to raid nearby homes for supplies. Otty agreed that it was a good idea, but asked him to wait. He explained his reasons and invited the two of them to attend the meeting scheduled at the church building the next morning.

"I know it is quite a hike, especially without snowshoes, but if you could come it would be great."

Otty finished his coffee and indicated that he couldn't stay, but had to "make tracks."

"Heading home?" Jarad asked.

"No, one more stop. Howard's place. You passed it last night. By the way, how did you make it up that road?"

"I don't know," Jarad said with amazement, shaking his head. "But I'm glad we did."

"Amen" Otty exclaimed.

"Amen," Jarad agreed, "and if you only knew."

+++

Chapter 9

They didn't have toothpaste. Jarad had made breakfast for everyone and Myla had begun to organize the house. The kids were getting set to explore their new home when Annie abruptly shared the disturbing news. "Mom, we are out of toothpaste. We gotta have toothpaste."

Myla smiled. "Honey, just brush with water, you'll be fine," she assured her.

"Mom, my teeth will rot out. I need toothpaste," she insisted.

"Have you had any candy?"

"No."

"Then you're fine. Trust me, your teeth won't rot out if you didn't eat candy."

"Okay," she said grudgingly. Myla knew that Annie wasn't expressing concern about not having toothpaste so much as she was expressing her need for normality. The toothpaste was part of her routine and routine was something she hadn't had in months. Like mother like daughter, Myla thought to herself.

The cabin was small, but very livable. It was nicely laid out, with a small loft overlooking the living room which allowed the heat from the wood stove to waft upstairs. The entire south-facing wall seemed to be windows, which Jarad explained allowed the cabin to be passively heated by the sun. "Did you notice that the floor was warm last night?" he asked his wife. "The sun heats the concrete below the floor, which radiates after sunset. That's why the front room is stone and not carpeted."

"Clever," Myla responded thoughtfully, "and nice."

The only other rooms in the house were a small bedroom and the kitchen. The front room overlooked a wooden deck. A mudroom was positioned at the rear of the house, off of the kitchen. Jarad, Myla and the kids had visited here quite frequently when Jarad's parents were still living in the area, and then used it as a weekend retreat after they moved. They had moved to southern California three years earlier, keeping the cabin as a summer home. "But Dad," Jarad remembered joking with his father, "you're supposed to move *from* California, not to it." His father chuckled with that deep bass laugh that he is always remembered by. "Yes, maybe so, but it is a hell of a lot warmer in the winter and very affordable. Plus, your mother loves the ocean." Jarad had been wondering how they had been fairing recently. He worried about them. He hadn't spoken to them in months. They were older, but both still in good health. He knew that they could take care of themselves, but nonetheless not knowing how they were caused him to pine for them.

Jarad listened to the voices of the kids outside. They were building a snowman in the little front yard. Kids can adjust so quickly, he thought. But then, they didn't have to provide for themselves. That was the parents' concern. He contemplated Otty Oleson's words. He was interested in this meeting, if only because it would possibly provide an avenue for him to support his family. He got dressed to go outside. He wanted to scout around. He wondered if that elk herd was still in the proximity.

He tugged on his boots. Myla didn't want to go outside. She wanted to make up her new nest and went about organizing the bedrooms and putting things away. In a fashion, Jarad was happy for his wife. She didn't have to carry the burden of both her family and her work. Until things returned to normal, her family was enough. Just as he was about to step out the back door, Myla shouted down from the upstairs loft.

"You going to scout out the perimeter?" she said with fun in her voice.

"Yes, ma'am, I am."

"You're a good husband, Jarad. Go make us safe!" He heard her loudly kiss the air, a kiss he knew she was sending to him.

"Thanks for the kiss, baby. It keeps me warm."

"You just wait," she shouted down, saucily. "I'll keep you warm."

Jarad chuckled to himself as he stepped out into the heavy, though softly falling, snow. He trod around the house, looking at the area with fresh eyes. Previously this little cabin had been a weekend getaway. Now it was home. And he wasn't ready for it to be home. There wasn't enough of this or that, and he was severely limited on what he could do to improve their situation. But as his father always said, a man has got to play the cards he was dealt. Even a marginal set of cards can become a winner if played right. Jarad intended to have a winning hand.

It was such an eerie landscape. The snow covered everything, including the road in front of the house. He wondered how they had made it! Without the plowed road to provide a point of reference, the cabin looked like it was simply plopped down into the snow from the sky. The only tracks were those of the Otty's snowshoes and those of various animals. The ruts from the Chevy leading to their house were already beginning to fill in.

He started to walk up the road, but it was slow going. He suddenly realized his first task and he headed back to the house. He was going to fabricate a pair of snowshoes, somehow.

+++

The church was busy. Myla and Jarad sat in a pew toward the front. They had never been inside the building before, though it was quite predictable. The pews were wooden and padded, the fabric well scrubbed. The floor was carpeted in a short pile which was surprising clean. But then everyone had removed their shoes and boots after entering. Some people wore slippers. The altar was a raised platform decorated with a simple table and large cross posted to the wall. Jarad searched the small group for familiar faces. There were few, but each of the men gave him a friendly nod of the head and every woman a kind smile. He felt safe and comfortable.

Otty walked out from a back room and centered himself on the podium. People quit visiting and talking among themselves and quited down, those standing taking seats. He greeted everyone with a smile and went directly into the business at hand.

"Hello everyone, glad you are here. Let's go ahead and start with a prayer."

He bowed his head and spoke aloud in his prayer, primarily asking that God would give them guidance, but also that a strong sense of community would develop among those gathered. Afterward, he briefly explained to the congregation what he had in mind.

He shared his believe that everyone in the area was now, for better or for worse, part of something bigger than themselves. Specifically, that people had to start putting the interest of others at the same level as they had been putting their own interests. This meant viewing themselves as being part of a community, which meant responsibilities and obligations. He delineated a list of specifics.

All eyes were on Otty as he slowly wandered from one side of the room to the other, speaking directly to each and every individual face, beginning the process of weaving the web of shared interests that he knew was essential for the survival of many people here. He spoke softly, but convincingly and passionately.

"We need to start considering our collective well being. Who is going without? Who is hungry? Who has needs? And how do we, as a community, meet those needs? We need to start considering the education of our children. How much longer will this new life go on? We don't know, so we can't wait. And probably most of important of all, we need to consider our collective security. So far, we have been lucky. There hasn't been any real problems with raiders and so forth. But we cannot assume that we will remain so fortunate. I anticipate that sooner than later we will need to start protecting our homes and resources from those who would take them from us."

He spoke a bit more before finally pausing and then began taking and answering a few questions. People raised their hands, registering their own concerns or sharing ideas. Jarad felt a sense of collective relief in the room, but also a real enthusiasm for what Otty was proposing. As more and more people began to request specifics or foist opinions, Otty had to raise his own hand to put a pause to the talking.

"Yes, those are all good questions and ideas, and each needs to be addressed. We need to discuss, collectively, as a group how we are going to implement these ideas. But that is for another time, though assuredly sooner than later. My intent tonight was to get the ball rolling."

"But just as important, let's get to know each other. I propose that we all gather in the other room and break bread, in the form of some freshly baked cakes, and share in some coffee. Let's get to know each other on a first name basis before we begin the process of figuring out what needs to be done and how we are going to do it." He raised his left arm and pointed in the direction of an accordion door that opened as if on cue. The smell of fresh coffee and hot, just-out-of-the-oven cake wafted into the room. It was mesmerizing. People began to stand and move towards the other room, the noise of chattering voices rising with the enthusiasm of the collective adventure that stood before them, let alone the thoughts of desert.

Otty smiled, touching hands and patting shoulders as he waded through the wake of people as he made his way directly over to Myla and Jarad. He extended his hand in greeting. "I hope you are going to stay," he said kindly and with a warm visage. "I really want you two to be involved in this process."

"Well, I don't have any reason not to stay, Pastor," Jarad replied, calling him by the polite address others in the room had been. "Anyhow, that cake sure smells good."

+++

It was dark before Jarad and Myla finally got back to the cabin, each wearing a cedar shake tied to their boots as improvised snowshoes. The kids had fun, too, and made some new friends. The whole atmosphere had been rejuvenating. A psychologist might say that the positive interaction among everyone would be an expected, even anticipated result of the return to predictability and normality, but that would be an error. There was nothing predictable nor normal about the immediate future.

As Jarad was stoking the fire and Myla fiddled with the kerosene lamps, a bright vibrating light projected into the room, careened across the wall and then back out the window.

"What was that?" Myla called from the kitchen.

"I think that it was a car, mom!" Cameron shouted with certainty and excitement, running to the closet to grab the coat he just moments earlier had taken off.

Jarad himself had dashed to the window to catch a glimpse of whatever it was that had passed. Prior to the "calamity," as Pastor Oleson had labeled it tonight, that light would have been attributed to a passing vehicle. But there hadn't been any traffic on the road, especially able to travel at that speed.

"Maybe so, Cameron," Jarad agreed with his son, his breath fogging the window as he peered outside. Suddenly, another similar light dazzled the room, coming from the same direction as the earlier one and traveling just as fast.

Jarad reached the door and dashed outside to watch the light pass, accompanied by his son. He stared as it rushed by, marked only with the soft whine of an electric motor and the crush of snow being swept along. Two dark bodies swiveled their helmets to notice him as they passed. Jarad continued to follow the light as it briefly ignited the darkness in the harsh whitish blue brightness of a xenon beam, before finally disappearing down the grade. He scanned again to the left, up the hill, before quickly jumping back into the cabin.

"Just as a I thought," he said to aloud to himself as much as to whoever was listening in the house. "Snowmobiles." He paused. "Odd, I don't remember seeing any snowmobiles at the church."

"Not only snowmobiles, but ones that were in quite a hurry. They were going pretty fast considering how dark it is, don't you think," Myla offered, as she returned to the kerosene storm lamp to hang it on the wall, illuminating the room in a soft, warm, glow.

+++

Early the next morning Jarad dressed and returned to the road. For whatever reason the passing of the snowmobiles had nagged him the entire night as the subconscious cop in his mind tried to sort it out. Consequently he slept poorly. But he had a hunch and rose early to check to see if it just might be right.

It had snowed lightly through the night, but what he was looking for was still clearly visible. Jarad had only noticed two snowmobiles passing that night and the tracks in front of him confirmed this. The distinctive chevron patterns ran from west to east, sometimes parallel and sometimes converging, one tracking over the other, but still the evidence was obvious. They led only in one direction, which meant that the snowmobiles had either come from a place further up the road to the west, or had somehow circled around from another direction. How that was possible, Jarad didn't know, but he was determined to find out. But from wherever they may had come from, he didn't know why this information was so important. He just knew it was.

He shuffled through the snow back to his house, shaking the powder from his hat and shoulders before entering. He decided to see Otty this morning to share his concerns. He wanted to discuss the significance of the two snowmobiles last night, and while he was at it, the issue of raiding unoccupied homes for supplies.

He turned to the kitchen to see what was available for breakfast. The bare shelves took away his appetite. The only thing edible were two envelopes of instant oatmeal. He knew that he would rather leave them for the kids than eat them himself. Instead he jotted a note for Myla and left it on the table. He dressed to return outside, putting on an extra shirt for warmth. As he left the house and tied on his cedar shingle 'snowshoes' he offered up a quick prayer. He needed this day to be a profitable one.

+++

"I share your concern. We are having parallel thoughts." Otty stood up from the big chair behind his desk and walked over to the large bookshelf that took up the far wall. It was filled pell-mell with books, journals, and miscellaneous printed material. He pulled out a large bound folder with faded red covers from underneath a stack of of oversize books laying on their sides. Returning to his desk he opened the folder in such a way so as to share it with Jarad. Jarad stood and joined him at the desk, examining the pages. He recognized immediately that this was a collection of old Forest Service maps that detailed the county.

"Here we are, at the church," Otty said, stabbing the page with a finger. "Here is Blue River Road." His finger traced along a line on the map that indicated the road from where it branched off from the highway, up past the church, and to its terminus at a trail-head. This was some six or seven miles west of the church. Jarad noticed that as the road traveled from the right to the left, that is from east to west, the topographical lines drew closer and closer together. The road climbed up in altitude from the highway and followed a narrow ledge as indicated by the slight widening of the sweeping brown lines.

"Now look here," Otty said, again daubing the page with a finger, this time a little distance to the left of where he had previously indicated. "If you cut here to the north, there is a short flat section that parallels the road. It starts here and moves to there." His finger danced over the paper like a paint brush, back and forth, up and down, and back and forth again, before being suspended in the air.

Jarad scrutinized the area that Otty had outlined with his finger. To the right of the church, approximately nine or ten miles to the east, was a broad area that was checkered with little icons that indicated buildings. Jarad new where this was. It was locally called Blue River Junction. He also noticed that to the north of the junction another road, probably an old gravel access trail, ran parallel to Blue River road, circling around to and connecting with the road about a mile to the west of them.

Jarad ran his own finger over the paper. "So what you're saying is that those snowmobiles originated here and then ran up this ridge, emerged over there and then followed the road back to where they started, passing by our place?"

"I suspect so, but we can't know for sure where they originated. But that is what I think."

"Why did they pass through last night?"

"I think that they are checking out their neighborhood, seeing who is up here and looking for resources to exploit."

Jarad thought for a moment before replying. "You mean, they are looking for houses to raid."

"Probably," Otty agreed. "And to see who is up here. They are doing the very same thing I would do if I were in their position. Which I am, and so are you and everyone else up here." Otty returned to his chair.

"So, why haven't you? Why hasn't everyone already scoped out the empty homes? Who knows what might be going to waste?"

"I'll tell you why," he said. "We haven't had to, until now. But first, let me explain something to you." Otty then gave details to Jarad about the warning from his brother and how he and his wife, as well as a few well-to-do parishioners, used that information in the most practical way they knew how.

Otty then stood and headed for the door out of his office. "Follow me, I'll show you."

They both left the office and made for the reception hall where everyone had gathered for coffee and cake the night before. From the windows it was apparent that the snow had resumed in earnest and the large flakes reflected a subtle white glow into the room. Otty led his guest to a set of nondescript folding doors against the far wall. Reaching them, he opened them up, collapsing the doors upon themselves so Jarad could see what lay upon the formerly hidden shelves. Before him was an array of canned goods and boxed dinners, as well a bric-a-brac of miscellaneous items. He could tell that the stock had been drawn down, though there was still a good supply of basic foodstuffs.

"Help yourself," Otty said, pointing at some empty boxes on the floor in the corner. Jarad hesitated, but he didn't know why. It wasn't that he wasn't appreciative, nor that he was indifferent to the needs of his family -- he could sure use everything here. Perhaps it was because he didn't know what to do. He had never had to get help in this fashion before. What should he take? How much should he take? What is expected? It should have been such a simple thing, but it was outside of his previous experiences and he had no schema to use as a guide. He felt catatonic.

Sensing his unease, Otty said, "Anyhow, I need to get back to the office. If you can, why don't you come by and see me tomorrow and we can plan our 'raids,' for lack of a better word." He walked away and then stopped, turning around. "Oh, I forgot. There are two freezers outside with ground beef. And don't forget toilet paper." Both Otty and Jarad smiled.

+++

Chapter 10

Myla felt dirty. She hadn't had a proper bath or shower since she had left the hospital. In addition, she was tired of wearing dirty clothes. She wished she had, if only for a couple hours, access to a washer and dryer. That would be heaven! But worse of all, she started her period and she had cramps. She hadn't had a period for a decade – at least not since the twins were born. And the birth control injection that she had received two years ago that kept her menstrual cycle at bay had worn off. How did women live like this!

When she awoke she noticed that Jarad had already left. The cabin was warm since he had made a fire. She went to the kitchen to make herself a cup of coffee. She noticed that there were no dishes in the sink or any other evidence that Jarad had prepared himself breakfast. She had suspected that he was cutting back on his eating in order to save what they had for her and the kids. "I wish he wouldn't do that," she said to herself quietly. But then, she had no other solution. They would need to get more food quickly or even the children would go hungry. That thought both angered her and made her ill with guilt and worry.

Well, if Jarad could go without eating, she could too. Anyway, she wasn't really that hungry. The kids at least had one more breakfast meal. Flavored instant oatmeal without milk. And she knew that they had already become so accustomed to this new life that they wouldn't complain. They wouldn't know why to complain. If only she could adjust as well as the kids.

The dog met her at the kitchen and sat, staring at her. Myla knew that this was his way of saying "feed me." She reached under the counter and scooped a cup of TVP from the bag and filled the dog's dish. He waved a thank you with his tail and began to eat his breakfast. She gave him a passing pat on the side. "And you're the only one getting fat," she said softly to the dog. She paused. "Why am I feeding you this?" she said in a mock scolding voice. "This is tonight's dinner. Meatloaf."

+++

Myla had joked with Jarad that his timely return that morning had saved him from a fate worth than death, if only he knew what she was planning to cook for dinner. But that box of groceries was a blessing and who would have imagined that toilet paper would be such a treasure. They both returned the next day to visit with Pastor Oleson, bringing the children in tow. Both Jarad and Myla wanted to know what they could do to lend a hand, and the children wanted to search for their new friends from a couple nights earlier.

Otty was glad to see them. He shared with them that he was excited that everyone was coming together to turn their little grouping of neighbors into a genuine community. But he did have concerns because not everyone was doing well. Besides the chronic need for food and wood for heating, there were those who had medical issues and others who were homebound. Otty also confessed that he felt the need for security was paramount. "This keeps me awake at night. I think that it is only a matter of time before we have to defend our turf, so to speak." Lastly, he wanted to somehow continue the education of the community's children, which had been temporarily disrupted. "Besides," Otty reminded them, "resuming classes would not only be good for the children, but also the adults. Give them both something constructive to do."

While Jarad and Myla visited with Otty, other people were constantly coming and going at the church. The church building really did serve as a community center. Of course, Otty was really the anchor of all of this activity. Without being asked or appointed, he had become the community leader. Sort of the *de facto* mayor. Perhaps everyone, including Otty, simply saw all of his effort as being a natural extension of his position as the church pastor. Without a doubt, some sort of governance was required and Otty by default was probably the best equipped to provide it. Not one complained or had yet challenged this development.

The visit with Otty was very calming, but came to an end when he said that he had to be going because of a prior commitment. "But I have a proposition for both of you," he said. "Myla, hear me out before you say yes or no. You have the most medical experience of anyone for miles around. I would really like you to somehow use your expertise to help some of our people. Maybe you and I could make some rounds, tomorrow perhaps?" And then he turned to face Jarad. "Jarad, you're a police officer. Maybe you would be interested in using your experience to somehow put together a security force. I don't know what that would entail, but I think you know what I have in mind. Lastly, I need you to talk with Genis Bullock. He is coordinating the exploitation of extant resources!"

Otty laughed at his choice of words. "I can give you directions to his place. He is expecting you, one of these days."

They shook hands and all walked together toward the wooden doors, Otty dragging along a heavy knapsack from his office. Stepping out, he pointed with this arm to the west, indicating where he lived and inviting Myla and the kids to drop in on his wife. She had the grandkids and they would love to visit with other children. Myla said that she would find the time and that it would be nice to visit.

Otty strapped on his cross-country skis, hoisted the knapsack onto his back, and then he was off down the hill, toward the east away from 'town.'

+++

"Did you bring my package?" Howard asked as Otty stepped through the door.

"I did, and some other supplies as well." Otty swung the heavy knapsack onto the kitchen table, glad to be rid of the burden. It was all he could do to ski downhill on cross-country skis with a twenty-pound load on his back and shoulders. He then carefully emptied out the canned goods and sundries and stacked them on the table. When he had finished, he fished a plastic bag full of shotgun shells out of a pocket sewn onto the front of the knapsack. He handed the bag to Howard, who took them with a matter-of-fact, but dour, look on his face.

"By the way, what is this I hear about strangers visiting your property?" Otty asked as he sat down in his usual place in the front room. He had noticed that a path had been tramped down in the snow which circled around his property.

"Well, my friend, that is why I need these," he said, holding up the bag of shells.

"I tell you, life is getting me down. I am too damn old to be worried about my safety. I'm sick of these people coming around my property. Now I gotta keep a light on all night, which wastes fuel." He signed heavily. "And I'm tired, Otty, patrolling my own property, back and forth.."

He did look tired, Otty mused to himself. Old and tired.

"Now is the time that you take me up on my offer and come and stay at my place."

"Otty!" Howard's voice raised in irritation and then quickly quieted down. "I don't want to leave my house. Would you leave yours?" He patted the bag of shotgun shells. "Thank you anyways. But this buckshot will help me to feel better now that I can at least protect myself. And the dog." He swung his head in emphasis, his long white beard dragging on his chest. "I swear I'll shoot the first person that touches my dog. Damn vandals."

"Anyhow," he continued, "what makes you think that your house is any safer than mine? You might not realize it, but there is a path down below with traffic going both directions. I think that you folks up there west of me are getting visitors, too. You just don't realize it yet."

"Well, perhaps, but I haven't seen anyone."

"That might be very true, but that doesn't make them any less real. Come here, I'll show you."

Howard got up from his recliner and reached for a pair of binoculars from a wall peg. Otty followed the short, stout figure out the back door and onto a small deck that overlooked the railroad bed some thirty feet below. He handed the binoculars to Otty.

"Look there," he said, pointing. "Down there alongside the tracks."

Otty put the glasses to his face and maneuvered and adjusted them until he found the place Howard had indicated. Sure enough, there were bootprints clearly in the snow, going in both directs, east to west.

"Well, I'll be," Otty said softly, trying to follow the tracks as far to the right as he could, in the direction of his own home. He suddenly realized that the rail bed was a perfect route from the Junction area up to Blue River, as he now thought of the little community. Typically no one bothered with the railroad bed because it was too difficult to get up and down the bank that separates it from the road that paralleled it, instead preferring to use the existing paths already cut into the snow through regular use.

Otty put down the binoculars and handed them back to Howard. Both men hustled back inside since neither had put on a coat. Resuming their visit, Otty conveyed to Howard that he knew it was only a matter of time before folks from the Junction area began to expand their search for resources. "There are only so many empty homes you can ransack before you have to move on. I just hope that they don't get presumptuous."

"That . . ." Howard said, raising a finger for emphasis, "is an interesting comment." He smiled for the first time since Otty had come to visit, albeit a wry one. "So, are we already dividing up the territory? Ours and theirs; us and them?"

Howard's words rattled Otty for a moment. "Am I really thinking like that?" he asked himself aloud. As a historian, Otty knew that that communities would spontaneously form whenever there was a breakdown in the existing social structure, but of course, he had never lived through such an event. Until now. But that was no excuse.

"Howard, you are right. I must remind myself that Blue River is not the center of the universe." He shook his head as he reflected about his previous thoughts. "Yup, I need to talk with folks and maybe we can send a delegation down to . . . our neighbors at the Junction."

+++

Jarad didn't get a chance to knock on the front door. The loud and excited dogs made sure of that. A tall young fellow, with a woolen sweater and full, red beard appeared at the multi-paned window that filled most of the door, just before he had a opportunity to rap his knuckle. The man opened the door and welcomed Jarad with a loud and generous greeting as two large mixed-breed dogs danced around their legs, sniffing Jarad intently.

"Hello, there," he said with an outstretched hand. "You must be Jarad Traverson. I am Genis Bullock."

Jarad met the proffered hand with his own, which the red-bearded man shook firmly. Jarad quickly scanned the youthful face and detected a hint of tension. He understood this sense of unease.

In the present situation, one had to quickly ascertain who was an ally and who wasn't.

Jarad knew that Genis was a bachelor the moment he stepped into his home. He was living at a level of unkemptness that few women would tolerate. Jarad sat down on a leather recliner, one of the few places in the small front room not being utilized for some alternate purpose. As with many homes at that time, living had been reduced to a single room – whichever one had a fireplace or a wood stove. If a home had neither, it was abandoned. Genis's front room was a combination living space and workshop. A few articles of clothing were hanging to dry from a clothing wire suspended over the wood stove and hand tools were roughly stacked on one side of a small dining table. Open maps covered the remaining area of the table.

Jarad and Genis bonded instantly as friends. They were of similar age, but more importantly, of similar purpose and motivation. Professionally Jarad had worked most of his adult life in a position of serving others. Therefore it was only natural to extend this effort to this recently adopted community of Blue River. This leap didn't even require a conscious effort, so much so that Jarad hadn't as of yet even given it any thought. And a natural extension of this was his overwhelming desire to provide for his family. At this time both needs could be met in this one place.

Genis, on the other hand, didn't have a family to provide for. At least not in the sense of kin. Instead, he had adopted and been adopted by the dozen or so retirees in the area. Through the course of the past years this seasonal logger, truck driver, and handyman had become everyone's favorite adopted son. For Genis satisfaction in this life was best found in helping those who could not help themselves and enjoying home-cooked meals that he neither had to prepare nor clean-up after. And it was a rare evening in his calendar where he didn't have a plate waiting for him at some household.

"Would you like a beer?" Genis asked, playing the host.

"Beer?" Jarad asked incredulously. "You have beer?"

"Sure, I make it myself. My own recipe." He removed the caps from a couple of unmarked brown bottles, handing one to Jarad. Jarad sniffed it cautiously and then took a sip. He paused, swirling the home brew around in his mouth. He took another quaff. "This is excellent," he said, smiling. "And not because I haven't had a beer in I don't know how long."

Genis chuckled lightly, removing his hat and giving his head a scratch. He had sat down across from Jarad on one of the wooden chairs next to the table. "I don't know if I can brew very many more batches since I will soon run out of hops. But I'll make it as long as I can." He laughed again, his eyes staring forward as he pondered a thought. "And I don't know if I'll be giving it away as I have in the past. If you know what I mean."

The two men bantered about the two inane subjects that men everywhere seem to enjoy discussing, the weather and dogs, before moving on to the issue which had brought Jarad to Genis's door. "I can see that you are already planning our first excursion," Jarad said, pointing his now empty beer bottle at the maps on the table. "What do you think?"

"Well, I know almost every house there is in this area, having worked on most of them. But I guess that is one reason why I've been dragging my feet. Most of these homes belong to friends of mine. I suppose they won't be needing them now. And I am sure that they won't blame me for making use of some of their belongings."

He turned in his seat and faced the table, pulling a map toward himself. "And I know where I want to start," he said, pointing with his thumb toward some unspecific place on the map.

"And where's that?" Jarad asked, curious.

"The Anderson's place, about a mile from here, near the tracks."

"Why there? A big house? Lots of stuff?"

"No, not at all. In fact, its kind of small. It's just that I never really cared for the Andersons and they never really cared for me. Nor anyone else, for that matter."

Jarad snorted. "Well, that's as good a reason as any. When do we start?"

+++

Jarad had brought Champ along with him, but not intentionally. It just sort of happened that way. The dog was barking at some people standing along the path that cut through the snow near his home. Jarad knew that these were the fellows he was going to accompany on this first raiding excursion. And when he opened the door the dog bolted out to fulfill his duties as part watchdog, part greeter. The men enjoyed Champ so much that they insisted he be allowed to come along.

Jarad was excited. To him this whole endeavor was a cross between exploring and hunting. Perhaps gathering was a more appropriate term, but terminology could be argued later, hopefully over a couple more of Genis's beers.

The three men were making friends with Champ when Jarad joined them on the path. Jarad recognized the faces of both of the other men with Genis since he had met them at the get-together a couple of days previous. But to Jarad's relief, Genis went ahead and reintroduced them anyways, which spared Jarad the embarrassment of not having remembered their names. Jarad had always struggled with remembering names, which was sometimes a handicap as a police officer. He compensated by always carrying a small pocket notebook. And now, out of habit he reached into his breast pocket like a recent ex-smoker groping for a pack of cigarettes. The pocket was empty.

Genis led the way away down the path and to the east, following the road. Each man pulled a sled. James, the older of the two, also packed a deer rifle. Meat was always in need and the local deer population provided a generally reliable source, though it was only a matter of time before the build-up of snow drove the animals to lower elevations.

The grade of the road gently descended for about a quarter-mile before leveling off for a similar distance, and then descended again. The group was animated and walked quickly, partly out of excitement and partly to keep warm. Their conversations sent plumes of steam from each person. Out of habit they talked quietly in order not to alarm any deer that they might come upon, but

Champ continually flushed hares, which served as a warning for any thoughtful prey animal that understood the significance of a hare in mad flight.

Their first stop was a small wooden home that was perched along an outcropping overlooking the railroad bed that lay behind it. Genis had mentioned earlier that he wanted to check on its occupant, a widower that lived alone and who was one of his friends. The three men and the dog waited along the road while Genis talked with the old man, who had come to the door wielding a shotgun. Snow tended to stifle the spread of sound, therefore the conversation between Genis and the old man was a silent pantomime of head nods and hand motions. Genis and the other man would occasionally point to the east as they continued what was obviously an emphatic conversation. Finally, they shook hands and the old man stepped back into his house. The four resumed their trek, with Genis carrying on a monologue as they tramped along in their snowshoes.

"He's been having visitors, prowling around his property," Genis told them, his frozen breath leaving a slight crust of ice on his beard. "Vandals, he calls them, and they've been coming from that a way." He pointed in the direction they were going. "He also said that these same people having been walking up to our area using the railroad tracks." The other men commented that they hadn't seen anything strange or noticed anyone prowling around, but then they also admitted that they hadn't felt any reason to be on guard.

After another half-mile they finally approached their target, an unremarkable white-paneled single-story house with dark windows and a battlement of snow under its eaves. But snow keeps records and the party of men realized that they hadn't been the first to visit this abandoned house, as evidenced by the multiple paths of footprints and sled runners that ran to and from the building. "Well," Genis said matter-of-fact, "I guess we're the last to the party."

The men searched the home. It was easy to enter since the front door had been left open. Snow drifts had invaded the front room, stretching white windblown tendrils into the kitchen and the hallway as if offering directions to Genis and his companions. The earlier visitors hadn't been kind guests as evidenced by the mess caused by upturned drawers and the scattered clothing strewn everywhere. Surprisingly, there was still a fair amount of desirable items, though most of the food had been taken.

"I think that there were only a few of them and they could only carry so much," Genis noted as he carefully placed some plastic bags of rice and a few canned goods into one of the sleds. "Otherwise they wouldn't have abandoned so much good stuff. Unless, of course, they meant to come back."

The men went room by room, taking anything of practical use. According to their shopping list, food was the priority, but it also included warm clothing, boots, bedding, medicines, toiletries, any large cooking containers, and select hand tools. As if to demonstrate how quickly the world had changed, the men ignored the expensive electronic items they encountered, as well as any tokens of wealth such as jewelry. Firearms and ammunition were desirable, but none were found. As they prepared to leave, one of the fellows lamented that they couldn't take any of the firewood that was stacked alongside the garage. "Too damn heavy," he said with disgust.

Jarad and the other two men were outside strapping on their snowshoes when Genis appeared, vigorously shaking a can of spray paint. "I got an idea," he said as he pulled down the garage door. Standing to the left of it he began to paint lettering with broad sweeps of his hand, pausing every few moments to reshake the can. When he was done, he stepped back from his effort, smiled, and tossed the can into the snow. The other men took a look at his work, which spelled out in black paint NO TRESPASSING. One of them laughed.

"Can't hurt," Genis said with a smile and a shrug of his shoulders. "Let's go."

+++

Chapter 11

The four men slowly trod up the path, each leaning forward like small two-legged beasts of burden as they dragged the heavy sleds behind them. There was less conversation among them than the earlier trip, but even larger steam plumes. As the grade steepened, talk came to a halt as he man focused on the next step forward as their snowshoes dug deeply into the snow, making forward progress arduous. If the need weren't so great and the drive to provide so compelling, each man would have chosen not to undertake this difficulty. But the thought of these treasures going to waste, even more the idea that someone else would beat them to the supplies, was sufficient motivation for these men to undertake the task.. Champ acted as the vanguard, his tail in continuous motion as he anticipated the movement of something to chase, for which he swept the air constantly with his nose, like a radar on continuous guard.

The men would pause and rest every few minutes, but they didn't dally long. It was already late in the day and all were hungry and cold. Each simply wanted to get this task done and be home. All found new energy when they finally crested the last grade and set themselves on the final straightaway to the church. Champ abandoned his new friends when they arrived at the house, but Jarad continued on to the church. The supplies gathered did not belong to any one man, but to the group. And the church was the distribution center. Jarad would take home what he needed only after these supplies were consigned to the church pantry.

After they had made it to the church, a couple of women helped them organize and put away the "loot," as Genis called it. When everything was finally out of the sleds, the men realized that they had done surprisingly well. James talked about returning in a few days to gather up the firewood. Jarad didn't know if that was practical, but he did acknowledge that he would have to find some wood for his own supplies before too long. But right now, all were tired and each was ready to go home and settle down for the evening.

As they were leaving, Genis asked Jarad if he would interested in exploring the extent of the pathway that the alleged visitors had been using alongside the tracks. Jarad indicated that he would be very interested. They agreed to check it out in the next day. Then, with final goodbyes, the men each drifted off into the darkness.

+++

A house never looked more inviting. As Jarad approached his home through the darkness, the postcard perfect image of a cabin nestled in deep snow and the warm glow emanating from the windows stirred his spirit. These near-desperate times had brought a gravity of meaning to every facet of his life, whether it be a meal that filled him so full his belly hurt or a warm bed that allowed him to sleep deeply through the night. He appreciated everything, especially those things he had previously taken for granted. Right now, this moment, he loved life. And he was never more happy to be home, at his home, coming home to his wife and his children. His hearth.

A chorus of greetings met him as he opened the door and stepped quickly into the warm envelope of light, his kids wrapping themselves around his waist. Perhaps it was simply the moment or the swoon of his feelings, but his children appeared to him to have never been more content. Odd, he thought. Here they were having to go without all of the things one would expect in a 'normal' childhood, but not one complaint. No toys, no computers, no music, and no complaints. Instead, now they find their own diversions. Jarad didn't understand it, but was glad nonetheless. Because they were happier, he was happier.

Myla blew him a kiss. "Perfect timing, as always," she said with a smile. "And I got a treat for dinner."

She walked over to the wood stove and fiddled with some sort of metal-box contraption that was placed on top of it. Something did smell seductively delicious, his stomach growling in both approval and anticipation.

"Ellie lent me her camp oven. It's an antique." She used a hot pad to flick open the sheet metal door of the square gray box that sat perched upon stove. She then reached in with that same hot pad and pulled out a pie, its golden crust a magnet for Jarad's steely appetite.

"Chicken pot pie," she beamed. "Homemade." She set the dish on the table which had been set for dinner. She then stepped back into the kitchen and returned to the the wood stove with a bread pan. "And cinnamon rolls for desert," she announced triumphantly, inserting the pan into the sheet-metal oven. The kids cheered. Life was good, almost too good. If were superstitious, he would have been unnerved.

They sat for dinner and said grace, a habit that was infrequent before and regular now. They discussed their day. Myla describe in busy detail how she and Otty went visiting some of the older and medically needier members of the community. She related to her husband her concern for some of them, describing in rich medical verbiage the maladies and conditions of each one, like a biologist describing recently discovered species. At the same time, she lamented what little she could offer them, since she had few medicines and little experience as a doctor. "I'm a nurse, not a doctor," she said in exasperation, expressing her thoughts aloud. But, she was glad that her presence did seem to encourage some of them and she promised to visit them regularly, no less than once a week. "And one old sweetheart gave me a bottle of cinnamon. So thank her for the rolls."

Jarad was more than glad to allow his wife to be the first to share her day. Not only was he interested in what had transpired, for whatever impacted her was always of interest to him, but also because it allowed him to satisfy his hunger. He ate an entire quarter of the pie, plus polished off what Annie couldn't finish of her serving. "Daddy," she said in mock alarm, "you're as bad as Champ!"

"Sorry, honey, but I had a very demanding day." He smiled at her to let her know that he hadn't taken offense. He then described in detail his adventure, what they had discovered and how difficult it was to bring the supplies back. "If anything, I don't have to worry about not getting enough exercise." He also explained to Myla the concern about the movement of strangers along the railroad tracks, and that he and Genis were going to check it out the next day. He assured her that it was probably nothing, but it still needed to be investigated. Suddenly he was overcome by a yawn. He was tired and his thoughts turned toward bed. "No cribbage for me tonight baby, I need to turn in."

"And what about the cinnamon rolls?" she asked, a bit petulantly.

"Oh, I forgot," he said, honestly. He raised his nose and took in the smell of cinnamon and fresh homemade bread. "Something smells heavenly," he said encouragingly. "Bed can wait." He smiled. "Your deal or mine?" he asked, fishing the deck of cards and the cribbage board from the hutch.

+++

"Jarad, wake up. I smell smoke." Jarad sat up in bed. Was he dreaming? Was he having some sort of flashback to Purcell, that day he had to escape? He couldn't think. Where was he? The room was dark and cold. He shivered.

"What?" he asked his wife, who was somewhere near him in the darkness.

"There is a fire somewhere. I smell smoke. And Champ is upset about something. I'm worried."

Jarad shook his head sharply to rouse his mind. Fire? Not again, he thought to himself. That's bad. Where's the fire? He clambered out of bed and put on the clothes that he had laid out for the morning. It was dark and he didn't notice any light coming from the window, but he did begin to faintly smell an odd scent. Was his house on fire? Was there a chimney fire?

He moved quickly out into the front room and slipped on his boots and coat. The dog was whining and anxious to go outside with him. He stepped outside into the darkness. It was clear out as evidenced by the starry night that peeked through the tree canopy. It was also very cold, which helped to clear his mind. He shivered as he fastened the front of his coat. His nose felt like it was being pinched as the frigid air froze the flesh in his nostrils. A breeze was blowing softly from the east, carrying that smell which had alarmed his wife. He moved away from his house so as to see the roof and chimney. No evidence of fire there. But from where he stood a very faint glow to his right captured the attention of his subconscious, and he turned again to face the east. Peering into the darkness he thought he saw a glow, but he wasn't sure. He moved a dozen or so yards toward that direction to find a clearer view devoid of trees.

Then he could see it. About a mile, more or less, something was burning. A bonfire? No, it was larger. But it was difficult to tell. To be honest, Jarad was simply relieved that it wasn't his own home. In addition, he didn't feel compelled to act, as he would have just months ago in Purcell. Now, he knew that there was nothing he could do to help these people and he surely wasn't going to dash off into the darkness to tackle a fire about which he knew little. He turned away and trod back toward the cabin, his boots crunching the hard, crusty snow in which he no longer sunk into. He was tired and wanted to get back into bed. Champ had also seen all that he had wanted and was waiting by the door.

He stepped into the house, kicked off his boots and rehung his coat in the small closet near the door. Since he was up, he checked the wood stove. It was still sufficiently stoked with wood, which indicated to him that he hadn't been asleep for very long. Either way, he was going to bed.

Myla was waiting for him when he returned. "Well," she asked expectantly. "Where is the fire?"

"Don't know," he replied indifferently, shaking off his clothes and quickly getting under the covers. "It's a long ways away, about a mile."

Myla continued to talk softly, not wanting to waken the children but also wanting to vent her concerns. Who were they? Are they safe? Do they need shelter? She then concluded that she was going to go out tomorrow and find out the answers to these questions. It was the least she could do. She then laid on her back and stared unseeing into the darkness, lost in her own thoughts.

Jarad had already began to drift off, when, again, he sat up suddenly in bed. "What," Myla asked, alarmed. "What's wrong?"

"Nothing," he responded softly. "Go back to sleep. I just figured it out. I bet my bottom dollar that someone was letting us know that they didn't appreciate the no trespassing sign."

"What are you talking about, Jarad? Who? Us? What sign?"

"Nothing. I don't think it's not important," he mumbled. "I'm too tired to know. I'll tell you in the morning." And he lay down again and fell immediately asleep.

+++

Jarad slept in that morning, which was unusual for him. But the previous day was so exhausting that he needed the rest. When he did finally appear in the front room, he was greeted by both his wife and Genis.

"Oh, man, I'm sorry Genis. I didn't mean to sleep so late," he said apologetically, running his hand through the tousled hair of his head.

"No apologies necessary. I am having a very pleasant visit with your wife and enjoying, what, my third cup of coffee? Pure indulgence and that includes the coffee!"

Myla laughed with that and got up from the table to make her husband some breakfast. Jarad disappeared to the bathroom and returned after a few minutes.

"Well, Genis, what's on the agenda?" he asked as he found his wife and planted a kiss on her cheek. She handed her husband a plate of fried potatoes and a cup of coffee. "Potatoes, again?" he said in a mock whiny voice. He smiled. He knew that it would be potatoes tomorrow as well, and the day after that, just as it was potatoes yesterday. And he felt genuine gratitude just to have something hot on his plate.

As he sat down he learned that Genis had already explained to Myla about the no trespassing sign. "So, what is your take on the fire last night, assuming it is the same place?" he asked Genis.

"Well, I didn't know anything about that until this morning when I stepped outside to let the dogs out. Then I smelled the smoke. So I got dressed and moseyed on down the hill to take a peek. It is amazing how much easier it is to get around when you're not dragging a sled." He smiled with a crooked grin and shook his head as if in disbelief. "I got just close enough to know that it was the same place."

"But to answer your question, I can't imagine why they burned it down. It is too far from the Junction to have been visited that late at night. It could've been been an accident. Maybe someone had moved in and accidentally knocked over a lantern or something. Who knows. But if it was intentional, that is darn wasteful, don't you think?"

He was staring at his coffee, lost for a moment in his own thoughts. "Still, if it was intentional," he continued slowly, drawing out each word, "then I suppose that it was meant to serve as a warning. Can't imagine any other reason."

"What kind of warning?" Myla interjected.

Genis gave her a kind smile, his pale blue eyes expressing empathy with the concern in her voice. "Don't know. Maybe, "this is our territory and you stay out?" Makes sense to me. Maybe we need to draw some lines between what's theirs and what's ours."

Jarad finished his breakfast in silence. He had thought that his world had become so simple recently, but now realized that that was a deceptive view of reality. Nothing is simple when people are involved, especially those whom you love.

The conversation resumed and soon the two men left to reconnoiter along the railroad tracks. It was a simple matter locating the tracks, but not as simple finding a way down to them. Though the tracks and the main road followed parallel paths, the tracks sat down closer to the river, whereas the road, and all the homes that straddled it, were up on a rise. The difference between them was a tangle of trees and underbrush that clung to the steep bank separating the two roads, a bank that was more often than not a cliff. Genis led Jarad to a place about half the distance between Jarad's cabin and that old man's place where the bank wasn't as steep. They lowered themselves down by clinging to the bushes as gravity tugged them downward on the slick surface.

Once at the bottom of the bank they bounded up out of the snow-covered ditch and onto the track bed. "Look at that," said Genis with a hint of genuine surprise, looking down at the collection of scuff marks in the snow, an indication of the passing of boots. "Who would have thought?"

Jarad eyed the tracks. They didn't appear fresh, at least not from the past couple days, but he wasn't really sure. Recently the weather had been without snowfall, so the tracks were still fairly distinct. What was more interesting to him was where they led. As if on cue, both Jarad and Genis began to follow the tracks to the west, back toward the main part of the community.

Genis thought out loud as they trudged on both sides of the marks in the snow. "It seems to me that it would be hard to know how long or how often this path as been used. I don't think it has been used anytime recently, but it sure gets my neck hairs up to think that someone has been scouting us out. I don't like that."

It wasn't a difficult hike. The ground was level and the snow was hard, allowing them to move fairly rapidly over the surface. They had progressed about a half mile before they came upon the first evidence that someone had scaled the bank, as demonstrated by the deep bootprints that punctured the snowbank filling the ditch between the bank and the rail bed. There were long gashes in the snow that covered the bank, caused by a boot digging for traction. They continued on for another mile before they came to the end of the tracks, having encountered evidence of another half dozen points of incursion up the bank side.

"Well, it looks like they've been checking us out," Genis said, matter-of-fact. "I suppose we could follow the track the other way, but I think I can guess where they lead to. Either way, they've probably seen all that they've wanted to see."

Jarad was just about to comment when a deep, deep rumble began to move the ground beneath them. "What in the world," he said excitedly, as the vibrations made the shards of hard frozen snow dance in the snowshoe tracks.

"It's a train," Genis practically shouted in alarm. "Come on, let's get out of here." He dashed across the tracks and practically threw himself over the bank, hiding himself in the naked tangles of willows and thimble berry bushes. Instinctively, Jarad followed Genis's lead though a more thoughtful part of his brain was asking why they had to hide. What was the danger, it kept repeating, it's only a train?

Jarad whispered these same questions to Genis. "Why are hiding, Genis? What's the danger?" Genis was holding himself flat against the ground, though he had shimmied into a position from where he could watch for the oncoming train. He looked back over his shoulder at Jarad when he heard Jarad's questioning. "I don't know. But I would rather be safe than sorry, if that makes any sense."

The rumble increased in intensity and loudness as the train moved closer to their position. It wasn't going very fast, probably because of the fairly deep canopy of snow that was draped over the rails. Jarad didn't know how well he was hidden, but he couldn't resist trying to see the oncoming engine. But he was too close to see it clearly, and then the rush of driven snow made visibility impossible. The ground vibrated strongly as the train passed immediately next to them, the noise surprisingly loud. Jarad simply buried his face into his gloves and allowed himself to be content with simply laying there, since there was little else he could do without betraying his presence. If that mattered.

When the train finally passed, both Genis and Jarad craned their heads for a better view, but neither jumped up. What they saw startled them. Though they could only see the last quarter section of the train due to the fact that the tracks followed a curve in the rail bed that led away from their point of view, they saw enough to know that this was not a typical freight-hauling train. Instead of box cars, the train was hauling over-sized flatbeds that carried huge military tanks and dark, camouflaged trucks. Following last of all were two olive-drab passenger cars, both of which were topped by what appeared to be turrets.

Both men slowly stood up, gawking at the sight of the train as it passed just around the bend. Suddenly, Genis let out with a stream of profanities as he grabbed his hand, blood being flicked everywhere as he waved it about in pain. The echo of automatic gun fire quickly followed and caused both men to pause and look at the train, before returning quickly to their previous hiding places along the bank. Genis was breathing hard as he laboriously tried to tie a handkerchief around this hand which was now missing a finger.

"I do believe that those sons of bitches have shot my finger off," he said through clenched teeth. "What the hell is going on?"

Jarad helped him bind his wound. The pinkie finger on his left hand was missing, nipped off by a bullet right above the bottom knuckle. The handkerchief was already sodden red. Genis clenched his wounded hand tightly with his other hand and Jarad helped him to stand. The snow around them was spattered with bright, red speckles of crimson.

"That wasn't just gun fire, that was machine gun fire. I don't think that those boys were intending to scare us, but to kill us," Jarad said, stating his thoughts as he breathed heavily from the excitement.

"I agree," Genis said with a wince. "What in the world is going on?"

+++

"I saw it happen, from right outside the house, along the road. And the two guys were laughing," Myla said disgustedly as she tied off the splint she had secured around Genis's hand. "I was wondering what they were shooting at."

"It was weird enough to have a train appear out of nowhere, rumbling and noisy and everything," Genis replied. "But then those soldiers started shooting. I'd never heard a machine-gun being fired before. At least not in real life. Scary."

Myla recounted to Genis and Jarad how the appearance of the train had captured her attention. And she had seen the entire thing pass, commenting on how strange it appeared with everything painted olive-drab, including the two engines. "And no markings anywhere," she added. She also recounted how there seemed to be gun enclosures everywhere, front and rear, and upon all the cars except the flatbeds. All manned by soldiers. "The whole things was ominous."

Genis was lucky. The wound, though potentially serious, was probably going to heal alright. Myla complained about the lack of proper antibiotics and sterile bandage, and fretted about the fact that she had never sutured a wound before. Still, she was optimistic that considering the circumstances, Genis was very fortunate. "Sorry I can't do anything about the pain. It is really going to hurt."

"You mean worse than it is now?" Genis groaned. He had agreed to spend the rest of the day and possibly the night at Jarad and Myla's, if only because he was so exhausted. The trek back from the tracks combined with the loss of blood and the pain he was enduring had sapped him of energy. Myla sent Jarad to the church to let the word out that prescription pain relievers were needed. And the need for someone to attend to Genis's dogs.

By the time Jarad had returned, Genis was sound asleep on the sofa in the front room, his arm propped up on some pillows. He was successful in tracking down some strong pain relievers, but he didn't know what they were. He handed them to Myla, who nodded in approval after scanning the label.

The kids had accompanied Jarad home. They had been at "school," which recently had begun meeting at the church. A couple of retirees in the area were former teachers and they were delighted to be working with the children – all eight of them. They were incessantly talking to Myla in whispers about the train and how exciting it was. They didn't get to see it, but they felt it and heard it. They didn't hear any gun fire, but were awed by Genis's wound once they heard about his travails. Surprisingly, none conveyed any concern about the safety of their father, whom, in the naivety of their youth both assumed him to be invincible anyhow.

They were also excited about the fact that there was going to be a Christmas party at the church in a month and a half. "Christmas! Not Solstice, momma," Annie said excitedly, "but Christmas! I've never been to a Christmas party before."

Christmas, Myla thought to herself, Christmas! "I haven't thought about Christmas."

+++

Chapter 12

It had not been months since the collapse of the grid and for most since then life had become an effort to simply survive, an effort that had shifted the perspective on time. Today was now the most important day of anyone's life, and longterm planning amounted to looking no more than a week or two ahead. The lack of electricity had quickly become normal. And for the children, who are so ready to adapt to new surroundings and who truly do only live in the present, it was as if no other life had ever existed. Neither had airplanes, the Internet, or the televisor.

Therefore it was disturbing to the entire community, though for each generation in a different way, when the train passed alongside the town. For the adults the train represented both hope and anguish. Hope because the movement of the train demonstrated that life was continuing normally somewhere. After all, the train was leaving one area and going to another, suggesting at least two places in the United States that were functioning. But it wasn't the usual type of train, one hauling freight and with engineers in brightly colored engines who waved at you when it passed by, or that sounded their horns at every road crossing, a sound in the distance, especially at night, that told all who listed that everything was fine, that life was moving on, that everything was normal. Go back to sleep.

No, this train was nothing like that. The engines were olive drab and no one waved from the dark, tinted windows. And the freight was not lumber or coal, but army tanks, military trucks, and other symbols of war secured to oversize flatbed rail cars. Soldiers with light machine guns were posted in gun emplacements at various points on the train, providing security against unknown foes. The adults of Blue River could only ponder the significance of such a sight, for none had any experience with the movement of troops and military equipment within the borders of their own country.

For the children, the train evoked wonder. The monster's engines roared and the ground and houses shook. All were excited, but some were afraid and turned to the nearest adult for reassurance, but few found immediate comfort there, for the adults themselves were afraid. Afraid not of the train itself, but what it represented. Or might represent. And not knowing made it all the worse.

+++

Otty was stressed. He had been doing pretty well, feeling really positive about how well things had been developing in Blue River. People had been cooperating with his efforts to organize and they had all begun to try helping each other. He saw them really bonding into an effective community. Myla Traverson had made the rounds with him and he was confident that she would become an integral and effective member of the network of caregivers he had wanted to put together. School had resumed for the children of the community, something he thought would really benefit them. Genis Bullock had taken the first steps in gathering all the resources available in the immediate area, which would help them all get through the winter. But the last couple days had complicated the little world he was trying to organize.

The knowledge that the community had been scouted out by others had made it through the grapevine and was causing alarm. Otty felt that he needed to get the right people together to solve this potentially dangerous situation. And now that Genis was hurt would impact more people than simply himself. And the train, that was just weird. To Otty it was symbolic of how much the world had changed and how it might never return to what it was before. He muttered to himself that it was an interesting time to be alive.

But Christmas was coming. This he was excited about. For once he could celebrate Christmas without any apologies. He could lead a celebration of Christmas the way, in his mind, it was meant to be. He couldn't wait!

And he still had to find a solar cell for Howard. He remembered how years ago, for while they had become quite ubiquitous, but with the never ending economic downturn and the availability of increasingly cheap electricity, people quit investing in them. If only he could find one! He knew that in the great scheme of things it didn't really matter if Howard got his radio up and operating or not. It wouldn't change his little world. But he really did want to know what was going on in the bigger world. Still, one part of his mind was always cautioning the other part. Maybe ignorance was bliss. It was just that his ego didn't know which angel on his shoulders to listen to.

He would have time to contemplate these things later. Right now he was busy making his rounds. His first stop this morning was also the closest. His daughter's place. Otty struggled with his relationship with Breann and even now he hesitated going to visit her. Often she seemed less of a daughter and more of a stranger. Sometimes he felt that he didn't really know her. Maybe he didn't. People change. Lord knows that he had changed over the years. But what was most bothersome about his daughter, and that which he least understood, was her hostility toward all that he treasured. He often reflected back on his life and what he might have done or said to cause his daughter to be the person she was. But in the end he had to agree with Ellie, Breann was simply their "Esau" and had to be loved just the way she was.

Before he knocked at the white, metal door he half prayed, half thought, Lord give me wisdom. No . . . patience. No . . . . both. He rapped the door with his mitten. It opened to the sullen face of his daughter. "Hi, dad," she said neutrally, retreating back into the darkness of her home.

By the time he entered she was already someplace else. Otty was always trying to keep up with her! He took off his knitted cap and scarf, pulled off his mittens, but left his coat and boots on. He remained standing in the front room. He noticed the GILM literature on the table. He didn't know if this was on display in order to bait him or if she had other purposes in mind. He knew that GILM was her current spiritual mania, though they didn't discuss it. Yet, she knew that he did not hold a favorable opinion about the organization. That was reason enough for it to pique her interest.

After a few moments she wandered back into the room. She sat down on the small sofa, an open bag of chips in one hand, the other hand smoothly transferring the potato wafers from the bag to her mouth. "Breakfast," she said, leaning back and crossing her legs. She said nothing more and stared at the wall, waiting for her father to speak.

"Just checking in on you, seeing how you are doing," he said with a mild sing-song.

"I'm fine," she said without enthusiasm. "Are the kids behaving themselves?" She had dropped off her two children at Otty and Ellie's house and never returned to get them. This was not atypical for Breann. She figured that when Ellie got tired of caring for them, or when the kids tired of their grandmother, they'd return. After all, they lived next door to each other. But Otty knew that his wife would never tire of them and the two kids had smoothly integrated themselves into his household. He was content as long as Ellie was content. And this way he knew that the two grandchildren weren't being neglected.

"Is there anything you need, Breann?" he asked quietly. She sighed heavily as if in boredom and said with false sincerity, "I'm doing alright."

She finished her chips and delicately and precisely folded up the empty bag, standing with the completion of her task. "Thanks for coming by," she said, dismissively. She disappeared again into a back room.

"Bye," Otty replied to the emptiness, exiting out the door he had entered just a few moments before. He signed heavily as he set out across the yard toward his next destination. He was both bewildered and relieved.

+++

"I didn't even know that you had raided the Cupperton's place," Otty said with a perplexed but interested look. "Do any good?"

James laughed lightly and pulled a spiral notebook from a plastic folder. He opened it to what must have been the correct page and offered it to Otty. Otty looked at it with a bit exaggerated interest, quickly scanning the pages that were listed under the Cupperton's name and address.

"Genls thought that it would be a good idea to catalog everything we take from each house. That way, if things ever right themselves, we know how it was before. If you follow what I mean."

James stood almost at attention, his long, gangly arms held to his sides. His face was posited on Otty's, as an attentive soldier might stand before an expectant officer. Otty sensed James's need and congratulated him on his thoroughness and initiative. James blushed unabashedly, his eyes bright with accomplishment.

"So what do you have planned for next? I am sure that your schedule is full now that Genis is out of commission for a while."

James explained in a uncharacteristically confident voice that he and the other fellows in his group were going to rest up. Raiding homes was very tiring. But they still needed to make at least one more trip to the Cupperton's house. "We aren't going to let that firewood go to waste, not like that last time. It's just gonna be a heck of a lot of work."

"Oh," he added with a start. He quickly left the room and disappeared around the corner, out a door and into his garage. He returned carrying a large, black, rectangular bundle with a wisp of wires hanging from underneath. "I almost forgot. This is for Howard," he said. "It's kinda old, but I am sure it still works." He handed the open plastic sack to Otty who peeked inside.

"It's beautiful, James. Bravo! He's going to be tickled." It was a solar cell.

+++

"So what are we going to do for the kids for Christmas?" Myla asked Jarad as she gathered her equipment for her day. She was going to make her first solo visitations and she wanted to be prepared. Though her tools were meager and she lacked virtually everything she thought necessary, she hope that she could at least convey the appearance of competency. After all, she understood that for many perception was reality. She knew more than anyone else the limitations of what medical care she could provide, but she was all they had. That was good enough reason for her to try.

"Christmas?" Jarad responded with a smile. "We're gonna have Christmas? That'll be interesting." It wasn't that Jarad had never celebrated Christmas, but like the rest of his generation, it was considered a bit old-fashioned, therefore most people didn't celebrate it in any traditional way. Only those who were considered to be more on the fringe still celebrated it like past generations. Instead, most people had lumped Christmas into a broader seasonal holiday called Solstice, which was considered far more inclusive. This made sense to most people since the majority of Jarad's generation affiliated themselves to some religious tradition other than Christianity, if at all. Even more, all the mainline churches had integrated themselves into the concept of Solstice, claiming that Christmas was simply the same festival anyway. And they didn't want to offend anyone.

"So what do we do, since we can't exactly run to the store and buy them a present?" Jarad asked his wife.

"I don't know. I'll see what the other parents are doing. Maybe I can get some ideas. But we'll do something special." She had filled Jarad's old knapsack with her supplies. She sat to put on her snow boots. With the advent of the colder weather, the snowshoes weren't necessary, which was just fine with Myla. She could get along fine on the hard crusted snow. "I'll be back before sunset. What are you up today? Another raid?"

"No, I'm bushed. We are going to wait a day before returning to that one place we just raided. James wants to get the firewood, which I think is a good idea though it will be a ton of work." Jarad paused for a moment as he considered his inadvertent pun. "And Otty is coming by. We are going to talk about security issues." He shrugged his shoulders. "I am not sure what he has in mind."

"He's trying to tap your police experience, which would be a smart thing to do. I agree with the ladies down at the church. We don't need any strangers snooping around. We got enough problems for ourselves. Bye."

"Bye," he responded to the shutting door. He rubbed the tips of his fingers over the growth of beard that was developing on his chin. He didn't have any more razors, and he had decided that there was no reason why he shouldn't just let his beard grow out. So he did, though it still felt strange. And he knew it looked strange as well, as he wasn't endowed with the ability to grow a really decent beard.

Christmas, he mused. What shall we do for Christmas? He looked around the room, appraising the space around him. We need a tree, he decided, and I know just where to get one.

+++

Cameron and Annie were content. They hadn't been living in their new home for very long, but such is life that when it is overfilled with adventure time loses its normal dimensions. This is especially true for adults. But for the children it wasn't as if they had lived in their grandparent's vacation home for a certain number of weeks or months or even years, but always. Always in recent memory. And that was the key. For a child – even an adolescent – recent memory is all time, any time, every time.

Annie and Cameron really enjoyed school. It not only gave them an opportunity to interact with other young people, but it also filled their day with activities. But probably most important of all it gave them a schedule. Their days were planned and relatively busy. Plus they were fed a meal, taking a burden off of their parents. And they were warm, which allowed Myla and Jarad to not aggressively heat the home at least part of the day, which conserved the difficult to replace firewood.

Typically the kids would get up with the sun. There was no reason to get up any earlier. Often they would wait in bed until their mother or father had made a fire. Otherwise it was too cold! When they heard a parent stirring, they'd quickly get dress and race each other to the bathroom. Breakfast was typically very simple: fried potatoes, sometimes with onions, or soupy oatmeal with brown sugar, *sans* milk.

Then they would walk to the church. The school at the church was effectively nothing more than an old-fashion one-room school. No computers, no electronic equipment of any kind, and very few books. There was only one small white board and they were down to their last two markers. But what they did have were two motivated teachers who had the luxury of spending a lot of time working with the kids one-on-one. Reams of computer printer paper and cups full of miscellaneous pens and pencils were available for assignments and classroom work. There were scissors but no glue, until one of the ladies at the church made a paste out of flour. And the first art project was an advent calendar. No concerns here about separating church and state.

Grade levels were not assigned. That would be too impractical with the limited resources at hand. Instead, each student was individually assessed in various content areas and then put on a unique academic schedule. Of the eight students, three were younger than the Traverson twins, and three were older. To Annie's delight, two of the older students were boys.

Besides those subjects typically taught in any academic circle, the students were also working on a stage presentation: a Christmas pageant. The first for all of them. And more than anything else, this is what excited the students. Because the pageant was a secret, it was going to be a surprise Christmas gift for the parents. Christmas couldn't come soon enough!

+++

The setting sun ignited the hilltops in glorious alpenglow, providing a dramatic riposte to the lengthening shadows in the deep valleys below. The dark, hooded figure ignored the former and welcomed the latter, as he trod stridently to the east, following the crusty ridge of snow along the rail bed. As he neared the small collection of houses, he paused to check his watch. He had some time to spare. He wasn't cold as long as he was moving, but standing idle quickly brought a chill to his broad figure. He drew closer to the houses, but mostly for the sake of doing something rather than nothing. Minutes later he glanced again at his watch. The time was near.

For the last time he drew out the map that had been repeatedly folded down into a small square. He estimated the lay of the tracks against the houses indicated by small, black squares on the map. It was getting so dark now that he could no longer see on the map what he already knew to be true. He was in the right place.

He scanned the landscape for movement, not knowing who might be around to notice his presence. It was too cold for people to be outside without some compelling reason, even more so to be on the rail bed. He didn't see anyone, nor did he really anticipate seeing anyone. But he was still playing it safe.

Suddenly, he saw what he had come for. In a drab little home, buried among the trees in a growing veil of darkness, he saw a flashlight in a window flicker on and off, on and off, beckoning him in a prearranged signal. He fixed the position of the house in his memory and set off in its direction. He was almost there. And he would soon be warm. Bless the sun, his guide, and the moon, his lover, he thought to himself.

+++

Myla got home a little later than anticipated. She discovered that, more than medical care, many of her 'clients' simply needed a willing ear to listen and a few words of encouragement. Many of the retirees in the area were quite elderly, which only compounded the acuity of care that they needed. Some were truly beginning to suffer. The lack of medicine, difficulty in preparing their own food, the labor required to keep warm, the struggle to maintain good hygiene, all these things and more conspired to slowly drag down the general health of this population. Add to this the prevailing unease about the future and Myla knew it was only a matter of time before some would begin to die. A few had already started the process.

The demographics of Blue River were a microcosm of the nation at large. A lot of older people and a dearth of younger. Perhaps the balance in Blue River did favor the seniors somewhat, but this only added to the caregivers' burden in the community. That was one reason why Myla arrived at her home so late, which had caused her husband a bit of worry. When she did finally push the door open she was greeted with such an enthusiastic "surprise" that the dog began to bark in excitement. Annie was clapping her hands with excitement as she anticipated her mother's discovery of the wonderful thing her father, her brother, and herself had been up to.

Pulling off her scarf and stocking cap Myla was confronted with a small fir tree perched in the corner of the room opposite the wood stove. Little scraps of fabric had been tied into bows and hung on the branches. A paper star covered in tinfoil was affixed to the top and a bowl of popcorn sat on the floor in the middle of the room.

"A Christmas Tree!," she said with delight. "How wonderful. And it is so beautiful."

"Yah," Cameron agreed. "And we are stringing popcorn. Dad is showing us how." He held up a long thread and needle, the tail of which dragged on the floor, half strung with the white cotton balls of popcorn. Little specks of white dotted his chin. "I can see that some of it isn't going to make in on the tree," she teased, as she dusted her son's face with her still-gloved hand.

"This is so lovely! What a wonderful idea." She gave her children hugs, and then gave her husband a long soft kiss on the lips. "You're such a good daddy," she cooed. Jarad reached his arm around her waist and pulled her close to himself. "I always try to please," he said in a whisper.

"Really," she said coyly. "What you got cooking?"

"What do you want?" he asked, suggestively.

"Dinner," she said, with a tease in her voice. "I'm starved."

The family sat around the little kitchen table and feasted on a casserole dish. It should have been tuna casserole, but since there wasn't any tuna available, it was made with what ingredients came in the box. No one complained and none was wasted, to Champ's regret.

Sitting around the table for dinner was a treasured moment in the Traverson household. Myla shared what had transpired during her day, without sharing her concerns. She didn't want the children to fret. She would unload her emotional burden later to Jarad, with what she called her "talk therapy." The kids talked about school, giggling when Cameron confided that there was something important happening at school but he couldn't name what it was. Annie told him to hush. Jarad talked about his brief visit by the pastor, whom he now felt at ease to call by his first name. Otty expressed his concern about the security of the neighborhood and wanted Jarad's ideas about how to address that concern.

"Oh, and by the way Myla, we got a date tomorrow," he added.

+++

Chapter 13

Otty sat at the table with members of what he called his
advisory board, elders from the church and the community who
helped Otty develop strategies for addressing issues and problems.
The advisory board was originally just for the church, but since then
their responsibilities had seamlessly extended to the community.
Joining them at the table were Jarad, Myla, Genis, and Ellie. Jarad
knew the the members of the board, but only casually and only since
he had moved to the cabin. The only exceptions were Emil and
Sarah Silverman who used to be residents of Purcell and retired to
Blue River a couple years ago. Jarad liked them both and had been a
regular patron of Emil's namesake restaurant.

"Jarad, it makes me very happy to see you here at this
table," Emil told him as he sat down. He was a small man, heavy
set, with kind but drooping brown eyes, and a thin, white pate. His
wife was his mirror in many ways except for the fading brown tinted
hair.

But if there was ever an example of how opposites attract,
these two old lovebirds were textbook illustrations. Emil loved
people. He was gregarious, animated, and enjoyed nothing better
than sitting and visiting with customers. For Emil no one was a
stranger. Perhaps that was one reason why his little diner had been
such a success. And also why the diner failed so miserably after he
sold it. For many people came to his restaurant not for the food, but
for him. "And the new owners offered nothing kosher, either.
Nothing," he reminded whomever cared to listen. Sarah, on the

other hand, was quiet, almost to a fault. Though she had spent part of everyday at the restaurant, for years on end, few customers ever saw her. She was always behind the scenes. Her primary job was taking care of the books. A responsibility she now did for the church. She was the church treasurer.

"And considering the topic on hand, I feel safer already," he said aloud, giving Jarad a wink. Others around the table echoed Emil's sentiment, which made Jarad a little uncomfortable. He recognized the fact that had the most experience in the community in the area of law enforcement, but at the same time he always knew that he had simply been just a big fish in a very small pond. He had no delusions. But, too often, when people saw a cop, they couldn't get past the uniform or the gun. That fact cut both ways.

The discussion at the table was quite frank about the security situation for Blue River. Otty admitted that when he and Ellie, along with the Silvermans, began planning for the possibility of a crisis as intimated by his brother, they never considered safety and security issues. Food, fuel, and medicines became the priorities. "And warm clothing," reminded Sara, which drew a smile from everyone, surprised to hear her voice. She blushed.

Jarad opined that this reasoning was logical then, but obviously everyone in the area faced the same problem of limited resources. And some people might be more willing to take than to ask or borrow. Ellie countered she felt that it is important to share. "Granted, we have limited means, but we might have something that other's could use, and vice versa. We actually don't know all that we do and do not have, since we haven't stripped all of the abandoned houses of their resources."

With that Genis jumped into the conversation. "Yes, we'd be further along if I hadn't been hurt," he said defensively, holding up his bandaged left hand. "But James is doing a good job. Look at all the firewood he and the others brought back. I'm glad I missed that!" He smirked, but his eyes remained serious. "It is a lot more work that I originally thought it would be, that's for sure."

The group sensed that Genis was taking the delay personally and the whole table spontaneously erupted with kudos for his good work. The praise evidently soothed him, because he began talking about the list of houses he had compiled and how these raids should help replenish the pantry and meet other needs. "Why, one of these days I want to tackle the dome house," he boasted.

"The dome house, what is the dome house?" Myla asked.

"The dome house? Why it is practically a landmark up here, though I don't think anyone here has actually been there. Only seen it from the road." Genis responded.

Otty laughed. "Yes, it exists about seven miles up the road, but it has become almost mythical in proportions."

"What do you mean?" she replied, her curiosity growing.

Genis leaned forward, the topic obviously interested him. He also seemed to be a self-avowed expert on the subject. "Well," he began judiciously, "it was built by this gal from back east. New York City, maybe. And she had it built as a refuge for her husband, her children, and herself."

"You mean a refuge, as in a vacation home?"

"No, something crazy." Genis laughed as he thought about what he was going to say. "No, a refuge from the winds!" He went on and explained that the woman was an heiress and had inherited some ungodly amount of money. "Billions," Genis said. She was also a follower of some strange prophet that predicted the world would end soon and be destroyed by great winds sent by aliens. "I kid you not. She really believes this malarkey. She even had the contractor who built the place put copper sheeting in the roof to protect them from bad karma rays, or something like that!" Genis chuckled lustily. "She is a certified nut. But a rich nut." He continued with gossip he had learned from some of the people he knew who had actually worked on the construction, Myla encouraging him with further questions.

Emil sensed that this story-telling wasn't useful, so he tactfully interjected. "Yes," he said, "the house is alleged to be quite sophisticated, being self-sufficient to high degree, it generates its own electricity, has special security walls, etc. All this is interesting, but we need to return to the business at hand, securing our own safety." Otty smiled at him, tacitly thanking him. Both Myla and Genis squeaked out apologies.

Getting back on topic, Jarad shared his concern that it probably wasn't practical to maintain a twenty-four hour surveillance, the community was simply too limited in manpower. "And woman power, too," added Myla. "Yes," Jarad agreed, brushing his hand over his wife's. "Healthy adults who can tolerate the cold for hours at a time."

"And," Jarad continued, "there is no reason why we can't develop a response team if we could devise a way of calling everyone together."

"You mean something like a siren, which was used in Purcell to call the volunteer firefighters?" asked Emil.

"Exactly," Jarad agreed. "Something that can be heard in the entire community, and is distinctive. But it might be tough since we don't have any electricity."

"No, it will be a snap," said Otty, smiling with a twinkle in his eyes, like a person has when they know a secret. "Most of you don't know it, because they haven't been used in probably forty years, but this church has bells!"

"It does?" Ellie asked. "What kind of bells?"

"You know, old-fashioned bells. Ding-dong, ding-dong. That sort of thing."

Everyone was excited about this revelation. Not only for using the bells as a general alarm, but also in a traditional way, to call people to worship on Sunday mornings. Hobson, one of the fellows who served on the board and who Jarad was only recently introduced to, recalled how he used to hear church bells as a child, until noise pollution legislation abolished them. "I guess they were disturbing the sleep of too many people," he snorted derisively.

As they were still discussing the bells, Jimmy, the 15-year boy that Annie had a crush on, rushed into the room. He was panting hard and wasn't wearing a coat, his boots untied and flapping as he stumbled into the room. "Raiders," he said excitedly between breaths. "Come quickly! There are raiders!"

+++

Out of instinct, Jarad hurried out of the room but didn't run. There was no reason to hurry to a crime scene out of breath. As he zipped up the front of his coat, he wished that he had brought his gun, something he hadn't carried since he arrived at Blue River. He mumbled to himself that things were turning into the Wild West and maybe everyone would have to start carrying a gun. What a life, he thought.

Genis and Otty were trying to keep pace with him, as he made long strides down the path towards James's house. Everyone else remained behind, with Myla going home to check on the kids, dragging Jimmy along with her.

"Keep your eyes peeled," Jarad hollered as they parted. His voice was firm and commanding. Though he hadn't changed his clothing, subconsciously he had put back on his uniform and badge.

"Shit!" Jarad exclaimed as the sound of gunfire echoed through the trees, one of which Jarad immediately took shelter behind. He heard a few more shots in the distance and then the sound of harsh electric motors reverberating everywhere, the sound emanating the strongest down toward the rail bed. The noise quickly ebbed away as what ever caused it disappeared to the east..

By now Jarad was scurrying along, avoiding the path directly and favoring the trees, stooped over slightly as he tried to avoided falling down in the slick conditions or hitting his head on the low-hanging branches. For some reason he knew that the worst was over, a thought that was confirmed when he saw James standing along side the path, beckoning him on with a wave of his rifle barrel.

"What's going on?" Jarad asked him as soon as he was in hearing range. James was visibly shaken and didn't seem to be pleased with the situation. His mouth was pursed like a child before he cries. Jarad could appreciate his being upset.

"Raiders," he said firmly. "Damn fools." He pointed at the yellow house down the path, again using his rifle as a pointer, both hands still keeping it at the ready.

"That's my place, though we live over there." He jerked his head in another direction. Jarad knew where James lived, though he hadn't realized that his actual house was abandoned. "I came out of the house and I saw two people carrying stuff out the back. I told them to stop and one of them waved a gun at me. Hell, I ran home and got my deer rifle and sent Jimmy to tell you all at the church. When I got back one of them was waiting and he fired a shot in my direction. I fired back, though mostly to scare 'em. I didn't want to hit anyone." Talking helped to calm him down. He slung the rifle over his shoulder.

By this time Otty and Genis had caught up with them. As James reiterated with them what had happened, Jarad walked over to the back of the yellow house. He saw multiple tracks leading up and down the bank. Boxes of miscellaneous items were abandoned both above and below the steep bank. Evidently James had surprised the raiders and they escaped on their snowmobiles. Jarad was both amazed and alarmed that no one had heard the snowmobiles earlier.

Otty approached and silently looked at the same things Jarad had just reviewed. "Maybe we will have to reconsider posting a twenty-four hour guard after all," he said.

+++

When he finally made it home, he found Myla in what she called her 'damage control' state of being. He knew that she was very upset, but her demeanor suggested otherwise. The children would never know that she was very anxious and concerned. The relief in her eyes was obvious to Jarad when she saw him enter the house. She was calmly playing cards with Cameron. What was especially interesting to Jarad was the fact that Jimmy and Annie were playing cribbage together. This can't be good, he chuckled to himself. Life goes on, he supposed.

"Oh, hi Mr. Traverson," Jimmy said, rising from his chair. "Is everything okay? I've been really worried."

"Yes, everything is fine. You can go home now, if you'd like."

Jimmy looked at Annie and then back to Jarad. "Yes, I really need to go home. But I would like to come back again, if I can." He looked again at Annie, whose eyes were bright and watching him. To Jarad, her eyes seemed, for lack of a better word, womanish. He hadn't ever seen his daughter look the way was she was appearing now.

"Of course, Jimmy, you can come back anytime." Myla said with a smile. "I'm glad that everything has worked out okay. Why don't you go home and then let us know if you need anything."

"Okay, thank you," he said. The tall, gangly boy stooped over to put on his boots. "Here," Jarad said, reaching into the closet. "Why don't you take one of my extra coats. You can get it back to me whenever. No hurry." Jarad handed the boy a heavy green canvas jacket. Jimmy put it on. It fit him surprisingly well, which caused Jarad to realize that the boy was practically his same size, just not quite as filled out. "Thank you, I'll be back," he said, with out indicating a time.

Jarad sat down where Jimmy had been a moment before and looked at his daughter. She hadn't moved or said a word, but seemed transfixed by some thought. My goodness, Jarad thought, she is too young to be thinking any thoughts besides what 12-year olds are supposed to think. But then, what do 12-year old girls think about? Father and daughter both sat looking at each other, neither saying a word.

"Well," Myla said, breaking the silence. "What happened?"

Jarad recounted what he saw and what he had heard from James, who was Jimmy's father. Myla expressed her concern that the raiders would be so bold and to come to Blue River in the middle of the day. "Doesn't that seem odd to you, too, Jarad?"

"I thought about that very same thing as I walked home. And I have come to two conclusions, both of which may not be accurate, but it is the only thing I have to go on. First, they must not have scouted us out as effectively as they had thought. Maybe James genuinely surprised them. Second, they probably don't want to waste kerosene or propane for their lamps, preferring like us to raid during daylight hours. But what really bothers me is the fact that they shot at James, without provocation." He scrunched his brows as he considered another thought. "But then, maybe they just fired a shot off to scare him, who knows. They were both close enough to easily hit their marks if they wanted to. James himself said he shot over their heads to scare them, maybe they did the same. We'll never know."

"I hope not," Myla agreed.

"What?" Jarad asked.

"That we'll never know. I've had enough of this raiding business. I've only had to treat one gunshot wound and I don't plan on treating another." She crossed her arms in frustration. "I hate guns," she said with a sigh.

Chapter 14

Otty made sure that James and his family were fine before he moved on to his own house. In hindsight, Otty could understand why the raiders found the yellow house an attractive target. It was located near the railroad bed and the bank up to it wasn't excessively steep. Also, it was a fairly large target, which would suggest that it might be well stocked with loot. Unfortunately for the raiders, James had already removed many items of value after he had moved in with his mother. Otty did find it interesting and notable that the raiders seemed to be just as surprised by James as he was by them. Perhaps they hadn't done their homework, so to speak, or were just sloppy. Worse yet, maybe they were getting desperate. That is not good, Otty mused. Desperate people tend to take desperate actions. He decided that they needed to communicate with these people, whoever they were.

He checked in with Ellie. She was handling this new development stoically. The grandkids were coloring scraps of paper on the kitchen table, completely oblivious to the events around them. And Ellie would have it no other way.

"What is most surprising to me is why we didn't hear their machines until they escaped on them," she shared. She was sitting with the children at the table, spinning her teacup on the coaster it sat upon, as was her habit at times. "It must be a combination of the snow, the trees, and the difference in heights that conspired to keep everything so quiet," she mused.

"I agree. Hey, I know it's my turn to make dinner tonight, but I need to go check on Howard. Hope you don't mind."

"No, I don't mind. And I've already started something. Here, take him these." Ellie removed some homemade ginger snaps from a plastic container, putting them into a plastic bag. "I know that these are his favorites." She sighed and returned to her tea. "Life around here is never dull."

"Yes, I agree," said Otty, a bit tired. "I prefer dull." He grabbed his gloves and headed out. "Be back in a bit," he said in leaving.

+++

Otty was glad to finally be on his way to see Howard. He was sincerely interested in how things had been going for him, because he worried greatly about Howard's safety since his home was the nearest toward the raider's territory. What a thought, he mused. Raider's territory. Us and them. It was easy to fall into that mindset. But Otty also wanted to know how it was going with the radio. James had delivered the solar cell to Howard and helped him to set it up. They had perched the solar cell on Howard's deck where it would get a good dose of sun and from where Howard could keep it free of snow.

Howard met him at the door, mumbling a greeting. He took the cookies like an autistic child, automatically and without any acknowledgment. Otty could clearly see that Howard was upset, but he didn't want to start his visit with prying. Instead, he pointed at the radio.

"So, what have you heard? Anything?"

Howard raised his head to respond to Otty and then paused. He seemed to be at a loss for words, which was very unusual. "What?" Otty kindly cajoled him. "I've never seen you not having something to say, relevant or otherwise."

Howard normally would have taken the bait, but not this time. He was truly upset, in a quiet sort of way. "Well, as you know my Spanish has much to be desired, but from what I can gather, we appear to be at war."

"At war. Oh, no! And who are we at war with this time?"

Howard's complexion blanched. "Ourselves," he said softly. He choked on a sob and wouldn't talk again for a long while.

+++

Jimmy came by to visit the very next day. He was eager to resume his game of cribbage with Annie, claiming it was the funnest game he had ever, ever played. Annie was very happy to see him. Jarad did notice that his daughter had brushed her hair especially nice and seemed to have more color to her cheeks. The previous night Jarad had shared with his wife his concern over this sudden transformation in his daughter. Myla reminded him that she had a crush for an older boy at the very same age as Annie. Plus, if he would remember, Annie had started her menstrual cycle five months earlier, so she was feeling very much like the young woman she was becoming. "Besides, Jarad, she is almost thirteen," Myla reminded him.

"And by the way, father of my daughter, have you noticed her chest?" she had asked him. Jarad hadn't. He laid in bed thinking to himself. My daughter has breasts! Well of course she has breasts. Why hadn't I noticed this before?

"Oh, my goodness," he lamented with a whisper, "I am not ready to be the father of a woman. I want her to remain my little girl." Myla snuggled with him and reminded him that Annie would always be his little girl, but someday she would become some man's special lady.

"I don't want to think about it," Jarad said softly. "I'm not ready."

Myla laughed. "Well, ready or not, our little girl is becoming a woman." She laughed again. "You're so funny, Jarad." He grabbed her hand and held it tight as they lay along side each other in bed.

"Life goes on," he said.

"Yes," she agreed. "Life goes on."

+++

The next day Genis came by to see Jarad. Jarad was glad to see him, since he and Genis were developing a really nice friendship. If life had been normal, they would have already gone fishing together or watched a football game on the televisor. But life wasn't normal. Or at least, it had changed. The two men spent all of their time either being extremely busy or resting. One or the other. No balance.

Genis showed his hand to both Myla and Genis. The wound was still quite red, though Myla said it was healing nicely. She made sure that he was still on his pain pills. He said yes, but there wasn't very many more left and he only took one at night to help him sleep. But he felt he would be fine after they ran out. Myla went ahead and changed the bandage and then reminded him to come back in about three or four days. She would then remove the stitches. "If you say so, doctor," he said like a good patient.

"I'm not a doctor," she reminded him in a flat voice.

"Well, you are now," he said.

Then Genis shifted the conversation to an issue that was of grave concern to him.

"I don't know if you heard it, but yesterday there was quite a bit of gun firing going off in the far distance. East of here. I could barely hear it. It must have been five or miles away. You didn't by chance hear any of it, did you?

"No, not a peep," Jarad responded. "What do you think if was?"

"At first I thought that maybe someone was out deer hunting. But there was far too much shooting. So, I figured someone was sighting in their rifle. But then I heard different rifles, some I could have swore were automatic."

"Automatic. Who in the world has an automatic rifle?" Jarad asked inquisitively. Then he snorted. "Except me!" He left the room and retreated to his bedroom. A moment later he reappeared carrying the assault rifle the chief had given him weeks before. Genis whistled.

"Wow, I haven't seen anything like that since I was in the service. This is practically an antique."

Jarad explained how he had come into possession of it. "I can't imagine anyone else having this kind of firepower around here."

Genis agreed. "Well, like I say, it was a long way off. I was lucky to hear the gun fire at all. But, I guess what makes it most bothersome is that it sounded like a firefight."

"What do you mean," Jarad asked.

"You know, a firefight. A bunch of soldiers firing at each other. Like we did in Afghanistan and Syria. I know a firefight when I hear one."

Jarad became instantly tense with concern. "That is not good news," he said candidly. "I can only imagine that raiding parties from different parts of the county are starting to run into each other. Lord help us if that sort of action moves up our direction."

"Agreed," replied Genis. "I think that we are probably okay in the short-term, while there is still snow on the ground. But come spring, all bets are off."

Jarad stroked his beard for a moment as he considered an idea. "Then let's plan accordingly."

"Aye, aye, captain," Genis said with a wink. "And I must say, I am sure glad to see that piece of hardware," he said, nodding his head at the rifle.

+++

"Otty, I'm a bit concerned about Breann," Ellie whispered. The grandkids were in their pajamas, sitting by the wood stove and playing on the floor. They hadn't seen their mother in days, nor had they asked about her. They were very content living with grandma and grandpa. "I haven't seen her, except for one time these past three days. And that was only because I saw her coming back from the church with a box of groceries. What is she doing over there, all alone?"

Otty understood her wife's concern. He, too, was worried about his daughter, but he felt that there was little he could do. "I don't know, dear," he said gently, "everybody's world has been turned upside down, including Breann's Maybe she just needs this time by herself."

"Needs it or not, she's getting it," Ellie said sadly. "I just wish. . . ." She stopped and sniffed. "I just wish she was more normal. Is that a mean thing to say?" She looked at her husband with pained, teary eyes. She glanced at the children and then back at her husband. "I hurt for her." She watched the kids playing with the dog, who never seemed to tire of their attention. "Her children would rather spend time with the puppy than with their own mother," she lamented.

"Unfortunately, maybe she is simply reaping what she sowed," Otty opined. Elly looked at him. "Then is my relationship with Breann, our relationship with Breann, our own harvest? Were we that bad of parents?" She pulled her hand away from her husband, hurt by his words and her own thoughts.

Otty reached over the table and touched her face, cupping her cheek. "I'm sorry. That isn't what I meant to say. I love you," he said.

She kissed his hand. "And I love you, too," she sighed.

+++

James and Jimmy tromped around the rail bed, trying to see if there was anything worth recovering from what had been discarded by the raiders. When James had surprised them they abandoned what hadn't been packed onto their snowmobiles and made their escape. There were a couple of boxes sitting in the snow, filled mostly with empty canning jars and some cooking utensils. "I can't imagine why they'd want this stuff," James said. They then turned to examining the snowmobile tracks in the snow. "Yup, there were two of them. And look there," he told his son, pointing with his gloved hand at some smooth parallel marks superimposed over the snowmobile tracks. "They were pulling little trailers. Quite a set-up they got."

"Hey Dad, look at that," Jimmy said, pointing across the tracks. "There's a set of tracks over there, too. But only one person."

James acknowledged the fact, but didn't pause to consider it to be important. Jimmy followed them for a few yards, before calling back to his father.

"Dad, these are going the wrong way."

"What do you mean, the wrong way? What's the right way?"

"No, Dad, these tracks are going that way." Jimmy pointed toward the east. "That means the person who made them came from that way." He twisted his body to point his arm to the west. "Why would someone come from that direction?"

James became curious and he walked over the snow to be by his son. He squatted down to look at the track marks, which were obviously made by boots. "Wow, whoever it is they sure has big feet." James followed the tracks for a while, stopped and then followed them further with only his eyes. He then reversed his course and returned to where his son was, passed him, and continued following the tracks like a hunter on a spoor trail.

The tracks stopped where the snowmobiles had passed over them, obliterating all traces. "You're right. That is very peculiar. We'll have to remember this." He turned to his son and called to him. "Good eye, son. You are always a bright one." Jimmy smiled hard.

+++

The church service that Sunday was pleasant but unremarkable, except for two important things. First, and most abstractly, was that Otty shared with the congregation that the United States might be in some sort of civil war. "We really don't know what's going on, except Howard's source says that US Army troops are fighting rebels – those were his words – in both California and Michigan. I'll let you know more when I find out, but we need to commit this to prayer." This report caused so much consternation among the congregation that Otty wondered if he had erred in choosing this time to mention it.

The second thing was almost forgotten in the hubbub, even though, ironically, it was this thing that was probably more directly impacted the members of the congregation. From now on someone was going to remain on guard duty for the community and volunteers were being solicited. Otty directed interested persons to

Jarad, who unfortunately was currently unavailable. He was pulling duty.

Earlier, Jarad had wrestled with how he was going to provide security for the community. There were too few adults able to commit to standing guard. It was simply too cold for the older people and too dangerous for the younger. So Jarad had to find some compromise.

What he decided to do was to put one person at the one point where the probable points of entry into the community would occur, but not too far from the church – which was the de facto center of the community. The place chosen was approximately fifty yards east of Howard's house, down where the road and railroad tracks almost met. Here a guard could watch both the road and tracks and still remain in Blue River territory.

To buttress his words with actions, James and a couple other fellows strung a heavy cable across both the road and the railroad, about two feet above the snow and marked it with white strips of cloth. This cable was passable by a person on foot, but would slow down a vehicle, such as a snowmobile. The strips of cloth fluttered listlessly in the breeze, making the cable more visible and hopefully less dangerous. In addition, signs were improvised at both the road and the railroad bed that said No Trespassing and Keep Out. Genis couldn't resist and added a skull and crossbones to the sign as well. "Worked in Syria," he said knowingly. The person on duty was armed with both a gun, for security, and a air horn, for alarm. In addition, there was a rake. In this way the person on guard, or at least on inspection, could maintain a nicely raked field of snow near the border, as the cable and signs were collectively called. In this way, it could be readily determined if someone had recently trespassed over the border, as evidenced by bootprints, etc.

This was the best Jarad could think up and it was approved by the advisory board. Now, he just had to make it happen. And that first Sunday morning, there he was. Freezing. Alone. And bored.

+++

Chapter 15

The church bell was finally in place. Ideally everyone wanted to install it in the steeple, but it simply wasn't practical at that time. The purpose of the bell was to act as a community alarm and the sooner it was functional in that capacity the better. Everyone could then sleep better. It's use as a call to worship on Sunday mornings would be secondary. Therefore, for the sake of expediency, the bell was hung on a wooden framework outside the front of the church building. It was was rigged to rock back and forth on a cam, allowing the person ringing the bell to stand to one side and not be deafened by the sound. The rigging was quite elegant and everyone was dutifully impressed.

But the bell had more value than its obvious function. That is because it became a symbol both of the community that the people around it had become and of the dire situation that they found themselves in. The bell existed to call together all who could hear it, or more accurately, all who understood the significance of its peal. In that function, it existed for *them*. And it would call *them*. And bring to their attention a matter that concerned only *them*. Unfortunately, outside of Sunday mornings it would be a sound that all would dread, because its very ringing would indicate danger and alarm. There was no incongruity between the two functions of the bell. Because the ideal community, like the ideal marriage, was for better or for worse. And no one ever married hoping for the worst.

That first Sunday when the bell was to be first struck as a call to worship was a delight. Everyone assumed that Otty should be given the honor of ringing in the first call to worship, but he declined. He said that this honor rightfully belonged to the oldest of the elders, which was Emil. Emil accepted the honor and he was proud, in a humble sort of way, as he stiffly walked up to the crank and started to turn the wheel. The bell began a painfully slow lean upward, before suddenly swinging downward and forcing the clapper against its curve side, rousing a deep resonance that hadn't been heard in those hills for over 50 years. Once Emil got it started it, momentum made it easier and round and round he turned the crank, and round and round the wheel would turn, rocking the bell back and forth, back and forth, a euphony of intonation with every swing.

Enough. Emil stopped and the bell quickly settled, the last reverberation dying in the clutch of trees and snow. And then he began to cry. Cry because of the honor to be first. Cry because all were now, officially, one in community. And cry because by being there, they all had committed themselves to each other. For each other's security, and welfare, and love. Beyond community, they had become family. And that made Emil so happy he cried.

+++

That next day, Myla was sad. The community had just suffered its first death, though Myla knew that there would be more. The more frail members of the community were not coping successfully with the changes in their world. Most were now without the prescription drugs that had previously ensured their health. And the chronic cold, the insipid food, and for many the constant, nagging worry, constantly lapped at their strength like a wind-whipped sea against an eroding bulwark. But the very thing that Myla knew would be the most dangerous, and least avoidable, would be the rise of contagious infections. A simple sinus infection for a healthy adult would prove to be a fatal case of pneumonia for the frail.

And this was the very thing that struck down Marie, James's mother and Jimmy's grandmother. Prior to the Event, she was a robust, over-sized woman. Busy with her family, her work, and the collection of pure-bred Shih Tzus that were always milling around her. But since then she had become a caricature of herself; thin, listless, and often indifferent to the needs of her four-legged "children." She had become so morose that, at times, James wondered who she was. "That's not my mother. I don't know who that woman is," he had remarked once, candidly, to Otty. "And I live with her and all of her confounded dogs."

Myla wasn't sure why she had been called; there was nothing she could do. Maybe it was out of habit. Someone always had to be called after a person died and who more logical than Myla or maybe Otty. Myla found Marie laying flaccidly on her bed, the way a person who had far too much to drink would lay, without tone and awkward. Without a second thought she began to prepare the body for burial, asking James to bring her a large container of water, soap, and towels. He complied without question. She then directed him to go and find Otty. "He doesn't have to come here, but he does have to know. Okay?" she asked kindly.

"Yes, of course," he replied. "Hey I'm okay," he told her, noting the concern in her eyes. "I'm glad mother is at peace. She hasn't been for months."

Myla gave him a pat on the arm and return to her chore. No, not a chore, she said to herself. Never a chore. An privilege.

+++

The funeral was held the very same day. Genis asked a couple fellows to cobble together a coffin, while James and Jimmy dug the grave. They dug the hole for the internment in the church parking lot after Otty had decided that this would be the most suitable site for the Blue River cemetery. After softening the compacted surface with a pick-ax the digging went swiftly. Both James and Jimmy appreciated the opportunity to dig the grave themselves. The physical effort helped to assuage their grief.

There was no viewing of the body, because James knew his mother would not approve of such a thing, but the church service was warm and comforting. During the brief committal Jarad noticed that Jimmy was solemn with grief and that Annie was holding his hand. James stood like a statue next to Otty, his face as frozen as the air around him. Jarad didn't know much about the personal life of James or what sort of relationship he had with his mother, but he did know that the Event had changed her personality for the worse. Perhaps James was feeling guilt that his dominant emotion right now was one of relief rather than loss. Anyhow, things would work themselves out in time. They always did. Well, they generally did, Jarad chided himself.

+++

Jimmy could really talk up a storm! He had come to Jarad and Myla's house following the funeral. He didn't want to go home. He knew that his father needed to be alone, anyhow. He had assured his father that he would be home before dark. Myla and Jarad didn't mind and there was no doubt that Annie didn't mind either.

Jimmy was a little less animated than before. He had shared that he had never seen a dead body. He missed his grandma, because in many ways she had become a substitute mother. His own mom had never married his dad and she had abandoned the family when he was about ten. "It still hurts when I think about it," he said in a candid moment. "So I don't think about it." Jimmy was really a sweet and sensitive young man who freely shared his feelings. This endeared him not only to Annie, but also to Myla. Jarad realized that if life continued on the path it currently was, Jimmy was going to be a familiar sight. He pondered that idea..

But Jarad was sympathetic toward the boy and he knew that talking was good therapy, and Jimmy needed to talk right now. So to encourage him to keep sharing, Jarad asked him about the raiders and what they had taken from his house the other day.

"My dad said it was sort of surprising, because the boxes they left down on the railroad bed were filled with mason jars. Dad was wondering why they took those things, but maybe it was all that was left. We had pretty much cleaned out the house a long time ago." He talked about walking the tracks and looking at all trails in the snow, and that the snowmobiles were also pulling trailers. "My dad figured that one out," he said proudly. Then, as a little boast for himself, he shared about the other boot tracks he found on the far side of the rail bed. The one's leading from the west and going to the east. That comment perked up Jarad's attention.

"What tracks?" he asked. Jimmy described them in detail, how they must have been made by a very big guy, "huge tracks," he said, holding his hands up to show the size. He also mentioned that the tracks terminated somewhere close to the bank, but the snowmobiles had covered them up.

Something sounded amiss to Jarad, though he wasn't sure what. "Could you show me the tracks, Jimmy?"

"Sure. I'd be happy to," he said proudly. "How about when I go home?"

"How about now?" Jarad asked, probably a little more firmly than needed.

Myla and Annie both objected. "He doesn't have to go home yet, it isn't dark." Annie insisted. She looked to her mom for support, but her mom cautioned her with a raised hand. Myla realized that Jarad was concerned about something.

"Do you think you need to go right this instant?" she asked cautiously.

Jarad nodded. To soothe hurt feelings he said, "This might be important. I want Jimmy to lead me there while we still have some light. You don't mind, do you?" he asked the boy.

"Not at all. Not if you think its important. Let's go," he said with enthusiasm, sensing adventure.

"Can I come, Dad?" Cameron asked. Reflexively Jarad was going to tell him no, but he paused. "Sure," he said, "if your mother doesn't mind."

She didn't and Cameron rushed to put on his snow gear. Annie didn't want to come. It was too cold! But Champ would have it no other way and danced with excitement near the door as the others put on their boots and coats.

They hiked the distance to Jimmy's old house at a pretty good clip. Jarad tended to make long strides when he was concerned about something. For some reason this idea of tracks coming from the opposite direction was compelling to him. He was unsure why he needed to check them out right at that moment, but he had learned to trust his instincts. And quite frankly, he had nothing else planned for the day.

All three slid down the bank side without incident, though Jarad knew that going down was the easy part. Jimmy pointed out everything that he and his father had looked at a couple day's earlier. Jarad could clearly see the snowmobile tracks and the sled marks of the trailers they must have been pulling. What really interested him were the other tracks, the ones Jimmy had discovered. He examined them closely, and sure enough they led from west to east, turning abruptly to the north where they were intercepted by the snowmobile tracks. But instead of stopping there, Jarad looked on the bank side and immediately saw what he was looking for.

The over-sized bootprints continued along the ditch for another fifty yard before continuing directly up the bank side. Someone left deep gashes in the snow as the person clawed up the bank side. Jarad backed up on the rail bed to pinpoint a location and then headed back to the spot where the three of them had originally climbed down.

"Come on, let's go guys," he said, encouraging them to hurry.

Once at the top of the bank he dismissed both of them. "Jimmy, why don't you head home. It's dark now. And thank you for your help." He shook the boy's hand. And then he turned to his son. "Cameron, you too. I'll be home as soon as I can. And take the dog, please." Cameron huffed a bit, his face a bit downcast. He was disappointed, especially since he knew his father was on to something, but he recognized by the tone of his father's voice that he wouldn't be able to tag along. If there was any consolation, it was that Jimmy had to go home, too.

"Come on, Champ," he said, slapping his thigh. "Let's go, boy." He dashed off toward home, the dog running with him.

When the boys were safely gone, Jarad marched quickly along the top of the bank to the place he had mentally plotted where the bootprints had crested the bank. He found what he was looking for, and sure enough they led straight to the little house next to Otty and Ellie's place. It was already dark, but he could still make out the prints and he followed them to the back door.

Jarad went around to the front door and knocked. No one answered. He looked in a window but could see nothing. It was dark inside and there was no evidence of movement. He knocked again, this time quite a bit harder. Still no response. He tried the doorknob, but the door was locked. Stepping back, he appraised the situation. He decided to go see Otty and Ellie to get more information about the house. What he really wanted to do was to put a shoulder to the door and force it open, but decided against it for the time being. No need to be too rash, he thought.

He quickly crossed the thirty yards to the pastor's house. He knocked at the door, and only had to wait a moment before it was opened by Ellie. "Hi, Jarad, good to see you. What brings you by?" she asked, a big smile on her face, though he could see the questioning in her eyes.

"Is Otty in?" he asked, as nonchalantly as he could.

"No, he's at the church. He won't be home till later. Can I help you with something?"

"No, I'm fine. Maybe I'll just wander over there."

"Alright. Well then, good night." She nodded her head and softly closed the door. Jarad headed into the darkness toward the church.

+++

Instead of his office, Otty sat in community room by the big wood stove. He often would sit by himself there. It not only made him more accessible to the congregation, since he was not sequestered in his office, but he didn't have to use up lantern oil for light. Like the birds, most residents of the community were in bed with the setting sun. I guess that it is instinctual, Otty thought to himself. He had had also observed that most people had taken on the habit of not rising from bed until the sun was up, it only made sense to hit the sack with sundown. He knew that he felt tired now staying up late, which was anytime after it was dark outside. He had fallen out of habit of using time determined by the movement of the clock.

Instead, like the rest of the people in Blue River, the movement of the sun had become the determinant of time.

He mused over his Bible as he sat near the big wood stove that heated the building, its open door providing the necessary light needed to read. It was a dim light and barely sufficient for reading, but it was a warm, almost healing light. He was at peace.

He had intended on getting a jump on next Sunday's sermon since his days had become so busy he seemed to never have enough 'free time' to prepare. Who would imagine that life without electricity would be more, not less complicated? Of course, there was no simplicity in such a seemingly simple lifestyle, only complexity as everyone adjusted to a life without televisor, automobiles, medicines, clean clothes, and other countless amenities of modern life. Otty had become convinced that the two greatest invention in the modern era was hot water and toilet paper, the two very things that were the most difficult to get enough of today.

He looked up as the old door that accessed the community room rattled as someone entered. He wasn't surprised that a person might be coming this late to the church. He didn't expect anyone, but still people would drop by for a chat or to get something from the pantry. The person was obviously a man, but his size was greatly exaggerated by the shadows cast from the flickering light projected from the stove. But as the figure drew closer, he realized it wasn't an exaggeration. The man was huge. Otty didn't know him. Or did he? His neck hairs raised in alarm, but he didn't move. Where could he go? And he was unarmed. So he simply watched the man approach.

"Hello pastor," the man said in a neutral voice. He had dragged a chair from the side of the room and over toward the light, positioning himself opposite Otty. Otty peered at him in the orange light, recognizing him but not sure from where.

After a moment, he realized who he was. "Welcome, Jonathan," he said with as much confidence as he could muster. Otty felt a strange combination of bewilderment and curiosity, laced with a strong dose of caution. This is odd, he thought to himself.

"You are not a person I ever expected to see tonight, or for that matter, ever again."

"Yes, I can understand that," he said calmly.

"And. . . . what brings you to Blue River?"

"I am on a mission," he said. "We are purging the area of obstinacy."

"We?" Otty responded, more reflexively than as a question. After his initial apprehension, Otty settled back down to genuine sense of self-assuredness. What have I to fear, he thought to himself. My life? My life is nothing. Otty was surprised to be thinking such thoughts. His subconscious must be working in overdrive. Is this what people did when facing death? Whose going to die? Don't get over dramatic, he cautioned himself.

"GILM, myself, my brothers, and Reverend Swess," the giant responded to Otty's question.

"Ah, yes, Reverend Swess. And how is our friend?"

"He is well. He has returned to Spokane. His work here is done."

"Done? I thought that GILM was here forever? Was the ground not as fertile as Reverend Swess had hoped?"

Jonathan shifted his weight and relaxed a bit on the chair, the wood creaking in protest as he learned back. If he had come to cause harm, he wasn't in any hurry. "Purcell started to be promising. We had our hopes, but the people there proved to be . ." he paused as he sought the right word, "*resistant* to the gospel."

Otty gently nodded his head. "I see, resistant to the gospel. And what gospel is that? GILM?"

"There is only one gospel, all others are either lies or distortions," he said with rote confidence. "And lies must be confronted and refuted. Otherwise, they grow and spread and harm people. For the sake of truth, lies must be refuted."

"But I thought GILM believed that all paths lead to the same mountain top? Aren't all religions valid as long as they practice love, as Reverend Swess was fond of saying?"

"Yes, but some don't love, therefore they need to be rebuked."

"So, tell me, did Reverend Swess leave Purcell because he had converted everyone or rebuked them?"

"Both." Jonathan paused, looking at the fire. He seemed to be gathering his thoughts. "Those he could save, he saved, and those who resisted, he refuted."

"And how did he rebuke them?"

Jonathan looked at him, the warm glow of the fire revealing his face but not his eyes. The man smiled. "With fire," he said, staring at the wood stove.

He then described how some of the misguided people had turned away from GILM. "At first we were hopeful, especially before the rally. But it didn't last." Otty asked him why not and the giant man said that it was because of the house churches. Only the few members of the mainline churches saw the light, the rest of the people lost interest and returned to their house churches. He recounted how Reverend Swess stated that he would give the people of Purcell what they wanted. So if they rebuffed GILM, GILM would rebuff them.

"So we set fire to the town," Jonathan said.

"You what!" Otty shouted, incredulous. "You set fire to Purcell!"

"Yes, but we were forced to," he responded calmly, continuing to stare at the fire. "They were given an opportunity to come to the truth, but they didn't want the truth. They wanted to continue in their lies. Therefore, the right Reverend allowed them to continue in their error. But we had to contain the contagion."

"Contagion! You had to contain the contagion! How arrogant!" Otty bellowed.

The man looked at Otty, threatened by neither his anger nor his shouting. He simply looked at Otty with calm repose, assured of his own dominance and rightness in this situation, both theologically and physically.

"No, the arrogance lay with them. When they rejected GILM they rejected love. And only those who hate cannot love. Therefore, they must be purged of their hate. Only then can they learn to love. Therefore, they were purged with fire."

"Get out of here," Otty said with a steely voice, pointing in the direction of the doors. "I don't know from where you have come, but I demand that you leave. And my God forgive you of your vile ways."

With that the man stood up. He towered over Otty, who by most measures was a big man. But he was no match for this humongous human being. "I will go, but first I must do my work." With one hand he grabbed Otty by the front of his coat and spinning with his weight he threw Otty across the room. Otty landed on a table, which immediately collapsed under the impact. He would have screamed in anger, if not alarm, but his breath had been driven from his lungs and he could only lay there gasping for air.

The man approached Otty, who lay powerless to resist him. I'm to old for this, he thought. And what a way to die. He was surprised by how calm he felt as this man again grabbed him by his shirt and picked him up off the collapsed table.

"Why are you doing this," Otty whispered hoarsely as he forced the words out of recalcitrant lungs. The man pulled him near and Otty could feel his breath as he breathed heavily into Otty's face.

"You," he said through a slit of mouth, "you too rejected GILM, therefore GILM rejects you."

"So, you're going to kill me," Otty asked as he hung limply in the man's grasp.

"No, you are killing yourself. I am simply the tool of your own hardness of heart."

Again, Otty found himself weightless as he flailed in the air, landing with a crash on something very hard and unforgiving.

He heard himself holler in pain, and felt a sharp spasm of pain sear through his chest. Was he having a heart attack?

Otty knew he was going to die. He couldn't resist the strength of this giant. He didn't want to die. He had so much to do, and he had so many people relying upon him. Who would take of Ellie? Who would help her with the grandkids? And the old folks of the community? And the church? Who would preach on Sundays? Bury the dead? Who would bury him? And then everything went black.

+++

Jarad moved too quickly to regret not having his gun, though later he would wonder if he would have reacted differently if he had been packing it. When he approached the church he heard a terrible crashing noise, as if someone was kicking wooden chairs. When he entered the door of the community room of the church, he saw the dark image of a giant holding a man by the fabric of his shirt up to his face, growling at him like a cat does when playing with a mouse. But Jarad could see enough in the dim light to know that the mouse was Otty.

The giant heaved and flexed and Otty sailed across the room, landing hard on a set of metal-folding chairs. Coming up behind the man, Jarad scanned the area around him for a weapon. He grabbed a hefty piece of firewood and swung it with both hands as hard as he could against the neck of the giant. There was a dull sound at the impact and the giant figure collapsed to its knees, as if in pious worship, before toppling over to his side. Jarad thought he might have killed the unknown person, but he didn't care. He rushed over to part of the room where Otty had landed and found him laying prone in the shadows. He was unconscious but breathing. He then returned quickly to where the intruder lay. He didn't appear to breathing. Shame, Jarad thought to himself, but that knowledge made him feel safer. With that he rushed outside. The darkness was suddenly filled with the peal of a small, old, church bell.

+++

"He's dead. Who is he, again?" Myla asked as she pulled the lantern away from the large corpse which still lay on the wooden floor. The dead man's now pale face was frozen in an expression of shock. Otherwise, the man was undistinguished, except for his great size.

"He was one of the GILM goons protecting Swess. He was one of their missionaries. Missionaries my ass," Jarad spat. Now he was angry. He was angry at himself for not thinking about the 'back door' into the community. He was angry that there was someone in the community abetting this man. And he was angry that he had, again, found himself unarmed. But most of all, he was angry that Otty had been hurt. He found himself callously indifferent to the corpse that lay before him.

"Otty will be fine," Myla assured him. "I think he has a broken rib or two, but no internal damage that I can tell. He's going to hurt for a while, but nothing life-threatening. He's asleep in his bed right now." She put her hands around her husband's arm and gave him a tug. "It's going to be okay," she said softly.

People were still milling around, lanterns or flashlights in hand, gawking at the corpse, conversing in soft whispers. They had

all come running when Jarad tolled the bell. Many of the older folks had already returned to their homes, not wanting to be in the way. Others, mostly the younger or middle-aged folks, had lingered to be available to help or simply out of curiosity.

"I'm going to check on Genis and see what he has found out," he said to softly to his wife, excusing himself as he walked toward the exit. He hadn't even made it to the door when Genis himself was walked in, lantern in hand. Jarad greeted him with a question, "What'd you find?"

"She's okay. She was tied up in the bedroom. Looks like she and lover boy were experimenting with that S & M bondage stuff. He left her trussed up like a pig and came here to finish the job he had originally come to do." He swung his head in disgust. "She's with her mother now."

Jarad nodded and then asked, "How are we otherwise?"

"I'm going to head back to the border. Andy is supposed to work this shift, but I would feel better manning it myself for awhile. Gary is going to go with me. I am concerned that the bell might have attracted a different kind of attention. If you know what I mean."

"Okay, I'm not going to worry about it. You got it covered." He gave Genis a pat on the shoulder and returned to the dead man. It took Jarad and four other men to carry the body outside. They laid the dead man on the ground and covered him with a blanket. "He'll be fine here tonight. Hopefully the bears will get him," he said bitterly. "We'll bury what's left in the morning. Thanks, guys. Goodnight." He gave them a wave, and then followed his wife down the path toward their home, the lantern swinging in her hand, the light and shadows dancing off the trees and the snow. If anyone cared to have noticed it was a beautiful night, the heavens heavy with stars.

+++

Adam couldn't sleep, not after all the excitement that night, do he decided to go down to the border a bit early and visit with whoever was on duty. Was it Andy or James? He couldn't remember. He made himself a snack from two slices of homemade bread. The bread was already stale, but he didn't even notice. Everything tasted good anymore.

He pulled on his heavy coat and fumbled with his boots. Before leaving, he grabbed his deer rifle from the corner of the room and slung it over his shoulder. Nowadays, he carried it so much that he barely felt its heft. He felt his pockets for his gloves, finding them he stretched the woolen mitts over his hands. As he left the house, he made sure not to the let the screen door slap shut behind him. He didn't want to disturb his little brother who was still asleep.

Adam didn't hurry. Life was so busy, anyhow. He would sometimes pause to think about his former life, as he called it. He *was* an electrical engineering major, until this whole fiasco with the grid. How ironic, he thought to himself. He was working toward spending his life working with something that seemed to no longer exist. He had no doubt that someday he would return to school and things would be normal again, but the news about the fighting that was breaking out in the country discouraged him. He was just glad that he happened to be home when this crisis came. He couldn't imagine what life would be like now back on campus.

He strolled slowly down the path, trying to understand the events of that night. Wow, that man was big, he whistled softly to himself. What would it be like to have to fight someone like that! Jarad was brave, he thought, but then he was a cop. Cops are supposed to brave, aren't the?. He didn't know. Anyways, it was a beautiful night, he decided, mentally moving on to another thought.

He had turned his lantern to its minimum setting, because he loved to watch the sky when the stars were out. He passed along the Perch, from where a person used to be able to see the lights down below in Purcell valley. He could just see the change in color on the eastern horizon as the day began to push back the night. Out of habit, he stopped and stepped onto the huge slab of stone jutting out into the air. He just wanted to take a gander. He noticed a collection of bright lights flickering far in the distance, along the horizon where the town was located. He wished he had brought his binoculars to better see them. He figured that there still must be people down in Purcell.

He resumed his journey, past the houses and the church, continuing down the well-trod path. A few minutes later he was heading past Jarad's place and soon he would be coming up on Howard's. He liked Howard and reminded himself to go by and visit with the old codger. As he neared the border he began to whistle a tune, as loud as his frozen lips would permit. This was a sort of sign for the person on duty not to be startled by his replacement coming up from behind. It was more a rasp than a whistle, Adam noted, but then he never could whistle very loud. Chapped lips didn't help.

As he neared the post, he saw Gary fervently shaking an raised finger in front of his lips, telling Adam to be quiet. Gary also pointed at the lantern and then made rapid slashing motions across his neck Kill the light, he was signing, emphatically. Adam shook his head to indicate he understood and he switched off the gas. He approached Gary as lightly as he could, not saying a word.

Gary leaned close to him, his hot breath lashing Adam's ear with hoarsely whispered words. "There's someone out there!" Gary pointed off in the direction of dark, nondescript underbrush, which Adam tried to focus on with his eyes. As if in counterpoint, he quickly unslung his rifle and pointed it in the same direction. Both men's pulses raced.

About ten yards away a twig snapped. Like two cats, the men's heads pivoted to the noise, their eyes straining to see through the darkness. The tip of Adam's rifle bobbed gently up and down in rhythm with his heart beat, as his hands held the cold plastic and steel in a tight woolen embrace. The only thing both men could hear was the blood pulsing through their temples as they tried to force themselves to catch another sound.

Suddenly a dark mass fluttered overhead before crashing on top of Gary. Both men jumped like over-taut spring toys, Adam letting out a shout of surprise. Simultaneously, they heard someone crashing through the underbrush in the distance, making good an escape. Adam lifted his rifle up and pointed in the direction of the sound. He pulled the trigger, hearing only the snap of the bolt sliding into an empty chamber. He had forgotten to load his gun.

"No, put that down," Gary shouted harshly. "What the hell do you think you're doing? Trying to kill someone?" He glared at his companion, though he could barely see him in the darkness. "It is only a stick. Whoever it was threw a stick at us as a diversion. Looks like it worked."

He removed his hat, which had been knocked askew by the unexpected piece of airmail, slapping it against his hip to knock off the snow. He replaced it, pulling it down securely around his ears. "Someone has been lurking around that side of border for about an hour now. I wasn't really worried, but I was hoping to see who it might be. Heck, maybe I might know him." Gary was tired and more than happy to be relieved of duty and going home to bed, but he wasn't sure Adam was up to the challenge tonight. He seemed a bit shaken up.

"Are you going to be alright down here alone? You aren't going to shoot someone, are you?" Adam didn't answer. He was still breathing too hard as he tried to master the adrenaline rushing through his body.

"Well, I got a good idea," he said flatly, "Let's build a fire."

"A fire," Adam responded, finding his voice. "Not a fire? They'll see us."

"That's the point, Adam. Our whole purpose here is not to stop anyone. Not really, but to let them know that we are watching the border. If we build a fire, they'll know that we are here and they won't be coming through. Do you understand?"

"I guess so," Adam responded unconvinced.

"Anyhow, it is too cold out here. My toes are about ready to drop off." He stomped his boots in the dirty snow, trying to drive circulation through his feet.

"Come on, help me gather some wood. We can use the kerosene in my lantern to get it started."

Within minutes the men were illuminated by the yellow tongues of a bonfire. "All we need now," Gary added, with his hands over the flames, "are some marsh mallows."

+++

The next morning, Jarad felt out of sorts. He was still tired, but he couldn't sleep. He didn't want to stay in bed, but then, he didn't want to get out of bed, either. He didn't know what he wanted.

"I hate life, right now," he told his wife. "I truly, truly hate life."

"What a thing to say," said Myla, surprise in her voice. She had gotten out of bed, but returned under the covers and snuggled up to her husband. He didn't respond to her closeness, like he normally did. "Why do you hate life?" she asked softly.

Jarad inhaled deeply, held his breath, and then slowly and heavily released it. "I guess I'm sick and tired of being a cop."

"A cop, honey, you've been a cop for . . ." she paused as she did the calculations in her mind. "For fifteen, sixteen years. Anyway, you're not really a cop anymore."

"No, I am" he said in a tired, slightly defiant voice. "I guess it is just expectations. People are afraid, they don't know what to do, so they become weak, demanding that others around them become strong. Become strong for them, so they don't have to be. Anyhow, they won't let me *not* be a cop."

"I don't think that you should let others expectations decide what you will or will not do," she said encouragingly. "You just be a dad and a husband. The others can take care of themselves."

"Oh, is that so, doctor?" he said peering at this wife, his voice frosted with sarcasm.

"I am not a doctor, people know that," she said defensively. "I just like to help."

"Yah, well, people seem to expect you to be the doctor, if you want to be or not." he retorted. "I know you're a nurse, you know you're a nurse, but they all run around calling you doctor. So if you're a doctor, I'm a cop."

"And how can I not be the cop," he continued. "It's my own dumb fault. I've made my own bed. I was the one who volunteered to set up security for the community. I was the one who ran off half-cocked to check out those footprints. And I was the one. . ." he paused. He pulled both of his hands to his face, grinding his knuckles into his now misting eye sockets. He then rubbed his face vigorously with the heels of his palms. "I guess I just don't want to be the one who has to kill people anymore," he said bitterly, pain in his voice

Myla didn't know what to day. She just laid near him, held him close and thought her own thoughts.

+++

Chapter 16

"You doing okay, old boy," a familiar voice said. "You look like hell." A deep, husky chuckle filled the room. It was Howard.

"Hi Howard," Otty said, cracking open an eye. "I feel worse than I look, trust me." He tried to move into a sitting position in his bed, but the pain was too great. "Am I dying? Did someone not tell me the truth. I must be dying if you're here. I can't think of any other reason why you'd leave your little den of iniquity."

Ellie came into the bedroom, two flour-covered hands held in front of her like a gloved surgeon ready to operate. She smiled at Howard, glanced at her husband, and then quickly left. She was baking, being a nurse, and being a grandmother, all at the same time.

"So, tell me what happened," Howard asked taking a seat next to the bed. Otty complained about being a captive audience, until Howard reminded him that *he* was the audience and could leave anytime he wanted. So the story better be good, he warned. He patted Otty's leg, his only overt concession to showing concern.

Otty described what happened that evening. But to give the whole episode context, he also had to explain about his earlier interactions with Reverend Swess and the GILM.

"Ah, yes. GILM. Those zealots. Bastards, all of them if you ask me," Howard replied. Otty hurt too much to argue. "Those are not my sentiments, Howard, but I appreciate your sympathy," he said. He wanted to laugh, but it wasn't worth the pain. Plus, he was so trussed up in fabric, he didn't know if laughing would cause him to pass out from oxygen deprivation. He chuckled weakly.

"But let me share with you the real tragedy. Swess, because he couldn't convince everyone to come to his party, had his 'missionaries' torch Purcell. That's why Purcell burned down. Swess set fire to it!"

Howard didn't know what to say to that. He just nodded his head back and forth, his sad eyes unseeing. After a while he said softly, "That's being reasonable."

"So where do you fit in all of this?" he asked Otty.

"I'm a heretic!" he said gruffly.

"Well, I know that," Howard agreed, matter-of-factly. "Tell me something that I don't know." His eyes had recovered their luster.

"I don't know," he said in a tired, confused voice. "I guess Swess took it upon himself to purge the area of hate. And if you weren't for him, you were against him. And in his own twisted sense of logic, your hate was evil and his hate was justified. Actually, in his mind it wasn't hate, it was a rebuke."

"I don't understand any of this. You're the historian, maybe sometime you can fill in my blank spots. I'm content with a little Bible reading and wrestling with Polkinghorne," Howard said, wanting to shift the conversation to another topic.

"By the way, when is the Polkinghorne Society going to meet, again?"

"By Jove, that is a grand idea!" Otty said with enthusiasm. "Obviously I'm not going anywhere soon. How about today!"

"By golly, I was hoping, so I came prepared." Howard reached into his pocket and fished out a small tin, flashing it in front of Otty. Otty knew instantly what it was, Howard's favorite brand of genuine English tea. Like he always insisted, one can't discuss Polkinghorne unless one could understand him, which, obviously, required imbibing only authentic British tea.

"Now, to go beg of your bride for a kettle of boiling water," he drawled in his best English accent, leaving the room.

Otty sighed contently. I sure do love that man, he said to himself.

+++

Oddly enough, Breann was being ignored. Her mother was the one who rescued her that evening from her fetishistic trappings, finding her handcuffed to the bed and gagged with a silk scarf. Breann had a slight case of hypothermia since the house was ice cold and the only thing she was wearing was a broad leather dog collar around her neck. Breann had been wholly ignorant of what had gone on with her father and she screamed at her mother when she was told what had transpired that evening. "You lying bitch," she said with venom. Her mother, for the first time her life, slapped her hard across the face. "You foolish, foolish, self-absorbed. . . .whore!" she screamed. "How dare you!"

Both women left the other crying. Ellie for her husband, who could have been murdered, but also for her daughter, who had been the foolish though unwitting accomplice to the violence. And Breann cried in anger and shame. Anger that she had been betrayed by her lover and shame that she had been played the stooge.

But the travesty of her sordid involvement in this whole event caused her to both further isolate herself and to be ignored by others. It was awkward for others to be around her as no one knew what to say. She knew that is was time for her to leave Blue River.

+++

Finally, Jarad finished getting dress. His wife had gone down to make breakfast for the children, though he knew that they were perfectly capable of making it for themselves. He suspect that Myla wanted an excuse to let him have some time with himself. But he knew that the solution to his melancholy was to get up and be active. Plus, he had a body to bury.

The day really was quite beautiful. The air was crisp and still. The sun seemed especially bright, and where the sun rays hit the snow little diamonds spontaneously formed. He could have waited to walk with the children to the church, since they had school that day, but he really wanted to be by himself, excluding Champ who always insisted on coming and who now ran on ahead of him. The walk helped him to feel a little bit better, but he did regret sharing with his wife. Not that he normally minded sharing his feelings. She always complained that he never shared enough. It was just that he knew she had her own issues to deal with and the times being what they were he didn't want to add his own problems to hers. Women tended to carry the burdens of the the world on their own shoulders. Especially those of whom they loved. At least, this was true of Myla.

Jarad felt he was really running behind schedule as he slowly strolled to his destination, but the later it got the less he cared.

Genis had made a comment last night about getting to the church early to bury the body, and Jarad knew he was undoubtedly expected to be there to help. But he wasn't there and maybe that was okay. Myla was probably right. Perhaps he did need to scale back on his commitments.

By the time he finally did make it to the church, he learned that he was even tardier than he had first thought. The body was already six feet under. Gary and James were standing along side the grave, leaning on their shovels, panting frosted breath into the still air. They nodded when Jarad approached. He looked down at the heap of freshly turned earth, large brown clods mixed with gravel and dirty snow. Someone had posted a temporary sign of wood and permanent marker at the head of the grave that read, Jonathan GILM. Looked like Genis's writing.

"Sorry I missed the party, guys," he said, with narrow smile.

James shrugged his shoulder. "No reason to be here, Jarad. I figured you'd just hang out at the house today. You've had enough excitement for a couple days." He stabbed the shovel into the ground and came over to Jarad, tugging off his glove and offering his bare hand to him. Out of habit, Jarad shook the hand, making eye contact with him. He sensed mixed emotions in James's countenance, but he wasn't really in the state of mind to try to analyze them. "I'm sorry if this sounds corny, Jarad, but thank you for following up those tracks. I really regret not figuring that one out, myself. As far as I'm concerned, you saved Otty's life."

Genis came out of the church, carrying three steaming mugs of coffee. "Well, hello Jarad," he said with surprise. "What are you going here?" He handed each of the men a mug, offering the third one to Jarad. Jarad took it, though he was a bit perplexed. Why are these guys surprised that I am here, he asked himself. Shouldn't I be here? Didn't I kill that guy? Wasn't he my responsibility? He was confused. This was a new thought. Was he the one that had been making all the assumptions about himself, and not people in the community?

Suddenly it was as if he could see more clearly. He knew exactly where the problem lie and the source of his funk. Himself. None of these people knew him before, especially as a police officer in Purcell. They only knew him as the guy that lived in the Traverson's cabin, was married to a really pretty lady, and who had a couple kids. Otherwise, there was a lot of blank information about Jarad that they didn't know and evidently didn't care. They just liked him for who he was. It was Jarad who had been filling in all the blanks.

He was really enjoying his coffee, more than he normally would have, but hey, he was a fellow who just had an epiphany! He looked around himself with fresh eyes, like a man who had just been exonerated from false charges. He was truly happy. This was the first time he felt that he was part of the community. That's an odd thought, he smiled to himself.

"What's so funny?" Genis asked. "Coffee okay?"

"It's fine," he said, with a lilt in his voice. "But I think I got your cup."

"That you did, but you deserve it. I'll just grab another cup when we go in for seconds. Have you had breakfast yet?"

Jarad was about to answer, when he heard a familiar voice calling out from behind him. It was Cameron and he was running toward him, his steps faltering as if he had been running farther and faster than he was capable. Champ went out to greet him.

"Cameron," he called out to the boy. "What in the world is wrong? Where is your coat?"

Cameron stopped, his chest heaving under his light T shirt as he tried to catch his breath. "Mom," he gasped. "They took her. . . mom!"

"Who?" Jarad asked, his voice rising. "Someone took mom?"

"Yes," he said, as his breath caught up with him. "Men with guns. They took mom away on a snowmobile."

+++

There was a sound outside the house that Myla hadn't heard in what seemed like forever. An electric motor! Instantly, there was a knock at the door.

"I got it," said Annie. But before she could get to the door it opened by itself and two men stepped in, one brandishing a gun. Myla immediately stepped forward, putting herself between the men and Annie.

"Who are you and what do you want," she demanded, her voice even and in control.

"Are you the doctor?" one of them asked, the man without the gun.

"Yes, I mean no, " she answered firmly. "There isn't a doctor here. But I am a nurse, and I have been doing what I can. If you need a doctor, I am sorry. There isn't one. Now, you have to go."

"She's the one," the man holding the pistol said to the other. He remained in the open doorway, and kept scanning his surroundings, as if looking for someone.

"Come with us," the first man said to Myla. "We got an emergency and you're the only one who can help us."

"I'm sorry. Truly I am. But I can't leave my family. And I'm not really a doctor. You understand."

The man with the gun growled at her. "Get dressed into winter gear and get your medical kit. You're coming with us," he said threateningly. The other man looked on, the sympathy in his eyes mixed with firm resolve. "You must come. Please!"

Myla hesitated for a moment before grabbing her snow pants and winter coat from the closet. Annie pleaded with her. "Momma you can't go," she insisted, tears welling up in her eyes. She tugged at her mother's arm. Then the back door shut with a soft thud as a lanky figure dashed past the kitchen windows. It was Cameron and he was fleeing the house, escaping down the road toward town. Myla saw him go and knew that he was off to find his father. The man with the gun cursed as he saw the boy disappear down the path. Myla turned to her daughter. "Annie, it will be alright. I won't be gone long, correct?" she said, looking at the man with the nice eyes.

"Yes, but hurry," he said.

She grabbed her bag and gave Annie a kiss. "I'll be back soon, honey, I promise."

Annie cried as she watched her mother mount the snowmobile, sitting behind the man with the kind eyes. The other man jumped onto another snowmobile that had been parked further back. The two snowmobiles then disappeared down the road and toward the east.

Approaching the border the two machines veered to the right and toward the bank. The man in front of Myla shouted. "Hold on," he warned her. They plunged down the bank and almost as quickly bucked back to the level, as the machine scooted across the whiteness and down a path previously beaten into the snow, parallel to the rails. As they crossed the border, a single observer, rifle in hand, waved to them as they passed. Both men returned the gesture and continued around the cable and on toward the east.

+++

"Oh, Lord!" Genis said in shock. He stood there staring at the boy, as if not fully comprehending his words. Jarad, too, seemed momentarily addled, but then carefully set the coffee cup down and took off down the path toward his house. Genis followed. Champ ran ahead, his tail high with excitement, anticipating adventure. Cameron lagged far behind them both, exhausted and unable to keep up with either his father or Genis.

Jarad was in a rage. How dare someone touch my wife, he shouted in his thoughts. Emotions flooded his mind: concern for his wife's safety, feelings of anguish that she was probably afraid, and bewilderment that this was even happening

When he reached the house, he saw the fresh tracks of two snowmobiles. Nothing else. Entering the still-open door, he found Annie sitting alone on the couch, upright, with her hands knotted on her lap, crying softly. Her eyes were puffy and she was shaking from both the cold and fear. She called out "daddy" when Jarad entered, and threw herself into his arms. He held her against his chest, cooing whispers to calm her, all the while looking around the room. He saw no evidence of violence.

He dragged his daughter to the couch and sat her down next to him, pulling off his coat and draping it over her shoulders. "Tell daddy what happened, baby," he said softly.

"She's coming back, dad. She even said so." She sniffled. Jarad cupped her face in his hands, using his thumbs to wipe the tears from her sodden cheeks. "Tell me what happened," he repeated, softly.

There was a shuffling noise at the door and Jarad looked up to see a man's head peeking around the door frame. It was Genis. He glanced at Jarad and Annie. Sensing the cold, he made to close the door, but first saying he wanted to have a look around outside. Jarad nodded, indicating that he understood. He shifted his attention back to his daughter.

Annie explained everything that happened, giving special emphasis to the fact that her mother went willingly and that she promised that she'd be back soon. Annie didn't like the fact that one of the men was wielding a gun. "Didn't you hear the snowmobiles, daddy?" she asked.

"No, I didn't honey. I was too far away. I wished I had. I would have come if I did."

Now it was Cameron who appeared at the door. Slamming it shut he joined his father and sister on the couch. He was breathing hard, from both sobbing and the effort from running so hard and long. Jarad hugged him close with his other arm, suddenly noting how cold the boy was. He looked around for something to cover him with, and then stretched to grab a quilt from the armchair, wrapping it around him.

There was a knock at the door, with Genis letting himself in. He looked around, trying to decide where he wanted to sit. Instead, he attended to the fire in the wood stove. It was cold in the house. Jarad turned to his daughter. "Tell Genis just what you told me." Genis listened while he quietly added wood to the stove, carefully positioning each piece.

Annie told the same story she had told her father, but this time Cameron chimed in, sharing what he saw. He distilled it down to a 'mean man' and a 'nice man,' with the mean man the one waving the gun. Jarad listened thoughtfully. He was trying to work out a course of action to get his wife back. He knew what he needed to do.

"Kids, I want you to stay here for a day or two. I'm going to go get mom. I know that she said she was coming back, but I don't want to wait. I need to go find her. You understand." He spoke softly, hoping his voice didn't betray the concern he felt waxing in his mind. "Can you do that for me? Can you two be alone here for a night or so?"

They both nodded. "If you need anything, just go over to Ellie's, alright?" Jarad was surprised, but relieved, that they both agreed so readily, but he knew that these were not the same kids that first arrived here, weeks earlier. In many ways, they were older than their ages. Jarad was not sure that this was necessarily a good thing, but was simply the way it was. He was equally surprised at how calmly he was taking the fact that his wife had been abducted. Or has she? Either way, he was going to be get her. He just needed a few minutes to get ready.

"I'm coming with you, Jarad," Genis intoned. Jarad looked at his friend. He hadn't considered anyone coming along with him. He wasn't willing to share the risk. "No, Genis, that isn't necessary. Plus, you're still recuperating," he responded, glancing at his still-bound hand. "No, I'm fine. And I know this area much better than you. I'll know people down there, assuming they took her to the Junction. You don't. You'll need me."

Jarad paused for a moment, realizing that Genis was correct. He did need him. "Okay, good enough." Genis headed back to his home to get himself ready.

Jarad moved hurriedly to prepare for his departure. He stuffed a small knapsack with things that thought he might need. He then pulled his holster and pistol out of the closet. He held it in the air, feeling its weight and considering it. No, he decided. He wasn't going to need it. He would use other means. What those other means were, he didn't know. He'd figure it out as he went along.

Before heading out, Jarad headed back up the hill and made a brief stop at Ellie and Otty's place. He quickly explained what had happened and what he and Genis were going to do. He asked Ellie to check on the kids later in the day. She said that she would be more than glad to and for him not to worry. Otty insisted that Jarad wait half a moment so he could say a brief prayer, which he did.

Within an hour after first arriving at the house and finding it devoid of his wife, Jarad and Genis were quickly jogging down the path, following the deep snowmobile tracks in the snow. They only paused to talk with the person on guard. "Who is it today, Genis. Do you know?" he huffed at his friend as they approached the border. "Andy." he said.

They paused for just a moment with Andy, asking him about the two men on the snowmobiles. "Sure, I know them. They were here to see your wife, Myla. Didn't you know? They didn't tell you?" he asked, perplexed. "I told them to tell you and they said that they would."

"Who?" Genis asked, sharply. Andy paused, sensing trouble. "It was Marty Anderson. You know Marty. I didn't know the other fellow, but Marty said that someone was hurt really badly and needed a doctor."

"Well, how'd they know we had a doctor?" Jarad wondered aloud. Andy didn't answer, but appeared troubled.

"What's up, Andy?" Genis asked firmly, sensing there was more going on here than either he or Jarad understood.

"Because I told them," he said, matter-of-fact. He explained how a couple days earlier when he was standing guard, he was approached by a couple of fellows from the Junction. He happened to know one of them and they spent an hour or so getting caught up on what was happening in their respective worlds. "I guess I must have mentioned that we had a doctor, and word got around. I hope I didn't do something wrong." He fidgeted under the firm stares of the two men.

"Lord, help us," Genis lamented with a strong tinge of sarcasm.

"Well, that changes everything," Jarad said to Genis. "We can assume that they will be expecting us."

"My thoughts exactly," Genis agreed.

Turning their backs on the boy with nary a word, the two men tromped off down the path, the sound of their passing fading into the trees.

+++

Otty slowly shuffled over to his daughter's house. It was always awkward for him to approach her, but this time doubly so. He knew, or at least hoped, that she would admit at least a shred of culpability for what had happened. It is not that he wanted his daughter to feel badly about what had happened the night before, but that she might begin assuming some responsibility for herself. He truly believed that good things could come of this event. Such was his faith.

He knocked at the door, but there was no response. He waited, knocked again, but still no response. He tried the knob, but it was locked. How odd, he thought to himself. I hope nothing is wrong. He went around the house and tried the back entrance, but had the same result. He hadn't brought any keys, so he slowly walked back to his own home to find the extra door key.

He met Ellie inside and explained what had happened. She was instantly worried and they walked over together, key in hand. Ellie held on to her husband to steady him. The bandages around his chest, as well as the pain in his ribcage, hindered his movements.

They were able to unlock the door and upon entering were greeted by the cold. The wood stove had obviously not been tended for many hours, and they feared for the worse. "Oh God, I hope she hasn't hurt herself," Ellie exclaimed as she began to search the house. Fortunately, the search was brief, beginning and ending with a note left on the kitchen table. Ellie read it aloud to her husband.

"Dear Mom and Dad. I have left. Do not come and search for me. Please take care of the kids. Besides, they love you more than me. You can have anything you find in the house. I don't know where I am going, but it doesn't matter. Obviously, I can't fit into your world. And you most definitely can't fit into mine. Breann"

Neither said a word, but simply looked at the other, each thinking their own thoughts.

Chapter 17

Though the day had started out beautiful, it quickly began to deteriorate. A warm front was coming in and the snow had turned into sleet. How strange the weather had become. Wasn't this December? This became most problematic for the two men when the formerly crusty snow quickly become sodden with moisture, making their forward progress much more difficult. They now tended to sink into the snow, requiring more energy to maintain their pace. They stopped often to catch their breath. In addition, the snow on the branches above them began to melt, showering them in a haphazard pattern of heavy droplets of water and ice, much of which seemed to more often than not find its way down a collar. The weathers gods were conspiring against them.

"Well, I guess the cable wasn't much of a barrier," Genis lamented as the two men stood side-by-side, huffing like a couple of smokers, their breath drifting off to mingle with that ever increasing mist that began to enshroud them.

Jarad agreed. "But, I never anticipated that one of our own guards would be in cahoots with the Junction people. But maybe that is my fault. I kept looking at the Junction people as being the enemy." Jarad cringed when he said that word. "At the very least, competitors. Maybe I was just being paranoid."

"I don't know," Genis cautioned, "they always had guns, and one of them shot at James. Remember, one of the fellows that took Myla had a gun. I don't know. ." he repeated, his voice trailing off.

"Hell, they are probably just as scared as we are," Jarad opined hopefully. "I just think we gotta go slow here."

Genis chucked. "Well, we're unarmed. You're not going to get any heroics out of me."

They had long passed the house that they had first raided. The smell of smoke still lingered faintly in the air. It served as a reminder that they were in 'foreign' territory, in spite of Jarad's words to the contrary. They paused after a couple hours and sat under a rock outcropping along the rail bed that offered a dry area to rest. They consumed some sandwiches, crackers, and hot tea from a thermos. "What'd I give for an apple right now," Genis said.

Jarad nodded his head in sympathetic agreement. Except for a rapidly shrinking supply of potatoes, he hadn't had a fresh piece of fruit or vegetable for months and found himself craving such things. This was odd, he would muse at times, because prior to the Event he tended to not eat enough fresh foods. Now that was one of the things he missed the most. Besides normality. He missed normality. Previously, the only time he had to rescue his wife was from an encounter with a drunk co-worker at an office Solstice party. That would be nice, he thought. He could deal with that.

As they finished their meal they looked out at the surrounding landscape. It was deathly silent. Except for the occasional small groupings of snowbirds that flitted and twittered among the trees, the forest was devoid of noise. All of the larger animals were either hibernating or had migrated to lower elevations to avoid the snow and the cold. Was it arrogance to assume that they could live here with impunity? What would happen when their stores of food ran out? Could they grow their own? Jared suddenly remembered a lesson from a high school history class. Even the Indians that lived here so many generations ago abandoned this area in the winter. But Jared dismissed this idea and forced his thoughts to return to the immediate present. The task at hand was enough to worry about right now. The rest would come later.

By now the rail bed was lifted high above the river channel, which had began to veer off toward the southeast, dragging itself and the canyon it created away from the men. Eventually the river would wander down toward Purcell, losing energy as it emptied into the shallow channel which weaved through the flatland in a series of looping oxbows. They could no longer hear the river. The trees in the surrounding forest were returning to their normal green color as the heavy snow melted and cascaded to the ground.

"Do you know where we are," Jarad asked, slipping the coffee mug back into his knapsack, preparing to return to the slow march down the rail bed.

"Yeah, roughly" Genis said, as his motions duplicated Jarad's. "But we aren't really anywhere, because I don't know where we are going. We are about seven or eight miles from the highway, which means we will be meeting up with houses pretty quick. The land will start to even out some and the woods will thin. We'll need to keep an eye out for others." He shrugged. "Besides that, I haven't clue. I guess we just follow the snowmobile tracks."

They continued down their path, keeping talk to a minimum. The rail bed seemed to meet up with road, as both came to be on the same level. They passed two empty houses in the distance, which appeared to the men as forlorn witnesses to another era. Suddenly Genis stopped and smelled the air, making motions to Jarad to do the same. Jarad did so and then nodded to Genis that he understood what he had wanted. There was a distinct scent of smoke in the air, which could only mean that there was an occupied residence nearby, probably somewhere ahead.

They found the house sooner than expected. As they cleared a bend in the tracks they stumbled upon what were once a couple of travel trailers that had now been cobbled together to make a single, less-than-unified, whole. Plywood had been hastily inserted around the base of the trailers to provide thermal insulation from the wind and a galvanized-tube that served as a chimney drizzled dark smoke into the air through a makeshift snow-roof of mismatched timber and fiberglass sheeting secured with old tires and gray cement blocks. It wasn't the dilapidated structure that surprised them; through the past couple decades an increasing number of rural people were forced to live in converted travel trailers as the affordable housing of choice. Instead, it was the four children that were playing outside.

The men paused when they discovered the four small faces staring at them, looking across the ditch that separated the house from the rail bed. They were warmly dressed, albeit in stained and ill-fitting clothing. The men felt naked and exposed. They were unsure how to precede, until their dilemma was solved by the smallest of the kids, who waved at them with a dirty, green mitten. Jarad waved back, and soon all the children had joined in waving before summarily dismissing the men by returning to their play.

The two men moved on, each giving the other a quick glance. "Let's get out of here," Genis whispered to Jarad, "before grandpa comes out with a shotgun . . . or worse."

"I'm just glad that they don't have dogs," Jarad said with relief. "Damn it, that's why I should have brought my pistol. All we need to do is have a run in with someone's pit bull."

In total, the men had been at their task for about three hours, having traveled some five or six miles and still the snowmobile track led them forward, still following the rail bed. They also began to notice more and more homes, some of which were quite grand. The larger places were perched on the high ridge that overlooked the land below and were probably summer homes for the wealthy. None of them seemed to be occupied. A waste of space, Jarad thought to himself. He wondered if they had been raided.

By now the sun was low on the horizon and they knew that they were at the first real hurdle of their mission. Where were they going to spend the night? During their next rest they discussed their options. They could easily break into one of the abandoned houses, but they were sure that building a fire would give away their presence. Or, they could simply continue on through the night, hoping that the darkness would offer them protection from inquiring eyes and allow them to get closer to their target. But before the men could come to a decision a friendly voice called from a distance.

"Hello, there," it said. They looked up to the grizzled face of an old man, looking on from the opposite bank. There stood an nicely dress man, leaning on a ski pole. "Hungry?" he asked. He waved them forward, toward his direction. "Come on, I'll make you some dinner." He left them, assuming that they would follow. They did.

The two men tramped across the rail bed, abandoning the snowmobile tracks that they had been following like slow, patient bloodhounds. They trod to the opposite side and across the ditch and then up the low, swept bank and toward a large wooden home that came into view as they passed through a line of trees. The old man continued shuffling toward the house, using the ski pole as a cane, his snow boots sinking deeply into the wet snow. Why was he leading them to his home? Jarad wondered. Why was he waiting for them along the tracks?

Genis and Jarad paused to take in the scene. The house was a large cedar home with oversize picture windows facing toward the west. There was also a large attached garage. The man was leading them to the front entry way, which was set in stone and rough timber. From outward appearances the home was quite elegant, though most of the windows were dark. There was a warm glow emanating from a side window, which was very attractive to the two men, who were starting to feel cold as the temperature dropped with the setting sun.

Sensing their hesitancy, the old man slowly turned around on the front step and called again to the men. "Welcome, welcome," he said with a raspy voice, a large grin on his face, his eyes reflecting genuine delight. "Come in, come in," he repeated as they finally approached the entry way. He opened the door. Light tumbling out, which proved to be very inviting. The man extended his hand to them as they entered, repeating himself with a soft, soothing voice. "Welcome, welcome," he said. "My name is Stanley Merton and welcome to my home."

Jarad noted that the room was very warm, but even more inviting was the smell of sausages and something familiar that he just couldn't place, but was nonetheless triggering his hunger. He handed the man his coat and reached down to unlace his boots . He stepped out of his overalls and hung them on a hook, setting his boots and knapsack below on the wooden floor. He followed the man and Genis forward through a wide doorway.

The room they entered was broad and high, with a vaulted ceiling and with one wall that seemed to be all glass. A large wood stove was situated in the corner and fed into a black stovepipe that exited into a central stone fireplace, the rock work continuing on up to the ceiling. Blankets covered the two doorways that led out of the room. A frying pan was sizzling on the wood stove next to a copper casserole, which steamed gently from under the lid. Sauerkraut, Jarad realized. And never in his life had sauerkraut smelled so delicious nor seemed so desirable.

He directed Genis and Jarad to the dining table. "I've been expecting you," he said softly, as he placed a plate in front of each of them, each laden with a fork. "Well, not you two exactly, but someone. I knew someone would probably be coming."

"How is that," Jarad asked with a steely voice. "Do you know where they've taken my wife."

"Ah," he said with a nod, as he busied himself with tea mugs and a kettle of water. "So, it is your wife? I can imagine your concern." He handed Jarad a mug of instant cocoa without asking if he'd even care for it and looked at him with soft eyes, the kind that seemed to embrace you when they were cast in your direction. "She's fine," he said with assurance. "She's perfectly fine."

"Where is she?" he asked, pointedly. Jarad didn't intend to be impolite, but he wasn't in the mood to play games. He wanted to get his wife and leave.

"She is very busy right now, I'm afraid. There's been an emergency. She's delivering a baby. If she can."

Their host went on to explain how one of the women in the Junction had gone into labor, but the birthing wasn't going well. The husband had heard that there was a lady doctor up in Blue River so he decided to get her. "He was in a hurry. A panic really. I cautioned him, but he wouldn't listen. But I can hardly blame him." He went on to explain how he figured that someone might come in pursuit. "You two were right on schedule." He paused again to embrace Jarad with is eyes. "She's okay, and you can see her tonight if you would like. But tomorrow would be better."

"Here, let's eat." He slowly walked over to the wood stove and returned with the griddle holding a mound of sausages. Big, plump, sausages spat oil in protest as the unsteady hand set the pan on a trivet in front of the men. He then returned to the stove for the copper casserole. "I made the sauerkraut myself," he said, as he positioned the casserole next to the other pan. "I was never a fan of the stuff before, but sometimes you can acquire new tastes." He smiled. "Jump in."

Genis was not bashful and heaped a big spoonful of sauerkraut over two of the sausage links. He had the giddy look of a man who was about to indulge into a secret fancy. Jarad was hesitant. He was very hungry and the food smelled and looked delicious, but it was difficult sitting here knowing his wife was near. His hunger won out and he reached for the food. He followed Genis's lead, spearing two sausages with his fork and then smothering them with a blanket of the hot shredded cabbage. It tasted as good as it looked.

The food helped Jarad to settle down a bit. He ate silently, watching his elderly host. The old man took one sausage and a small serving of sauerkraut. He seemed to be enjoying the company. "And tell us about yourself," Jarad said with some measure of politeness. "You seem to have a handle on what's going on around here."

The old man nodded his head again in a broad rocking motion. He had closed his eyes as if savoring the bite of sausage he was chewing. "Ah, this is good," he said with obvious pleasure. "I'd been saving these for a special occasion."

"To answer your question, I don't know where to begin. I am an orphan." He explained how he was a retiree who had moved to the Purcell area with his wife. "She had always wanted to live in the mountains," he said. "She just had to get away." They had moved to the house about two years ago, but his wife died unexpectedly. "She's gone now, so I have no reason to remain here. It is lovely, but. . . ." he paused, as if not wanting his words to offend his guests. "I guess, it is just too cold for an old man like me. I want to return to San Diego. Someplace a bit warmer. You understand, I'm sure."

Both Genis and Jarad nodded. The men would agree that it was a difficult winter, especially without the luxury of central heating. "And to imagine that people used to live like this in the normal course of their lives," he said with wonder. "But I can't bear it any longer. Ironically, I really don't own this home anymore. It was sold just before we lost power. I haven't even had a chance to pack." He looked around the house and lightly sighed. "Not that it matters."

Genis continued to eat, slowly but steadily. He didn't even pause to join in the conversation, though he added color with nods and grunts. He seemed at ease which helped to calm Jarad's spirit. Maybe it would be okay to spend the night, he admitted to himself.

"Has the Junction formed any sort of . . ." Jarad paused as he searched for a word, "local government?" he asked.

"Oh yes, we have. We have a committee, which I sit on. Why? I don't know. I don't really know the people here very well, and I don't have any real skills to contribute. In fact, I suppose I'm more of a liability that anything else. But they seem to bear with me." He smiled wanly.

"Who," Genis asked, his first word since sitting down to eat.

Stanley looked at him with neutral face, as if searching his mind. "Well, there is myself, Elaine Stevenson, John Stevenson, Serena Turner, and Peter Rafferty. Do you know any of them?"

"I know the Stevenson pretty well," Genis answered. "They own the gas station on the highway. And if I'm not mistaken, Serena Turner is a school teacher. Right? But I don't know any Peter Rafferty."

"I know Rafferty," Jarad said. "He's a retired from Homeland Security." Jarad explained how he had first met him professionally and then recently in the hospital. "I guess he's recovered," Jarad added.

"Oh, yes, he's quite an asset. He really seems to know how to manage a crisis. I don't know where we'd be without him" Stanley shared how Rafferty had organized search teams to gather up all the resources in the surrounding houses and how everything was kept in a central warehouse that also served as a community hall.

"But then we've ran into some problems. Serious ones."

"And what are those?" Jarad asked, his curiosity piqued.

"Armed men from south of here, Purcell I suppose. They've been moving up and pushing against our borders, so to speak. I guess that they are probably spreading out, looking for supplies, like the rest of us. Unfortunately, they are quite aggressive."

"I heard a lot of gunfire a few days ago," Genis added. "Was this related to those raiders?"

"Yes, we had a real run in a few days back. A lot shooting. I'm glad to say that no one got hurt. At least not our people. I think it was the stress of that excitement which pushed Cammie into labor. Poor thing." He paused and glanced at the food. "Eat up, gentlemen, I don't have a refrigerator. Or at least one that works."

"Tell me more," Jarad said, leaning forward in interest, as Genis speared the last sausage. "My family and I fled Purcell on the day it was burning. I thought that it pretty much burned down."

"Yes, that was quite a sight, especially that evening. But it is my understanding that only the north side of town was lost. That is why it seemed so dramatic from our perspective up this direction. From what I heard, accurately or not, most of the town actually came out okay. I hope your house was a survivor," he said kindly.

The men talked well into the night. Finally, they all retired. Stanley made up bedrolls on the floor near the wood stove. "You are welcome to sleep in one of the beds," he told them, "but I am sure that you will find this more comfortable." They agreed. They both slept well that night.

+++

The two men were up early, or so it had seemed. But Stanley had beat them both and made them a breakfast of coffee, toast, and jelly. "Unless you would like more sauerkraut, I really don't have anything more," he said apologetically. The men agreed that the toast was just fine and they complimented him on his hospitality. "And your insight. I don't know what we would have done if you hadn't taken us in," Jared reminded him.

Instead of following the railroad tracks, the three men followed the lane that Stanley's house was at the terminus of. A well defined slash had been cut through the snow and down to a well-compacted trail, which made the going easy. In addition, both men felt better having Stanley with them, even if he did slow their pace a bit. If anything, they felt safer and less exposed.

Inside, Jarad could barely contain himself with anticipation. He was very glad to be seeing his wife. He wanted to hold her, to touch her, and to tell her that he loved her. But at the same time, he wanted to scold her, to challenge her and ask why she left so promptly, without so much as a note. But immediately he would chide himself, acknowledging that in fact his wife was abducted and probably had no choice. She simply had the good sense to see this. Part of him understood this as well, but at the same time it made him angry. Was he simply being selfish?

It was a relatively short distance to their destination, what Stanley called the community hall. It was a squat green building with a tacky cedar shake mansard roof. To Genis's delight it proved to be what once was Stubby's Tavern, one of his old watering holes. "Oh, the good times that were had here," he shared. When Stubby's went out of business, the building was converted into a real estate office and then finally a combined county social services office. I think that was its final purpose until the event," he explained.

As they approached the building, Jarad could see in the near distance what appeared to be an animal hanging from a wooden framework. Getting closer, he identified it as a yearling moose suspended by a rope under a tripod of rough timbers. A man and a woman stood in front of the eviscerated beast, each with rolled up sleeves and blood up to their wrists. The man waved a red-hued salute to the party, which Stanley returned with a nod of his head, his own hands being planted deeply in his pockets.

They entered the front door of the building which ushered them into a reception area of dingy white tile, fronted by two counter tops buried in cardboard boxes. A well trod path of dirty boot prints guided the men, though Stanley obviously knew his way around. It was barely warm in the room. Voices could be heard in the back, which drew the three men toward that direction, their boots adding a freshness to the grime that gilded the floor.

The further they made their way toward the back the clearer the voices became. Women chatting, Jarad noted as he drew nearer. And one of them was Myla and she didn't seem distressed at all. A dark shroud was immediately removed from Jarad's heart. Myla was fine.

He saw her before she saw him. Peering over Stanley's low shoulder, he spied his wife leaning against a counter, wrapped in her heavy sweater, with a coffee cup in hand. She was discussing something of light importance with another woman, whom Jared couldn't see. Both women looked up simultaneously to see the visitors and it was then that Myla saw her husband.

"Oh, my knight!" she said in mock surprise, her eyes betraying her words. She seemed to be both excited and relieved to see him. "I was wondering when you'd get here. I knew you would never wait at home." She gently reached her arms around her husband and planted a kiss on his lips, looking at him squarely in his eyes. She seemed to be perfectly at ease, which confounded Jarad. He had expected her to be far more distressed, which only caused him to realize how much he had misread the situation. He was glad that he did not make a grand entrance last night!

Myla introduced the two strangers to her new friend, a thirty-something red head who was really quite attractive. Her name was Emma. Both Genis and Jarad shook her hand, though Genis with much deliberation. The interest seemed mutual.

"So how was your adventure?" Jarad asked his wife, still holding her hand. Though happy to see him, she did not seem anxious to go anywhere.

"Fine," she said. "I delivered my first baby, well my first baby by myself, or maybe I should say, as mid-wife because Emma proved to be such a help." Emma smiled with the acknowledgment.

"You should be proud of your wife, she is quite a gal," she told Jarad.

"I am," he said with a smile. "She is amazing. How is your patient?" he asked, turning toward his wife. "Or should I say patients?"

"Mother and child are fine. They really didn't need me after all. The father-to-be was just a little over-anxious, as men tend to be," she said, poking her husband on his chest with a finger. "Ever met anyone like that," she asked him, playfully. "Just the usual first birth of a young mother, minus the pain meds, of course. I can understand why all the men around here thought she was dying." She rolled her eyes in mock disbelief.

Stanley let out a small chuckle. "Well, there were some terrible noises coming from behind those doors," he said, pointing at the double-doors behind the women. "I was with John, go get help, go get help, I told him." He smiled. "So here you are, and the cavalry too."

The conversation continued, but not in a cohesive manner. Jarad and Myla were sharing with each other what had transpired in each their lives the past twenty-four hours, as well as her concern about their children. Genis and Emma seemed intent on getting to know each other a little bit better. Still insisting on playing the role of host, Stanley led the four of them back toward the front of the building and then around the corner to what served as a meeting room, obviously a large office space in its previous life. A collection of well-stuffed chairs circled a large faux-marble table. In the far corner, a small, hastily installed wood stove perched on cinder blocks provided heat to the room. Loose bricks were stacked between the wood stove and the adjacent wall to provide the semblance of a heat shield. Similarly, the flue pipe of the stove had been haphazardly forced through a rough-cut hole in the wall and chinked with what appeared to be wadded-up aluminum foil. It was obvious that whoever installed this stove was not concerned with the fire code.

Stanley served tea from the ubiquitous kettle of hot water. After all were served, he took a seat among his guests and asked them to be patient. "I know that you will all want to return home as quickly as you can, but I would like you to wait for a bit, if you can. I know that Peter would like to speak with you before you leave. He would be here now, except he had to go and inspect our . . ." he paused, as he gathered his thoughts. "Our line of defense, for lack of a better term. As I told you last night, we've been having a problem with the Others. We've had to take steps to protect ourselves." He smiled, knowingly. "I'm sure you understand."

This information changed the tenor of the conversation. All five people began to converse in a flurry of suppositions about how best to protect themselves. The conversation ended as quickly as it began when Stanley ventured the opinion that it was shameful that neighbors were arming themselves to rob neighbors. "I thought communities were suppose to help each other in times of trouble. Not take advantage of them. Surely, not to rob them at gunpoint."

"Let's not go there," Jarad snorted. Stanley looked at him and then nodded his head. "Yes, I am sorry, Rigby did act a little rash. But, if its any consolation, I think that his actions speak a volume of words about what we were just discussing." He shrugged with his hands, rolling them over and exposing his palms. "But, hopefully, that's behind us now." Myla reached over and squeezed her husband's arm, as if to second Stanley's words.

The group didn't have to wait long, for a few moments later a short, wiry figure stepped into the room. The man was dressed in a stocking cap pulled low over his head strands of gray-blond hair framing his face and hiding his ears, a ski coat that was a couple sizes too large, and dirty jeans stuffed into snow boots. His countenance was one of strain and exhaustion. It was Peter Rafferty.

He introduced himself, shaking hands as he went around the table. "Hello, Jarad, we meet again," he said with a tired voice, taking Jarad's hand. "I'm sorry about this mess. I couldn't believe my ears when Stanley told me what happened. Just dumb. I've already read the riot act to Rigby and told him he's lucky he wasn't shot. Hell, I would've shot him! I told Stanley here to keep an eye out for you. I see he did." He gave Stanley a grateful nod of the head.

"Am I that predictable?" Jarad asked.

"Well, you did what I would have done." Peter responded. "So, yeah, I guess your are." He smiled. In contrast to most men any more, Peter was still clean shaven. This only accented the deep furrows that the strain of his current existence had formed on his face. The man was carrying a lot of burdens, Jarad thought to himself.

"And thank you for being such a good sport," he told Myla when he reshook her hand. He then introduced himself to Genis and gave Emma's shoulder a fatherly pat. "Ah, Emma, as beautiful as ever. Using your enchanting wiles on our guest?" She blushed and gave Peter a glare. And then she smiled. Peter was obviously a person that no one could be angry with.

He sat down with a wince and gratefully took the tea proffered by Stanley. He slumped slightly in the chair, obviously uncomfortable. "Butt bone still hurts," he said with a smiling grimace to Myla. "But its getting better." She gave him that sympathetic look that was the domain of mothers and nurses.

"So how are things at the front," Stanley asked.

"I don't know. I think we are doing all right. There are some nasty fellows out there who want to play king of the hill." Peter went on to describe how raiders from the south were pushing north toward the Junction, looking for houses to plunder. Unfortunately, their practice was to shoot first and ask questions later. When they finally reached one of the outlying houses of the

Junction community, they peppered the house with so many random shots that it was a miracle that no one was killed. All that gunfire drew a response from the Junction, and a group of men were able to chase the looters away. "Fortunately, no one else was hurt, let alone killed," he said with a sigh. "Lord knows we can't afford to waste ammunition."

"So do you think that they'll come back?" Jarad asked, knowing the ramifications to Blue River if they did.

"Yes, I imagine they will. They keep an eye on us. I think that they are just biding their time. But, if we don't have to worry out this same problem coming down from the north, we should be able to hold our own. But if not, we can always fall back to Blue River." Though the tone of his last comment indicated he meant to be playful, his eyes said otherwise. "As long as we can hold the bridge, we should be fine. For now."

"Enough of this," he continued, pushing himself away from the table. "Come on, let me show you around."

They all stepped out through the front door, except for Emma who went to check on what were now "her" two patients. The day was cold and gray and a breeze had picked up from the west. The warm front that had plagued Jarad and Genis the day before, had already passed, as quickly as it has come.

As the small coterie wandered among the houses, Peter would indicate points of interest with his hand, waving it around like some small town realtor pointing out the potential of the area to a big-time developer. What Peter called their "second to last" stop took to them a large shop building that had been formerly used as a repair facility for log trucks. A point of interest was the collection of solar panels propped up on fifty-five gallon drums, all connected with an umbilical of bright wiring.

"And here," he continued, "is where we keep our vehicles charged-up, among other things." They entered the small metal door into an vast open area – a large, shadow-cast concrete floor enclosed by high metal walls. Toward the center were three snowmobiles, each with a sled trailer attached to it. One of the snowmobiles had its service panel open. Wires ran from an electrical apparatus to the power pack. It was obviously being recharged.

Peter inspected the machine, looking at its charge level. The digital meter was slowly approaching the full mark. "This one is for you. It should be able to get the three of you home. You can return it later. It is the least we can do for you."

"I don't understand," Jarad said, a little apprehensively. "You're giving me a snowmobile? That's kind, but . . . . I have no way to charge its batteries."

Peter laughed lightly. "No, actually I am lending it to you. It has enough charge to get the three of you up to Blue River. There is a second battery in the sled to get you back again. Perhaps we can use it to run a courier service between our two communities. I think that we might need each other through the course of time."

The four discussed the possibility for a while. Then Genis offered an additional idea. "How about if I stay for a couple more days or so and take a look around. Maybe I can help out in some way. Or at least get an idea of what we can do to help each other out."

Myla smiled and looked at Genis from the corner of her eye. "Are you sure that it is the only reason?" she chided. Genis furrowed his brows, as if he didn't understand what she was talking about. "I can tramp on back in a couple days," he said, ignoring the comment, though a ruddy hue on his cheeks indicated that he did, indeed, understand. "Assuming, someone is willing to put me up."

"Of course, I would welcome having you here. And I am sure Stanley wouldn't mind the company."

Peter disconnected the snowmobile from the wiring, returned and fastened the cover, and then flicked on the indicator switch to confirm that everything was set. "All systems go," he said, matter-of-fact.

"Okay, before you two gather up your things to leave, I have one more stop and it is a surprise. For that we'll have to return to the community hall." They all exited out the small door and walked directly toward the green building, conversing little, all of them thinking about the new opportunities that lay in their collective future.

Reaching the hall Peter led them to the rear of the building and through a single door that Myla hadn't entered before. Inside was a small storage room, in the back of which was another closet. It was here where Peter took them. "You have children, correct? How old are they?" he asked them as he opened the door. Myla told him and mentioned how she was looking forward to seeing them. "Well, when you get home, make sure you keep this stuff hidden. Help yourself and happy Solstice," he said, pointing into the closet. Though the light was dim, Myla could see what she needed to see.

The shelves were stocked with games and new clothing. She gave Peter a hug. She was going to do some Christmas shopping for her kids.

+++

Chapter 18

Myla and Jarad didn't have many things to pack onto the snowmobile. They bundled up as best as they could, since Jarad was going to turn off the foot and seat warmers to save power. Genis was there to see them off, Emma at his side. Romance was in the air. And so was the wind, as snow began to whirl around them. A storm was coming in.

With a wave to their friends, Myla and Jarad boarded the snowmobile. He flicked on the power switch with his thumb and sped off toward the tracks. It was exhilarating not only to be riding the sled through the snow, but the thought of getting home, and in only a matter of minutes rather than hours, added to the thrill. Though the both of them had only been away for less than two days, each felt like they had been away for a week. Granted things had worked out very well, especially considering how the whole affair began, but still it would be nice seeing the kids and sharing their news with the community.

He didn't travel as quickly as he could have, partly because it had been years since he had driven a snowmobile and he wanted to be safe, and partly because he wanted to conserve power. The snow blowing every which way posed more of a nuisance than a visibility problem, but that could quickly change. Still, even at a leisurely pace they'd be home in a little over an hour. Myla was content to hug him from behind, her face buried in the back of his coat and snuggled in a long scarf.

The world looked differently going in reverse at speed. It was only when had passed the little pastiche of a house that he recognized where he was. The children were not out playing in the developing tempest. Then, immediately, the road pulled away from the tracks and moments later Jarad was able to spy sections of the river down to his left. Maybe he sensed it more than he actually saw it. He couldn't hear the river over the whine of the motor and grind of rubber tread, but he still imagined it in his mind. Was he homesick? How odd. Was this little cabin now his home? It must be, for his life in Purcell was increasingly a distant memory, a separate existence. Time and memory were strange bedfellows.

But he was feeling very complete. He was on his way home with the woman that he loved, who was clinging to him stronger than she needed to. Perhaps she is feeling the same way that I am, he thought. He wished he could hug her, right then and there, but he kept his hands on the steering bar and watched the trail ahead. He was wondering how his kids were. Did they go to school today? What was today? He was losing track of time and that feeling was both strange and delicious. Was life better? It was surely more simple, in spite of everything. No, he reconsidered. Sometimes it was simpler, other times less so. Life was still life.

He became lost in thought as he considered the world around him, his world, where he was, but not, yet, where he was going. Except down the trail. He thought no further than that. As he continued in this fugue of mind the mirage of a dark train appeared in the distance ahead of him, slowly taking shape in the dancing snow fairies that spun in the cold naked air. He contemplated this phenomenon in dream-like way, when his conscious mind suddenly warned him. Train! It is real! Turn around!

His eyes refocused and he suddenly became aware of the huge, monstrous, oncoming threat that the train posed. He looked around himself and realized that he was in a narrow gully, where the embankment on his right was nearly vertical and and far too high to scale. His alternative to the left was a steep, sheet of scree that plunged down to the river. He could not escape off the rail bed, whether on the sled or on foot. He thought about turning around, but the area between the rail and the cliff side was too narrow for him to maneuver. A more experienced rider might have managed it, but Jarad knew that he could not.

For a moment, he wondered if he was insane. He was still driving forward toward the train and the train was heading toward him, their combined speeds quickly devouring the space that separated them. He didn't know what to do. Then, ahead, halfway toward the train he saw what appeared to be the remains of an access road that was cut into the bank side. But he couldn't be sure, since the whiteness of the snow both on the ground and whirling in the air confused him. He shouted at his wife, "Hold on!"

Instinctively, she wrapped her arms around him and knotted her fists together, pulling herself tight against him. "What's wrong?" she shouted in return.

"Train!" he roared, louder than necessary.

He curled the throttle control with his palm and the snowmobile accelerated rapidly forward, throwing both of them backward. Myla let out a brief scream, but held on tight. The snowmobile weaved back and forth as Jarad struggled to both hold on to it and maintain steering control. He cursed for having to go so fast, but he knew he had no other choice. In spite of the suddenly serendipitous blizzard, which was probably helping to conceal him, he knew that he would soon be spotted. He remembered his last encounter with a train. The thought of being murdered here, so close to home and yet so far from his children, grieved him. He grit his teeth.

Seconds had only passed, but he was now able to make out the straight, upright lines of the engine as it came increasingly closer. He thought he could hear its rumble and feel is vibration, but he knew this was his imagination. The two of them bounced on the seat of the snowmobile as if on a short-legged bull, twisting and bucking to shed them from its back, as it crashed down the trail, faster than. was safe. Unsafe, but not unreasonable, he knew. The train was sure death for him and his wife and his fear turned to anger.

The train seemed to be closing in on him quicker than he was closing on to his escape route. Where is it? His view was stymied by the swirling snow which seemed to increase in intensity by the moment. Pathetically, he realized he wasn't going make it. His heart raced. He felt so trapped, so helpless, so frustrated he could scream. He did. "God, this isn't fair," he shouted as loudly as he could. He looked up to see the bright orange engine approaching menacingly, grimly wondering if he would be able to see the soldier in the gun turret whose intent would be to kill him. Or more morbidly, the flash of the gun barrel. He felt a sense of resignation growing in his spirit. Is this how people feel when they know that they are going to die, he pondered in some corner of his mind.

Orange? The engine was orange, not black. He took another quick glance. Indeed it was orange. How could he miss it? A bright, glorious, beautiful orange! He knew that he had lost the race, so he pulled as far over to the shoulder as he could, away from the train. The sled settled into the snow, tilted at an angle. Jarad craned his head to the side, trying to look past the engine. Coal cars. The train was hauling coal cars. He let out a wild hoot of joy, pumping his fist into the air. He then spun in his seat and covered up his wife's face with his chest just as the train rushed by, driving a shroud of snow over them. Jarad was laughing. "It's a freight train, honey. It's a freight train," he said, in a muffled voice. "And I love you."

+++

The rest of the drive home was uneventful, though Jarad had to constantly remind himself to slow down. The adrenaline that filled his body energized him and it caused him to move more quickly than was economical for saving battery charge, especially since the loss of charge wasted trying to outrun the train.

Passing the cable barrier, Jarad noticed that no one was manning the border, which was just as well. The whole idea of keeping a constant surveillance on the border seemed good at the time, though in hindsight the effort was amateurish, if not impractical. You're being too hard on yourself, he thought to himself. After all, it did work in a fashion.

The kids were greatly relieved to see their parents. They had taken well care of themselves and had even gone to school, but it had ended early because Mrs. Hobson was sick. But they were glad to be one again as a family. Jarad and Myla both realized that their children were growing up. Life continued, regardless of the circumstances, they discovered anew. They shared their experiences with the children over a late lunch of soup.

Cameron was delighted with the snowmobile and asked his father to give him a ride. At first Jarad declined, explaining the purpose for the machine and their inability to keep up its battery charge. But then he relented when he remembered the second battery. Since the first one was just about completely depleted, he let his son motor slowly around an open area near the house, Jarad monitoring from a distance. Cameron parked the sled when a warning light flashed on the dash, indicating the pending loss of charge. He then helped his father to remove the power pack in the trailer to store it in the house. The warmer environment would help maintain the charge, he explained. Afterwards they covered the machine with an old plastic tarp from the woodpile to keep off the snow and ice. This didn't stop Cameron from sitting on the machine and fantasizing about speeding over the snow.

Afterwards, Jarad told Myla that he and Cameron were going to drop in and see Otty, to let him know that everything has worked out fine and to inform him on all that is happening down at the Junction. Myla was agreeable, but she did ask Jarad to drop a hint that she was not available today to make the rounds. She wanted to stay home with her daughter. "The rest of today is officially my day off!" she declared with a smile.

Cameron was excited about spending this time with his father. It was not that he didn't get to see his father often, they saw each other every day. If anything, this change of life from Purcell to Blue River increased the time that they had with each other. But Jarad was so busy so much of the time, that he probably spent less time one-on-one with his son. Such was the novelty of being a leader in building a from-the-ground-up community. Granted, countless others had done this before in hundreds of generations, but it was new to Jarad and it was new to this generation. And it was new to his son, too.

Otty was glad to see them both. He was up and about and didn't look any worse for wear. He was still terribly sore, but knew that he was on the mend. "I wish I could say this for the rest of the folks. There seems to be a lot of sickness going around, mostly chest colds. I fear for the worse," he lamented. Otty thought that pneumonia was developing in a lot of the older folks, and he feared it was only a matter of time before they would have a lot more funerals to attend. "I wish I could do more," he said with a grim smile. He then gave Cameron a mock hit on the shoulder to break the tension that had developed. "My," he said in admiration, "you're turning into quite the young man." Cameron didn't know how to respond, whether to smile, to blush, or to thank him. So, he did none of them, but he felt different inside. Maybe he was turning into a man. After all, he was almost a teenager.

Otty was disappointed to hear that Genis had remained in Junction, if only for an extra day or two. "He's my right arm, and I need him especially now since I've been hurt." He shrugged. "But, as always, I am sure things will work about better than we can realize. For instance, look at Myla's abduction. Who could have imagined?"

Jarad asked if there was any other news that he might need to know since he was gone, albeit only for a couple days. Otty thought for a moment, as he sifted his brain to separate those things of macro-importance from those of micro-importance. "Howard is sick. I worry about him. He has that same flu bug as the others. And his radio quit again, something to do with the solar cell. Christmas is coming soon. Other than that, just one day at a time." Jarad agreed. That had become his motto as well. It was something that Jarad had remembered from a recent sermon by Otty, something to the effect of "don't worry about tomorrow, tomorrow will worry about itself, each day has enough trouble of its own." In many ways, Jarad had no other means of dealing with the present.

"And one last thing," Otty choked, obviously bothered. "Breann has left." Jarad looked at him for a moment, searching his eyes. He knew what grief Breann had brought into Otty and Ellie's lives, but he also knew that they both loved her very much.

"Where did she go?" Jarad asked softly. Otty could only shake his head. He didn't know.

"How long has she been gone?"

"I discovered her gone right after you left our place to go after your wife. She left us a note," he said with sadness. "I don't know, Jarad. I have no answers. But strange as it might sound, perhaps it is for the best. Maybe she is doing the right thing. I only hope she is safe." Otty gasped, repressing a sudden sob.

Jarad and Cameron got up to leave. He laid a hand on Otty's shoulder, his touch both telling him not to get up and that he had his sympathies. Leaving the house, Jarad drew Cameron close to himself as they walked down the path toward nowhere in particular. It felt good to have his son close to him.

+++

Otty felt morose. Things were not going well. He worried about his daughter. He wanted to take off after her, but he knew that as an old hobbled man that wasn't practical. And a part of him wanted her to have her space. Deep inside, though Otty might never admit this openly – even to himself – he was relieved. But he would have to ponder this another time. Right now he had a large number of older people who were down with sickness and fever. And Genis was gone. He didn't blame Genis for staying and he was optimistic that only good would come from this news about Junction, but right now he needed him. Howard was ill, and his radio was no longer functional. Food stocks were getting low and the last few houses that James raided brought some good supplies, but little that could be eaten. Still Jarad did bring some good news. Maybe they could trade or barter supplies with the Junction for food. He would give that some thought and then discuss it with the council. But right now, he also had to think about Christmas. Time was running out.

He turned and faced the window, watching the snow swirl under the eaves. "Oh, Breann!" he blustered softly to no one.

+++

"Hey Dad, let's go to the Perch and take a look. I love it up there. Maybe we can see Purcell."

"Okay, sounds good Cameron. It's been a while."

The two turned away from their wandering and made off to the west and toward the overlook. The walking was easy, though the wind hadn't ceased since they'd been home. It was still kicking up the snow and knocking it from the trees, but it wasn't unpleasant to walk in. Not now. Now that he was home and had a moment of ease.

They wound through the trees, hands buried in their pockets. They would intentionally bump into each other as they slowly meandered along, talking about little things. Cameron wanted to go hunting. He would often see varying hares and thought that it would be fun to tan their hides. "Well, I've never done it, but I am sure Genis knows how," Jarad said in encouragement. "But I do like fried rabbit, that is for sure." He promised to take him hunting in the next few days.

They reached the overlook and carefully walked out toward its end. There was a narrow section that normally wasn't difficult to traverse, but in the snow they had to be careful. They both pretended to be walking on a balance beam as they shimmied toward the wide end of the overlook, carefully stepping one foot in front of the other with their arms out horizontally from their sides. Cameron went first and when he made it to the end, he twirled around with a jump, as if he had accomplished something difficult and daring. Jarad encouraged him with a loud whoop. He followed his son's lead and slowly but steadily met him at the terminus of the big stone slab.

They turned and stared out into the airy abyss cast before them. The trees below swayed rhythmically as the wind pushed them hither and yon. They could track the movement of the wind, like wheat in a field, as the tree tops moved in the gaseous currents. Cameron became fascinated by this and would wait patiently for the wind to accommodate him. "Three seconds Dad, for the wind to hit us. Watch." A moment later the trees in the immediate distance bowed and Cameron began his count. Sure enough, when he said three the wind brushed their faces. "Good job, son. You are very observant."

Jarad watched his son for a bit and then turned his gaze toward Purcell. Nothing could really be seen during the day, especially with the snow flurries. From this vista, Purcell only became evident at night when its lights would betray its presence. But that was no longer true. Now if was always dark. But if he felt that if he were to live the rest of his life here in Blue River, Purcell would forever remain a distant memory. Out of sight, out of mind, he supposed.

"What is this?" Cameron asked, kicking at something in the snow. His boot cleared away the dusting of snow and exposed a piece of clothing. He reached down and gave it a tug, liberating it from the crusty ice that held in against the stone. He held it up to display to his father. "It's a sweater," he said. He gave it to his father and then dropped to his knees, digging into the snow with his gloved hands. "There's more," he said. Before long he had pulled out a pair of pants, a shirt, and various underclothes. "Did somebody take their clothes off?" he asked his father quizzically. He looked again at the collection of clothes. "That's weird," he said definitively.

Jarad helped him clear more of the snow, making sure that there wasn't anything more to be found. He noted to himself that there weren't any shoes or socks. Maybe someone had left them from earlier in the year, he pondered. No, his own mind replied, it is just on the surface. It had only been there for a couple days. His mind was then quick to make a connection with his visit with Otty.

Without saying a word to his son, he carefully looked over the edge of the Perch. He knew what he would see, and sure enough it was as he had figured. Far below a naked, twisted corpse lay semi-buried in the snow. It was Breann.

"What are you looking at Dad," his son asked, aping his father's movements. "Oh, nothing," he replied softly. "Just trying to watch the wind, like you were," he lied. He quickly got up. "Say, let's go get our guns ready. Maybe we can go hunting in the morning." Cameron readily agreed and jumped up as quickly as he had gotten down.

"And let's gather up these clothes. No reason for them to go to waste," he said to his son, as he stuffed everything into the pants.

+++

Chapter 19

Reality had become, again, surreal. Jarad was lost in thought as he and his son made their way back to the house. He tried to keep his son engaged in conversation, or he at least be an attentive listener, but the problem of facing Otty and Ellie with Breann's death was consuming his thoughts. What a strange world he lived in! It seemed to be some bizarre, Darwinian exercise in the survival of the fittest, whether physically or emotionally. Who was going to die next? Who was next to develop some psychosis? He wondered where he sat on the continuum.

When they neared Otty's house he paused, as if forgetting something. "You know what Cameron, I forgot to talk to Pastor about something. Would you mind waiting outside for a moment?"

"Sure Dad, I don't mind. I would rather wait outside anyhow." He sat down on a round of firewood that was waiting to be split.

"Great, I'll just be a moment."

Jarad knocked on the door and he was quickly welcomed in by Ellie. The door closed and Cameron turned on his wooden perch to see what lay around him. He watched the snow flakes, allowing some to alight on his outstretched glove. He examined them closely, wondering if it were really true that no two snowflakes are ever the same. He couldn't ascertain the facts from the few he had captured, so he licked them up with his tongue. Soon, he was trying to capture as many as he could with his tongue, wondering if a person could quench his thirst with snowflakes alone. After chasing them for a few minutes, swinging his tongue in the air like some sort of electronic sensor, he decided it wasn't possible. All he did was get a cold, dry tongue.

No sooner had he settled himself down again, when the door to the Pastor's house opened. He saw his father stepping through the dim outlet and softly closing the door behind him. He also noticed that his dad no longer had the clothes.

"Ready?" his father asked.

"Yes, sir!" Cameron said with a smile. "I'm gonna make a hat?"

"What?" his father asked, befuddled.

"Out of the rabbit skin. I'm gonna make a hat."

His father smiled. "That is the coolest idea ever." As they continued on their walk toward the house, Jarad again drew his son close to him. What a happy and sad world, he mused to himself.

+++

When they neared the house, Champ raced up to greet them. He had been keeping an eye out for them. "Can we take Champ with us?" Cameron asked his dad, as they entered the house.

Before Jarad even answered, Cameron let out a loud gasp of surprise. Underneath the Christmas tree were four presents, all wrapped identically though varying in size. Jared looked questioningly at his wife. He knew about the two presents for the kids, but what were the extras? "Hey dad, there's one for you, too!" Cameron exclaimed with delight. Myla looked away, ignoring his silent inquiries. Then he laughed. "Girl!" was all he could say.

Myla smiled and giggled lustily. She knew that he knew that she knew. .

Jarad wanted to tell Myla about his discovery, but he didn't want to spoil the moment. He gave his wife a hug from behind, and explained how he and Cameron had plans to go hunting. She expressed the opinion that that was a grand idea, because she knew that Cameron had been waiting in the wings for some activity with his father for weeks. But Myla could sense that something was pressing on Jarad's emotions.

"What's wrong," she asked him, with that I-know-something-is-wrong-and-you-can't-hide-it look. Jarad sighed and whispered into his wife's ear about Breann. He knew that he should help retrieve the body, but he was concerned about his son and he didn't want to spoil the moment, the day, the holiday – he could go on and on.

Myla turned around and grabbing his hand she dragged him into the kitchen and out of sight of the children. In a low voice, Jarad explain in more detail what had just transpired in the previous hour. She nodded as she listened, and then paused for a moment as she gathered her thoughts. She then suggested that maybe Jarad needed to be straightforward with their son and include him in the process. Hmph, he snorted.

He paused for a moment to ponder her words. He hadn't considered sharing this problem with Cameron, only devising ways to protect him. But maybe Myla was right. Maybe he need to stop treating his son like a child. Granted, he was only thirteen, or soon to be, but he probably was old enough to handle some of the uglier sides of life. Would either of them ever be old enough, Jarad ruminated in his mind.

"Cameron, come here, I got something to say," he said to his son, sitting down with him on the couch. "You, too, Annie. This something that you need to hear as well." For Annie's sake, Jarad explained what he and her brother had done and about the clothes that they had discovered. But then he admitted what he actually did see and where those clothes came from and why he had to see the pastor and his wife on the way home. Cameron listed intently, and then looked away, his forehead crumpled as he considered what his father had just shared.

"That's tough," he said in a surprisingly matter-if-fact tone of voice. "I feel badly for Pastor and Ellie. But Breann was really weird." He turned in the sofa and faced his father. "So, when are we going to go get the body? Somebody has to do it."

"I was thinking about asking James to help," Jarad said. "I know that he would be willing and able to help."

"Me, too," Cameron offered, optimistically.

"Well, son, I appreciate it, but this is really an unpleasant task. I don't think. . ."

"Dad," Cameron interrupted, "I am not a baby!" Jarad was surprised. Rarely had Cameron every spoke to him in that tone of voice. He looked into his son's eyes,and realized that he was looking into the eyes of a young man, growing up quickly. What was I like when I was thirteen, he asked himself.

"Okay," he said softly and with a shrug. "But, trust me, this is not an adventure."

+++

Later that afternoon, Jarad and Cameron went over to James's place. James met them at the door. After Jarad explained the reason for his visit, he responded with an invitation. "Let me show you one of my morbid secrets," he said with a wave of the hand. He led them to the back of his house and out under a large covered outdoor area that once served as a patio, but was now converted into an outdoor shop. Large, long, oddly shaped boxes in various stages of assembly were being constructed. Jarad immediately recognized that they were coffins. "I knew it was only a matter of time, and nobody wants to wait for a coffin to be built. And with my own mom dying . . . I guess I just got to thinking. I have the time, the equipment, and with no mortuary. . . ." his voiced trailed off. "Sad to hear about Breann. She knows how to continue giving her folks grief, even after she's dead," he said bitterly. He shook his head. "Why wait until tomorrow? Let's get it done. I'll get Jimmy. The four of us can make haste of it all."

Twenty minutes later the four of them were lugging the empty coffin down toward the tracks, each holding onto a handle. James had brought a long length of rope, just in case, which was now coiled up inside of the coffin, along with some old blankets, a hammer, and a bag of nails. The coffin was sturdily built out of old siding and other miscellaneous scraps of wood, but still exuded evidence of craftsmanship. James did good work.

James and Jimmy were in the lead and steered the party down past Jarad's house and toward that low section of the bank halfway to Howard's place. Reaching it, they lowered the coffin onto the snow and slid it down the bank, being caught by sure hands below. The group reassembled on the rail bed and continued their march toward the body. Little was said, everyone thinking their own thoughts. Only the wind provided any diversion in the way of sound.

Past the very last house, the railroad grade began to gently but perceptively descend relative to the embankment on the right, which soon turned into a very steep and high cliff. When the railroad began to curve south, James led the group onto a secondary bank that formed under the shadows of the increasingly high rocky up-thrust. Through the trees the group could begin to see the Perch, high up in the air, which provided a reference point for their search. They were close.

It became increasingly difficult to maneuver the coffin since they had to now thread it through the trees and underbrush, much of which had been sheltered from the snow by the canopy of branches overhead. While they took a brief rest, huffing from the exertion, James went on ahead to spy out the body. He only had to follow the sounds of the ravens to know where to find it.

Exiting the grove through a narrow game trail, he knew he had found what he was looking for,directly under the Perch. Though he couldn't yet clearly see the body due to the snow and being on the same plane of ground, he knew exactly where it was. The presence of the two black forest denizens squabbling noisily over the sky-sent bounty, told James where to find it. He paused for a moment watching them hop on their strong legs, flicking their black wings as they challenged each other for first fruits. "Scat!" he bellowed as he rushed toward the scene. The two big birds flew off to nearby trees, croaking in protest and keeping vigilance from high, bare branches.

James found the body under the imprints of raven's feet in the snow. Fortunately, they hadn't yet disfigured the corpse, which surprised James since the body had been there for at least two days. The eyes were intact, generally the first item to be consumed by the birds. They were still in their slumber under closed lids.

Reflexively, James began to dust the snow off the body. Why was she naked, he asked himself. "You always were an odd one, weren't you?" he asked the partially frozen corpse. "Now how in the world are we going to get your bent frame into that straight coffin? Dumb fool. Why couldn't you have jumped into the river and been swept away? Then we'd be rid of you!" He snorted. This was an unpleasant task and he blamed her for it. "I'm gonna nail that coffin shut so nobody can see you. You hear me? I'm not gonna allow you to cause your mother any more grief."

He went back and joined the others. "I found her," he said flatly. "Let's get over there before the ravens make a meal out of her."

They turned the coffin on its edge and carried it as quickly as they could down the game trail. Clearing the trees, they jogged over the rocks to an open area of snow and frozen scrub. The body was a stiff puppet thrown violently into the snow. The four of them gathered around it. Simultaneously Jimmy and Cameron turned and staggered over the rocky terrain to relieve their stomachs of their lunches, splattering the snow and rocks with tokens for the ravens.

Neither James nor Jarad could blamed them as their own stomachs turned.

    With some effort they were able to get the body into the coffin. Though rigor mortis had passed, the semi-frozen body was still resistant to some manipulation, causing them to leave the corpse on its side and not face up. Instead of shrouding the body with the blankets, James balled them up and stuffed them around it, using them to hold it in place rather than drape it from view. "I suppose I should have brought a smaller coffin," he said to no one in particular.

    Once they had the body in place, James nailed the lid shut. He drove in extra nails, intending that it never be opened. He felt in his heart he was sparing both Otty and Ellie grief, for he was sure that they would want to view the remains. Not if I can help it, he thought to himself. "Not if I can help it," he repeated in a mumble.

    "Help what?" Jarad asked. James looked up, a single nail held in his lips. "Nothing, just thinking out loud," he said from the corner of his mouth.

    When the coffin was secure, James wound the rope and draped it over his neck and shoulder and hung the hammer through a loop in his pants. "Let's go," he said, each fellow lifting on a handle. The load was surprisingly light, but then Breann was not a large person. She was like her mother in that respect, Jarad thought to himself And only in that respect.

    The return trip was uneventful though more tedious. Along with the increased load, the men had to deal with an inverse in the grade, which was now uphill rather than down. But with frequent rest periods, they managed to make pretty good time.

They used the rope to pull the coffin up the bank, and the maneuver was executed with a minimum of fuss. Finally, they approached the pastor's house, their tiredness held in check by their anticipation. Otty had been keeping an eye out for them and met them as they approached his property. His eyes were puffy from tears but he was full of praises and thanks for their efforts. He had tried to keep the mourning to a minimum to spare his grandchildren, but he was a man of feelings and obviously he wasn't entirely successful.

He led them to Breann's house. "Let's just let the coffin rest on the kitchen table," he directed. The men drew the coffin through the door and balanced it on the white, marble-like surface. "It will remain cold enough here, so we won't have a worry. I must rely on you fellows to dig the grave as well, since I am not in any shape to help, to my regret." He sighed deeply. "But that can wait for another day. No one is going anywhere," he said softly, patting the wooden box. He shook hands all around and then returned to his home.

As Otty left, James and Jarad made plans to dig the grave. They agreed on an early hour for the next morning. And with that and another round of hand shaking, the two men and their sons went their separate ways. It was time for dinner.

+++

They didn't have one grave to dig that morning, but two. Sarah Silverman had died that same night. And as befitted her character, she died quietly and unobtrusively. Not even her husband knew until that very morning. Fortunately James had another coffin ready, and while Andy, Jarad, and the two boys dug the graves, Myla and Hobson took care of the body. Otty sat with Emil and they shared each other's grief. Ellie stayed with the grandkids, who had now become as her own children. She would bring them only when the funeral started. She was worried about them, knowing that their mother was to be buried. But to date they had been strangely indifferent.

Annie helped out by making coffee at the church for everyone, and she seemed all the world like a wife as she handed Jimmy his cup. "Extra sugar, just as you like it," she said with a smile in her eyes.

Everybody who could came to the funeral. Some didn't even know that Sarah had passed away and only discovered the fact when they arrived. The weather cooperated in a strange way. A brilliant sun was out and its rays splayed through the trees, as if casting spotlights directly on the grave sites. Some recounted later that the sun rays only lit upon Sarah's grave and not Breann's. This was observed by others, but few discussed it. Surely it was simply a trick of the light, that could be replicated by similar conditions any day, but few accepted that. Sarah was loved by most everyone who knew her, but few, if any, would lament the passing of Breann. But it was impolite to mentioned such things.

Otty was in good form for the committal services. He skillfully wed the two memorials together, weaving and separating his words as each life was celebrated and its loss lamented. But in some ways, a burden had obviously been lifted from both his shoulders and his heart. He would always privately question what he could have done differently with his daughter, but now that she was gone he was at peace. Yes, he had two new children to raise, but they were a joy to him, something his daughter never really was. Never chose to be. Still, for all her faults, Otty loved her and would miss her. After all, she was his flesh and bone.

After the services the four men lowered the caskets and filled the cavity with the wet, crumbly dirt. And then each went to his own home. Officially there was no wake for either woman, but many did gather at Emil's home. That was good. For Emil needed the company and Otty and Ellie did not. They were fine to be alone with the kids. Their kids.

+++

Myla gathered up her things. She was going to make her rounds. Annie was coming with her to lend her a hand. Her timing might not have been the best, but she was surprised at how awful many people appeared at the funeral. Many should have remained at home. With all the hacking and coughing she was afraid that they were only spreading the illness. Otty was right; for many persons pneumonia was just around the corner. She didn't know what was going around, whether something viral or bacterial, but it wasn't good. She feared for the worst.

"Here, honey, you'll need one of these," she said to her daughter, handing her a surgical mask. Annie took it, but with questioning in her eyes. "I'm not contagious, mom. I'm not going to make anyone sick," she insisted with a voice a bit too insistent.

"I know dear, I'm not worried about you making them sick," her mother replied, ignoring her daughter's tone of voice. "I worry about them making you sick."

As she was leaving the house she shouted to her husband in the kitchen. "Have a good time hunting. Please be careful. And please bring home dinner!"

Jarad popped his head around the corner and gave his wife a wink. "Always aiming to please," he said with a silly grin, pleased with his pun. "We're taking orders. Anything particular?"

"Yes," she said with playful seriousness. "Something with a lot of meat!"

Jarad chuckled. "Well, that's pretty specific, but we'll do are best. We're gonna have a bang up good time."

He gave his wife a stern, but soft look in the eyes. "Seriously, babe, be careful."

His wife nodded. "I will be. But I got my helper here, I'll be alright."

+++

Myla's first stop was Otty's house. She didn't get to talk with him at the funeral and she wanted to see how he was doing with his ribs. Physically, he said, he felt fine. He believed that he would be near normal in a couple of weeks. Perhaps his ribs weren't as seriously hurt as they first thought. Myla agreed. That was good news. An omen she hoped.

Her next two stops were not as hopeful. Each was an elderly couple and all of them showed signs of pneumonia: fever, deep chest congestion, shortness of breath, and a heavy cough. And there was absolutely nothing she could do. Surprisingly, this didn't bother her. Was she becoming hardened, she wondered. No, just realistic. But she wasn't indifferent. She encouraged them to maintain fluid intake and keep indoors. She also promised to send over one of the older boys to help stock up their wood supply and do any other chores that might be needed. Then she moved on.

She got no response from her tapping on the door at her fourth stop. She pounded louder and called out, "Chelsea" in a loud voice. She twisted the handle and felt it release in her hand. Unlocked, of course. She helped herself into the warm but dark house. "Chelsea, are you here," she called. First she searched the two rooms that Chelsea had made into her quarters, and then the rest of the house. She was afraid that she would find the old woman slumped over and dead in a cold room. Instead, there were no ghosts to be found.

"Maybe she's visiting someone," her daughter suggested, her voice muffled by the mask. "Maybe she is at Emil's house."

Her mother nodded. "I'll leave a note," she said, glancing about for a scrap of paper.

She skipped a couple stops as she had visited with those folks at the funeral. So she headed for her final and farthest stop: Howard's house. As she walked down the narrow, snowbound path back toward her own home, she wondered what would become of all of them. Not just herself and her family, but the people that made up the community of Blue River. She had little doubt that more of the elderly would perish. There was nothing that could be done to help them fight this battle, beyond the most basic assistance. Either they would survive or they would not. And there was still a lot of winter to come. She wasn't optimistic.

As they passed their house, Myla told her daughter that she could go ahead and stay at home if she wanted. Annie declined. "I like being with you, mom, and this is interesting."

Myla chuckled. "Interesting? I figured you'd be bored."

"Not at all, mom. I feel like I'm helping. And I like wearing the mask." Myla reached over and wrapped her arm around her daughter's shoulder and pulled her close. The two walked side-by-side, heads touching. Neither saying a word. "I wish this was a normal world for you, honey," she said softly to her daughter.

"I like it mom, its a better world. I like living here better than Purcell. Though I sometimes miss my friends. Cameron and I both like it better."

Myla stopped and looked at her daughter with a quizzical mien. "Really? I thought you'd have missed the televisor, shopping, school, all of those things."

Her daughter shook her head. "No, not really. Sometimes. But I like it here. Its slower and I get to see you and dad a lot more. I like that. And I get along with Cameron better. And I like Jimmy." She blushed. "The only thing I really miss are potato chips and long, hot baths. I miss hot baths!"

"Me, too, sweetie," Myla said, giving her daughter a kiss on the head. They continued down the path toward Howard's house, arm in arm.

A small flock of crossbills chattered overhead in a grove of Douglas-firs, indifferent to the two women walking down the grade below them, while the Blue River gave up a dull roar that faded in and out as the path weaved to the left and right following the path used by animals and humans alike. The walking was easy, though a good snowfall would necessitate the return to snowshoes.

Myla liked Howard. She found him to be an independent spirit who spoke his mind and who was wholly indifferent to what people might think of him. He was a kind soul who only veiled himself behind the stern visage of an old coot. This book, she knew, should not be judged by its cover. Though she hadn't known him long, he always seemed to surprise her.

Arriving at the door of his house Myla removed her mitten and gave the door a couple of raps with a knuckle. She waited for Howard's normal command to enter, but only heard the staccato of barks coming from Bitsy, his dog. She waited a couple moment more, but still Howard hadn't responded. She gave the door another series of raps. Still no response. "Oh, no," she said in a fearful hush.

She tried the door, but it resisted her efforts. She swore, which surprised her daughter, who had rarely heard her mother ever use profanity. This only worried Annie, seeing her mother in such a state.

The two of them moved to the back of the house. Myla wanted to try the back entrance or at least peek in through the windows to see if she could see Howard. Her mind's eye imagined him on the floor or dead in bed. She was determined to get into the house even if she needed to force an entry.

The back door was locked as well. She cupped her hands against her face as she peered through the glass panes, trying to see inside the shadow-darkened interior. She knew that the wood stove was operating because of the smoke that lingered lightly in the still air. The dog had stopped barking, though Myla could hear it whining on the other side of the door. This added to her concern.

"We need to get inside," she told her daughter as she looked around the outside of the house as if searching for ideas.

"Can we open a window?" Annie asked.

"Grand idea," her mother said with encouragement. "I'm glad I brought you along."

The two of them started testing windows, trying to push up on any that they could reach, the heels of their palms under the window frames that held the sliding panes. Nothing budged. "Damn it!" Myla exclaimed in frustration.

"Find a rock," she shouted at her daughter, "or something hard. I'm going to break a window." The two of them looked around the area, trying to find something in the snow covered deck and landscape that might serve as a means to bust a window pane. "Here," Annie shouted at her mom, coming from behind the corner with a small ax. "Perfect," her mother said, taking it from her.

Myla returned to the back door, determined to break the lower pane and reach in and unlatch the lock. She waved her daughter away and then swung the little ax with both hands, which met the window with a sharp and loud shattering of glass. A roar came from inside the house.

"What the hell is going on!" a man's voice called out in anger. A dark shadow moved in the interior and the curtain was pulled away from the now pane-less rear door. The grizzled, but bewildered face of Howard stared out at Myla and Annie. Howard, without his glasses, squinted as he tried to focus on the surprised faces. He saw the ax in Myla's hand. "Myla," he growled, "why the hell are you trying to break into my house?"

"Oh, I'm so sorry Howard. I was making my rounds, and. . . you didn't respond when I knocked. I was worried you might be sick in bed. . . or worse."

"I'm fine!" he said with a wheezy cough. "Or at least I was until you started breaking down my door."

A woman's voice called from the bedroom behind Howard. "Who is it Howie?" Myla knew that voice instantly. It was Chelsea. She closed her eyes, suddenly realizing why Howard didn't respond like he normally did. He was busy. Howard didn't answer Chelsea's questioning. He just glared at Myla.

"Well, I see you're fine. I'll let you get back to . . . . whatever you were doing. So sorry. I'll send Jarad down to fix your window. . . ."

"It's fine!" he snapped. "I'll fix it myself."

"Howie?" the voice called out again.

"Coming," he responded over his shoulder. He gave Myla one last glare and then flung the curtain over the gaping hole. Myla gently set the ax down near the door, away from the snow, and grabbed her daughter's arm. "Let's go. He's fine." And the two headed back quickly in the direction they had just come.

+++

Jard should have been exhausted, but instead he felt energetic and ready to go. He supposed he was finally getting into shape physically, at least better shape than he had ever been in his adult life. His ability to dig two graves, well, at least help dig two graves and then spend the rest of the day tromping through the snow in pursuit of game proved that he had never been stronger. But he knew he would sleep well that night, assuming life didn't deal him any more surprises.

The day had become indifferent, neither particularly sunny nor overcast, not cold nor warm. In fact, it was quite still. Oddly so. Perhaps a storm was coming? he asked himself. It was times like this that Jarad realized how disconnected he was from the world around him. Even though he grew up in a very small town, he was still a city-boy at heart. And nothing demonstrated this better than his inability to read the signs of nature around him. But he was learning.

Champ proved very adept at flushing hares. The key was to not accidentally shoot him when they shot at the hares. But invariably, as Champ took off after one hare, another stood near by, frozen against the backdrop of snow, betrayed only by the black tips of their long white ears. It didn't take Cameron long to figure this out and it was these by-standers that he would turn the sights of his .22 on. Soon they had themselves four hares. Enough for the day, Jarad decided. "We want to save some for next time," he joked.

They had intentionally hunted to the west of Blue River. This was because Jarad knew that there we no homes here, and also because he was curious. He knew that somewhere far to the west, some six or seven miles, was the dome home. He was forever curious about this building. If anything, he did find that the road was level and clear, only criss-crossed by animal trails.

They were done hunting, but Jarad wanted to hike a little bit further down the road. As they did so, Champ suddenly came bursting through the underbrush toward them. He was yelping in fear. Jarad immediately kneeled down to hold the dog and brought a finger up to his mouth, indicating to Cameron to be silent. Something had spooked the dog and Jarad wanted to see what it was. Suddenly a huge dog pushed through the underbrush, but skid to a stop when it caught sight of Jarad and Cameron. The large animal tried to quickly return in the direction it had come, but it lost its footing on the snow and fell on its side. Just as quickly, it recovered and bounded up and disappeared in the thickets.

"That was a wolf," whispered Jarad to his son. Cameron's eyes grew in size as he considered what his father had just said. He handed the rifle to Jarad. "Here, dad, just in case." Jarad noticed that his son was shaking a bit in fear. He cast him a smile to let him know that there was no danger; trying to calm his nerves. Taking the gun, he waved at his son to follow him and he took off in the direction of the wolf. Champ trailed reluctantly behind both of them.

Jarad followed the tracks through the snow, which headed off to the northwest. The terrain quickly got steep, causing him to lose interest in the pursuit. But he knew that if there was one, there were probably more.

"Why are they here, dad?" Cameron whispered to his father as they both rested, while scanning the underbrush for signs of movement.

"They were probably hunting and Champ stumbled upon them. Wolves will eat dogs. But they are probably coming down from the mountains, following the game. I suspect that since it is quiet around here now, no vehicles, chainsaws, and that sort of thing, they are coming closer than they normally would. Kind of exciting, huh?"

"Kind of," Cameron agreed.

"Come on, let's go home."

They turned toward the downward slope when Champ began to growl, his ears back and his teeth bared. Looking up, Jarad and Cameron found themselves almost surrounded by a dozen ghosts, so silently did the wolves appear. Some of them paced, but most just stood at guard and watched with inscrutable eyes the two people and dog. The hairs on Jarad's neck rose in alarm, sending a shiver of alarm through his body.

Jarad hadn't intended to be afraid of the wolves, for he knew that they didn't hunt or attack people. But now he wasn't sure. They appeared to be very threatening. He pulled the bolt back on the rifle and fired a shot into the air. Instantly the wolves scattered in all directions, as silently as they appeared. Champ's growls turned into whimpers. "It's okay, boy," he said to the dog, rubbing his brown curly flanks, feeling the animal shivering under his caresses. He looked at his son, who still wore an expression of disbelief. "Let's get out of here," he said with a forced smile and chuckle. With one last glance around them, they dashed down the slope as quickly as they could.

+++

It was nice to be home and sitting around the table. Myla had commented with a mouthful of roasted rabbit how a good meal put everyone in a good mood. Myla and Jarad had both shared with each other their experience from that day. Though Myla expressed concern about the wolves after hearing about her husband's and son's adventure, Jarad had laughed so hard when he heard about the window at Howard's house he almost fell off of his chair. He was still guffawing, tears streaming from his eyes, when there was a rap at the front door. With a shout of welcoming the door opened to reveal the bright eyes of Genis. "Something smells good," he said with a smile. "Room for one more at the table?"

Jarad and Myla were both delighted to see Genis and they met him with a barrage of questions. "I see I'm going to have to earn my dinner," he said in jest. "Well then, food first, words second." So, while Genis ate the other two adults were able to recapitulate their stories afresh. He expressed interest in the wolves, and like Jarad, laughed so hard at Myla's tale about the window that she blushed.

"I guess it is funnier than I thought," she said with a grin. After a bit, they were able to share other news about the community, such as the increasing sickness among the elderly and the deaths of Breanne and Sarah. Genis was saddened to hear about Sarah, but predictably seemed indifferent about Breanne. "And so it goes," was all he said.

Genis polished off everything that was left over. Of anything in the world he enjoyed food most of all, which one would not suspect judging by his lean figure. Finally, after every last scrap had been consumed and with a cup of coffee in his hand, he got up from the table and said "My turn." He then retired to the single overstuffed wing-backed chair in the front room.

"Alright, where do I start," he said with a look of satisfaction. He said that he really only had a couple things to share. First, he was getting married! "Emma has decided to make an honest man out of me," he said with grin.

"When?" Annie asked with excitement.

"As soon as I can, which brings me to my second announcement. "We've all been invited to move to Junction."

"Whose we?" Jarad asked, unsure.

"All of us. The entire community," he replied. He then when on to explain how the leaders of Junction wanted the folks at Blue River to join their community. "It only makes sense," Genis explained. "They have more resources, plenty of homes to occupy, and they need our help."

"That's interesting though," Jarad mused, "that they need our help. What do we offer them?"

"Us," Genis stated succinctly. "Myla knows medicine, you know security, and I'm a decent roustabout. And, they don't have a preacher. Otty can do that. But most of all, they are facing a threat from those damn raiders. I promise you this, either we go help them or they're going to be pushed our way." He shrugged. "Anyhow, I'd rather have access to their resources down there than our very limited resources up here," he said with a swirl of his hands. "I told 'em, sign me up!"

Genis got up and poured himself a second cup of coffee, weighing the pot in his hand to see how much was left. Resuming his seat, he talked about the other things he saw and the people he talked with while visiting the Junction. But mainly he talked in worried tones about the threat posed by the raiders and how they were requiring constant vigilance at the border. "Anymore, they have to keep two or three people constantly on guard. Fortunately, it is fairly easy to control the bridge." Jarad knew that Jarad was referring to the bridge that spanned the deep Blue River gorge as it sped southeast toward the flatland. In the winter and spring, at least, it would be impossible to cross the river without using the bridge.

"What about to the north?" Jarad asked.

"They keep it manned, but only with one person. So far, no problems with any people from the north."

They talked a bit more, but after his second cup of coffee was finished Genis got up to leave. "I'm gotta go see Otty and then check on a few folks. Then I'm gonna hit the sack. We'll talk more later."

After he left, a melancholy mood lingered in the room. Without expressing it, neither Jarad nor Myla liked the thought of leaving. It wasn't because what Genis had to say didn't make sense, the problem was that it did make sense. Perfect sense. It was the thought of leaving. Neither of them were ready for that big of a change in their lives. Not so soon. They were still finding their way after that flight from Purcell and they felt safe here. Secure. But now Genis goes and throws a monkey wrench in the gear works and suggests the very opposite. Effectively, Genis reminded them that their sense of security was a mirage, soon to be revealed by an onslaught of marauding raiders. Images of those men firing through the breach in the brick wall at the Liberty Ranch appeared before Jarad's eyes. He knew it was going to be another restless night.

+++

Chapter 20

Jarad stayed home the next day to split wood. He didn't want to go anywhere and he didn't want to see anyone. He just wanted to stay home and spend time with his son, and since firewood always needed splitting, it was as good excuse as any. So that was what he did. The next day was Christmas, which meant that he would be attending the community dinner and church service. He would be plenty busy tomorrow with errands and visiting. Excuse enough to make the day a stay-at-home day.

But that didn't preclude others from coming to visit him. First it was James and Jimmy. They just wandered by and decided to help Jarad with his chore. Jarad knew that they were being neighborly, but he didn't want any help. He wanted to be alone, but he was unsure how to tell them without hurting feelings. Finally, he told them about the wolves and where they might see them. Jimmy got the idea that he would love to have a wolf hide to tan, so he and his father gracefully backed out of helping Jarad and dashed back home to get their rifles.

Jarad's next visitor was Otty. He was on his way to see Howard. He had a chess board tucked up under the arm of his overcoat. Otty asked him if he had a chance to talk with Genis about the proposed move and what his thoughts were. Jarad indicated that he and Myla weren't opposed to it, but that they were quite content in Blue River and weren't particularly interested in moving at this time. Otty agreed with the sentiment, but he thought that a move might be best for most of the people in the community, and he might end up supporting it for that reason alone. But he said that a meeting was planned for next week and he and Myla were, of course, invited to attend. Jarad said that they would come. With that Otty continued on his way with a wave and a hearty "Merry Christmas."

Jarad stopped and took a deep breath of the cold air, glancing around the premises. This was his home now. This was the home of his parents, at least after a fashion, and he did have some memories that tied him to Blue River. And the past few months had welded his sentiments to this place. He felt he had invested a part of his soul into Blue River and, rational or not, he wanted to continue his life in the here and now. But just looking at his son, who seemed to be growing physically and emotionally by the week, reminded him that nothing ever stayed the same. And if he had paid attention, he would have seen this in Purcell.

+++

It was Christmas and Jarad was both curious and excited about the evening service as he slowly strolled with his family through the cold, but starry night toward the church. The last time he had attended a genuine Christmas service was as a child. As he and his children weaved through the darkened trees, he explain to them how churches many years ago had abandoned the term Christmas and adopted "Solstice" instead, because it was considered more friendly, and perhaps socially and politically expedient. In time, this idea was taken on by the larger community and soon children came to expect a Solstice break from school during the winter rather than a Christmas break. It was only recently that Jarad had begun to consider the significance of the difference, so easy and smooth was the transition made during his youth. It was a strange feeling to be intentionally going to this evening service, since only those labeled as ignorant, intolerant, or zealous still observed "Christmas." Cultural baggage was often a load to bear, he mused.

The meal was a communal affair, though people now sat closer together and more as a cohesive unit. The conversation was more animated and there was a general sense of ease and amity. Jarad enjoyed this, for it was a feeling that he really hadn't felt often before in his life. Perceptively, he began to better understand why his children preferred living in Blue River with all of its shortcomings and deprivations, than in Purcell, which seemed to have everything. Everything but a true feeling of community. Otty had once described this feeling as a product of something he called *gemeinschaft* association. Jarad didn't really understand intellectually what that meant, but he could understand it with his heart.

One thing he did notice, though, was the fact that there were fewer people here than he expected. People were sick and were either unable or unwilling to make the slow, slog through the dark cold to the church. For a moment, Jarad wondered if he should be offering rides on the snowmobile and be shuttling people back and forth. But, just as quickly he dismissed the idea, knowing that he couldn't sacrifice the battery charge. That sled still needed to return to Junction and it would be worthless without power. In some ways it was their life line.

After a few words Otty gave the blessing and everyone got up to pass through the line of food. The selection was surprisingly rich and varied. Obviously some treats, such as yams and apples, had been hoarded for this occasion. Jarad was glad because the thought of fresh apple pie and candied yams was almost too good to be true. He felt like a child and wanted to dash to the front of the line or take extra portions. But he used restraint in both areas. He caught Myla's glance and knew she felt the same way. They both smiled over the feast to be had.

Jarad couldn't believe his good fortune. Roasted turkey with gravy, green beans in mushroom sauce, real mashed potatoes, and fresh stewed cranberries. Plus there was more pies and cakes available afterwards than everyone could eat. This was truly a merry Christmas! But he also knew that the community had used up much of its reserves and the pickings would be slim after this. Hopefully the next few house raids would make up the difference. Immediately, a deep-seated fear of the future began to express itself in his conscious mind. Reflexively he pushed it back by concentrating on an over-sized mouthful of gravy-drenched turkey. Everything in its time, he thought to himself as he moaned audibly. "This is so good," he said slowly.

"Yup, it is," agreed Cameron with enthusiasm, "but I want some of that cherry pie. Did you see it dad? Cherry pie!"

No one hurried through their meal, because to the hungry food is the staff of life. The needs of the heart and spirit would be met in time, but there was still a variety of other dishes to explore. And then, of course, dessert and coffee. Conversation had ebbed as folks focused on their meals. Even the children were still, each begging permission to get a second helping when the opportunity presented itself.

Slowly, forks and knives were retired to rest on empty plates and coffee cups were drained for a final time. Otty made a remark that maybe the evening service would have to postponed a day so everyone could recover from the orgy of eating. Some laughed, but others agreed, not realizing that he made the comment in jest.

Finally, people began to move toward the sanctuary, first a few and then the rest of the flock followed the lead. Dirty dishes were set in tubs of water to soak and would be cleaned another day. It was already late and many felt that nice, smug, rummy feeling that comes from culinary indulgence, and each hoped that the coffee would keep them sufficiently awake during the service.

But there was little to fear, for the service was both artistically and spiritually satisfying. To everyone's surprise, because they never realized he possessed such skill, Emil played a solo rendition of Bach on his violin. The music was perfect for the moment and Emil played on and on, everyone hoping that the tune would never end. But it did as he slowly eased the piece to a masterful and loving end, tears tracking down his white whiskered cheeks. No one dared to clap, instead they loudly whispered their thanks. Emil acknowledging them with a mute smile and nods of his head as he slowly moved from the front of the congregation to a wooden pew to his left.

He was replaced by the stout figure of Brittany Freese, who slowly made her way up the steps to the piano that sat to one side of the altar. After making herself comfortable and effusively praising Emil, she led the congregation through a series of old time Christmas hymns. Everyone sang boisterously, expressing the joy of the moment. But Jarad wondered if these feelings were transcendent to the moment. Tonight he was really feeling good about his predicament, this new life in Blue River and the sense of belonging he felt. Inwardly, he was silently amazed that at his age he had never felt these feelings before. He had talked with Myla about these feelings a few days earlier, during a quite spell at home when the kids were out and the two of them had a rare opportunity to make love during the day. She acknowledged that she, too, was feeling similarly. It was, as she described it, a Little-House-on-the-Prairie moment.

"As a family, these hard times have brought us closer together. I guess we are more of a team that we've ever been. Just like in those stories," she had mused as she lay in his arms. He looked at his wife, who was singing with vim, her body swaying to the tune. She didn't notice him. He smiled at her anyway and returned to the music. Life was good, he thought. No, life was great – at least right at that moment.

The singing eventually faded, if only because as voices began to fail people began to resettle on the pews, their bodies played out from the excess. Otty then took the pulpit and, as it was his turn, thanked both Emil and Brittany for their efforts. He then gave his Christmas address, though he didn't speak long. His message compared the hope that came with that new beginning in Jerusalem, so many years ago, with the hope of this new beginning in Blue River. He spoke of what he knew and what he saw, and how the small community of Blue River was on the cusp of a new start. Indeed, this was true for everyone present. Jarad knew the message rang true and though his mind was willing his body was weak, and the meal, the singing, and that morning spent splitting wood, all worked together to cause him to fade. He was falling asleep!

He found himself climbing a snow-covered hill when suddenly he began to slide backwards. He grasped at the underbrush around him, but couldn't secure his grip. He fell on his back and saw branches overhead blur past his field of view as he slid backward, flailing, down the hill. Suddenly, he hit a tree or some other obstacle and he was startled . . . awake. Someone was shaking his arm.

"Jarad," he heard his wife whispering loudly in his ear, "wake up!" He opened his eyes to see that all the faces in the congregation were pointed at him, some smiling, some frowning. He looked up at Otty, you returned his look with a bemused grin.

"You were snoring, dad," said Annie. He blushed and instantly the congregation erupted into laughter, albeit a kind laughter. Jarad looked at his wife. She was laughing along with everyone else.

"And with that I close, but. . ." he paused, building expectation in the congregation, "now we have a special presentation from our students."

With that cue all the students got up from their pews and hurried off with rapid steps and squeals of delight to the makeshift stage to the right of the podium. Then with the encouragement and couching of Lori Hobson and Brittany Freese the children gave their various performances. Annie sang a song with her friend Trina and with Jimmy. Her brief solo part brought damp eyes to her mother. Cameron limited his public performance to playing the part of the innkeeper in a brief skit. His dialog was limited to "no room, nor\ room in the inn" to an eleven year old Mary with a plastic baby Jesus.

Afterwards all the students were called out for their collective bow, which was greeted by an enthusiastic and partisan standing ovation. The kids were obviously proud and each felt a keen satisfaction with a job well done.

Otty returned to the podium and with a grin sent everyone home. "Merry Christmas Blue River," he said "Let's all get to bed." As people were standing, a voice called out to the congregation. It was Genis.

"Hold on a second, everyone, I want to say a word." Everyone turned to see him, as he walked quickly to the front of the pews.

"First off, Merry Christmas," he said loudly. Voices called out in kind. Then he continued. "Some of you have heard and maybe some of you haven't, but I'm gonna get married." In response those words, there was another uproar of voices, intermingled with clapping. Genis put up his hands, batting the air with his palms out, a large smile on his face, as he tried to continue with his words. "But that isn't why I am keeping you all here for a few extra moments. I also want you to know that I am moving to Junction. And, on behalf of that community, I want to invite the rest of you to follow me there." He then went on to explain the broader outline of his idea and invited everyone to a community meeting to discuss it. "I just wanted you to have something to think about. See you in a couple days."

Then, people again made their way toward the exits. But now the voices had died down and the laughter had been replaced with silence. The moment had lost its magic.

+++

It was a beautiful night as Jarad and Myla and their children made their way home. The stars seemed exceptionally brilliant. They didn't carry a lantern, since they had long learned to make their way through the darkness, though the quarter moon was trying to do its part to simplify their task. But Jarad and Myla were quiet, considering Genis's words. Too bad he hadn't spoken earlier and not after Otty, Jarad thought to himself.

The kids were chatty all the way home. They were pleased with their performances tonight and excited about finally discovering what lay under the Christmas tree. And their enthusiasm proved contagious and soon Jarad and Myla were infected. Jarad challenged them to a race home to see who would get to open their present first. But Myla nixed the idea. "No broken bones," she warned. With their melancholy lifted, Jarad and Myla began to enjoy the night sky and the beauty around them.

Getting home they quickly went through the routine of stoking the fire and bringing in wood for the night. While the kids hurried through these minor chores, Myla put on some water to boil. She had been saving some packets of instant hot chocolate for weeks, for this very occasion.

The family gathered around the tree. It had begun to dry out, as Jarad had simply nailed the tree to a couple of crossed boards. It had no water and needles were beginning to shed. But it was still beautiful with its red bows made from colored paper, the strings of popcorn laced with the occasional cranberry, and topped with a tinfoil star. Champ especially enjoyed the Christmas tree, once he discovered the popcorn which he deftly nibbled off the twine where he could reach it. This explained why most of the bands of popcorn had migrated toward the top of the tree.

The two children sat in anticipation, eyes shifting from their presents to their parents and then back again. This behavior by her kids really pulled at Myla's heart as she didn't want them to be disappointed by their gifts. Her choices had been so limited and . . . she just hoped for the best.

"Here's your cocoa," she said as she distributed the cups, "careful, they're hot."

Jarad watched from the table. He felt a strangeness in this moment. He knew that the tree really was pathetic and the children were only getting one gift each. This was so unlike previous years. When they packed the car to flee Purcell they did not take their tree ornaments. Only essentials. He also rued the fact that he hadn't even gotten his wife a single thing and there lay a present from her to him. He blew on the cocoa before taking a sip. Quit the pity party, he said to himself. "Wow, great cocoa, honey. Thanks" He gave her a wink.

"Okay twins, you can open up your presents one at a time," Myla said. "Who is first?" The two kids looked at each other and

said simultaneously "rock, paper, scissors," and immediately began
pounding a fist over an open palm. "Best two out of three,"
Cameron insisted.

First round, rock beats scissors. Annie won. Second round,
paper beats rock. Cameron won. Last round, scissor beats paper. "I
win!" shouted Cameron, victoriously taking his present from under
the tree.

He carefully untied the string that secured the colored paper
to the present.   Myla hadn't been able to find any tape. His actions
were in stark contrast to prior Solstices when the kids would rip
recklessly through the wrappings of paper, tossing them aside. But
now he was careful to save both the string and the paper, without
being asked to. Truly his perception about the world around him had
changed and he was adjusting on his own.

"Holy cow! Binoculars!" Cameron shouted. "Awesome.
Dad, we can use these for hunting!" He lifted the small pair of
binoculars to his face and tried to focus on things in the room. He
took them to show his father. "Aren't they cool?" he asked, more in
confirmation than in question. "Lucky duck, son," Jarad said
approvingly. "Maybe I can borrow them sometime?"

"Always dad, anytime! I'm going to go look at the stars. . .
can I mom?"

Myla was glad her son was happy. It was always stressful
for her when she got the kids presents which they hadn't requested.
"Yes, of course, but wait for Annie to open her gift."

Annie also carefully untied her present. It was smaller than
her brother's. Once the little cardboard box was free of it wrapping,

she lifted open the top. Immediately she cooed in delight, "Oh!" she said, flashing a knowing smile at her mother. Carefully she pulled four little bottles of nail polish from the box. "Mom, these are beautiful," she said as she carefully laid them on her lap. "Can I try one?"

"Of course you can, honey," Myla said kindly, relieved that her daughter was pleased. In so many ways, Annie was the more challenging of the two twins when it came to presents. "But there is still one more thing in the box. You better check again!"

Annie's face showed that she was both perplexed and excited. She reached into the cardboard and fished out a long, plastic elastic thing that looked like a stretched out comb. "What is it?" she asked, with a hint of confusion in her voice.

"Let me show you." Myla responded, "It is perfect for your long hair"

Annie brought it to her mother, who patted the seat next to her, inviting Annie to sit down. Annie sat and then her mother guided her through the process. "Lean forward and let all of your hair hang down," she said. "That's right! Now wait and let me show you." She reached around her daughter's shoulders and place the fancy contraption around the base of her hair. "Now flip your head up and let your hair fall back." Annie did as she was told and her long locks folded over the plastic piece, which Myla then clip together at the top. "Now shake your hair," she instructed her daughter. Annie did. "It's staying in place," she said with satisfaction. "That's cool!"

"And it makes your hair look beautiful," her father added, encouragingly. Annie gave her mother and father both kisses on the lips. "Thank you mom, thank you dad, this is a *wonderful* gift," she said, dragging out the vowels. She then ran off to the bathroom to look at her image in the mirror.

"And now for our gifts," Myla said, crinkling her nose playfully. "You first, I already know what mine is." She chuckled and handed her husband his present.

Like his children, Jarad carefully opened the package. "You're so sweet, and I didn't get you anything," he said.

"Yes you did, keep unwrapping," she said, putting her hand out to retrieve the string and paper from her husband. These things would be put away and reused.

Jarad's present wasn't in a box, but a paper bag. Having removed the string and wrapping paper, he unrolled the top and reached inside. He pulled out a large jar of peanut butter. "Peanut butter!" he said with a shout. "I love peanut butter. And I have been craving it for months!" He looked around the room and noticed that the kids were gone. "Do I have to share it," he asked with mock seriousness.

"Yes you do, but I'll share mine with you." With that Myla quickly opened up the present she gave to herself, giggling as she as did so. Teasing her husband she slowly pulled the surprise out of bag. "Chocolates!" she said with relish.

"Looks like we got some negotiating to do, sweetheart," he said with a hint in his voice.

"Yes, and let the negotiations begin," she responded with a smile, moving near to her husband. He drew her close to himself and gave her a long kiss on the mouth. "Merry Christmas, lover," he said softly. She rubbed his nose with her own. "So, what do you want to trade for a piece of chocolate?" she whispered.

Suddenly the room erupted. "Peanut butter!" the twins shouted at the same time. Jarad was shaken from his reverie. He laughed at the kids. "Ask me again, tonight," he told his wife, patting her on the arm. " I am sure we can come to terms." As he got up from the chair Myla playfully smacked him on the rump. "Darn tooting!" she said, giggling.

+++

Chapter 21

The Christmas season was a difficult time for the Blue River community. Not only because of the specter of death and illness that seemed to touch every thought and conversation, but the season itself reminded everyone of their deprivation. They were truly living a hand-to-mouth existence and most realized that they – individually and collectively – could not survive another winter under these conditions. If this was the future then the future was bleak.

Genis's news about his upcoming wedding and move to Junction set in motion a general movement toward that community. Few could argue against the logic of moving to Junction and even fewer could defend the saneness of staying put in Blue River. The world seemed to be a dangerous place and there was no evidence anywhere that it would be getting better soon. Strength was in numbers and not the other way around. Otty had commented that if the threat of raiders hadn't existed, people might be content to stay where they were. But most came to the realization that Junction had more resources than Blue River, and there was no way that Blue River could accommodate Junction if they were forced to come their way.

In addition, people respected Genis. On par with Otty, Genis was adored by the people of the area and his opinion carried a lot of weight. He was a proven quality and if Genis thought that moving to Junction was in everyone's best interest, than it was. Simple as that. Yes, people did not want to give up their homes, but living on the cusp of life and sanity was a powerful motivator to seek security. And Junction seemed to offer this in spades.

Genis acted as liaison for the move. He shuttled between Junction and Blue River almost daily on a snowmobile. Even before News Years Day, which was also set to be his wedding day, people were being transferred. Genis began with the oldest members of Blue River, most of whom had long ago "adopted" him as a son. Though the majority were still quite sickly due to the continuing illness that none could ever seem to shake, each was fostered into a home that could provide the care and shelter necessary for their recovery. Hopeful recovery, any how. This opening of the family homes by Junction people for Blue River folks only endeared the one to the other.

Not surprisingly the pressure on Myla to move to Junction was even greater than that placed on Jarad. After all, she was their "doctor" and the very person that Junction was most interested in obtaining as a resident. "But I am not a doctor and I don't want to leave," she insisted to Genis. "I don't care what you say, this is my home"

She was adamant, which suited Jarad just fine. He didn't want to leave their home, either. And it was simply that: Blue River was their home. As he reminded Genis, and anyone else who would listen, he was only eight miles from Junction. Three hours by foot in the summer. It wasn't the other side of the county!

Nonetheless, it was obvious that most everyone was going to move within a month's time. Otty himself suggested that it was in everyone's best interest and he and Ellie would probably make the transition later in the spring. Until then, he agreed to hold Sunday services in Junction. "I might as well," Otty thought to himself, "since most of my flock was heading there already".

But until then, there was still life to be lived in Blue River. New Years was approaching. Genis was going to be married. Jarad and Myla were making preparations to attend the ceremony and spend a few days in Junction. That is, until they got word from Otty who had just asked them to stay.

"I don't want to sound paranoid, and I especially don't want to sound as if I need to have my finger in every pie, but I do not feel comfortable leaving Blue River so . . ." he paused as he searched for the right word, "vulnerable. Does that make sense?"

Jarad nodded to Otty who sat across from him at the little table in their home. He knew that Otty often found himself in the position of a politician: every decision he made would make some people happy and some people not. He couldn't win.

"I understand. You want someone to watch over Blue River while you're gone. Makes sense. I would be just a guest at the wedding, you're the preacher. A wedding needs a preacher."

"Yes, thanks, that's right," he agreed with a masked sigh. Noticeably, Myla and Jarad both saw how relieved Otty looked.

"And there is one more thing." He paused again. "I am not sure what to make of this." He explained to Myla and Jarad what he had just heard from Howard, not twenty minutes earlier. "You know how hit and miss it has been with Howard on that radio of his, and of course his Spanish is pretty rusty, but he just told me about something he heard last night from a contact in Mexico. Their news is reporting that there is going to be a sign on New Years Day in the United States."

"A sign?" Jarad grunted. "That's weird? What can that possibly mean?"

"I have no idea. That is all we know," Otty replied. He raised his eyebrows and shrugged his shoulders. "It's supposed to be seen across the county, or at least what used to be the country. It is meant to somehow demonstrate federal control over the rebelling sections."

This shift in topic led the three of them into speculation of what this sign might be. They came to the conclusion that it had to be some sort of demonstration in space. "How else could the whole country see it?" Jarad ventured.

"And especially not with the televisor system down," Myla added. Both men shook their heads in agreement.

"Well, I got to go," Otty said, getting up from the table. "Thank you for agreeing to stay. That puts my mind to ease. And like you said, a wedding needs a preacher." He reached over and put his hand on Jarad's shoulder, who had also risen from the table. "We are both a lot alike, Jarad. Neither of us like change."

"Count me in with that, too," Myla laughed. "Sometimes I feel like I've lived my whole life here. For sure, I've lived here the most interesting part of my life!" She laughed again, which did Jarad's heart good. He was glad to see his wife relaxed. With most of the most sickly folks already moved to Junction, her burden had been lifted proportionately.

"Well, I am glad that the two of you are so flexible. I know that Blue River will be in safe hands." Otty moved to the door. "I'm off to get the wife and kids. Genis's coming later with a couple of snowmobiles pulling sleds. He insists that he can get all of us, Ellie, myself, the kids, and the dog to Junction"

Otty smiled one last time and left. "Happy New Years to the Traversons," he said with a wave.

"Good," Myla said, after the door closed. "I'm glad I don't have to pack. I'm glad we don't have to go. And I don't have a wedding present, anyhow!"

Jarad nodded in agreement as he sat down again and returned to his coffee. He stared at the dark mirrored surface, lost in his own thoughts. He was curious as to what was going on in the larger world, the one far from Blue River and the one that he once belonged to.

"What are you thinking about," Myla asked as she topped off his cup from the percolator. She sat opposite her husband, setting her coffee down in front of herself. "Are you worried about this 'sign'?"

"No, not really." He looked over at his wife. He appreciated her concern. They were truly a team. "Though it might be fun to spend New Years on the perch. Who knows, maybe we'll see something memorable. Like the first Mars landing. You know, memories to share with our grandkids and great-grandkids." He chuckled at the thought. "Grandkids, where did that come from?"

"The perch? We'd freeze to death," Myla chided him.

"We'll bundle up," he offered.

"Sounds fine. Hopefully we'll see something. Either way, I got a special treat for all of us planned for New Years."

"What, tell me," Jarad said to his wife, anticipation in his voice.

"Nope, I can't tell you, otherwise it wouldn't be a surprise," she insisted. "And don't get too excited, it isn't anything over the top. Just a treat. . . you'll see."

With that, Jarad got up from the table. "I'm heading to the church," he told his wife.

"What's at the church?" she asked.

"Maybe nothing. Maybe something. I need to look at Otty's maps. I just want to take another look at the area." He shrugged his shoulders. "No reason."

Myla eyed him with mock suspicion. "No reason, I bet," she said sternly, but with a smile. "Well, I'm not going anywhere. I have a date with a book."

+++

Jarad stopped long enough at the Oleson's place to get Otty's permission to review his maps. "Sure, go ahead. It's unlocked. Always feel free," he said, taking a break from his packing. Genis was had arrived and wasted no time in getting the few things the Oleson's were taking onto the snowmobile sleds. Jarad explained the decision he and Otty had come to and apologized for not coming to the wedding.

Genis gave him a hug and a smile. "Jarad," he said, "I just appreciate you willing to do whatever is needed." With that the two shook hands and Jarad headed for the church.

The church wasn't nearly as busy as it usually was. This was partly because there was no school scheduled for the week and partly because people were either busy preparing to move or had already moved to Junction. When Jarad first entered the building he notice how oddly quiet and dark it was, like one of the deserted homes that they raided. The only difference was the lingering warmth from the embers in the big wood stove. It would be cold again by tonight, he mused to himself.

He entered Otty's office and made straight for the bookshelf. He knew exactly what he was looking for and it only took him a moment to find it. He pulled the county atlas out from under a stack of papers and set it on the table in front of the window. He sat down and quickly found the page he wanted and examined it intently, elbows on the table and his chin resting on the foot of his palms.

"What am I looking for?" he asked himself. He wasn't sure what he wanted and he wasn't even sure he knew what he was doing. But for some reason he had convinced himself that this map was important. So he simply stared at it, following the contour lines has they ran east to west, north to south, and every other which way.

"There," he said quietly, positing a finger over a very small black square. He estimated the distance from the that black square to the church building, using the map scale as a reference. "Seven miles," he thought to himself. "Seven miles to the dome."

But this discovery didn't satisfy the subconscious prompting of his mind. "What am I looking for?" he asked himself again as his eyes traced the roads and ridge lines and . . . tracks!

That was it. He looked carefully at the tracks, following them from Junction to the left edge of the paper. He had to flip to the previous page to see where the tracks continued. And there it was. Now he knew why he was so unsettled about this whole issue of the map. Previously he didn't have the whole picture, but now he did. The tracks came up from Purcell, west to east. The grade wasn't steep, though it was a bit of a distance. And then it all made sense. Big foot, the giant Jonathan GILM. The man that attacked Otty had come up the tracks. And if he could make the trip. . .

At one level he found this realization very satisfying, answering a nagging question that had sometimes woke him up at night without consciously understanding why. But it unsettled him at another level. "Should I be worried about this access to Blue River from the West?" he asked himself. No, he realized, it wasn't Blue River that anyone would be interested in. It would be Junction. He just found the chink in Junction's armor.

He rushed back to Otty's place. He felt that he needed to warn Genis or Otty, just to be safe. But the web of snowmobile tracks in front of Otty's home told him he was too late. Damn, he thought to himself and cursed the fact that he didn't have a phone. Oh well, he tried to reassure himself, there was still time to warn them. After all, this was only conjecture and not fact. But that thought didn't ease his mind.

+++

The next day found Myla singing in the kitchen. She had decided that what she wanted was a clean house to welcome in the new year, so she might as well get started. It wasn't that this was something she did every year, but there was absolutely nothing on her schedule. No demands, no expectations, no tasks – nothing. As she didn't have anything else to do, why not clean house. It definitely needed it!

Actually, cleaning the house was a simple chore. Without electricity there were absolute limits as to how clean it could be gotten. A broom did most of it, though it wasn't very useful on the carpeting in the bedroom. Maybe Jarad could pull out the carpet in the summer, she thought. She would prefer just to have a wooden floor, even if it was only particle board. Assuming they were still living in this house. She paused for a moment. No, we're going to stay, she assured herself.

The only cleaner she had was automatic dishwasher detergent. It couldn't be used for its intended purpose since the dishwasher didn't work. But the detergent worked well in the wash bucket. And it did do a good job on the clothes. That was the biggest chore, washing clothes. James had made a bunch of wooden washboards which he handed out to whoever wanted them in the community. These washboards helped immensely, but the clothes still had to be wrung by hand and hung to dry. There was always clothes, or blankets, or other articles hanging over the wood stove. But Jarad and the kids had all learned to hand wash their own clothes, so it didn't all fall on her shoulders. And forget about ironing! Everyone wore wrinkled clothing. Clean was good enough. As she liked to remind herself, this was just like *Little House on the Prairie*. She was a pioneer.

+++

The family had played just about every game they knew.
Every board game, every card game, even charades and dictionary
game. Currently they were playing poker. Jarad had taught the kids
how to play, using green peas to bet with. "Save them when you're
done. This is tomorrow's dinner," Myla teased the kids, at least in
part. The hard peas would most assuredly be saved and used another
day in in a soup. But Cameron had developed an affinity for the
peas and was nibbling on them one at a time while he played. "You
better win or you are gonna starve," his father chided him, pointing
at his shrinking reserve of green bullion. Cameron thought that was
funny once he figured out the joke.

They were simply waiting for midnight. The kids knew all
about the "sign," and they each had their own idea as to what it
would be. Annie thought that the new international space station
would drop fireworks from space as it travel overhead. "You could
see them from across the world," she insisted. Cameron thought that
her idea was dumb. "How can you shoot off fireworks in space?
There's no air!" he said as if stating the obvious. His thesis was that
there would be special trains heading from the east coast to the west,
carrying important people around and telling everyone that things
were going to be okay. Jarad's thought was that Howard's contact
was wrong and nothing would happen. "Besides," he reminded
them, "it wouldn't be possible to send a sign to everyone in the
country without the televisor. Simply not possible."

After Jarad said this, Myla got an idea and shouted, "I know
what it is! I know what the sign is!" Jarad and the kids stopped

playing and looked up from their cards. "And?" Jarad asked, waiting.

"They are going to turn the electricity back on," she said with certainty. "Don't you see? *That* is the sign. Because whoever turned it off can turn it back on."

"Brilliant," Jarad said with sincerity. "But why?"

"Because whoever it is, General Abrahmson or whoever else it is that controls the government, would be proving themselves to be in control. At least, of the grid. And since the grid controls everything, everywhere, they would be flexing their muscles, so to speak. Especially if they coordinated turning on the power with the time zones. That would be something?"

"Yah, assuming anyone knew what time it actually was!" Jarad teased her.

They discussed it a bit more, Jarad becoming convinced that his wife was right. Oh how he wished he could tell others! He wondered how life would change with the power restored. Would they return to Purcell? Would he go back to being a cop? Was the country still the *united* States? And to finally know what was going on in the rest of the world. Oh my, he thought to himself.

"So, that means we can wait here. We won't need to go and freeze our noses off on the perch," Jarad said to his family .

"No!" the kids shouted. They both began to loudly insist that they still wanted to go to the perch. "We've been looking forward to it all day and night," Annie reminded him with exaggeration. "It wouldn't be fair. And what if mom is wrong? We'd miss something really important."

Myla laughed. "Come on Jarad, it's not like we have anything else to do."

He laughed in agreement. "Fine," he said with a smile.

Myla got up from the table. "Deal me out, I am going to make our special treat. It's going to be tricky, but I think I can do it."

"What is it," the kids asked, offering up their guesses. Candy? Pie? Pizza?

"Well, those are all nice treats, but it is something a bit more humble. I'm making us fresh, hot, home-made potato chips."

"Wow," Jarad thought. "More potatoes!" He laughed to let his wife know he was only teasing. "That would indeed be a treat. And now if we only had ketchup."

Myla opened up the cupboard and pulled out a bottle. "Voilà!" she said with a flurry. "You are full of tricks, woman," Jarad said with a smirk. "Kids, I think your momma is a genie."

"You mean a genius," insisted Cameron.

"That's my boy," said Myla.

+++

The potato chips didn't work out. Myla couldn't quite get the lard hot enough over the wood stove, and the resulting product was quite soggy. But, as Jarad noted, ketchup covers a multitude of sins and everyone found the chips to be delicious. Or more accurately, the ketchup. The four of them almost consumed the entire bottle.

They stayed close together as they marched to the perch. Jarad didn't want the kids to cross the narrow neck by themselves. Once they arrived and settled themselves it, the view was stupendous. The moon was waning and now just a sliver of itself. And the stars were bold and they flickered gamely in the crisp, night sky.

And then they waited. Cameron keep a vigilance facing downward, hoping to scope out any trains with his binoculars. Annie keep her vigil directed at the stars, knowing that at the strike of midnight there would be an eruption of fireworks. Jarad and Myla directed their attention toward each other, hugging closely. What a great way to keep warm, Myla thought to herself.

"One minute," Myla said with a glance at her watch. She had to dig to find her watch, since her life in Blue River didn't require it. Instead, time had become less absolute, but also more instinctive. It was hard to explain. A person always knew what time it was, but not according to a number.

Moments later Blue River was awash in light. Myla was right! All four of the Traversons turned around to see the fanfare. It was spectacular! Probably every structure in the community had at least one light come on. For the children it was a dazzling display They couldn't remember seeing such vivid imagery. For the two adults, it took their breath away. Not because of the lights themselves, but what they represented. The lights were manifestation of electricity. And electricity meant Purcell, a normal life, hot water, jobs, trips in the car, visits with the family, late-night television. It was the summation of all that they ever had, and all that was now lost. Did they want it back? Could they? Would they?

Compelled to see, Jarad turned away from Blue River and directed his face to the south. After his eyes readjusted to the dark, he noticed that much of Purcell was dark and still in the abyss. "Well, even if power does return," he thought to himself, "we could never go back to how thing were exactly before. Life had changed."

Though it only seemed like a few moments, the lights had shone for ten minutes. And just as suddenly they turned off, returning Blue River to her nocturnal sleep. The entire community was black except for a single lamp in the church, which flickered brightly and insolently. Both Jarad and Myla saw that defiant light, but were so absorbed in their own thoughts that they didn't consider what it meant. It was their daughter's questioning that brought them back to the present.

"Why is there still a light on at the church?" she asked her parents. Both of them turned in her direction as they grasped her words, and then toward the light that peeked through the trees. It didn't seem right. The power had been severed, but the light continued to burn. In fact, it was growing brighter.

"Oh no!" Jarad shouted. "That is not a light, that is a fire!"

He gathered up his family and safely ushered them across the isthmus of the perch and back to safety of the mainland, and then he dashed through the trees toward the church. To his horror the light grew in intensity and size the closer he approached the building. By the time he arrived, he was unsure how to proceed as flames were now reaching out through the windows of the community hall. He pushed through the entry way into the foyer and then stood helpless. The smoke was overwhelming. "Where are the fire extinguishers," he bellowed. He looked around, but the smoke and embers pushed him back. He couldn't breath, he couldn't see, and he realized that there was nothing he could do now except save his own life. He fought his way back toward the way he had come and stumbled out into the night, falling to the ground as he tried to regain his breath. His wife found him and kneeled down to hold him as he coughed harshly, barely able to snatch breaths. She then tried to pull him up and away from the developing firestorm that now had command over the complete building. Both of them stumbled to safety toward the shadows of the on-looking evergreens.

Once he regained command of his himself, Jarad leaned against a tree to watch the inferno. He didn't even speculate how the fire came about. It didn't matter. As far as he was concerned, the heart and soul of Blue River was lost. Forms moved among the trees as folks gathered to watch the flames. In the background, someone wailed forlornly. Jarad had had enough. He turned, hooked his arm through his wife's and headed back toward his home,

+++

Chapter 22

The destruction of Blue River Community Church was complete. Even the chimney had collapsed. The only thing that survived were the bells. Some said that the fire was a sign that God wanted Blue River to move to the Junction, but Otty wasn't convinced. "God works in his ways, but he doesn't play hardball," he said to the congregation that following Sunday.

Either way, the moves from Blue River to Junction continued unabated. Within a week's time only Jarad and his family remained. They still hadn't opted to move. They were going to stay. They were content. They would visit Junction frequently, but until their hearts were changed, they were going to sit tight. Try as he might, Genis couldn't convince either Myla or Jarad otherwise.

"Fine, but when you do change your mind, there is already a place – a very nice place – waiting for you," he reminded them. He was a little miffed, but he also knew that Myla and Jarad were doing what was right for themselves. Just as he did, when he made his move to Junction. They left Jarad and Myla a snowmobile and a sled, so when they did visit they wouldn't have to walk. "It has enough charge to get you there, but only enough." Genis reminded him.

Jarad did get the opportunity to address his concern about the rail bed being used as a point of incursion for raiders coming from Purcell. Both Otty and Genis were surprised and alarmed by the idea.

"I hadn't thought of that," said Otty, candidly. "It is so patently obvious now." Genis agreed, and felt that maybe this would be a good reason after all for Jarad to remain where he was. "You can be our advanced warning system, so to speak," he said in all seriousness. Jarad didn't say anything in return. He didn't want the responsibility.

It was strangely quiet in Blue River now that everyone had gone. But neither Myla nor Jarad had any regrets, at least not yet. They were truly at peace. At times Jarad felt almost guilty. Not quite, but almost. He had served so long in a position of public service that to not be continuing in that capacity felt selfish. Still, he understood that he was only one of many. Anyone in Junction could do what he did. He was not unique, he was not irreplaceable. He was just a man trying to make his way in the world.

Unfortunately the same could not be said of Myla. She was perceived by the people of both Blue River and Junction as being irreplaceable. And the pressure put on her would have been overwhelming if Jarad hadn't headed it off. He bluntly told Otty and Genis that his wife was not going to move to Junction and that they would have to figure out how to get along without her.

"She is not a doctor, how many times do I have to tell you that?" he practically shouted at Genis. "And a nurse is not some fifty-percent doctor. They are completely different. If Junction wants a doctor, then maybe they should raid Purcell for one! Okay?" That tirade wasn't really helpful, but it made him feel better.

Neither did Myla have regrets about staying. She felt that the sooner Junction weaned themselves off of this false perception of who she was, the better. Myla's deep fear was that something horrid would happen to someone and people would turn to her to make it all better. And she wouldn't know how. She could insert an IV, she could assess a patient's response to a medicine, and she could take vital signs. But she did not know how to set a bone, diagnose a disease, nor remove an inflamed appendix. After all, she was not a doctor and the sooner she could step out of that play-acting she was forced into by others, the better she'd feel.

There was plenty to do. No one was bored. Jarad spent his days gathering wood, hunting game, and scrounging for supplies. Myla helped in all of these things, as well as keeping the family together as a cohesive whole.

"You are our glue, baby," he once told her.

"And I love being stuck to you," she responded.

They were so busy and active in their lives that the first month passed so quickly that they could scarcely believe it. The trigger that reminded Jarad of the passing time was the moon. He was getting more dependent on nature to provide him with the ambient information he needed, as he became more skilled in assessing it. The moon was only a diminishing sliver on New Years day, and tonight there might very well be a new moon, that is, no moon at all. It would be dark. The significance was not lost on him.

By the middle of the afternoon he was pacing the floor. He couldn't help himself. Myla felt the building tension and asked him to explain what was wrong. He said, "I'll show you." He led her outside and up toward a clearing that gave a view of the tracks.

"That's what's wrong," he said pointing down toward the rail bed. "Now follow that track to the right and who could go all the way to Purcell. And it is an easy grade."

"What are you talking about, Jarad? You aren't making any sense."

"The moon!" he said emphatically. "The problem is the moon. It is going to be black tonight. Pitch black."

"And?" Myla asked, gesturing with her hands, laying them outward, questioning.

"And. . Oh shit!" he said quietly, pulling Myla down suddenly as he hunkered behind some shrubs. "Shhh" he repeatedly manically, obviously very upset. He stumbled backward onto his seat, breathing heavily.

"Jarad," she whispered sharply, "what is going on?" There was alarm in her voice. She had never seen her husband so upset.

"Raiders," he said as calmly as he could. "Follow me. We need to get back to the kids and get out of here."

He scrambled out on all fours directly away from the shrub and the tracks, heading for a cover of cedars to the far side of the path. Myla followed him as best as she could, though she couldn't quite keep up. Once she also reached the protection of the trees, they both stood and peered through the branches. There were men on the rail bed, all of them armed and walking single-file to the east. Some of them looked and pointed up toward the homes of Blue River.

Jarad and Myla followed the trail to their home, keeping a shield of trees between them and the raiders down below. Once they neared the house they quickly, but quietly entered from the front entrance instead of the mud room to the rear.

"Annie, Cameron, come here," Jarad shouted as quietly as he could. "Quickly."

The kids were in the loft playing a board game. "What," Annie called down. "Is that you, dad? What's wrong with your voice?" Cameron appeared looking over her shoulder. He was starting to pass her up in height.

He put his finger to his mouth to indicate their need to remain silent. "Come, we got to go, quickly," he told them with an earnest tension in his voice.

Myla was gathering up their snowsuits and boots. They would need to be warm. She dressed them as quickly as she could, while Jarad gathered up the automatic rifle and the cartridges. "Get what we need, honey," he told his wife as he peeked out of a window.

He went up to the loft to try to get a better view from up there. "Damn it!" he spat in a sharp whisper. "They are already at the border. We'll never make it to Junction now." Jarad felt cornered and wasn't sure what to do.

"We're going to take the snowmobile and head west," he told his wife. "Let's load up the kids. Champ will have to follow as best as he can."

Jarad peeked out the front door and then waved his family to follow him. He got the twins set in the sled and told them to hold onto the bundle of supplies that Myla had quickly gathered. "Hold on tight," he warned them. "Myla, hold on to me." Myla sat behind him on the snowmobile.

Before they took off, Jarad adjusted the sling on the M16 so it was draped over his left shoulder but under his right arm. This way he could pull it up quickly if necessary. He chambered a round. He hoped it wouldn't be needed.

He turned on the switch and curled the throttle. The snowmobile began to ease forward. Champ thought it was a game and began to bark. Jarad glared at the dog and whispered as loud as he dared, "Shut up, dog!"

He pulled ahead to follow the path forward. He had originally hoped that he could get out of harm's way and then return later, after the raiders had passed. But now he wasn't so sure. He realized that they might use Blue River as a resting spot before their assault on Junction. He wanted to be gone before they arrived.

Too late. As he crested the rise where the church had stood he came upon two armed men examining the ashes. When they saw Jarad they turned to fix their rifles on him, but he was able to fire first and he dropped them both with two short bursts. He scanned quickly to his left and right, and seeing no one else he directed the snowmobile past the church, down the trail and toward the end of town. He knew the gunfire would attract more raiders.

"Dad, there's more guys. Tons of them," his son shouted from the sled. "I think they're shooting at us." Jarad was surprised by the calmness in his son's voice. "I wish I felt the same," he thought to himself. Jarad couldn't hear any gunfire over the sound of the snowmobile, but his ears did detect bees zipping by his head.

He wondered if they were bullets or simply his imagination. When he passed Hobson's place he allowed himself a look over his shoulder. They seemed to have passed immediate danger.

He stopped the machine to consult with his wife. "Are we okay, are we okay," she kept repeating.

"Yes, yes, we seem to be," he said, consoling her. He checked on his children. They just stared up at him from the sled. "Where's the dog?" he asked. They looked around, just now realizing he was gone.

"That's okay, he'll find us," he said unconvincingly. Right now, the dog was his least concern.

He stood up on the snowmobile to get a better view from behind him. He couldn't see anything, but the sound of gunfire reminded him of his vulnerability. He didn't know if people were firing in his direction, but he didn't want to wait to find out. "Hold on, everybody," he shouted. The snowmobile bounded ahead for another couple hundred yards before he stopped again.

"Are we safe, Jarad. Should we stop?" Myla asked after the machine quited down. "I think so," he said softly. He was breathing hard, more from excitement than exertion. He dismounted from the snowmobile and got the binoculars from his son, who had to fish them out of a pocket. He ran a short distance down the path that the treads had made in the snow. He scanned the landscape with the glasses, the rifle hanging from his chest. He then returned.

"We're safe," he said, but looking around he wasn't so sure. He didn't know where he was. He had never traveled this far west from Blue River. "Where are we?" Myla asked. "I don't know," he said curtly.

He looked at his wife. She was concerned and she needed him now. There was no reason to be short-tempered. "I'm sorry honey," he said lamely, "too much adrenaline." She waved it off and checked on her children. They were silent and simply watched their parents. Neither making a sound.

He took off a glove and removed his hat, running his fingers through his hair. He didn't want to sit. He had too much energy flowing through his veins, and a little guilt as well. "This is my fault, I should have known," he said with a moan.

"What do you mean by that? How is this your fault," Myla challenged him. "Did you know the raiders were coming?"

"Yes!" he spat. "Just like you knew that the electricity was being turned on for New Years. I figured it out. The problem was, I didn't want to believe it."

He quickly explained to Myla how he had a hunch that the raiders were going to eventually figure out that the best way to take Junction wasn't by storming the bridge that spanned the Purcell River gorge, but by following the tracks. And if they were going to raid, they would do it on a moonless night, like tonight or tomorrow night. What he didn't calculate was the travel time to Junction. Blue River is easily ten or more hours from Junction by way of the rail bed. That explained why they showed up now. They would spend the night in Blue River and then continue on to Junction tomorrow.

"So where are we going to go?" she asked, looking around.

"We only have one choice: the dome house," he responded, replacing his hat and glove. He explained that they didn't have enough juice in the battery to take them the long way back to Junction, and he knew the kids couldn't hike the remaining ten miles or more through the snow. And the dome house was less than seven miles ahead. "We could make that in an hour," he said, confidently.

Suddenly Jarad gave a grunt, slumped to his knees and fell forward onto the snow. A distant gunshot reverberated through the ridge line behind them. Myla screamed and jumped off of the snowmobile to her husband. A slight stain of blood appeared in the fabric of his coat under his right arm.

"Jared," she screamed again, grabbing him around his shoulders and trying to peer at his face. He seemed to be unconscious. She prayed that he wasn't dead. But a moment later he rolled onto his back and let out short gasps as he tried to speak.

"I've been shot," he said laboriously. "We gotta go." With effort he was able to get to his knees. He was holding his side, resisting Myla's efforts to examine his wound. "No, no," he kept insisting . "We gotta go."

Myla quickly assessed the situation. "Kids, move, I need to put your father into the sled. The children quickly scrambled out, both of them alarmed at the sudden misfortune to their father. Jarad half slid, half fell, into the empty sled, laying on his back, with his legs splayed over the top and hanging off the edge.

"Jarad, I need to look at your wound," she told her husband, giving him no choice. She unfastened his coat and pulled up his blood-sodden shirt. Jarad gasped in pain. There was a puncture wound on his side, just a few inches below his armpit. It was bleeding, but didn't appear to be arterial.

"Kids, both of you," she yelled louder than necessary, "give me your shirts!"

"What?" Annie asked. "My shirt?"

"Both of you, give me your t-shirts!" their mother ordered, almost at a shout. " I know you're both wearing t-shirts!"

"Okay," Annie said as she grasped what her mother wanted. She quickly unzipped her jacket, letting it fall over her shoulders, and pulled her sweater off over her head. She then slipped off her undershirt and handed it to her mother. She stood in her bra as her mother took the shirt and ripped in lengthwise. Cameron had done the same and also tossed his undershirt to his mother. While the kids both redressed, Myla took the other shirt and quickly folded it into a square and then pressed it firmly against Jarad's wound, causing him to groan.

"Sorry honey," she said in firm voice as she worked quickly. "I need to stop the bleeding." She then took the shirt that she had ripped and wrapped it around her husband's chest, tying it tightly. "This is just going to have to work," she said to herself. She slipped Jarad's arm out of the coat sleeve. "Hold your arm against the bandage," she directed him. "This is important Jarad."

Jarad complied with his wife's command, though he began to shiver. She covered him up as best as she could with his jacket. "We are going to go to that dome house," she said to herself, speaking her thoughts out loud. "Lord help us if we can't find it."

"It's there," Jarad responded with a croak. "It's there. . . west."

Suddenly a dog appeared and jumped onto Jarad's prone form in the trailer, who responded with a holler. It was Champ. Myla pushed the dog down into the sled between Jarad's legs and shouted at him, "stay!"

She then looked at the machine. "I don't know how to run this," she said aloud. "Damn it!"

"Momma, I can," Cameron said. "I know how. Let me try." He sat at controls and turned on the power. "Ready?" he asked, looking over his shoulder at his mother. Myla sat behind him, pushing herself forward to make room for her daughter. "Annie, hold on to me, tight," she ordered. When she felt Annie grab a hold of her waist, she told her son "go." He immediately applied the throttle.

The machine bucked forward in a series of lurches, before Cameron was able to smooth out the acceleration. He searched ahead for a route, but that proved to be an easy task. As they moved along over the crusty snow-covered road, he turned to speak to his mother.

"Where are we going?" he asked.

"Go straight," she said into his ear. "We need to go about seven miles."

He looked at the gauges on the machine and then back toward the road. "How far is seven miles, mom?" he asked, uncertainty in his voice.

"Stop," she ordered him. She then shifted her body to crane over his head. She peered at the gauges and found what she wanted. She pushed the reset button on the odometer. "There," she told him, "watch that till it counts out six miles and then tell me. Okay?" He nodded that he understood. She glanced back at her husband's form in the trailer. He hadn't moved. The dog's head watched her from between Jarad's legs. It would have been comical any other time. "Then let's go!" she said impatiently.

They sped along a snow path that would turn into a gravel road once its covering melted in the spring. It was a gentle, continuous grade upward. Shadows increased as they hurried on toward the setting sun. Cameron switched on the single headlamp. It didn't help much, not yet anyhow.

After about ten minutes, Myla told her son to come to a stop. She dismounted and went to attend to her husband. He was still laying in the same position. She leaned over him, trying to assess his state. He sensed her presence. "I'm fine," he said in a surprisingly steady, though pained, voice. "Let's keep going, honey. Don't stop." The dog sat up to and stared at Myla, awaiting any commands. She ignored him, so he relaxed again on the floor of the sled and returned to his slumber.

She took her position again on the saddle and directed her son to continue. They resumed their journey.

She looked forward over her son's shoulder, monitoring their path and his driving. Her thoughts wandered into dark places. What if we can't find this dome house? What if we get stranded and have to spend the night in this cold wilderness? She had no answers, but simply offered up prayers that God would help them. She secretly prided herself on rarely asking God for anything, which is common for strong, self-confident personalities who come to God on their own terms. But she didn't feel that way now. She needed and sought all the help she could get. But the only thing at that moment that truly felt real was the wind against her face, the movement of her son's shoulders as he steered, the clasp of her daughter's arms around her waist, and the pain of worry in her heart.

After a half hour or so Myla had Cameron stop so she could check on her husband again. The rudimentary bandage was soaked with blood, but the it appeared to have stemmed the flow. She felt his pulse and felt his temperature. There was little else she could do. She stood and looked back toward Blue River. No one appeared to be following them, which made her feel a little bit better. But resuming her place on the snowmobile only reminded her how cold it was. And it was going to get colder as the setting sun too quickly retreated behind the horizon. They continued their travel west.

Cameron had been focused and silent so it startled her from the timelessness of her worried thoughts when he suddenly mentioned that they had reached six miles. "Should I stop," he asked. She looked around them, the landscape seemingly unchanging from one mile to the next. "No . . ," she paused. "but keep an eye out for a house."

By now it was just after sunset and the only effective light was what projected from the headlamp. Myla had no idea as to what she was looking for. At the very least she wanted some sort shelter for the night. She didn't have to wait long before a fence line appeared incongruously on her left. "Follow the fence," she told her son, pointing it out.

The fence itself was evidence of wealth. It was not a simple construction of barbed-wire and inexpensive metal posts, but a costly affair with wooden rails and uprights. It seemed to go on forever. Finally they reached a break in the railing as it changed to stone and the stone terminated at a large wrought iron gate. Cameron parked in front of it, the headlight pointing inward through the imposing black defense. "Turn off the light, honey," she reminded her son. "We need to save juice."

"Are we there," a weak voice called from the sled.

"Yes, we are at the gate," Myla responded encouragingly. "We need to get it open. Just hang tough, Jarad. We'll figure it out."

She stood in front of this last obstacle, which lay half-buried in the snow. "Come on kids, help me get this open."

The two children climbed over the barrier as Myla inspected it in the semi-darkness. It didn't appear to swing open, instead it evidently rolled laterally by way of a track. She pointed this out to the kids. Annie quickly found the mechanism, though it, too, was mostly buried in the hard, white permanence of mid-winter snow. Myla scaled the fence with effort and joined her children, examining the puzzle.

She found some windblown branches and used one to start digging at the snow. The children duplicated her efforts and soon they were making progress in uncovering the mechanism. The fence was evidently opened by being drawn by a chain, but Myla discovered this mostly from feel rather than sight. She ran her hands over the savagely cold steel.

"Let's pull together," she said. On the count of three they all gave the railing a tug, but it did not so much as budge. They sat down to contemplate their next move, exhausted by their efforts. As they each stared into the night, Annie thought she saw something glowing in the darkness, reflecting in the headlight of the snowmobile. She scrambled the wall and discovered LED lights illuminating a touch pad.

"Mom, look what I found," she called excitedly. Cameron and her mother both stumbled through the growing darkness to join Annie. Myla looked closely at the keypad, which illuminated her face in a soft greenish-white light. She hadn't noticed it a moment earlier. Perhaps their actions had triggered it on or maybe it was the growing darkness that allowed the dim light to show itself, but either way it was an important find.

She started pushing buttons, but nothing happened. "There is no way we will ever open it this way," she said shrilly in frustration. She picked up one of the hefty branches and drove the butt of it into the face of the touch pad. Suddenly the fence mechanism started to grind and began to pull open the gate. But it was balking under the strain of the snow that still encumbered the wrought iron railing.

"Come on kids, push" she called out in excitement. The three of them grabbed a hold of the gate and pushed and pulled with all the effort they could muster. Slowly the barrier began to retract, opening about four feet before it suddenly switched off, filling the surrounding air with the smell of ozone. It had overheated.

Myla ran through the opening and directed her children to get back on the snowmobile. Champ, who had long left the sled, decided to follow alongside. His tail waving in the air betrayed the sense of adventure he was enjoying.

Cameron backed up the machine a couple feet and then maneuvered forward through the narrow entrance. He had plenty of room. Myla told him to go slow and to follow the road, which for their purposes was simply the lightest background coloration in the darkness.

They had traveled on about a tenth of a mile when they saw a light ahead through the trees. Continuing down the pathway a large, dome-like structure appeared before them, casting a dark hemisphere against the dark blue and russet sky. It looked occupied as light streamed dimly from a few of the windows visible from their position.

Both of the children turned to their mother on how to proceed. She simply hiked through the drifts to the front entrance and knocked on the door. When her knocks were not answered, she began to pound on it in frustration. "Open up," she shouted. "We have an emergency." The large, concrete half-moon remained silent.

In her anger she tried rattling the front doors by grabbing the large, brass knobs, which turned in her hands, the doors falling inward. They were unlocked. Myla stood there, unsure what to do, looking into the warm and inviting entryway. She hadn't anticipated this. She stepped inside, calling loud hellos. No response. Champ followed her and began sniffing out the new venue. His demeanor indicated intense interest and excitement. Myla turned on her heels and called to her children. "Come on, let's get your father. We are going inside."

Jarad had fallen into a groggy sleep. He woke suddenly from his wife's prompting as she shook one of his knees jutting up out of the sled. "What? Are they shooting?" he asked almost incoherently.

"No, Jarad, we're safe," she assured him. "We are at the dome house and we are going inside. Come on boy, I need to get you someplace warm"

With effort Jarad fitfully raised himself from the sled and then stood by balancing himself on Myla's shoulder. He was shivering. He held his right arm tight against his side, the hand making a fist as it gripped the fabric of his coat. He peered through foggy eyes at the lights and then allowed himself to be led toward them. "Get the gun," he said hoarsely to no one in particular. Cameron dashed back to the sled and grabbed both the gun and the bag of shells. Annie mustered the bag of supplies.

As they entered the house the children hovered with trepidation near Myla. "Someone close the doors," she said with a gasp, struggling under the weight of her husband. "Turn the on light," she ordered one of her children, but it switched on with her voice command..

The illumination revealed a large entry way that led to two stairways, one to the left and one to the right. A large front room beckoned forward below the stairways. "Hello," shouted Myla. "Is anyone home?"

She set her husband down on a small love seat in the front room. She looked around her new surroundings and was agog at the richness of everything she viewed. Someone has money, she thought to herself. The kids still huddled near her. Champ suddenly reappeared and greeted his family with a wave of his upright tail. He obviously wasn't distressed by encountering any strangers, which calmed Myla's nerves. Maybe there is no one home, she thought to herself.

"Come on kids, stay with me." she said. She looked at her son and shook her head. "No, Cameron, the gun stays with your father." He reluctantly set it against the couch and resumed his position next to his mother. They set out to explore this strange abode.

Minutes later she returned by herself and woke her husband up from his sleep. "Come on, baby, I'm going to look at your wound and put you to bed." She led him to an elevator and took him to the a different floor and then to a bedroom. She sat him on the bed and began to undress him

He looked around the room, taking it in but saying nothing. He was more aware of his pain than he was his surroundings. And he was utterly exhausted. Myla tore his shirt off in order to ease its removal, making softs sounds as she looked at his wound. Myla then carefully washed the area with something cold before putting on fresh bandage. She then had him lay down so she could remove his boots and pants. That task accomplished, she tucked him under the sheets and gave him some tablets and a glass of water. "There is a veritable pharmacy downstairs," she said with amazement.

"Where are the owners," Jarad asked lethargically, exhaustion overcoming his ability to stay awake.

"No one's home," she said, smoothing his hair. "You go to sleep, everything is okay."

Jarad slept fitfully. Though he was never roused from his sleep, he wrestled through the night in an endless battle with raiders. He exhausted himself climbing up snowy ridge lines, with his arm limp from the effects of firing his gun again and again, clip after clip, until he had run out of bullets and hills to climb. His right shoulder ached from the recoil of the gun. Then he awoke.

It was morning. He heard his wife singing, somewhere in an amorphous reality he was still trying to grasp. His eyes opened. He could see the room around him, draped in the angles of sunlight that entered through some window to his left. Myla's voice was now clearer and he knew she was nearby, but in a different room. Her singing put his mind to ease, as she only sang when she was happy and at peace.

He sat up in the bed. He reached up with his left hand and scratched his scalp. He looked down at the bandage wrapped around his chest. It looked professional, as if he had visited a hospital. He had a headache and his ribcage was very painful, it hurt to breath. But he was so glad to be alive and so thankful to be safe. And warm. Considering his condition, he was perfectly comfortable. What a strange place he thought to himself.

He stood and got his bearings. He was clothed only in boxers. He visited the bathroom. Afterwards, he went in search of his wife.

He found her in the bathroom of an adjacent bedroom. She was standing in front of a mirror, braiding her hair. She had just showered and she smelled like spring. She was wearing an outfit that he had never seen before. She smiled at him as he entered, the nurse in her quickly assessing his condition. She kissed him without removing her hands from their task, as they nimbly twisted a shock of hair into a braid.

"Have I died and gone to heaven?" he asked only half in jest.

"Just about," she said. "We are fortunate indeed."

"Where are the kids," he asked, surveying the accouterments of the room, wondering if he, too, could manage a shower.

"Sleeping," she said, "and will probably sleep for a long while more. They were utterly exhausted."

"How about you?" he asked, looking at her eyes by way of the mirror. "How did you sleep last night?"

"I didn't!" she chuckled. "I was too wired. So I explored the house. This is an incredible place."

She shared what she had discovered. Hot, running water. So much food stored away that they could eat for a year and not exhaust it. A televisor that worked, but only to play movies. "The net is still down," she said.

"I don't know where power comes from, but at this point I don't care. That shower was a godsend." She sighed deeply, out of satisfaction rather than discouragement. She was happy.

Completing the braiding of her hair, she wrapped Jarad in a housecoat and took him by the hand. "I want to show you something, before the kids wake up," she said. She led him to a large room full of comfortable looking furniture and a pool table. She paused to pick up an item sitting on an end table and handed it to him. He looked at the piece of metal. "What is this," he asked, "it looks like a bullet"

"It is," she responded. "It fell out of your shirt last night when I was undressing you." She explained that his would wasn't very deep, though he probably did have a cracked rib. "That rib might have saved your life. Who knows what damage that bullet could have done if it had entered your body between the ribs."

"It must have been a lucky shot," he responded, looking at the slug. "Some guy took a pot shot at me from a long distance and got lucky. It didn't have much energy if it bounced off of a rib." He tried to chuckle. "For which I am glad."

"Come on, we are not there yet," she said, again taking his hand and leading him further into the house.

They entered a large room, obviously a master bedroom. A huge bed sat unoccupied in the center of the far wall, looking out onto a sun lit deck. Myla led him to the a large window that filled the wall and which fronted the third-floor overlook.

"There is the owner," she said, pointing to a small form taking in the cold sun on a wooden chaise. "She's dead." Myla explained that the woman had intentionally poisoned herself with an overdose of tranquilizers. "She must have emptied out the bottle and then laid down on her deck to die. Probably three weeks ago."

Jared looked away."Nobody else, huh?"

"Not that I've found, anyhow, but. . ." she paused. "There might me a mister corpse somewhere." Without explaining she again took him by the hand. "Come on, I'll make you breakfast and show you the suicide note."

As they left the master bedroom Myla turn down the hallway in a direction opposite the game room. Jarad could see the circular form of the house taking shape as he was steered down the arcing carpeted hallway. They entered into yet another room, also sun-drenched. It was a kitchen and dining area. "Have a seat," she instructed him, pointing to a beautiful and substantial cherry wood table. She fetched a paper and brought it over to him before returning to the kitchen area. She busied herself with making breakfast while her husband scanned the sheet of writing.

The very first sentence captured Jarad's bemused attention: "To whom it may concern." What an odd opening to a suicide note, he thought to himself. As he read he became more confused rather than enlightened by the words of the writer. The handwriting was masculine, leading Jarad to agree with Myla that there was a second body to be found somewhere else on the premises. The author wrote of hopelessness and despair, "Happiness is an illusion," he carefully penned, and "life really isn't worth living." It was signed, but Jarad could not make out the name. Saving that task for later he turned to the post script: "Whoever finds this note is welcome to all the assets they find. They are worthless, no meaningless, to us now. Perhaps they will serve you better."

"What do you think," Myla asked as she set a cup of coffee before him.

"I got a splitting headache," he said, laying the paper down on the table. "Is there any ibuprofen?"

"That's it?"she asked, incredulous and disappointed. "That is the sum of your thoughts?"

"No, it is sad. Looks like their sanctuary wasn't what they had hoped it would be." He ran his left hand through his hair and stretched. "But who can really know another person's mind?" he asked with a yawn. He took a drink of his coffee and realized where his headache was coming from. He was going through caffeine withdrawals. He took another sip.

"It's a man, by the way," he said pointing at the note as his wife brought him toast and eggs. He kissed her hand as a thank you. He told her that he was afraid they'd find his corpse somewhere. She acknowledged that and told him that they needed to try to do so before the kids did.

"So, what are your thoughts?" he asked his wife as he dipped toast into the warm yokes. "This is wonderful," he murmured with a full mouth.

"That is one reason why I sat up all night," she said. "I was thinking about these poor people."

Jarad laughed. "Poor!" he said, looking around the room.

"I was reminded of Otty once said about tearing down barns to build bigger ones," she ventured. "These folks had a very, very nice barn, but maybe that was all they had. And when the world turned in on itself, they found that raggedy edge. Maybe they discovered how poor they really were."

Jarad nodded in agreement. His head was already feeling better. He tried to eat the remains of his eggs left handed. It wasn't going well. He set the fork down and reached over and took his wife's hand. "As long as I got you and the kids, I am the richest man on earth," he said. She smiled. She took his fork and began to feed him.   "Thank you, mommy," he said in jest.

After breakfast he got up to explore the house. It was three stories tall, each floor accessible by both a stairway and the elevator. There were two decks that faced to the south – one off the master bedroom on the third floor, and an even larger one off of the living room on the second floor. Jarad stood outside on the latter one, dressed only in the bathrobe Myla had put on him. He was cold, but not chilled. He felt, at least momentarily, safe. His wound limited his movements and, for the time being, his options. But he was content to heal before he did anything else. He peered off to the horizon, his thoughts drifting between Purcell, which he knew lay somewhere before him, and Junction, which he could only see in this mind's eye. He hoped that the raiders were thwarted, but there was nothing he could do. He turned to go back into the house. He needed a shower, badly.

A rope around the railing caught his eye. "What is this?" he asked himself aloud. Walking over to the heavy ice-crusted rope he peered over the edge, wondering what function such a stout rope was needed for. At its terminus he found the body of the man, a blanched corpse hanging stiffly in the cold vault of air under the deck. Jarad was unmoved by the sight, which surprised him. Was he getting hardened, he wondered. No, he assured himself, just accustomed. Just accustomed to death.

He went into the house and returned with a large knife. He carefully cut the rope and let the body simply fall where it may. He'd take care of it another time. Until then he would cover it up with a blanket, so as to protect the children from the sight of it. He knew that it would remain frozen until early spring. And the bears were still in hibernation, so that wasn't a problem.

Before he could return a second time to the house, Myla met him on the deck. She notice the knife and looked curiously at her husband. He smiled when he realized his wife's concern and shook his head no. He explained what he had discovered. Relief swept her face, but she didn't bother to look at the body. She didn't need to.

She stopped suddenly and looked across the deck, pointing her arm at a bird. "A robin," she said. "A sign of spring." She was delighted.

"Kind of early, don't you think?" Jarad wondered aloud.

"Nature knows," she assured him.

She lovingly wrapped her arms around her husband and rested her head upon his chest. "I love you," she said with deep conviction. "And I'll love you forever."

Jarad wrapped his left arm around her and held her as tight as he dared. "You could not make my life more perfect," he whispered.

"Can I try?" she asked. Jarad looked at her with curiosity.

"Sure, but how could you?" he challenged with a crooked smile.

She laughed a strange laugh, as if she knew a secret. "Oh, Jarad," she said with a smile. "I'm pregnant!"

The End

Made in the USA
Lexington, KY
30 March 2011